UNTIL PROVEN GUILTY

UNTIL PROVEN GUILTY

A NOVEL

BETSY BRANNON GREEN

Covenant Communications, Inc.

Published by Covenant Communications, Inc.
American Fork, Utah

Printed in Canada
First Printing: August 2002

08 07 06 05 04   10 9 8 7 6 5 4 3

ISBN 1-59156-061-6

Library of Congress Cataloging-in-Publication Data

Green, Betsy Brannon, 1958-
    Until Proven Guilty : a novel / Betsy Brannon Green.
       p. cm.
    ISBN 1-59156-061-6
    1. Mormon women--Fiction. 2. Custody of children--Fiction. 3. Divorced fathers--Fiction.
4. Nannies--Fiction. 5. Georgia--Fiction. I. Title

    PS3607.R43 U58 2002
    813'.6--dc21
                                                2002067668

DEDICATION

For my mother, Dorothy, who was easy to please
and my father, Wayne, who wasn't.

She gave me confidence.
He taught me to keep trying until I got it right.

ACKNOWLEDGMENTS

First and foremost I want to thank to my husband, Butch, and our children. Writing books has been a wonderful experience, but like faith, sacrifices preceded the miracle, and I will always be grateful to my family for giving me the chance to follow a dream.

I also owe a huge debt of gratitude to The Honorable Loring A. Gray, Jr., Superior Court Judge, Dougherty County Circuit. He has given me technical advice and support throughout the creation of this book. Attribute any legal errors to me and all authenticity to him.

And as always, I appreciate the wonderful editorial staff and the other good folks at Covenant who produce the finest LDS fiction books on the market. I am proud to be associated with all of you.

PROLOGUE

When Beth opened her eyes, the first thing she saw was her wedding dress hanging on the back of the closet door. Sunlight poured through the window, giving the fabric a translucent, unearthly look. She sat up and stretched, thinking of David and their wedding later that morning.

Her mother hurried into the room and told Beth that it was time to get ready. As the gown was removed from its padded hanger, Beth heard the distant rumble of thunder. She asked if it was going to rain, but her mother assured her the weather was perfect. Beth raised her arms, and the dress was slipped over her head. Then she heard the thunder again, more distinctly this time.

"Are you sure it's not raining, Mama?"

"Nothing is going to spoil your wedding day," her mother replied firmly, but without meeting her gaze.

Beth heard the thunder again, loud and insistent. "Mama!" Now the thunder was deafening, and Beth pressed her hands against her ears to block out the awful sound. Then the door burst open and she saw her father standing there with tears streaming down his cheeks. "Daddy! What's the matter?" Beth was screaming now. "Where's David? David! David!"

CHAPTER 1

Beth's cries awakened her, and she clutched a pillow to her chest, gasping for air. Once her breathing was under control, she rolled over to look at the clock on the nightstand. It was three o'clock in the morning. Since sleep was no longer a possibility, she walked to the bathroom of her efficiency apartment and flipped on the fluorescent light. After a long, warm shower, she put on a cotton dress that was now too big for her thin frame.

With a towel wrapped around her head, she went into the tiny kitchen and opened a cupboard to survey her breakfast choices. There was a strawberry NutriGrain bar and a can of milk-chocolate Slim Fast. She opted for the fruit bar and put the Slim Fast into the refrigerator so it would be cold in time for dinner. Then she turned on the television for background noise and settled on the couch, tucking her bare feet under the extra material of her voluminous dress.

She nibbled her breakfast and opened her library book to the page she had marked a few hours before. Occasionally she would glance up at the television screen. The weatherman was predicting hot temperatures and afternoon thundershowers. It was a typical Georgia August, so Beth didn't need a meteorologist to tell her that. She read another page and a half before a strident voice from the television reclaimed her attention. Displeased by the interruption and her own lack of concentration, she stared as a face filled the screen.

"I'm Veronica Smalls, reporting for Channel Five News," the woman said, then proceeded to give her viewers an update on Ferris Burke and his impending murder trial. Uninterested in the country music singer and his plight, Beth returned to her novel.

Beth read steadily and finished the book at noon. She took the time to brush her teeth and pull her hair into a ponytail, then locked her apartment door and walked out into the stifling heat. Her old Volkswagen Beetle didn't have air conditioning, so her dress stuck to her back as she drove through the industrial neighborhood where she lived to the Dougherty County Courthouse for her meeting with Bob Wells.

Bob was the director of the county's Department of Human Resources, and Beth had worked for him briefly before her life self-destructed. About once a quarter he insisted that she come to his office so he could give her his "you're wasting your education and your life" speech. Beth had no intention of working in her field of study ever again, but their meetings made Bob feel better, so she humored him.

After parking on the street, Beth walked into the lobby and climbed two flights of stairs. A rush of memories momentarily staggered her as she stepped out of the landing into the familiar corridor. She put a hand against the wall to steady herself, then heard Bob's booming voice.

"I thought you had decided not to come!"

"I'm five minutes early," she retorted, then brushed past him into his office, stopping short when she saw a man sitting on Bob's old couch. Afraid she had interrupted an appointment, Beth took a step back. Bob halted her exit by closing the door.

"Beth, I'd like for you to meet Jack Gamble. Jack, Beth Middleton." She and the stranger acknowledged each other with simultaneous nods. The man was slouched casually against the worn leather, but his clenched jaw and drumming fingers seemed to indicate extreme tension. "Please have a seat, Beth." Bob pointed to an empty chair.

Jack Gamble was studying her, so she stared back. He was a handsome man, almost beautiful, with dark, longish hair curling around his ears. His eyes were brilliantly blue, if a little cold, and his clothes looked expensive.

"Jack and I have worked together on several cases over the past few years, and he's earned my respect," Bob said by way of introduction.

"Which puts you in a distinct minority around here," Jack Gamble added.

The men looked at each other for a few seconds before Bob turned to Beth. "Jack is divorced and has custody of his five-year-old daughter. His career is demanding, and he's away from home quite a bit. His parents are concerned . . ." the DHR director faltered. "That is to say, they have decided—"

"They think I'm a bad father, and they have complained to a family court judge," Jack Gamble took up the narrative abruptly.

Beth's eyes widened, and Bob raised a hand. "That's an exaggeration. Chloe is a little withdrawn, and Jack's parents thought she might need some counseling—"

Jack Gamble's jaw tensed a little more. "They wanted to do a battery of psychological tests on my daughter—"

"Just to be sure that her shyness isn't an indication of anything more serious," Bob interrupted impatiently. "Jack wouldn't listen to their concerns, so they approached a friend of theirs who is a family court judge."

"To twist my arm," Jack Gamble contributed.

"To ask for advice. The judge offered to quietly file a court order for an evaluation, just to give Jack's parents some peace of mind."

"And force me to do something unnecessary and possibly even detrimental."

Bob sighed and turned to address Beth. "As you can see, Jack is very opposed to the testing. While I agree that it could have been handled more discreetly, I don't believe the testing itself would have been harmful to Chloe. But somehow the press got wind of the court order, and the whole thing has been blown out of proportion. They are claiming that Jack's parents are suing for custody of Chloe, which is not true."

"Not yet anyway," Jack Gamble muttered from the couch.

"All of this has put the family court judge in a difficult situation. He can't just ignore headlines claiming that Jack is an unfit father."

"He could if he wasn't up for reelection in November," Jack Gamble predicted.

"In any case, the judge felt that action was necessary. So he told Jack to hire an impartial observer to move into his house and evaluate the environment. This person would be a nanny of sorts, someone who will temporarily alleviate other concerns that Jack's parents have—such as Chloe's lack of supervision." Jack Gamble made a noise in his throat, attracting Bob's attention.

While the two men scowled at each other, Beth looked back and forth between them in bewilderment. "But what does any of this have to do with me?" she asked finally.

"With your degrees and experience as a social worker, you'd be a perfect observer for Chloe," Bob said, and Beth's mouth fell open. "Jack has a live-in housekeeper, and other employees are always around, so you wouldn't be in a compromising situation of any kind. And the fact that you and Jack were both raised in the Mormon faith is another plus."

"Religion is not an issue here." Jack Gamble dismissed Bob's remark.

"It may not be an issue for you, but it is for your parents."

Jack Gamble conceded this with a brief nod, and then both men turned to stare at her and Beth realized that they expected a response. "You want me to baby-sit his little girl?" she asked Bob, making no effort to hide her astonishment.

"Not baby-sit," Bob corrected. "You would spend time with Chloe, observe her and Jack together, and then give the court your educated opinion."

Beth took a deep breath, then turned to Jack Gamble. "I sympathize with your situation, but I'm not available. I've decided to go on a mission."

"That's a great idea!" the DHR director agreed. "But it's no reason to refuse this offer. The position is only temporary, and once everything is settled with Chloe, you could do mission work."

Jack Gamble leaned forward. "If I don't turn in a name soon, the court will appoint someone, and I can't risk that. So, this is the basic proposal—three months at a generous salary. You'd report to the court weekly, with a final assessment due at the end of the evaluation period." He extended an envelope toward her.

Beth accepted the packet automatically. "I don't know how much Bob has told you about me, Mr. Gamble." She stared at the envelope in her hands. "It's true that I spent years learning how to help children. I learned phraseology and techniques designed to comfort those in pain. For almost a year I used these methods to help children in crisis."

She took a deep breath and pressed on. "Then I experienced a personal tragedy and found myself, a grown woman, completely unable to cope with the grief. The phrases and techniques did nothing for me, and I realized they had been no help to the battered, neglected children either. And then I accepted the awful truth. There is no escape from the pain, no way to relieve the anguish. Everything I learned was a sham, and my job was futile. So at that point I made a decision never to work with troubled children again."

Jack Gamble had been watching her closely during this painful narrative, and as she finished, Beth clenched her hands together, waiting for the predictable platitudes. "Chloe's not in trouble," he said finally. "We don't need your skills, just your qualifications. And as Bob has mentioned, your religion will be a plus as far as my parents are concerned."

Beth blinked back at him, unable to formulate a reply. Anxious for somewhere to look besides into Jack Gamble's piercing blue eyes, Beth pulled a stack of papers from the envelope. There was a picture of a small girl clipped to the top.

"That's Chloe," Bob told her.

"A mug shot of sorts." Jack Gamble's tone was light, but his expression was angry.

Beth touched the photograph, and the hair stood up on the back of her neck. She had the oddest feeling that she already knew this child. "She's beautiful."

"Yes," Bob agreed.

"What symptoms is she exhibiting?" Beth asked, curiosity pushing past her reticence.

"There is nothing wrong with Chloe," Jack Gamble assured her. "She's shy, but otherwise, she's a normal, happy kid." He ran his fingers through his hair, then continued more calmly. "I've got a big trial coming up. If you take this job, you'll get the family court judge off my back and buy me the time I need to settle this case."

Somewhere on the edge of Beth's mind was a vague memory. Then she thought of the Channel Five reporter with the irritating voice from the early morning news. The reporter had shown a brief clip of the country music singer walking down the steps of the Dougherty County Courthouse. The man beside him had declined to comment, and Ms. Smalls had breathlessly announced that he was a local attorney who had been hired to represent the famous recording artist. "You're going to defend Ferris Burke," Beth said with certainty.

"I'm going to try."

Bob was more enthusiastic. "Jack is an excellent criminal lawyer. Ferris Burke could have hired anyone in the United States, but he chose Jack."

Beth had developed a healthy contempt for the legal profession during her short career as a social worker. In fact, for the last two years she had avoided contact with most people, but especially men and children. So she returned the papers and Chloe Gamble's picture to the envelope and put it on Bob's desk. "Well, it was nice to see you again, Bob," she told her friend, "and to meet you, Mr. Gamble." She nodded at the lawyer. "But I need to get to work. I hope you find someone to evaluate your daughter." She inched toward the door.

Jack Gamble acknowledged her words with a tip of his head, but Bob grabbed the envelope and followed her. "At least agree to consider Jack's offer," he asked as they reached the doorway. "The situation really is desperate." He looked over at Jack Gamble in silent appeal.

"I won't beg." The other man shook his head.

Bob leaned closer to Beth and lowered his voice. "Think about it, please. Jack's a good guy, and his daughter needs protection. Once the courts get involved . . ."

Beth glanced at the envelope he pressed into her hand. She had seen what bureaucracy could do to a family. "I'll let you know," she promised, then walked out the door.

Since the downtown branch of the Dougherty County Public Library was only a half block from the courthouse, Beth decided to walk the short distance. She paused by the car long enough to feed the parking meter and put the proposal from Jack Gamble on the passenger seat. Before closing the door, she reached down and removed the picture of Chloe Gamble from the envelope.

Long, dark hair, shining brown eyes, and a brilliant smile combined to create total perfection. Such a child in trouble was a disturbing thought, and whether or not Jack Gamble was a bad parent, until things were settled with the courts, the little girl's future was uncertain. Beth slipped the picture into the pocket of her baggy dress and hurried into the library.

She was a few minutes early, so she bypassed her chair at the return desk and went to the rare books department to see Derrick Morgan. At fifty-six, Derrick was an accidental bachelor. As an only child, he had spent his youth caring for sick and then elderly parents. After his parents died, he inherited their home in Albany's historical district and could have lived comfortably on the money they left him, but instead he chose to work long hours at the library.

From her first day at the book-return desk, Beth had discouraged familiarity, and everyone got the message quickly except Derrick. He brought her vegetables and flowers from his garden, recipes he found in magazines, and jelly he made himself. She had to admire his persistence and eventually gave in to his friendly overtures.

"Hey, Beth!" he greeted her.

"Hello," she replied while opening the cover of a book called *Cobb County Deaths—1890*. "Who would want to read something like this?" She eyed the volume with distaste.

"Someone trying to trace their family history." He ran a hand lovingly over the old book.

"So, what happened on *The Brave and Relentless* today?" Beth asked. Most women she knew followed the popular soap opera, but Derrick was one of the few men who did.

Derrick pursed his lips. "Nothing new. Results of the blood tests are supposed to be announced on Monday," he said, watching his computer screen.

"Well, I hope the tests show that the baby is Parker's so Tori can quit torturing herself," Beth wished out loud, and Derrick looked up sharply.

"What would be the point of that? Parker is not the baby's father. You can count on it."

Beth turned a page in the death book, discouraged. She really liked Tori and hated to think about what would happen to the girl's marriage when her husband found out that he was not the father of her unborn child. While she mused, someone came up and asked Derrick an obscure question. He had a ready answer, and as the patron walked away, Beth regarded Derrick thoughtfully. "Do you ever listen to country music?"

"Never," he responded. "Why?"

"I'm curious about Ferris Burke and his murder case."

"The man killed his ex-wife and her boyfriend with his nine-year-old daughter in the house! He's not only a bad musician, he's a sloppy murderer!" Derrick smirked. "The only person more contemptible than Ferris Burke is the scummy lawyer who's defending him when everybody in the world knows he's guilty."

Beth smiled. "Actually, it's the scummy lawyer I'm interested in. He offered me a job today, and I'm a little curious."

"Jack Gamble? Jack Gamble offered you a job?"

She nodded. "My old boss at DHR introduced us, and I just thought you might have read something about him." Years of caring for his parents had turned Derrick into a compulsive pleaser, and she saw the anxiety form in his eyes. It was going to bother him that he couldn't answer her question about Ferris Burke. "It's no big deal," she promised. "If I watch the news tonight, I'll find out more than I ever wanted to know about Ferris Burke and his lawyer!"

His troubled gaze followed her as she walked back to the book-return desk and Beth regretted mentioning Jack Gamble or the controversial case. During her break Beth ate a package of nearly fresh peanut butter crackers she found at the bottom of her purse. While she chewed, her mind strayed to the picture of Chloe Gamble in her pocket. Almost involuntarily, she pulled it out and stared at the beautiful little face.

At exactly 8:00 P.M. she clocked out and walked toward the side entrance. Derrick met her by the door. "Beth!" he gasped. "I'm glad I caught you." He waved a video. "I have a cousin who likes country music, so I called and asked if he had anything on Ferris Burke. He had two music videos and the Country Music Awards program from last year. He made you a copy."

Beth stared at her friend. "I feel bad that your cousin went to the trouble," Beth told him with complete sincerity. She really didn't care anything about Ferris Burke. All she wanted was a little personal data on his lawyer.

Derrick waved this aside. "Jack Gamble went to law school at Mitner, so on my way back from my cousin's house I stopped by there," he continued, and Beth's mouth fell open in horror. "I talked to the head librarian and asked if they had anything on Gamble. Grades and things like that are confidential, but she found a video of a mock trial he participated in ten years ago. She copied it onto the end of this." He waved the tape again.

"Oh, Derrick, you shouldn't have."

He shrugged. "I have a reputation to maintain as Albany's best researcher. What would people think if they found out there was a question I couldn't answer? Besides, I'm not even scheduled to work today. I just came in because I didn't have anything else to do."

This caused Beth's frown to deepen. "We've really got to find you a wife."

Derrick's eyes widened, and then he cleared his throat nervously. "It was nothing, really," he assured her as they walked outside.

Beth drove home through the quiet streets of Albany and parked beside an empty lot two blocks down from her apartment building. After tucking the video from Derrick and the manila envelope that contained her job offer under her arm, she climbed out of the car. She would watch the video during dinner, then call Bob Wells and decline Jack Gamble's proposal.

In her mailbox there was a bill from a book club, two credit card applications addressed to "Occupant," and a letter from her younger sister, Melissa. Since she couldn't remember ever receiving a letter from Melissa before, she opened it with rising anxiety.

Inside the apartment she put the video and the envelope on the counter in her kitchen. Then she took the chilled Slim Fast out of the refrigerator and sipped it while she read Melissa's scrawl. After a routine report on things at home, Melissa got to the point. She had been accepted to BYU for the upcoming school year. Melissa's high school grades were adequate but her ACT score was unimpressive, so this was quite a surprise. The letter said that a student loan would pay her tuition, but not room, board, or books. In addition to these fees, her parents would be responsible for purchasing warm clothing and a plane ticket to Utah.

Beth put down the letter and stared out her small front window at the street below. Her expenses were modest, but her salary at the library was even more so. As a result, her savings would only cover about half the cost of a mission. Ever since she'd decided to talk to her branch president about going on a mission, she had been trying to work up the courage to ask her parents to pay for the rest. Melissa's good fortune put an end to that idea.

Absently Beth reached over and opened the manila envelope. Jack Gamble was indeed offering a generous salary, and if she accepted the job for the three-month period, she would have enough money to pay for a mission. Her hand slipped into the pocket of her dress and pulled out the snapshot of Chloe Gamble. Beth looked at the small face for a few minutes, and then her heart started to hurt, so she put the picture on the kitchen counter and changed into sweatpants and a T-shirt.

It was too early for her nightly run, so she sat on the couch and watched the video Derrick had given her. She was familiar with some of Ferris Burke's songs but had never seen any of his music videos. The first had been recorded years earlier, introducing his initial big hit, "You're Killing Me Without Kindness." Ferris stood alone in a dark room, singing woefully and gesturing toward the camera. Occasionally he would tap his foot or swing a hip.

The next video, "You've Broken the Laws of Love," was more professional, indicating that Ferris's financial situation had improved. This time he sang to a beautiful girl who was removed in handcuffs at the end. The song Ferris performed at the Country Music Awards was one she had never heard before. Ferris was dressed in gold satin and surrounded by men and women in fuchsia leotards. With a shudder, she fast-forwarded to the mock trial.

She had always been a fan of *Matlock*, so Beth could identify the main players. The judge was an older man, probably the teacher. The prosecutor was a serious-looking young woman with a lot of hair and a distinct overbite. A youthful Jack Gamble was the defense attorney.

The hypothetical defendant was a garbage collector who had accidentally driven a city vehicle into an elementary school. His blood-alcohol level was above the legal limit at the time, so he had been charged with gross negligence and criminal endangerment. The evidence was staggering, and Beth didn't see how Jack Gamble could possibly win, but by the end she felt sorry for the pretend prosecutor. Mr. Gamble was well prepared and charismatic. He handled the witnesses, the opposing counsel, and even the judge with careless ease. The jury returned a verdict of *not guilty* and the fictitious garbage man went free. Unable to help herself, she rewound the tape to the end of Ferris's Music Awards performance and watched the trial again.

It was late by the time she left her apartment to run the familiar streets, and as she ran she couldn't keep images of Jack Gamble and his daughter from her thoughts. It took three miles to achieve the blankness of mind that she usually reached in one. Slightly resentful toward Jack Gamble and Bob Wells, she returned, took a shower, then sat down to watch the eleven o'clock news. She told herself that she just needed to check on the weather, but was pleased when the anchorperson introduced a clip of Ferris Burke's press conference.

The camera showed Ferris standing in the background looking sad and misunderstood while his lawyer described the police department's bungling ineptitude and the district attorney's unreasonable vendetta against his client. He concluded by assuring the viewers that justice would be served and Ferris would be making platinum records again soon.

Beth turned off the television and read her new book until she finished it at two o'clock on Saturday morning. She saw the picture of Chloe Gamble on her kitchen counter when she checked to make sure the front door was locked. It reminded her that she hadn't called Bob Wells to decline the job offer. Irritated with herself, she tucked Chloe Gamble's photograph into her pajama pocket and went to bed. And when she slept, she dreamed of brown eyes and dark pigtails instead of death and thunder.

Beth was scheduled to work from ten to four on Saturday, and she barely had time to get settled at the book-return desk before one of the catalogers came over and told her that the director wanted to see her immediately. In the two years she had worked at the downtown branch, Beth had never known Mrs. Wiley to come in on a weekend. Curious and a little nervous, Beth followed the cataloger back to the administrative area.

Mrs. Wiley was sitting at her desk and politely invited Beth to come inside. Once Beth was seated in one of the upholstered chairs, the director informed her that she had some rather unpleasant news. "I was notified last night that as a result of recent municipal cutbacks, your position at the library is being discontinued."

Beth shook her head in an effort to clear it. "I'm sorry, could you repeat that?"

"I know that finding another job will be inconvenient, but I'm sure someone with your education and experience can easily find a better position."

"You don't have another job I can do?" Beth asked softly.

The director shook her head. "I'd have to fire someone with less seniority and give you their job," Mrs. Wiley explained. "Arif in book bindings has only been with us a few months, but he's an exchange student and if he loses his job, he'll have to go back to Kuwait. Then there is Leslie in reference, but this job is her only source of income and she's a single mother—"

"I understand," Beth interrupted. She couldn't very well be responsible for deporting a teenager or for starving fatherless children.

"I hate to lose you," Mrs. Wiley sighed as she stood. "But I have been given no choice."

After receiving a brisk handshake, Beth walked back to the book-return desk in a daze. She needed a few minutes to compose herself, but it was not meant to be. Derrick was sitting in her chair, awaiting her arrival.

"I've just come from Mrs. Wiley's office," she told him. "My job at the library has been discontinued."

"What do you mean 'discontinued'?"

"I guess it means I'm fired," she responded. Derrick was outraged. He offered to call a lawyer, organize a picket line, or quit himself. "It's okay, Derrick," she assured him. "I told you that I was thinking about going on a mission soon and would have had to resign anyway. Besides, Jack Gamble's job pays a lot more than I make here!"

Derrick's eyes narrowed. "You're going to take his job?"

Beth shrugged, unsure of what she was going to do.

"What would he want you to do for him?"

"Move into his house and evaluate his relationship with his five-year-old daughter," she answered, and Derrick's expression reflected comical confusion. "I'm actually more qualified to do that than to work in a library."

"Why do you have to live in his house to observe his kid?" he asked. "Couldn't you just stop by for a few hours a day and see how he treats her?"

"I guess the family court judge doesn't think I'd get the full picture unless I'm there all the time," Beth told him.

Derrick was still frowning. "I'm surprised you'd even consider it."

Beth lifted a shoulder. "Well I've got to work somewhere, and the offer is only for three months. What could happen in that length of time?" Derrick continued to glower. "And you don't need to worry about me. He has a live-in housekeeper, so I won't be alone with Ferris Burke's sleazy lawyer."

A patron came up at this moment and asked for Derrick's help in locating a bill of sale from 1894. "We'll talk more about this later," he promised Beth as he rushed off to meet this new challenge.

During her first break Beth got a phone call from Bob Wells. "I'm sorry to disturb you at work," he said when she answered, "but I felt I had to make a final effort to hire you in Jack's behalf. He has until six o'clock today to find an evaluator. After that, he's at the judge's mercy. I don't know what kind of impression Jack made on you . . ." Bob paused, but when Beth made no comment, he continued. "He's a private sort of person, and that works against him in a situation like this—makes it look like he's got something to hide." A nervous laugh came through the phone line. "Which is not your problem, but I feel very strongly that you are the right person for this job. So I'm going to ask you to do it as a personal favor to me."

In all the time Beth had known Bob, he had never asked her to do anything for him. "You're desperate."

"I need a good lawyer in my back pocket," he teased, and Beth had to smile. "Seriously, though, it's not very often that we get to step into family situations early enough to prevent problems. I'd like to see if we can help Chloe now, without getting the courts more involved."

"I thought the evaluator was just to appease the press and Mr. Gamble's parents."

"That's the way Jack looks at it." Bob was silent for a few seconds, and Beth got the impression that he was reluctant to proceed. "Jack seems like a nice enough guy, but I've never been to his house or met his daughter, and his parents were concerned enough about the situation to consult a family court judge. So if you agree to take this job, you will have a responsibility to observe and report fairly. I don't want to see Chloe's name come across my desk again a few years from now when it's too late to do anything but repair the damage."

Beth's hand slipped into her pocket, fingering the corners of Chloe Gamble's snapshot. "They told me this morning that my job here at the library has been discontinued."

"That's wonderful!" Bob responded with inordinate enthusiasm.

"I don't know if getting fired is wonderful, but it does leave me at loose ends for a while . . ."

"You'll do it," he whispered into the receiver.

"For you," Beth answered slowly. "But just for three months."

"I'll call Jack and let him know." The relief in Bob's voice was obvious. "Can you start immediately?"

"How 'immediately'?" she asked.

"Monday if possible."

"That soon?" Beth felt the old anxiety surface. Too many changes in such a short time would upset the delicate balance of her life, so she searched for a plausible excuse. "I'll have to give them a two-week notice here."

"If your job doesn't exist anymore, I don't see how they could expect a notice," Bob responded.

Her mind raced again. "I'll have to get out of the lease at my apartment . . ."

"Explain the situation to your landlord and if there's a penalty or anything, I'm sure Jack will be willing to pay it."

"I'll let you know," Beth said, then ended the call abruptly. On her way back to the book-return desk, she stopped by Mrs. Wiley's office and asked when her employment with the library would officially end. She was hoping that the director would name a date far in the future, requiring her to call Bob and tell him that Monday would not be a possibility.

"You won't need to come back after today," Mrs. Wiley said with a polite smile. "We'll mail your final check."

Surprised and a little hurt, Beth went back to her desk. It wasn't that she thought the library couldn't function without her. She knew her job was routine and could probably be performed adequately by a fifth-grader. But she'd been there for over two years, and it was sad to think that they wouldn't even miss her.

During her lunch break she called her landlady, expecting resistance to a sudden departure. However, Mrs. Peterson said that several people were waiting for a vacancy and since new tenants could be charged a higher rent, she would happily release Beth from her contract.

Derrick stopped by later that afternoon carrying two Payday candy bars and a stack of computer printouts. "So, what did you think of the video?" He extended one of the candy bars and piled the papers on her desk.

She accepted the candy and replied honestly, "I couldn't bear to watch Ferris."

"I had some free time this morning, so I dug up what I could on Jack Gamble," Derrick told her with his mouth full of peanuts. "Newspaper articles, stuff like that. None of it's good."

"It must have taken you hours to collect this!" she scolded, already reading the top sheet.

Derrick shrugged. "It wasn't hard. I used the Internet."

"My old boss said Mr. Gamble is a very good criminal lawyer." Beth looked up from a handful of articles on a case involving a professional football player.

"Emphasis on criminal," Derrick muttered. "Take this guy." He tapped the picture of the huge man wearing a helmet. "He admitted that he was paid to throw a football game, but Gamble contended that the prosecution had to prove the man actually played below his potential on that particular day. Gamble swayed the jury and the football player walked. Then there's this doctor who was supposed to take out a woman's spleen and took out her appendix instead."

"How could anyone make such an awful mistake?"

"Gamble blamed it on everybody who had the misfortune of being in the hospital on that date." Derrick took another bite of his Payday. "He did a good job of spreading the responsibility around, but his real coup was finding lab results that showed the appendix was enlarged at the time of surgery." Beth raised an eyebrow. "According to an expert medical witness, this meant it could have been about to rupture," he explained.

"No way," Beth breathed.

Derrick nodded. "By performing the wrong surgery, the doctor may have saved the woman's life. What jury would convict under those circumstances?"

"He always seems to win," Beth murmured with grudging respect.

"Even though his clients are always guilty," Derrick agreed. "Now he's got his eye on Jeremiah Dobson's state senate seat. When Dobson announced a few months ago that health problems were going to prevent him from completing his term, Jack Gamble 'expressed interest'." Derrick indicated toward the "Gamble Enters Political Ring" article.

"He wants to be a politician?" Beth asked as she scanned the column.

"Show me a lawyer who doesn't," Derrick replied cynically. "And I promise you that a competitor like Jack Gamble won't be satisfied with a measly state senate seat." Beth studied a grainy newsprint picture of Jack Gamble standing beside a tall, heavyset man. "That's Oscar Fuller, chairman of the Georgia Republican Party. He was one of Gamble's professors in law school, and whoever Fuller endorses is sure to get the appointment."

"So Jack Gamble wins without a fight?" Beth asked as she studied the white-haired man.

"No, the Dougherty County district attorney wants the job too, and he's popular with the voters." Derrick handed Beth another article. The picture of Lance Kilgore explained his public approval rating. With blonde hair and straight white teeth, he appeared to be everyone's idea of the boy next door.

"They both seem young for the state senate," Beth mused, studying Kilgore's picture.

Derrick shook his head. "A lot of men begin political careers in their early thirties, and the state senate is a great place to start. Besides, Jeremiah Dobson is as old as Methuselah. Maybe Oscar Fuller thought the voters were ready for some younger blood." This last statement earned Derrick a little smile. "Mr. Fuller can't just give the appointment to Gamble, so he's focusing media attention on the Ferris Burke trial. Jack Gamble will defend while Lance Kilgore prosecutes."

"And whoever wins gets the senate seat?" Beth asked skeptically. "Like a contest?"

"Unofficially, I guess," Derrick frowned. "The accusations that Gamble is neglecting his daughter haven't come at a good time. That's not the kind of publicity he wants."

"Which is where I come in." Beth examined the article entitled "Gamble Unfit Father?" A fellow employee walked by for the second time, and Beth was afraid that staying in her section much longer might get Derrick in trouble. So she hastily stacked up the papers he had given her. "All this sounds like interesting reading, and you are unquestionably my very best friend. But since you still have a job here, you'd better get back to work."

Ignoring Beth's suggestion, he continued to stare at the computer printouts. "Derrick," she said firmly, and he looked up. "Today is my last day at the library." She paused when she saw moisture collecting in his eyes, then forced herself to continue. "But just because I won't work here doesn't mean I can't come to see you!"

"Beth." He reached over and touched her arm in a rare personal gesture. "I feel bad that you won't be working here anymore, but after reading this stuff, what really worries me is the thought of you dealing with Jack Gamble." Beth smiled, but Derrick did not. "I'm serious, Beth. He's rich and powerful, and one of those articles even hinted at ties to organized crime! If you have to report anything negative about him to the court . . ." He shuddered. "Why can't you find another job? Something nice and safe like a convenience store clerk?"

"I'm only going to be there for a few weeks," Beth tried to hide her amusement. "I'll watch his little girl while he tries to figure out a way to convince a jury to acquit the obviously guilty Ferris Burke. Then I'll leave his house and forget all about Jack Gamble."

Derrick refused to be distracted by her attempt at humor. "I mean it, Beth. I have a bad feeling about this," he whispered as he walked away, his forehead still wrinkled with concern.

Beth had no close attachments to any of her other coworkers, which made the rest of her good-byes brief and unemotional. At four o'clock, she packed her personal effects and the papers about Jack Gamble in a cardboard box and drove home. The bright sunshine put her in a good mood, so when she passed a deli, she stopped and splurged on a sub sandwich. Back in her apartment, she turned on the air conditioner, then the television, and curled up on the couch. As she ate, her hand slipped into her pocket and closed around the picture of Chloe Gamble.

She saved half of her sandwich in the refrigerator for later, then stared at Melissa's letter on the kitchen counter. It was only a sixty-mile drive to her parents' house in Eureka, and she knew her sister's acceptance at BYU was important enough to warrant congratulations in person. But her family would be so happy to see her, and they'd torment her with questions about her new job. She couldn't bear to even think about it, so she called instead.

Nancy Middleton answered the phone. "Is everything okay, Lora Beth?" Her mother was the only person in the world who continued to use her double name.

"Everything is fine, Mama," Beth spoke in a flat tone she had perfected for emotional situations. She wanted to speak to Melissa, but her mother said her sister was shopping. "Well, tell her I called to wish her luck at BYU."

"Isn't it amazing that she was accepted?" Nancy asked reverently. "It shows that miracles do happen."

Beth wanted to say this showed that some people had all the luck, but she told her mother about her new job instead.

"I had no idea you wanted to be a live-in nanny." Her mother didn't sound pleased.

"I wasn't looking for the job, Mama. Bob Wells suggested it." Her mother had always been fond of Bob, and Beth knew his name would carry a lot of weight. "The salary is good, and it'll be an easy way to make money."

"Bob Wells is one of the nicest men I know," Nancy still sounded hesitant. "He was so good to you after . . ." Her voice trailed off into an uncomfortable silence.

"I feel ready to do something different, Mom," Beth said into the quiet. "And Bob is determined that I help this little girl."

The conversation moved to safer issues, and Beth listened to her mother discuss an ill neighbor for almost thirty minutes before she ended the call. After an encounter with her mother, she needed stress relief, so she changed into her running clothes. The sweatpants didn't have pockets, and for some inexplicable reason she couldn't bear to be separated from Chloe Gamble, so she tucked the picture into her sock. After she returned, Beth stayed up late finishing a book about homesteaders in Wyoming and was groggy during church on Sunday.

When sacrament meeting was over, she waited her turn to speak to the branch president. Once he worked his way down the line of congregation members, she explained about her change of address. He said that by moving into Jack Gamble's home in Haggerty, Beth would transfer from the Albany third branch to the Albany second ward. He promised to send her records and notify Bishop Sterling to expect her in their meetings the following Sunday.

"They meet from nine to twelve," the branch president continued after consulting his stake calendar. "Sacrament first. And we are certainly going to miss you!"

Beth was anxious to leave before other members of the small branch involved her in a series of awkward good-byes. So she mumbled something appropriate, then hurried outside.

That evening, Beth received a phone call from Jack Gamble's secretary, Roberta Stark. She gave Beth detailed directions to the Gamble's house and confirmed that they would meet there the next morning at ten o'clock.

Usually Beth didn't run on Sundays, but the events of the past couple of days had left her nerves raw. While putting on her sweat-pants, she berated herself. She had built a predictable, safe life. Why was she risking change? Automatically her hand reached into the pocket of the dress she had worn to church and closed around the photograph of Chloe Gamble. Then, with a sigh, she transferred the picture to her sock and ran outside.

Beth woke up before dawn on Monday, nervous and almost excited. After showering in the tiny bathroom for the last time, she loaded her possessions into the trunk of her car. Then she gave her keys to the landlady and drove away. Her hands were shaking, but she did not cry.

CHAPTER 2

Traffic was light as Beth left Albany and headed west on Highway 11. She had passed the Haggerty City Limits sign often when making the trip to her parents' home in Eureka, but for the first time she took the Haggerty exit. Then she followed Roberta's directions into a new subdivision called The Crossroads.

All the houses were huge and had large, landscaped yards. Wide sidewalks lined the streets, and there was a park with a running track and expensive playground equipment surrounded by shade trees. Jack Gamble's house stood out from the rest because it was obscured from view by a brick security fence that extended all the way out to the sidewalk.

Beth approached the keypad cautiously and entered the code Roberta had given her. She watched the big gate open, then followed the driveway up to a red-brick mansion, vaguely aware of the gate closing silently behind her. She parked in the circular drive at the front of the house behind a bright blue Honda. A woman emerged through the double doors and came to the passenger side of her car. Beth leaned over and rolled down the window as far as it would go.

"I'm Roberta." The voice on the phone had created a glamorous image in Beth's mind, but in reality the secretary was about forty-five years old and at least that many pounds overweight. "You can leave your car here. I'll have someone move it and bring in your things."

Once inside, Beth's senses were bombarded with fresh flowers, antiques, and priceless oil paintings. She had expected a wealthy, single man to favor abstract prints, contemporary furniture, and a few bearskin rugs. When they entered a state-of-the-art kitchen, she was forced to make a comment. "This house is gorgeous."

"It is lovely," Roberta agreed as she walked through the kitchen and into a hall. "Your rooms are this way. Hipolita's suite is here," she said, indicating to the right. "She hasn't been in the country long, so you may have trouble understanding her at first. You are over here." Roberta opened the door to the left. A couch and two chairs were arranged around a television, and there was a dinette set against the far wall. They stepped briefly into the bedroom, where the big window offered a view of a rose garden.

"Hipolita cooks meals for the family, and you're welcome to join them, but the kitchen is well stocked, so feel free to help yourself," the secretary invited. "The laundry room is down the hall. Dry cleaner picks up on Thursday." They walked back through the kitchen and to the stairs. "Chloe's room is up here," she said as they climbed.

The child's room was painted a soft yellow and had high ceilings. Large windows admitted plenty of sunlight. A two-story playhouse was built into one corner, and a bookcase covered an entire wall. The door to the closet was slightly ajar, and Beth could see rows and rows of miniature clothes.

Roberta explained that Chloe would start school the next day, but Beth would be given access to her every afternoon so she could make her evaluations. Beth nodded as they heard voices below. "That must be them," Roberta predicted, walking toward the stairs. Back in the hall, Beth glanced to the left of Chloe's room and Roberta followed her gaze. "Jack's quarters are down there. He's a very private person, so you'll probably want to avoid that area."

When they returned downstairs Jack Gamble was standing by the front door, dressed in old, faded blue jeans and a T-shirt. Beth's subconscious registered these impressions of her new employer as she focused on the little girl clutching his hand.

Chloe was a little older than her snapshot and absolutely breathtaking in hot pink overalls. Most of her hair was pulled into a neat French braid, but a few loose tendrils framed her face. The large, brown eyes shifted nervously as she continued to hold onto her father's hand, and Beth swallowed hard. David's death put an end to her dreams of motherhood, and she had learned to accept it, but Chloe Gamble dredged up the old yearnings.

Roberta smiled at her boss, then spoke to the child. "Chloe, I'd like for you to meet Beth." Chloe retreated behind Jack Gamble's leg. "I guess your daddy told you that she'd be staying here for a while?" Roberta tried again, but Chloe had no comment.

Jack Gamble gave Beth a brief nod of acknowledgement. "Is that your Volkswagen parked out front?"

Roberta answered for her. "I told her to leave it there and I'd have it moved."

"I can't believe you drove that car all the way from Albany. I figured we'd need a tow truck to get it as far as the garage," he muttered as he pulled Chloe from behind his leg. "I'll see you tonight," he told her, then disappeared into the back of the house.

Without her father to shield her, Chloe seemed very small. A short woman wearing earphones walked in, and Roberta introduced her as the housekeeper. Hipolita's head bobbed when Roberta asked her to arrange for Beth's car to be moved. As soon as the other woman was gone, Roberta patted Chloe's shoulder.

"Well, I need to get to the office. Since you and Beth are going to be spending a lot of time together, you've got to be at least a little friendly," the secretary coaxed.

"Chloe's not being unfriendly." Beth chose her words carefully. "It will just take us a little while to feel comfortable with each other."

Roberta gave Beth an approving smile. "Well, you have my cell number?" Beth nodded. "Call if you need me." After giving Chloe another pat, Roberta walked out the door.

Before Beth had a chance to speak, Hipolita came back through. Moving the earphones to hang around her neck, she said that she served breakfast at seven, lunch only when Mr. Jack was at home, and dinner at six every day except Sunday, which was her day off. She reported that the things from the Volkswagen were being transferred to Beth's new room, and the car would be parked in the garage. Then she put her earphones back on and went into the kitchen.

Alone again, Beth studied the child. Chloe seemed nervous, so Beth decided to take things slowly. "Well," she said, "what should we do now?" The small shoulders shrugged. "I hate to ask you this . . ." Beth watched and was pleased to see a little spark of interest in the dark eyes. "Roberta took me around the house, but I don't remember how to find everything. Would you show me again?"

Chloe contemplated this request. "Can we take turns?" she asked finally.

Beth had a brother, two sisters, and a master's degree in early childhood development, but this question confused her. "Take turns doing what?"

"If I do something for you, you have to do something for me. It's fair."

"What would I have to do?" Beth was cautious.

"Maybe you could drive me in your wrecked car."

This seemed harmless enough, so the terms were accepted. Chloe was a very good tour guide. As they entered each room, she pointed out interesting features like a loose brick in the den fireplace and the laundry chutes, which she warned Beth that she must not ever climb into.

The backyard was large, with a swimming pool to the left surrounded by a six-foot wrought-iron fence. Chloe touched the padlock and said that children could not go in there without an adult. To the right was a continuation of the stone-paved patio scattered with potted plants and expensive outdoor furniture. There were some beautiful gardens close to the house, and a well-maintained lawn extended past the pool. Beth could barely see the roofs of the homes on either side of the Gamble residence over the trees that lined the fence.

They sat on the patio for a while and enjoyed the late summer weather. Then Beth glanced at her watch and saw that it was almost time for *The Brave and Relentless*. She knew she owed Chloe a ride in her car, but didn't want to miss the blood test results, so she proposed a compromise. "There's a television show coming on that I'd like to watch. Afterward we could drive to McDonald's."

Beth expected an immediate, positive response, but Chloe considered it carefully. "My dad doesn't like me to eat at McDonald's," she said finally. "He says it's not nutritious."

"You and your father are concerned about nutrition, are you?"

The child shrugged, her jaw set stubbornly in what was obviously an inherited trait.

Beth stood and led the way inside, proud that she made it to her room without a single wrong turn. Chloe touched Hipolita's door as they passed by and said that it was a private area and Beth should never go in without knocking first. She also pointed to the laundry room and confided that all items put into the laundry chutes would eventually end up there, even toys.

Once inside the suite, Beth covertly turned the television to Channel Five, then took a pen from her purse. They sat at the little table and Beth drew a pitiful sketch of the food pyramid while keeping one eye on the television screen. She listed the contents of a typical hamburger Happy Meal as *The Brave and Relentless* theme music ended and the camera zoomed in on Elena talking on the telephone.

Elena was whining about how hard it was to be a wife and a mother while making millions as a successful real-estate agent. Uninterested, Beth turned back to Chloe and continued the health lesson. "Now you can see that a Happy Meal has protein and grains, and maybe the pickle can count as a vegetable."

"Or you could eat a carrot when you got back home," Chloe contributed.

Beth smiled. "I guess you could. Why don't you draw a better food pyramid while I watch the rest of this show, and then we'll go eat a mostly nutritious McDonald's lunch."

Chloe accepted a clean sheet of paper, and Beth scooted her chair up close to the television. Chloe focused on her assignment as the doctor informed Tori that Parker was not her baby's father. Her pregnancy was apparently the result of a brief romance with Parker's half brother, Pierre, during a bout of amnesia Tori had experienced around Christmastime. Disappointed with this news, Beth picked up her purse. Chloe's drawing was not complete, but Beth told her she could finish it later, and they headed outside.

Chloe was very impressed by the old Volkswagen, and Beth let her open all the doors to prove that they worked. Beth didn't know where a McDonald's was, but entered the security code at the formidable gate with the intention of riding up Highway 11 until she found one. As she pulled out of the driveway, she saw a petite woman in a business suit two houses down and across the street, standing at her mailbox. Although the woman appeared to be older, her gray hair was cut stylishly, and she watched with interest as they approached.

Beth leaned over Chloe to roll down the passenger-side window. "We're looking for a McDonald's," she explained. "Could you direct me to the closest one?"

The woman studied Chloe for a few seconds, then looked back at the gates that separated Jack Gamble's house from the rest of the world. "My name is Annabelle Grainger," she said, and Beth recognized this as a polite demand for reciprocal information.

"Beth Middleton," she responded. "And I guess you know Chloe."

"Actually, I don't. I've seen her a few times," the neighbor added thoughtfully, then returned her attention to Beth.

"I just arrived today," Beth provided. "I'm sort of a temporary nanny."

Mrs. Grainger nodded. "I read the newspaper."

Beth sensed that additional inquiries would follow and reminded the neighbor of her original question. "The closest McDonald's is in Albany." Mrs. Grainger pointed vaguely toward the east. "There's a Burger King on Highway 11."

Beth looked at Chloe, and the little girl shrugged. "That will do," Beth assured her.

"Turn left at the entrance to the subdivision. You can't miss it." Mrs. Grainger smiled. "And welcome to Haggerty."

In five minutes Beth parked the Volkswagen in front of a Burger King. She ordered two Kids Meals, then led the way outside. Chloe ate most of her food while staring longingly at the huge tunnel-maze that towered over the playground. Beth suggested that Chloe climb it, but the child shook her head.

"It's okay," Beth comforted. "You would probably have to be at least seven to make it all the way to that spaceship on top." She pointed to the highest level.

"I bet I could do it," Chloe said with determination.

"Well, you could try." Beth purposely sounded doubtful.

The challenge was accepted, and minutes later Chloe was waving from the spaceship. She came down, went up, slid down head-first, and climbed up backward. Finally she sat beside Beth, tired but triumphant. Her hair was coming out of the neat braid, there were smudges on the knees of her overalls, and her shirt had a big ketchup stain on the left sleeve. She looked like an emotionally healthy child having fun, and Beth was pleased.

Once they were settled back in the car, Chloe concentrated on buckling her seat belt, then looked up at Beth. "Does riding here in your car count as my thing you have to do for me?"

Beth took her key out of her purse. "Is there something else you'd like me to do?"

Chloe lowered her eyes and answered softly. "Could you drive to my school?"

"Why?" Beth asked as she put the key in the ignition.

"Because I have to go there tomorrow, and I don't know where the bathroom is."

Beth gave the child her full attention. "Your father hasn't taken you to see the school?" Beth asked, and Chloe shook her head. "You haven't even met your teacher?"

"No."

It seemed like any responsible parent, no matter how busy, could find the time to take their child to a new school before the first day. Beth made a mental note of Jack Gamble's failure to properly prepare his daughter for kindergarten. Then she turned the key. Several times.

"Your car won't start?" Chloe's eyes were wide with amazement.

"It will start," Beth assured her, and it did, with the help of three Burger King employees and a jump from a customer's pickup truck. While she had a group of local residents assembled, Beth asked for directions to Haggerty's elementary school. The truck owner started pointing, but Chloe tugged on Beth's shirt.

"That's not my school. I go to Morrow Academy in Albany," she reported solemnly.

The truck owner saw Beth's confused expression and stepped into the conversation. "It's supposed to be a good school. Real expensive. It's on Lott Street, down from the old armory."

Beth was familiar with Lott Street, so she thanked her helpers, then put Chloe in the Volkswagen for the drive into Albany. The Frances F. Morrow Academy looked more like a college campus than an elementary school. They stopped by the gate, and a uniformed man stepped out of the guardhouse to ask Beth if he could help her.

She explained that Chloe was a new student, which he seemed to doubt. He gave the Volkswagen a long look, then went inside to check his lists. In a few minutes he returned with a temporary visitor's pass and pointed the way to the office.

The principal was an older lady with a white bun and perfect posture named Mrs. Elliott. She offered to give them a limited tour of the kindergarten building, and they followed her through the cavernous hallways.

"The teachers are all extremely busy today, since school begins in the morning," the principal reminded them as they reached Chloe's classroom. "I'll check with Miss Hyde and see if she can spare a few minutes to talk to you."

Beth and Chloe waited in the hall while Mrs. Elliott conferred with the teacher. There was a restroom directly across from them, and Beth pointed it out. Chloe nodded grimly. Then Mrs. Elliott returned and said that the teacher would see them.

Miss Hyde looked chic and sophisticated in a tailored linen dress and matching shoes. Her glossy, black hair was expertly styled and caressed her cheek each time she moved. The principal made introductions.

"Miss Hyde, this is Mrs. Gamble and her daughter Chloe."

Beth opened her mouth to make the correction, but Mrs. Elliott was already listing the teacher's considerable credentials. Beth learned that Miss Hyde was born in Boston and had a master's degree from an Ivy League college. Mrs. Elliott explained that this was her first year of teaching, and Morrow Academy felt very fortunate to have her.

During this discourse, Beth watched as Miss Hyde assessed her under demurely lowered lashes, taking in the cheap sandals, baggy dress, and lack of makeup in one quick sweep. When Mrs. Elliott finished heaping laud and honor on the teacher, the principal excused herself, and Miss Hyde's smile became less cordial.

"It's a shame that you weren't able to attend our orientation this morning with all the other new students."

Beth rarely worried about her appearance, but Miss Hyde's cool appraisal made her regret her shapeless outfit, and Chloe didn't look much better with the ketchup stain on her shirt. "I'm not Chloe's mother." Beth wanted to make that clear from the start. "And I'm sorry we missed the orientation."

Miss Hyde accepted the apology with a brief nod, then turned to Chloe. Under her scrutiny, the child seemed to wither. Miss Hyde asked several simple questions, but Chloe hid her face and refused to answer. With barely concealed irritation, Miss Hyde walked to a desk and pulled out the little chair. "This is where you will sit," she explained, but Chloe remained silent. Miss Hyde frowned and directed their attention to the reading and computer centers, but Chloe showed no interest. Eventually the teacher worked her way back to Beth. "We'll give Chloe a few days to settle in before we begin testing her."

"I guess you test all the children to get a base IQ."

The teacher lifted a shoulder. "Chloe will need a special evaluation."

Beth's forehead creased in confusion. "Special?"

"Surely you realize that her behavior is not normal. Her lack of verbal competence indicates possible learning deficiencies. Some kind of speech therapy may help, but she probably should be moved into a remedial class, at least until she learns to talk."

"Chloe most definitely can talk," Beth refuted this statement. "She is shy, but if you will be patient—"

"I have seventeen other children in this classroom," Miss Hyde interrupted. "Everything cannot revolve around one slow child."

"Slow!" Beth was outraged that the teacher would use such a term in front of Chloe.

"Her oral skills are certainly below average. Did she have difficulty learning to speak? Any stuttering, that type of thing?"

Beth paused, unable to respond because she didn't know the answer. Miss Hyde mistook her ignorance for embarrassment over Chloe's lack of ability. "It's nothing to be ashamed of," the teacher consoled. "With early intervention and the correct environment, Chloe can learn a number of useful things."

"I can't believe that someone as well educated as you are would classify a child based on five minutes of observation."

"My initial impressions are almost never wrong," Miss Hyde informed her.

"Well, you are very wrong about Chloe." Beth urged the child toward the door.

"Since Mr. Gamble is the parent, any further discussions on this subject really need to be with him," she said to Beth's back. "There will be an open house at the end of next week. Perhaps he can attend."

"I'll tell him," Beth promised as she pulled Chloe through the school and out the front doors. Still fuming, Beth returned her visitor's pass to the security guard, then negotiated the crowded streets of Albany while Chloe sat quietly in the passenger seat. Once they were driving down Highway 11, she turned to Chloe. "Why didn't you speak to Miss Hyde?"

Chloe's response was simple. "Because she has mean eyes."

"But now she thinks you can't talk. Tomorrow you'll have to show her how smart you are," Beth advised, but Chloe just shrugged.

"She'll still be mean."

Beth couldn't think of a comforting response, so they continued in silence. When they turned into The Crossroads, Beth saw that several families were taking advantage of the nice weather and the lovely park. "I'll bet you play out here a lot." She pointed to the playground.

Chloe looked across the car and out Beth's window. "My daddy doesn't let me. He thinks I'll break my arm."

The park disappeared from view as Beth pulled in front of the Gamble's house. She punched in the security code and noticed a little blonde girl about Chloe's age in the yard across the street. "Is she a friend of yours?" Beth asked, watching the gate slide open.

Chloe twisted around in her seat and stared at the girl. "I see her sometimes, but I don't know her name. She has a brother." There was a wistful note in Chloe's voice, and Beth added another black mark on her mental list. No McDonald's, no park, no friends. The evidence against Jack Gamble was mounting.

Beth parked beside the garage and was collecting her purse when the passenger door of the Volkswagen was jerked open. She looked up to see Jack Gamble leaning into the car.

"Where have you been?" he demanded through clenched teeth.

Ever since David's death, Beth had been uncomfortable with men. Jack Gamble had startled her, which made the reaction worse. As a result, it was a few seconds before she could compose herself enough to speak. By then he was holding Chloe in his arms.

"We went to Burger King for lunch and then toured Chloe's new school."

His expression darkened, and Beth started to list the nutritional values of a hamburger, but he cut her off. "You drove my daughter to Albany in this piece of junk?" He gave the car a critical examination.

Beth felt obligated to defend the Volkswagen. "My car is a classic," she stated firmly, hoping that Chloe wouldn't choose this moment to mention the faulty battery.

"The tires are bald, the tailpipe is dragging on the ground, and I doubt you could go more than thirty miles per hour downhill, which makes you a road hazard."

"I have driven over thirty miles per hour on several occasions," Beth denied the allegation.

He looked away, running his fingers through his hair. After a moment he returned his angry gaze to her. "My daughter will never ride in it again at any speed." He shifted the child to his other hip. "I want you to be perfectly clear on this, Miss Middleton. Anytime you take Chloe off this property, it had better be with my permission, in my car, and with my driver at the wheel. Otherwise it's equivalent to kidnapping."

Beth listened to him insult her car and her intelligence. He emphasized each syllable as though he were talking to a young child. When he finished, she nodded. "I understand." His expression relaxed and he turned toward the house. "But Mr. Gamble," Beth called after him, and he paused. "I want to make it perfectly clear than any further instructions you have for me had better be delivered in a polite, civilized manner. Otherwise I'll have to report your uncooperative attitude to the family court judge." She hooked her purse over her shoulder and left him staring after her.

Inside her new room, Beth changed clothes, then collapsed on the bed to recover from her confrontation with Chloe's father. She woke up hours later, completely disoriented. It took a few seconds to remember where she was and why. Her head felt dull—not quite a headache, but close.

It was 6:30 when she walked into the kitchen, expecting to find Chloe and her father eating dinner, but the room was deserted. Warming pans were arranged along one counter, filled with fried chicken and several vegetables. A cake and two pies were off to the side. After putting some food on a plate, Beth walked back to her room and ate at her little table. Fifteen minutes later, when she put her dishes in the sink, all the food had disappeared and the kitchen had returned to perfect order. There was still no sign of Chloe, so Beth walked upstairs.

From the hallway Beth could see that the yellow bedroom was dark and quiet. Roberta had said that she would have access to Chloe each day, but the term *nanny* seemed to indicate more responsibility, and Bob Wells had made a reference to concerns about Chloe's lack of supervision. With a sigh, Beth realized the only way to clarify her position in the household was to find her employer. She had taken one step down the forbidden hallway toward his room when Hipolita came around the corner and almost scared her to death.

"I can help you?" the housekeeper asked, looking pointedly at the area Beth had been warned to stay away from. Beth cleared her throat and explained that she was searching for Chloe. Hipolita's expression became even more suspicious. "She with her father now. He puts her to bed on time," she reported.

Beth thanked her, then turned away, feeling foolish. The housekeeper didn't reply, but stood and watched Beth's retreat, as if she were afraid the new nanny might reconsider and run to Mr. Gamble's door.

Beth returned to her room and changed into sweat clothes. It was just starting to get dark as she ran down the driveway, pausing at the metal gate to enter the security code. She followed the winding road to the park, then started running around the track, admiring the beautiful homes with lights shining through the windows. Occasionally she caught a glimpse of families gathered for the evening meal. She filled her lungs with flower-scented air and didn't count laps but ran until her knees forced her to stop.

That night she climbed into the strange bed expecting to lie awake for hours. To her surprise, she woke up with the sun at six o'clock on Tuesday morning. Beth stared at the alarm clock in amazement. She had not slept for that many consecutive hours in over two years.

After searching through her limited wardrobe, she found a decent pair of khaki pants and a shirt her mother had given her for Christmas. She didn't really think she could change Miss Hyde's original opinion of her, but didn't see any need to emphasize it.

Once she was dressed, Beth forced herself to look into the mirror. She had always considered herself passably attractive, but after David's death she had gotten into the habit of ignoring her appearance. Years of running regularly and eating sporadically had left her painfully thin. She examined the pale, tightly stretched skin of her face, the solemn gray eyes, and long blonde hair that hung over her shoulders. Her teeth were straight, thanks to three years in braces. She thought of Miss Hyde and wished briefly for chic and sophisticated. She settled instead for clean and neat.

Hipolita had breakfast arranged buffet style on the kitchen counter. Beth picked up a biscuit to be polite and was nibbling on it when Chloe came in. The child was wearing green overalls and a frown. Her hair was divided into two perfect pigtails, and Beth thought when she got to know Hipolita better, she might ask for braiding lessons. The housekeeper helped Chloe get some cereal and then settled the child at the table.

"Will your father eat with us this morning?" Beth asked, anxious to determine her responsibilities.

Chloe shook her head. "He won't eat breakfast too much for a while. He has to get to court early so the judge won't think he's late."

"I guess he's pretty busy right now with his new case," Beth ventured.

She regretted the words immediately as Chloe's expression darkened. "He says things will be better in a few weeks."

A tall, thin man with red hair and freckles walked into the kitchen while Beth was trying to think of a way to cheer up Chloe. He lifted Chloe out of her seat, swung her around with the cereal spoon hanging from her hand, then plopped her back into the chair. "You must be the baby-sitter," he said to Beth, taking a clean plate from the counter.

"I'm not a baby," Chloe objected to his terminology.

"What are you then, a monkey? A goose? A lizard?" the man teased, and Chloe giggled as he piled food onto his plate. He mixed eggs and bacon and fruit, then poured gravy over the whole mess. Beth watched jelly seep out of a doughnut onto his grits and shuddered.

"I know you aren't going to eat that," she couldn't help but say.

"Roy always mixes his food," Chloe explained. "He says it's the way real men eat."

"Roy Hankins." He sat down and extended his hand to Beth.

"Beth Middleton," she returned, touching his palm briefly.

"Born and raised in Albany," he supplied as if she had asked. "Taught to fear the Lord, respect my elders, and appreciate beautiful women!" He gave her what he probably thought was a charming smile. "Always been lucky, too. I mean, how much luckier can you get than to land a part-time job with Mr. Jack Gamble? He pays good, lets me live in the apartment over his garage, and all I have to do is run a few errands and drive Chloe around. Can't beat a deal like that!"

"Are you taking Chloe to school today?" Beth ignored the rest of his useless information.

"Sure am. Today and every day. That's what my boss, Mr. Jack Gamble, told me to do," Roy reported around a mouthful of mush. Averting her eyes, Beth said that she wanted to ride with them and asked if it would be a problem for him to bring her home afterward. "No problem at all," Roy answered slowly, looking up from his breakfast.

Chloe's posture improved after Beth's announcement. "You're coming with me to school?"

"Today and every day," Beth imitated Roy. "I don't think Miss Hyde will let me stay, but I can at least ride with you."

Chloe curled her lips into a brave little smile, and Beth's heart melted.

Once everyone was finished with breakfast, they walked out into the bright sunshine and Roy opened the back door of a new-looking Ford Expedition. He watched while they put on seat belts, then talked all the way to Morrow Academy. Finally Beth realized that he didn't expect any response from her, so she concentrated on Chloe. In an attempt to distract the child from their destination, Beth opened Chloe's new backpack and admired all her school supplies.

Despite her efforts, Beth noticed that the tension in Chloe's body was increasing steadily as they approached the school. Roy turned through the gates and pulled up to the curb, stopping behind several other cars. A man stood by the curb opening doors for the students, but Beth didn't give him a chance to assist Chloe. She stepped out and took the child's hand. Then they walked into the school and down the long hallways to the kindergarten building. Beth pointed out the bathroom again and Chloe nodded, her fingers clutching Beth's.

Miss Hyde was standing by the door wearing another beautiful dress. She waved her manicured hands as she spoke to a lady Beth recognized as the host of a local cooking show. Finally it was their turn to approach.

"Mrs. Gamble." The teacher's tone was cool. "Chloe," she added.

Beth opened her mouth in another attempt to explain her relationship to Jack Gamble, but people from behind surged forward and pushed them aside. As Miss Hyde's attention shifted to other parents, Beth bent down to Chloe. "I'll be waiting right here after school."

Tears slipped over Chloe's lashes and ran down her cheeks. "You promise?"

"Promise," Beth answered, then watched as Chloe disappeared into the classroom.

"First day of school," Roy said as she climbed back in the car. "Seems like just yesterday." He began a soliloquy about his early years, and Beth stared dismally out the window. They passed a school bus as they turned into The Crossroads, and Beth interrupted to ask why Chloe didn't attend the public kindergarten. "Have to check with the boss about that," he replied.

Although Mr. Gamble was not happy about Beth's presence in his house, they both wanted what was best for Chloe. Beth pictured Morrow Academy with a guard at the gate and Miss Hyde standing like an expensive mannequin outside her classroom door. After she described the situation to Mr. Gamble, surely he would admit his mistake and transfer Chloe to a public school.

Roy dropped Beth off behind the house with a promise to pick her up at 1:30. Inside she found Hipolita chopping vegetables. Beth told the housekeeper that she needed to talk to Mr. Gamble.

"He real busy," Hipolita answered, the knife suspended above her cutting board.

"I know, but it's about Chloe. Very important," Beth added for emphasis. "Should I write him a note?"

"I tell him," Hipolita said, then turned back to the vegetables.

It took Beth a full five minutes to unpack all her things and straighten her room. She opened a library book but couldn't get involved in the plot. She turned on the television, but none of the programs interested her. Restlessness finally forced her to leave the bedroom. She made it to the front entrance without running into Hipolita. Feeling bold, she stepped into the enormous living room. It was beautifully decorated and set up for entertaining on a large scale. Beth was examining a small oil painting when Jack Gamble spoke from behind her.

"You wanted to see me?" His voice seemed amplified in the large, open space.

Feeling like a trespasser, she turned to face him. "I need to know Chloe's schedule. I looked for her last night after dinner, but couldn't find her."

He stared at her without speaking for a few unnerving moments. "I am under no obligation to keep you informed of Chloe's whereabouts," he said finally.

"I'm here to evaluate the home environment," she reminded him, and his jaw tensed. "I should spend a lot of time with Chloe, and I'll need to observe the two of you together as well."

Jack Gamble frowned. "I am not a circus performer, Miss Middleton. I will give you time with Chloe after school. I will allow you to roam my house and critique the atmosphere. But I won't have you sitting in a corner taking notes while I watch television with my daughter." He turned to leave, and Beth took a step toward him.

"I also wanted to discuss Morrow Academy. Chloe isn't happy there, and I think you should transfer her to the local public kindergarten."

"Chloe's school is no concern of yours," he said over his shoulder.

"For the next three months, everything about Chloe is a concern of mine," she contradicted him. "Did she tell you about her teacher?"

"The subject came up," he admitted. "Miss Hyde is very well qualified."

Beth tried to think of a way to describe the teacher. "She's stiff and critical. And the school itself is extremely intimidating." When none of this seemed to make much of an impression, she pressed on. "Chloe cried when we left her this morning."

He was still facing away from her, so she couldn't see his expression, but his voice shook a little when he replied. "Most children shed a few tears on the first day of kindergarten. I investigated Morrow Academy thoroughly, and it is perfect."

"Perfect for some children maybe, but not for everyone. Not for Chloe," Beth disagreed.

He turned and stared at her. "You met my daughter twenty-four hours ago, and you think you are qualified to make decisions about what kind of child she is?"

"It only took Miss Hyde five minutes to determine that Chloe needs remedial testing." Beth was pleased to see the tension in his jaw increase. "I am giving you my educated opinion, Mr. Gamble. I have been to the school, I have met Miss Hyde, and if Chloe were my child, I would move her immediately."

He ran his hands through his hair in an impatient gesture. "I appreciate the fact that you are trying to help." His tone indicated otherwise. "But Chloe is not your child, and there is no question of her changing schools. The security at Morrow Academy is the best in the state."

"You missed the parent orientation yesterday," Beth continued doggedly. "But there is an open house next Friday you will have to attend."

"I don't *have* to do anything," Jack Gamble said.

Beth's eyes narrowed. "You're being uncooperative again."

He scowled and looked at his watch.

"If you miss that open house, I will be forced to mention it to the judge."

He smiled, although his eyes showed no amusement. Then he took another step toward the door.

"Do you want Chloe to be the only one there without a parent?" Beth persisted.

He stopped then. "Next Friday won't be a good day for me. Chloe understands."

"Do you really think so?" Beth decided she had nothing to lose. "No one is that busy."

"I've got a murder trial to prepare for, Miss Middleton. Leave my daughter and her education to me." With that, he walked out of the room and left Beth staring after him.

Discouraged, she went back to the kitchen and took an apple from a fruit bowl on the table for lunch. She ate it outside on the patio, enjoying the sunshine. When she returned to the kitchen to throw away the core, Hipolita was nowhere in sight but another shiny red apple had been placed in the bowl.

She was able to watch the first half of *The Brave and Relentless* before Roy came to pick her up. After setting the VCR to record, she hurried out and climbed into the SUV. On the way to the school Roy told her that he had interviewed to be a tour guide at the Veterans of Foreign Wars Museum. "Has flexible hours and it pays pretty good. All I'd have to do is walk around and explain what caused the Great Depression and World War II."

Beth wished him luck, silently thinking there wasn't much hope of him getting a job where he had to speak at all, let alone describe economic collapse and global conflict. Beth was standing in the hall across from Chloe's classroom when Miss Hyde opened her door. The women nodded to each other, then Beth watched for Chloe. She was the last child out.

"Come on now, Chloe," Miss Hyde said with exaggerated patience. "I asked you twice to be ready before the bell rang."

Without a word, Chloe joined Beth and they walked back to the car. During the drive they looked through Chloe's backpack. She had a homework sheet of circles and was supposed to find pictures of red things from magazines to share with her class the next day.

Hipolita had cookies and a glass of milk waiting on the kitchen table for Chloe when they got home. Beth took a cookie off the plate and, after a brief hesitation, the housekeeper poured another glass of milk. Then Beth suggested that they take the snack into her room and do homework there. Chloe agreed before Hipolita could object, although it was obvious that she wanted to.

Beth pushed the tape of *The Brave and Relentless* into the VCR as they settled in at the little table. Chloe finished a cookie, then said she was going to make extra good circles so that Miss Hyde would like them. Beth tried to imagine a circle perfect enough to please Miss Hyde as she listened to Cedric tell Marissa that he had been an alcoholic for years, which was no surprise to anyone except Marissa. During a commercial break Beth saw an advertisement for a local florist, and an idea started to form. It was so simple that she laughed out loud, and Chloe looked up.

"I was just thinking about how Miss Hyde is nicer to some of the other parents and kids than she is to us," Beth explained. "I think she might still be mad that we missed the orientation, and when I saw how happy that lady was to get roses . . ." Beth pointed toward the television.

Chloe assimilated this information. "So if we send Miss Hyde some flowers, she'll be nice to me?"

"I think it might help, especially if she thinks they are from your father." Jack Gamble was a minor local celebrity and unquestionably attractive. Miss Hyde seemed vain enough to enjoy attention from a handsome man and smart enough to recognize the advantage of knowing a good criminal lawyer.

"We're going to tell my daddy to give flowers to Miss Hyde?" Chloe asked, and Beth shook her head.

"No, we won't bother him at work. I'll order the flowers and have the florist sign his name." Beth opened the phone book and, with her Visa card in hand, dialed the number for the only florist in Haggerty. She ordered an autumn bouquet, then gave them Miss Hyde's name and the school's address. After dictating a carefully worded note, Beth hung up the phone and smiled at Chloe.

The child regarded her solemnly. "When will she get the flowers?"

"The florist promised that they would be delivered first thing in the morning," Beth assured her. Chloe nodded and returned to her circles with more enthusiasm.

They ate dinner promptly at six and without Jack Gamble. After the meal, Chloe invited Beth upstairs to play in the beautiful, yellow room. When Chloe opened a cupboard full of Barbies, Beth sat down on the floor and took out several. "I've always loved Barbies," she said from her cross-legged position. "I have a bunch at home."

"Barbies are my favorite," Chloe agreed, pulling out her Barbie Dream House. Beth arranged furniture while Chloe opened a box containing a bridal ensemble. They took all the pieces out and put the white outfit on Back-to-School Barbie. Then they chose three more dolls to be attendants. Beth placed a smiling Ken beside the bride, and then her hands started to shake. She jerked back and knocked over two of the bridesmaids. "What's the matter?" Chloe asked.

Beth didn't answer immediately. "I almost got married once," she finally forced past stiff lips. "But," she pointed toward the dolls still arranged for a wedding, "my Ken died."

"Oh, that's sad." Chloe's eyes clouded with concern.

"I don't like to talk about it," Beth said, afraid she would be asked for details. Then she started returning bridesmaids to the correct boxes. Chloe grabbed the Ken doll and hid him under the Barbie

Motor Home, then jammed the other dolls into the cupboard without regard for clothes or accessories.

Beth stared at the jumbled mess. "Aren't you afraid you'll lose things if you don't put them in the right boxes?"

Chloe gave her a mischievous grin. "Nope. Hipolita will fix them tomorrow."

Before Beth could object to the unfairness of this plan, Chloe said it was time for her shower. Beth offered to help, but the child insisted she could handle it alone. In response to Beth's doubtful look, Chloe took her into the bathroom and demonstrated her custom-made shower. The system controlled the water temperature and pressure automatically.

"I thought most children took baths instead of showers," Beth commented.

"My daddy says I could drown if I take a bath, so the shower is better," Chloe admitted matter-of-factly. "But I have to tell somebody before I get in," she said. Beth was impressed by the technology, but it did seem a little sad. Chloe was very young to be so independent.

After Chloe's shower Beth suggested that they watch TV downstairs, but the child shook her head and pointed to the clock. "It's almost my bedtime." Beth offered to read a book, but Chloe declined again, and it was obvious that she was politely ending their evening. This hurt a little, since Beth couldn't remember a day she had enjoyed so much.

She trudged down to her room and changed into running clothes. Then she ran laps around the park until her knees ached. Beth took some Ibuprofen and a shower, then slept until dawn.

CHAPTER 3

On Wednesday morning when they pulled in front of Morrow Academy, Beth started to get out with Chloe, but the child stopped her. "Miss Hyde said we have to come in by ourself today," she explained. Beth wondered if that was an official regulation or Miss Hyde's own idea, but Chloe's burst of independence was a good sign, so she stayed in the SUV with Roy.

Back in the Gamble's empty house, Beth went to her room and opened her new book. It was a predictable story about a middle-age couple who met and fell in love at an amusement park. She tired of it quickly and considered skipping to the next one, but that seemed like cheating, so she made herself continue. As she read, her mind kept drifting. Had the flowers arrived yet? Was Miss Hyde pleased? Was Chloe having a good day? When she started the same page for the fifth time, she put the book aside and spent thirty minutes changing the television channels. Finally she was bored enough to call her mother.

She gave her mother the new phone number, then listened to a description of all the family activities geared toward getting Melissa ready to leave for Utah on Monday. When her mother asked Beth if she would be able to come home for the holiday weekend, she used her new job as an excuse but promised to try and meet them at the airport.

Next Beth called the downtown branch of the Dougherty County Library and asked to speak to Derrick, but he had gone to lunch, so Beth forced herself to read until one o'clock. The entire first half of *The Brave and Relentless* was devoted to Elena's decision to leave the real-estate firm so she could concentrate on her personal life. At 1:30, Beth set the VCR to record and went outside to wait for Roy.

When Chloe came through the school doors, Beth knew that their plan had been successful. "Miss Hyde loved her flowers," the child reported breathlessly as she climbed into the SUV. "They came while she was saying our names to see if we were here. Miss Hyde has seen Daddy on television with Mr. Burke, and she thinks he's cute," Chloe added with a giggle.

"I thought she might," Beth murmured as she helped to fasten the seat belt. "So, you had a good day?"

"I had a real good day," Chloe confirmed. "Miss Hyde moved me up to the front row by her desk. Now I sit next to Briana, and she's my friend."

"Is Briana's mother the lady from the TV cooking show?"

"No, that's Horizon. I don't think she is my friend yet, but I'll ask her tomorrow." Beth went through the backpack while Chloe chattered. She was so interested in what Chloe was saying that they were turning into The Crossroads before she realized that Roy hadn't said a word for miles. She looked up to see him watching her in the rearview mirror.

"Are you okay, Roy?" His silence was so out of character that she was mildly alarmed.

"Things seemed a lot better at school today," he answered.

Beth's eyes widened in surprise. She didn't think he ever paid any attention to her conversations with Chloe. "Miss Hyde just appreciated a small gift we sent her." Beth admitted reluctantly. "But you're right about Chloe having a good day. Do you think Mr. Gamble would mind if we stopped to get some ice cream in celebration?"

"Only one way to find out," he responded, pulling a small cell phone from his shirt pocket and punching in some numbers. "Roberta!" he hollered a few seconds later. "Checking to see if a quick trip to that ice-cream place over on Highway 76 would be okay with the boss." There was a pause. "That's real good news." He returned the phone to his pocket, then made a U-turn and drove to a place called Fifty-Five Flavors.

Chloe chose a chocolate fudge sundae with colored sprinkles, and Beth had a scoop of vanilla on a sugar cone. Roy ordered a double banana split with extra cherries. Beth had intended to pay for the treats since the celebration was her idea, but Roy insisted. "I'll turn it in as a business expense," he told her with a smile.

They found an empty booth in the dining area and listened to oldies on the jukebox. "Do you think there really are fifty-five?" Roy asked as he licked melted ice cream from the sides of his bowl.

"Fifty-five what?" Beth tried to keep her distaste from showing.

"Flavors." He pointed to the lighted sign above the counter. Beth looked at the name of the shop and shrugged.

"If they don't have fifty-five flavors, it would be a lie," Chloe pronounced.

Beth laughed and Roy ruffled Chloe's hair. "And liars couldn't make ice cream this good," he said as he stood.

At home, Beth watched the last half of her soap opera while Chloe drew vertical lines on her homework sheet. They both finished just as Roy knocked on the door and invited them to go swimming. Beth was shy about wearing a swimsuit, but since no one could look worse than Roy did, she accepted. Chloe went up to change, and Beth searched through her own clothes. The only suit she owned was ten years old and way too big, so she put a T-shirt on over it.

Then she sat on the pool steps and watched Roy and Chloe play. Roy did innumerable awful dives, causing Chloe to laugh so hard she had to run into the cabana to use the bathroom. After they were sufficiently waterlogged, they dried and went into the kitchen. Roy stayed for dinner and bragged about Hipolita's cooking as they walked along the counter, filling their plates. Beth chose a piece of chicken, but he reached over and poked his fork into it.

"No grilled chicken for you tonight." He tossed the meat back into the pan. "Mexican food is Hipolita's specialty." He took the plate from her hand. "Let me fix that for you."

Chloe laughed when she saw the amount of food Roy finally placed before Beth. "I'll never be able to eat all that!" Beth objected.

"If you don't eat everything, you might get on Hipolita's bad side," he warned.

Trying to imagine Hipolita any less friendly that she already was, Beth reexamined the plate. Grateful that at least he hadn't mixed it all together, she ate a few bites. Luckily she had eaten her fill before she saw Roy's dinner. It looked like fresh vomit.

"How can you eat that?" Beth asked as he put a spoonful of brown goo into his mouth.

He lifted an eyebrow. "Bet you've never tried mixing your food together."

"Bet you're right."

Beth and Chloe left Roy working on his third helping of Mexican mush and went to Beth's room to watch *Wheel of Fortune*. Afterward they walked upstairs and Beth sat on the bed while Chloe took her shower. When the little girl came out of the bathroom, dressed in white pajamas covered with red hearts, she climbed up beside Beth. "Could we play something?" she asked. "Not Barbies," she added quickly.

Beth pointed to a stack of photo albums. "Maybe you could show me some pictures of yourself when you were little." Chloe selected a large, blue album, and Beth opened the book hoping to see baby pictures, but all the photos were fairly recent. In a Christmas snapshot she saw a stunningly beautiful woman with dark hair and eyes very much like Chloe's.

"That's Monique," Chloe said.

"She's your mother." There was no question.

Chloe nodded. "People might think she's old if they know she has a girl as big as me, so she said don't call her mom." Chloe's tone was matter-of-fact. "She's an actress in France."

"She's very pretty."

This drew a smile. "My daddy says she's the most beautiful woman in the world besides me."

Beth got so involved with the pictures that she didn't notice the time until Chloe mentioned that it was almost eight o'clock. Reluctantly, she surrendered the albums and watched as Chloe returned them to the bookshelf. Then she fluffed the pillows and waited for Chloe to settle in the middle of the big bed. Without thinking, Beth reached down and pushed the soft, damp tendrils of hair from the child's forehead. It was like touching silk and velvet.

On Thursday morning Chloe rushed through breakfast, anxious to get to school. "Miss Hyde said I get to be line leader today," she announced as she swallowed a mouthful of toast. Beth offered her congratulations, then Hipolita sent Chloe to brush her teeth.

After Roy dropped her back off at the house, Beth walked through the kitchen toward her room. Jack Gamble cut her off at the walk-in freezer. "You ordered flowers for Chloe's teacher and signed my name," he stated abruptly.

She was tempted to make him grovel, but decided to be gracious. "Actually, the florist signed for you, but I did order the flowers." *And paid for them,* she thought to herself.

He didn't thank her. "I have a regular florist in Albany who called me three times yesterday to find out why I had used a competitor. In the future, if you think I need to send flowers to someone, please let Roberta arrange it."

Beth was too surprised to respond. She watched him walk out the back door, then went to her room and called Derrick at the library.

"Can you believe that drivel about Elena quitting the real-estate firm?" her friend asked the minute he heard her voice. "They know all anyone cares about is Parker's reaction when he finds out that his brother is the father of his wife's child! They're holding America hostage!"

Beth laughed, and it felt good. "I have missed you so much, Derrick. You understand the intricacies of daytime television better than anyone I've ever met!"

"It's a gift," he agreed. "So, how do you like Jack Gamble?"

"I don't," she told him frankly. "But I love his little girl. She's beautiful and smart, and I wish she were mine."

"Hey! Is the FBI going to be calling me in a few weeks to say that you've kidnapped the kid?" he asked, and she laughed again.

"If that particular situation arises, tell them that I definitely did not take her to the mountains of Uruguay." Beth smiled as he groaned.

Her conversation with Derrick left her feeling optimistic, so Beth decided to drive through Haggerty. At first she was concerned about getting lost, but after a few minutes realized that this was not a possibility. The business district was concentrated around a town square, which she circled several times. Then she turned down a few residential streets, passing churches and a nice, new elementary school.

She didn't trust her battery, so she made no stops, but felt more secure about her surroundings when she got back to the Gamble's house. She parked by the garage and walked around a fancy pickup truck near the patio. Inside the kitchen she saw a small, balding man talking to Hipolita. He turned when she came through the door.

"You must be the nanny," he said. The man was a few inches shorter than Beth, and his slightly uncertain mannerisms reminded her of Derrick, so she was immediately drawn to him.

"I'm Beth." She extended her hand.

"My name is Malcolm Schneckenberger," he said as he clasped her palm enthusiastically. "Can you believe that last name? Fifteen letters! I was in the seventh grade before I could spell it," he told her, and Beth smiled at the weak joke. "I work for Oscar Fuller, chairman of the Georgia Republican Party, so you'll see a lot of me!" He glanced down at the papers he was holding. "I've brought a report for Jack and was just about to take it up to his office."

"I tell him Mr. Jack not home and the papers can stay with me," Hipolita said from across the room. This was a veritable speech by Hipolita's standards, and Beth was immediately on guard. For some reason, the housekeeper didn't want the little man to go upstairs, but his position near the hallway indicated that he didn't intend to respect her wishes. Without stopping to think, Beth stepped forward and blocked his path.

"I'll see that Mr. Gamble gets them, Mr. Schneckenberger."

After the briefest hesitation, he surrendered the report. "Thanks. And call me Malcolm. I can't stand my last name. Well, I'd better get back. Not enough hours in the day, you know."

Beth wanted to tell him she had plenty of hours in her day, but followed him out to his truck and watched until he was out of the gate. When Beth got back inside, she gave the papers to Hipolita and started to take a banana out of the fruit bowl.

"I make you lunch." The housekeeper pointed to a sandwich on the table. Beth assumed that the unscheduled meal was a reward for keeping Malcolm Schneckenberger out of Jack Gamble's office and ate every bite to show her appreciation.

On the way home from school that afternoon, Beth checked Chloe's take-home folder. The column for a parent signature was

Un mot de ...

Monsieur Michel Léger

B2B2C

TEL: 514-908-5420

WEB = B2B2C.CA

TEL + INTERNET

$ 38.00 PAR MOIS

blank for the past three days, so she checked each little square. Mr. Gamble got home so late every night she doubted that he ever even looked inside Chloe's backpack. But if he objected to her interference, at least that would give her another opportunity to discuss Morrow Academy and Miss Hyde with him.

Beth settled Chloe at the little table in her room, then watched the second half of *The Brave and Relentless* while Chloe practiced drawing squares. Later Roy came by and offered to take them swimming again. They had only been in the pool for a few minutes when a misty rain began to fall, and Roy helped Chloe out of the water. Beth hated storms, but since there was no thunder or lightning, she suggested they continue to play. Roy and Chloe both turned to stare at her. "It's so dangerous to swim in the rain." Chloe's tone was grave.

"Heard that where there's rain, there's lightning," Roy added as he directed them through the gate and toward the house.

Beth looked up at the sky. "I'm not sure this qualifies as rain. It's more like heavy humidity. And what you've heard is 'where there's smoke, there's fire'."

He grinned and held open the kitchen door. "Knew it was something like that."

On Friday morning Beth was reading the last chapter of the amusement park romance when Hipolita brought her an envelope that had arrived in the mail. Inside, Beth found her final check from the county library, which included a few vacation days and was therefore more substantial than she expected. When she finally finished her book, she decided to reward herself with a trip to Albany. She deposited her check, then visited Derrick in the rare book department. She got back to the house just as Roy arrived to pick her up.

He waited in the SUV while she put her new library books in her room. She was on her way back outside when the phone rang. She picked up the receiver cautiously. It was Jack Gamble's secretary.

"Jack's going to be late tonight. He said you can observe Chloe until dinnertime, then Hipolita will take over."

"I'll just keep her with me," Beth offered. "The more time I spend with her, the better."

There was a brief pause. "Jack said for you to give her to Hipolita." Roberta's reluctance was obvious.

"Tell him that giving me extra time with Chloe will look good in my report to the family court judge," Beth suggested, thinking that Mr. Gamble could use some points in his favor.

Roberta said she'd check with her boss and asked for Beth's cell phone number. Beth recited the number, then rushed outside and apologized to Roy for the delay.

"No problem. Always leave a little early anyway, just to make sure I'm not late. Can't risk losing this job until I find one full-time."

"The job at the VFW museum didn't work out?" Beth was sorry, but not surprised.

"Naw, they gave it to some know-it-all college kid, but I've got an interview on Monday with the Chamber of Commerce. Said they need somebody to show important visitors around."

Beth knew that the Chamber of Commerce was never going to let Roy get anywhere near "important visitors" and was grateful when her phone rang, saving her from a reply. "Jack says you can keep Chloe until bedtime, and since it's Friday she can stay up until nine o'clock," Roberta reported succinctly. "Call if you need me."

Beth told Chloe the good news as soon as the child climbed into the SUV. Then she checked the backpack and found that all the papers were stamped with smiling faces, and Miss Hyde had sent a thank-you note for the flowers. Beth added another check mark under the one from the day before and left the teacher's note in the folder for Jack Gamble to see.

Chloe said she had made two new friends, Allison and Haley. Allison's mom was divorced but had a boyfriend, and Allison wore only clothes from Gap Kids. Beth mentioned at this point that she thought Chloe's own clothes were very nice and Chloe shrugged. "They aren't cool like Gap Kids. Haley has to wear her sister's old clothes, but she has a dog."

"What did you tell them about your life?" Beth asked.

"I told them my daddy is a lawyer and my mom is an actress."

Unreasonably saddened by this response, Beth stared out the SUV window until they drove by a mall on the outskirts of Albany. When she saw the Gap Kids sign, she smiled. In a shameless attempt to win a place in Chloe's heart, she asked Roy if they could stop for a while. He made a phone call and got permission, then followed them into the mall and remained a discreet distance behind them as they shopped. Beth bought Chloe a red Gap shirt, a soft pretzel, and a lemonade. When they reached the front entrance they stopped and let Roy catch up.

Then Beth remembered that she needed nylons for church on Sunday, so they went into the nearest department store. While Beth was busy making her selection, Chloe found a rack of leopard-print pajamas. Beth was only mildly interested until she saw that they came in children's and adult sizes. The little size five was irresistible, so she put a pair for both Chloe and herself in the basket. They found pony-tail holders to match their pajamas, and then Chloe suggested that they buy black fingernail polish to complete the ensemble. Beth convinced her that this would be a fashion mistake, and they compro-mised with blood red.

Roy had stayed in cosmetics, sniffing cologne during this last shopping spree, but when they headed toward the cashier he joined them. "What have we got here?" he asked, taking the pajamas from Beth's arms.

"We're going to be twins," Chloe told him. He expressed interest in owning a pair himself, but Beth assured him that real men did not wear ladies' nighties. Then she retrieved the pajamas and paid for her purchases.

That night Hipolita served dinner outside on the patio. They all fixed plates then sat by the pool to eat. Roy offered to change into his swimsuit and perform some dives, but Beth convinced him to stay put.

When it started to get dark, Beth followed Chloe up to her room. After a quick shower, the little girl pulled open the door and jumped out wearing her new pajamas. She was so adorable Beth couldn't resist pulling her into her arms for a quick embrace.

"Now it's your turn," Chloe told Beth, and they headed down-stairs. Beth changed into her pajamas, then pulled Chloe's damp curls into a ponytail right on top of her head and wound a leopard print ponytail holder around it. Chloe insisted that they look just alike, so Beth gathered her own hair up into an awful spout. She had just put in the day's episode of *The Brave and Relentless* into the VCR when the phone rang.

"Beth!" Derrick's voice was almost drowned out by static.

"Derrick!" she answered. "I can barely hear you. Where are you?"

"In front of this house you moved into," he whispered frantically. "All it needs is a few bats swooping around and some eerie mist to look as sinister as Dracula's castle!"

Beth laughed. "This house is beautiful, Derrick."

"This house is surrounded by a twelve-foot brick fence with electrified spikes on top!"

"How do you know they're electrified?" She walked into the bedroom, away from Chloe, and glanced out the window.

"Because I called around and asked questions. You know what a fence like that means?"

"That Jack Gamble is security conscious to the point of being paranoid?" Beth ventured.

"Walls that keep people out can also keep people in," Derrick hissed.

"I'm not trapped! I have the security code," she assured him.

"You think he can't change it without telling you?" Derrick demanded. "You've got to get out of there right now. Pack your bags and then walk casually to your car. Drive slowly to the gate and enter what you think is still the security code into the keypad. On second thought, forget about your things. You could replace your entire wardrobe for twenty dollars at a thrift store, and if anyone sees you with luggage, they'll know something is up. Just grab your purse and run."

Beth knew that Derrick was serious, but couldn't control a giggle. "I'm not laughing at you," she hastened to say. "But you've let your imagination run wild. I'm completely safe here."

"There is no way you can be sure of that."

"I can't just leave. I signed a contract to stay for three months."

"He can hire somebody else to live inside this mini-Alcatraz," Derrick pleaded.

"I need the money." Beth tried to reason with him.

"No amount of money is worth risking your life!"

"I'm not risking my life." Her eyes strayed to the other room. "Besides, I can't leave Chloe." The very thought made her chest hurt. "At least not until I'm sure that everything is all right here."

"Haven't you been listening? Nothing is right there! That's why you need to get out!"

"Why don't you come in and see for yourself that I'm not in any danger?" Beth suggested.

"One of us has to stay on the *outside* of this fence," he declined as their connection started to fade. "My battery is getting low. You're going to stay?"

"I have to, Derrick." She was both touched by his concern and amused by his sense of drama.

She heard him sigh. "I'll call every day and if I can't reach you, I'll notify the police."

Even though she knew Derrick was overreacting, Beth felt a little uneasy as she stuffed cotton balls between her toes. Chloe was staring at the television, and Beth listened as Parker questioned Tori closely about the blood test results, obviously getting suspicious. Then she painted Chloe's nails while they watched Elena's farewell party at the real-estate firm.

Near the end of the program, the party was interrupted by a phone call from Elena's neurosurgeon. In somber tones he explained to the retiring real-estate agent that x-rays taken during a recent visit indicated she was probably going blind. Resisting the urge to call Derrick back, Beth propped her feet on the table and offered Chloe the opportunity to perform her first pedicure. The child was very pleased to accept and concentrated on the task.

When all ten of Beth's toes were mostly red, Chloe examined her workmanship with a satisfied smile. Then she put her feet beside Beth's as they watched Elena tearfully explain the awful diagnosis to her mother. They were in precisely this position when Hipolita opened the door. Before the housekeeper could say a word, Jack Gamble appeared behind her.

"Hi, Daddy!" Chloe called out loudly in order to be heard over Elena's copious weeping. Hipolita retreated into the hall as he advanced into the room.

"Hi, Chloe." His eyes moved from Beth to the television screen and back.

"We got matching pajamas!" the child announced the obvious. "And I painted Beth's toenails."

He looked at Beth's polish-spattered feet. "Thanks for watching Chloe," he forced out grudgingly.

"I enjoyed her company," Beth answered with a smile at the little girl.

"Come on, Chloe." He held out his arms, and she left with a wave.

After they were gone, Beth pulled the cotton from between her toes. The room that had been so full of life a few minutes before now seemed lonely. She took the ponytail holder out and let her hair fall in sad lumps around her shoulders. She was turning off the television when someone knocked on the door. Thinking that Hipolita had returned, she pulled it open.

"Chloe says you bought her a shirt in addition to the pajamas," Jack Gamble said from the hallway. Beth nodded, familiar enough with him now to realize that he probably had not come to express gratitude. "You'll never be able to pay for a mission if you spend everything you earn on Chloe."

"I won't spend more than I can afford," she assured him.

He got that look again, like he was talking to a very slow preschooler. "Well, I'll leave your personal finances to you then, but buying Chloe clothes is still not part of your job. She has more outfits than she can wear now."

"But only one red T-shirt from Gap Kids just like Allison's," she told him as she closed the door.

On Saturday morning when Beth went into the kitchen, she found the regular breakfast buffet set out on the counter, but the room was quiet. Beth poured some juice and ate a sausage biscuit, then a cinnamon roll. After putting a generous serving of cheese grits onto her plate, she went back to her room to eat.

Her next book was about a nun in Argentina, and she couldn't bring herself to open it. Since Saturday morning programming was dedicated entirely to cartoons, she didn't even bother to turn on the television but sat on the couch, absently nibbling her food. She never expected to finish all her breakfast, but when she caught herself picking up crumbs with her finger, she knew she had to find something to do besides eat. So she took her empty plate into the kitchen and lay in wait for Hipolita. The housekeeper finally came through carrying folded towels, and Beth asked if she needed help with the laundry. Hipolita shook her head and rushed away.

Beth went back to her room and took the sheets off her bed, then washed them with a small load of her clothes. The day seemed to stretch out endlessly in front of her until she saw Roberta's car pull around to the back of the house. When Beth met the secretary at the kitchen door, Roberta held out an American Express card.

"Use this anytime you make a purchase for Chloe," she said. "Just sign the back. You've already been added to the account."

Beth ran a finger over the raised letters of Jack Gamble's name, feeling completely off balance. "He said not to buy her anything else."

Roberta shrugged and picked an apple from the fruit bowl. "I guess you're all settled in by now," she said, taking a big bite. Beth nodded as she watched the secretary chew and wondered how long it would take Hipolita to replace the missing fruit. "Isn't Chloe great?" Roberta asked around a mouthful of apple.

"She is great." That was, of course, an understatement, but it didn't seem wise to admit her growing fondness for Chloe.

"I've worked for Jack since she was a little baby. She's so sweet and never any trouble." Roberta hefted her bag and started for the door. "Well, I've got to run. Call if you need me."

Beth took a step after her. "What I need is something to do during the day while Chloe's at school," she blurted out, hoping she didn't sound as desperate as she felt.

Roberta turned back and looked at her cautiously. "You're not here by Jack's own choice, and I'm not sure how he would feel about . . ."

"I know," Beth interrupted miserably. "But I'm willing to do anything." Then a thought occurred to her. "I can type. Maybe I could answer letters for Mr. Gamble!"

Roberta shook her head and smiled. "That's my job."

"Oh." Beth sighed. "It was just an idea."

Roberta reached for the doorknob, reminding Beth that she was a busy woman with things to do. "I'll think about it." She waved over her shoulder and was gone.

Alone again, Beth considered the rest of her day. The Argentine nun was still waiting, but she felt too restless to read, and concentrating on a cartoon was unthinkable. Finally she decided to drive into Haggerty. She experienced a split second of anxiety when she entered what she thought was still the security code, but the gate slid open and she rolled her eyes at Derrick's suspicions.

She glanced up as she drove by Annabelle Grainger's house and saw the older woman standing on her porch. Mrs. Grainger held up her hand and started toward the street. Beth pulled to the curb and rolled down the passenger window. "Good morning," Beth greeted.

"Do you have business in town?" Mrs. Grainger asked.

"Not really," Beth admitted. "I just thought I'd drive around and find the library. I read a lot of books and can't keep driving to Albany every time they're due."

"I need to check my post office box. Would you mind if I come along?"

Surprised by the request and embarrassed by the condition of the Volkswagen, Beth apologized in advance. "You're welcome to come, but my car is old—"

"I don't mind. As long as it gets us where we're going." Beth decided not to mention that there was some doubt about that as well. "Let me grab my purse."

When Mrs. Grainger returned, Beth pulled back onto the street and commented on their surroundings. "This is a lovely neighborhood," she said.

"I think the developer did a wonderful job, but you won't get the same opinion from my sister and the other ladies in town! They think new, modern houses are tacky. According to them, it's much more dignified to live with squeaking pipes, dripping faucets, and peeling plaster. But no house built inside the Haggerty city limits ever caused as much fuss as Mr. Gamble's."

"What kind of a fuss?" Beth asked.

"Well, for one thing, his house is built on two lots instead of one, and the developer didn't like that."

This explained the generous amount of property that surrounded the house. "Why would the developer care?"

"He thought it would make the other lots look small, but Mr. Gamble finally convinced him otherwise. Once that was settled, Mr. Gamble built that awful fence."

"The developer didn't like the fence either?"

"It was the other home owners that objected to it, but by the time they got around to making their complaints official, the fence was already up. So Jack Gamble won that round too."

Beth could have told her that he never lost, but refrained as they entered the business district of Haggerty. Annabelle pointed out the high spots around the town square. When Beth asked where the Haggerty library was located, Annabelle laughed and pointed to an old, dilapidated building.

"It used to be there, but after a patron fell through the floor last summer, the county condemned it. What's left of the library is housed in the basement of the city hall and is operated on a volunteer basis. All the books are older than I am, and business is slow—" this with a wry smile. "A group of old women, including my sister Eugenia, call themselves 'Friends of the Library' and run the show. But it's not open on Saturdays."

Beth squinted at the city hall. "Can anyone be a 'Friend of the Library'?" she asked, an idea forming. She had extra time, library experience, and needed access to fiction books, even if they were ancient. "I worked at the downtown branch of the county library before I came here, and I have some spare time while Chloe is in school."

Annabelle considered this for a few seconds, then changed to a seemingly unrelated subject. "Have you eaten lunch?" she asked, and Beth shook her head. "Then turn right at the corner." She pulled a small phone from her purse and called her sister Eugenia, asking her to meet them at Haggerty Station. "Take any empty space," Annabelle instructed as they approached the establishment.

All the parking spaces along the street were available, so Beth pulled into the one closest to the front entrance. Then she followed Annabelle up the stairs and stood aside while her companion pounded on the door for several minutes without a response. "Maybe it's closed," Beth ventured just as the door was yanked open.

"Annabelle, you know we don't start serving until 11:30 on Saturdays," an irritable woman said from the doorway.

"You don't have to serve us until 11:30, Nettie, just let us in. Eugenia will be here in a few minutes, so there's no need to lock the door again." Annabelle grabbed a couple of menus off a counter on her way to a table in the corner and earned another scowl from Nettie.

"Maybe we should eat somewhere else," Beth suggested as they took their seats.

Annabelle smiled. "Nettie's always cranky, no matter what time customers arrive, and there's nowhere else to eat in Haggerty." They studied the menu and had both decided on a grilled chicken salad when the front door swung open to admit a large woman wearing men's work pants and a T-shirt that proclaimed "*I fought the lawn and the lawn won!*"

"For goodness sake, Eugenia! Did you at least wash your hands?" Annabelle demanded, but her sister ignored the question and spoke directly to Beth.

"So, you're the girl who's moved in with the hermit." She pulled out a chair and sat down.

"We're having grilled chicken salads," Annabelle spoke quickly. "Why don't you look over the menu, Eugenia?"

"If you mean Mr. Gamble, I am living in his house, but just to take care of his daughter. I rarely even see him." Beth wanted her relationship with Jack Gamble to be clearly defined.

"The newspaper said you were sent by the court because they think he's a bad father."

"I can't discuss the terms of my employment."

The sisters exchanged a glance, and then the larger woman extended a hand to Beth. "Eugenia Atkins," she supplied. "But the young folks around here call me Miss Eugenia." Beth shook her hand as the unfriendly restaurant owner returned.

They all ordered salads, and Miss Eugenia asked for a club sandwich on the side, then took a roll from the basket in the middle of the table. "I see Nettie's in a particularly good mood today," she commented, then turned to Beth. "So, what's he like?"

"Mr. Gamble?" Beth clarified, and Miss Eugenia nodded. Beth continued, "I've only spoken to him a few times. I couldn't really say."

"We never see him either. Now that he wants to be a state senator, I thought he'd be a little more friendly." The old lady shook her head. "But apparently he only cares about the voters in Albany. Do you play bridge?" Miss Eugenia continued her inquisition in a different direction.

"I used to watch my mother play," Beth began hesitantly.

"We have a club that meets on Wednesday mornings. Of course, someone has to run the library, so I rarely get to attend anymore . . ."

"Beth doesn't want to play cards with a bunch of old ladies," Annabelle stepped in. "But she used to work at the library in Albany, and she's interested in helping you in the city hall basement branch."

Miss Eugenia gave her sister a cross look. "Our library is open from nine to twelve on Monday, Wednesday, and Friday," she informed Beth as the salads arrived. "This lettuce is wilted, Nettie. And we're going to need some more bread, fresh if possible." Nettie glared at the back of Miss Eugenia's head, then walked away. Oblivious, Miss Eugenia continued. "You can come with me on Wednesday, and I'll show you our system."

"That should take all of two minutes," Annabelle predicted.

Miss Eugenia sniffed. "Annabelle thinks she's above volunteer libraries and such. You won't ever see *her* donating time for civic service!"

"I can't volunteer at the library! I have a real job!" Annabelle defended herself.

"Where do you work?" Beth asked as Nettie slammed another basket of rolls down on the table.

Annabelle smoothed the napkin on her lap. "At the National Bank of Commerce in Albany. I'm a loan officer, so come see me if you ever need to borrow money."

Beth smiled. "Well, I don't need a loan right now, but I have plenty of extra time. I'd be glad to work at the library all three mornings, if you can use me," she told Miss Eugenia.

"It's good to see that someone has a social conscience," the part-time librarian approved.

"Really, I'm just bored stiff," Beth felt obligated to admit.

Other customers started to arrive and filled the tables around them. The sisters introduced Beth to several people, including a plump woman named Miss Polly Kirby. "Did you hear about Elena?" Miss Polly asked once the formalities were out of the way.

"Elena is a character on a soap opera called *The Brave and Relentless*," Annabelle interpreted for Beth, then rolled her eyes.

"Daytime television is another thing Annabelle is too good for," Miss Eugenia replied, and Beth chose not to comment.

"Poor Elena! So young to be blind!" Miss Polly added. Then she left to join her Sunday school class in the banquet room as Nettie delivered their check.

"It's all together," Annabelle complained, studying the list of things they had ordered.

"Can't you add and subtract?" Nettie asked before she moved on to the next table.

"Give me that." Miss Eugenia snatched the bill from her sister's hand, then invited Beth to attend services at the Methodist Church on Sunday.

"No, thank you," Beth declined.

"What? Are you an atheist or something?" Miss Eugenia demanded without taking her eyes off the figures she was scribbling in an attempt to divide $22.95 evenly.

"No, but my church is in Albany," Beth explained and Annabelle looked up. "I'm a member of The Church of Jesus Christ of Latter-day Saints. Most people call us Mormons."

"You're kidding!" Annabelle's reaction was stronger than seemed reasonable, but Beth shook her head.

"You can't be!" Miss Eugenia exclaimed.

The sisters faced each other. "That is a 400 percent increase in a year!" Annabelle whispered.

"The folks in town won't like it. It looks like infiltration."

"Almost an influx!" Annabelle agreed.

Beth had dealt with anti-Mormon sentiment before, so she took a deep breath. "Some people are not very familiar with the beliefs of my church, but we are a Christian religion . . ."

Annabelle nodded. "We know all about Mormons now, but none of us had ever even met one until recently."

"What about that woman who lived in the Yerby place?" Miss Eugenia interrupted.

"She was a Jehovah's Witness." Annabelle waved her sister's question aside. "But a Mormon couple moved in next door to Eugenia about a year ago. They go to church in Albany, and I'm sure they'd be glad to give you a ride in the morning."

Beth shook her head. Attending a new ward was going to be bad enough, but riding there with strangers would be unbearable. "Thanks, but I'd rather drive my own car. Chloe will probably be home soon, so I'd better go."

Beth pushed away from the table and stood. Miss Eugenia had obliterated the original meal charges with her ciphering, so Beth just handed Annabelle a ten-dollar bill and walked toward the door. The sisters followed her, still haggling over the check. Finally Annabelle put the whole thing on her credit card and returned the ten dollars to Beth.

"My treat," she said as they stepped into the hot sun and paused by Beth's battered car.

"This is yours?" Miss Eugenia asked, pointing to the Volkswagen, and Beth nodded. "I was going to tell you to pick me up on your way to the library Wednesday morning, but I'd better come get you instead. Be standing outside that eyesore Jack Gamble calls a fence at 8:45." Beth watched Miss Eugenia unlock a Buick, then she opened the passenger door of her own car for Annabelle.

"Eugenia can be a little much sometimes," Annabelle said as Beth pulled away from Haggerty Station. "I hope she didn't offend you."

"Of course not."

Annabelle smiled. "Then you're well on your way to being a Friend of the Library." Beth waited in the car while Annabelle went in to check her post office box, then took her new friend home. "Come see me anytime!" Annabelle invited as she walked up to her house.

Roy and Chloe were sitting at the kitchen table when Beth came in. Chloe reported that she spent the morning at her father's office, but Roy was now going to take her swimming. She invited Beth to join them, and the new nanny accepted with a smile.

Beth changed into her swimsuit and walked outside to find the gate open and Roy supervising Chloe's application of sunscreen. Beth sat on the steps, partially immersed in the warm water. Chloe challenged Roy to a series of races, and they asked Beth to judge their contests. She agreed, then consistently let Chloe win.

Finally tired of racing, Chloe settled on the steps by Beth while Roy entertained them with a diving exhibition. He splashed so much water that Beth eventually moved to a lounge chair out of his range. Chloe got a handful of waterlogged Barbies from the cabana and played on the steps in the shallow end. Once his audience deserted him, Roy flopped down on a chair beside Beth.

"Bet you've gained a few pounds since you've been here. Wouldn't hurt to put on a couple more," he added, and Beth had to laugh at his outrageous remark. Roy didn't have a perfect physique, and she pointed this out to him. "Not much to look at, but I'm healthy as a horse. A stiff wind would blow you away." Beth started to laugh again, but he wasn't smiling. "Don't have to get fat. Just need a little something to cover those bones."

She was searching for a reply when the pool gate swung open and Jack Gamble walked through. He was wearing a red bathing suit. His skin was deeply tanned, indicating that he took advantage of the pool often, and he didn't see Beth behind Roy until it was too late to retreat. Nor did he make any effort to hide his dismay once he became aware of her presence. She would have left, but Roy put a restraining hand on her arm.

"Thought you still had hours of work to do, Boss."

"I still have weeks of work, but I decided to take a break," Jack Gamble replied stiffly. He waded into the water, and Chloe abandoned her Barbies to jump into his arms.

Beth tried to stand, but Roy stopped her again. "Got something urgent to do inside?"

"Mr. Gamble will be uncomfortable if I stay," she answered.

"He'll get used to you," Roy replied. "Just give him a chance."

Beth pulled her knees up against her chest in an effort to make herself inconspicuous as she watched Chloe play with her father. When they started toward the steps, Beth stood up and hurried to the gate. Chloe intercepted her before she could push up the latch.

"My daddy has to work tonight, and he says I can stay with you again."

Beth looked up at her employer, who was now standing behind his daughter. "I'll be glad to have some company."

"Thanks. I'll bring her by on my way out," he said, then led his daughter into the kitchen.

"See, you're growing on him already," Roy claimed.

Beth changed her clothes, then left her room at six o'clock, intending to join Chloe for dinner. From the hallway she heard Jack Gamble's voice and stopped. This was the first meal he had eaten in the kitchen since her arrival, and she hated to intrude on more of his time with Chloe. So she went back to her room and called Derrick.

"I see you're still alive," her friend said when he answered.

Beth smiled. "Jack Gamble is holding a gun to my head, making me pretend to be okay so you won't call the police—" She was just warming up when he interrupted.

"That's not very funny."

Instead of teasing him further, Beth told him about her plan to volunteer at the Haggerty Library. When he didn't seem interested in this topic, she switched to the one subject she knew he couldn't resist. "Did you watch *The Brave and Relentless?*"

"If Elena doesn't hurry and leave that stupid real-estate firm!" Derrick cried. "They ought to have a federal agency control what soap opera writers can inflict on their viewers!"

"It's awful that she might be going blind," Beth commented.

"I can't figure where they're headed with that . . ." Derrick was off and running, and for the next fifteen minutes she listened to him theorize about soap opera plot twists. Finally someone knocked on her door and she ended the call. Beth looked out in the hallway and found Chloe, dressed in leopard-skin pajamas. The child had a video under one arm and a dish in her hand.

"Roy said to give you this." She thrust a roast beef sandwich and a huge piece of chocolate cake at Beth. "And I brought *Sleeping Beauty*. It's my favorite."

"Mine too," Beth said with a smile as she put the tape into the VCR. Then she settled Chloe under a blanket on the couch and became so involved in the movie that she ate her entire dinner without thinking. By the end of the video, Chloe was fast asleep against Beth's arm.

At nine o'clock, Beth moved Chloe upstairs, and the child awakened long enough to murmur "good night" before she curled into her pillows. Beth stood by the bed and watched Chloe sleep for as long as she dared. Then she went back downstairs and rewound the video. She folded the blanket and started to put it in the closet, but it smelled like Chloe so she spread it out on her own bed instead. After changing into shorts, she walked across the hall and asked Hipolita to listen for Chloe.

She ran to the park and circled the track, thinking about Chloe and her growing affection for the child. She knew she was getting too attached to Chloe, but couldn't seem to stop herself. On top of that, the prospect of attending a new ward for the first time the next day was terrifying. Struggling to control her growing anxiety, she finished her laps and started back to the Gamble's house at a slow jog. Then she remembered that she had promised to meet her family at the airport on Monday and shuddered. Caught up in her thoughts, she crossed the street without checking for traffic and ran directly into the path of an oncoming car.

The driver slammed on the brakes and swerved sharply to the right, almost hitting the brick fence that Derrick hated so much. Beth jumped back and missed the fender by a fraction of an inch. She lost her balance and fell onto the asphalt. Footsteps pounded toward her, and seconds later she looked up into the bright blue eyes of Jack Gamble.

"Are you trying to kill yourself?" he asked as he stooped beside her, and Beth smiled. She was tempted to reply that if she had seriously considered that to be an option, she'd have done it a couple of years earlier. "You think this is funny?" he demanded.

"No, no," she assured him, getting to her feet. Nothing seemed to be broken or sprained, but her knees were skinned up, and they hurt like crazy.

He regarded her for a few seconds, then tipped his head toward the car. "Get in," he instructed, opening the passenger door. Beth obeyed, careful not to smear blood on the leather interior. He climbed behind the wheel, then backed the Jeep up to the gate and punched in the security code. He parked beside the patio. "Come on."

He walked inside the house, through the kitchen, and into her room. He flipped on the lights and pointed to the couch. Blood was running down her legs, and she was anxious not to stain the carpet, so she complied. He went to the bathroom and came back with a damp towel.

Beth protested as he pressed the expensive towel to her wounds, but he ignored her. Once the blood was washed away she could see only minor abrasions on both knees. "Not too bad," she pronounced.

"I'll get you some Neosporin," he said, eyeing the oozing scrapes on her palms. Beth blotted her hands on the already-ruined towel, then rested her head against the couch. He was back in a few minutes with the ointment and watched as she applied it to her knees and hands.

"What were you doing outside the gate so late?"

"I was running."

"From who?" he demanded, and Beth couldn't suppress a smile.

"Not from anyone," she answered. "Just running."

He regarded her with disbelief. "Why?"

"I run every night, but I usually check traffic before I cross a street."

"Cars should be the least of your worries." He bent down in front of her. "You could have been robbed or mugged or even murdered." She wanted to smile again, thinking how much safer these streets were than the ones near her old apartment.

"I have to run," she replied and hoped he wouldn't ask her to explain.

He pushed himself up and walked over to the window, shoving his fingers through the curls at the back of his head. "Well, you can't run alone at night. For the rest of the time you're here, Roy or I will have to go with you."

Beth leaned forward. "That's ridiculous. I'm sure the park is perfectly safe, but if anything happens to me, it will be my fault, not yours."

"No matter whose fault it is, if you get hurt while you're working here, the family court judge will hold me responsible. So from now on, you'll run with an escort. Give me a time." She was too stupefied to answer. "What time do you run?" he enunciated.

"Usually about ten," Beth muttered.

"Stop by the garage tomorrow night at ten, and someone will be waiting for you." He turned to leave and she tried to protest, but only a moan escaped her lips. "The garage isn't convenient for you?" he asked over his shoulder.

"No, it's just that I wanted to warn you . . ." She searched for a polite way to say it. "I'm a serious runner."

She had his full attention now. "What do you mean by that? You think I can't keep up with you?" His incredulous glance took in her less-than-athletic appearance.

"I've been running several miles every day for two years, in all weather conditions, and I don't stop until my knees hurt."

His eyes dipped to the scrapes on her legs. "Looks like I picked a good time to join you," he said, then walked out, closing the door firmly behind him.

Without wasting the energy to change clothes, Beth laid down on the bed, then pulled up the blanket that smelled like Chloe and fell asleep.

CHAPTER 4

Beth had hoped her injuries and the trauma of her latest encounter with Jack Gamble might cause her to oversleep on Sunday morning and miss church, but she woke up at six o'clock with sunlight seeping through the blinds. Stiff and a little sore, she took a shower, then applied more Neosporin. At 8:30 she left her room and found Chloe and Jack Gamble in the kitchen eating breakfast. Chloe asked where she was going, and Beth explained that she was on her way to church. Setting her fork down on her plate of pancakes, Chloe turned to her father.

"Why don't we ever go to church?" she asked.

"We have a standing appointment with Aristotle and his famous Greek cuisine on Sundays," Jack Gamble replied.

Chloe laughed and explained to Beth that Aristotle's was their favorite restaurant. "Sometime I might like to go to a real church, though," she said thoughtfully. "Could I go with you, Beth?"

"I would like that," Beth answered, then waved good-bye and walked out to her car. The weather was nice, but Beth couldn't enjoy the drive into Albany as a knot of dread formed in her stomach. When she reached the meetinghouse, she parked in a far corner and waited in the car until nine o'clock so she could walk straight in without having to speak to anyone.

She found a seat on the back row of the crowded chapel. When the bishop dismissed the Aaronic Priesthood after the sacrament, the organist left the stand and sat in front of Beth beside a tall, dark-haired man and a baby with curly pigtails. The little girl was pleased to see her mother and emitted a blood-curdling scream of welcome.

During the testimonies Beth's mind started to wander, so she watched the couple in front of her wrestle with the restless child. The baby bit, threw her toys, and finally ripped a page from a hymnbook. At this point, her father stood to take her out. The baby's lip started to tremble, realizing she had finally gone too far. Beth gave her a look of sympathy as the child disappeared through the chapel doors.

Before closing the meeting, the bishop reminded the ward members about a youth fireside that evening. The organist used this time to collect toys, and Beth picked up a few that had landed near her, then handed them over the bench. "Thanks," the woman whispered with a quick glance up at the pulpit. "You're new."

"I'm just in this ward temporarily," she explained quietly. "My name is Beth Middleton."

"Oh, yes!" the organist replied too loudly, and several people turned to stare. "I'm Kate Iverson, Miss Eugenia's neighbor. She told me about your lunch yesterday." Kate stood when the bishop announced the closing hymn. "I'll be back," she promised.

After the prayer, the tall man with the baby returned to wait for his wife. The little girl seemed happier after her time in the foyer and smiled over her father's shoulder at Beth as the last organ strains faded.

The organist returned to her husband and they began collecting their paraphernalia as the bishop stopped to introduce himself to Beth. "I'm Bishop Sterling, and your branch president told me to expect you," he said cheerfully. "I see you've met Kate and Mark." He turned to include the couple with the baby in the conversation. "They live near you in Haggerty, and if you ever have a crime to report, Mark is the resident agent for the FBI in Albany," the bishop added with a smile.

They all shook hands as the baby hammered a plastic toy against her father's head. "Beth ate lunch with Miss Eugenia and Annabelle at Haggerty Station yesterday," Kate mentioned for her husband's benefit. He nodded vaguely, trying to dodge the toy. "She's living in Jack Gamble's house." This got his attention, and he studied Beth for a few seconds.

"You know Mr. Gamble?" Beth asked.

"Only by reputation," the man responded.

Bishop Sterling reentered the discussion by informing Beth that the Gospel Doctrine class met in the chapel and telling Kate Iverson that his wife was at home with the flu.

"Sister Sterling usually holds Emily for me while I play the piano in Primary," Kate explained as the baby threw her toy. It landed at Beth's feet and she reached down to pick it up. The little girl squealed with delight when Beth gave it back to her.

Mark Iverson said something about not being able to keep the baby during Sunday School, and the bishop apologized again for his wife's inconvenient illness. Kate told him it was not a problem, but the worry wrinkles between her eyes indicated otherwise. "I'll ask Sister Armistead to watch Emily," she proposed hesitantly.

"Sister Armistead is filling in for the librarian today," the bishop said with regret.

"I guess I could let one of the Primary children hold her." Kate tried to sound confident, but her eyes continued to scan the room for another possibility.

The baby dropped her toy again and watched with pleasure as Beth retrieved it. This time when Beth stood up, the baby lunged toward her. Brother Iverson was distracted by their baby-sitting dilemma, and his grip was faulty. Beth caught the little girl just before she hit the ground headfirst.

"Emily!" Mark Iverson cried.

"Mark!" His wife's tone was reproachful.

Beth clutched the little girl against her racing heart. "I could hold her for you," Beth suggested as Emily settled comfortably into her arms. The parents exchanged a dubious glance. "I'll stay in Primary so you'll be right there if she needs anything." The Iversons were still hesitant. "It will get me out of going to Gospel Doctrine class."

The bishop cleared his throat as Kate laughed and her husband blushed. "Mark is our Gospel Doctrine teacher, and he always prepares wonderful lessons," the bishop said quickly.

"But you've heard all that stuff before." Kate smiled at Beth. "So come with me. The kids are much more fun!" With an amused glance back at her husband, Kate picked up the diaper bag and led the way to Primary.

Beth settled in a corner near the door, then spent the next hour getting to know Emily. Beth barely remembered her sisters as babies,

and she'd made a point to keep her distance from her brother's two children. But in spite of her lack of practical experience with babies,
sharing and singing time passed without incident. By the time the children separated to classes, Emily was asleep and so was Beth's left arm.

"Emily is never that good!" Kate said when she came over to
collect her child. "You must have some kind of magic touch."

"I think she just felt sorry for me," Beth said while the baby was
transferred.

"Well, now it's time for Relief Society, and if we don't get there
fast, Sister Gibbons will come looking for us!" Kate said as they
hurried down they hall.

After the meetings, Kate thanked her again for helping with the
baby. "Miss Eugenia told me you're going to work at the library,"
Kate said, and Beth nodded. "Emily and I will come see you one
morning this week. At the library, I mean!" she was quick to add. "I
wouldn't even try to get past the Gamble's gate. I've heard a rumor
that it has a laser that can read people's corneas!"

"As far as I know, security isn't that tight, but I don't know much. My
cornea might be read every time I go inside," Beth responded with a smile.

She felt good all the way home. It had been a long time since
she'd enjoyed church so much, made a new friend, or held a baby. She
found the kitchen deserted, but there was a tray of sandwiches on the
counter so she knew Hipolita was around somewhere. After changing
clothes, she ate, then made an obligatory call to her mother. She
checked in with Derrick so he would know she hadn't been smoth-
ered in her sleep, and she was trying to decide whether to watch television or take a nap when there was a knock on her door.

She cracked it open to find Chloe standing in the hallway. "Hey,
Beth," she greeted, walking in and making herself comfortable on the
couch. "Was it fun at church?"

Beth smiled. "It was very nice. How was your lunch at the Greek
restaurant?"

"Oh, it was real good. Mr. Aristotle was so glad I cleaned my
plate, he let me count money in the cash register." She looked around
the room. "What are you going to do now?"

"I was just wondering that myself," Beth replied. "It's a beautiful
day. Maybe we could go to the park?"

Chloe's eyes widened in surprise. "I don't think my daddy would let me do that."

"Is he here?" Beth asked.

"No, Roy brought me home and said to stay with Hipolita, but I want to play with you."

Driven by the need to be more fun than Hipolita, Beth pulled on her tennis shoes and told Chloe to follow. The housekeeper met them at the back door. "Mr. Jack say I watch Chloe." Her tone was polite, yet firm.

"We're just going to the park. We won't be gone long." Beth reached for the doorknob, but Hipolita didn't move.

"I call Mr. Jack," she said.

Beth did not want to ask Jack Gamble for permission to play with his daughter, so she reconsidered. "Could we at least go outside the house?"

Hipolita thought this through. "You stay inside the gate?" Beth nodded. The housekeeper still didn't look happy, but she stepped aside.

Beth led the way outside, and Chloe ran onto the manicured lawn like a prisoner set free. They walked around the perimeter of the Gamble's property twice, and the second time they passed the big gate, they could see the blonde girl and her curly headed brother in the yard across the street. Chloe stepped up and pressed her little face between the metal bars. Remembering Derrick's claims about electrification, Beth told the child to let go. Chloe's expression was sad as she backed away from the gate and the neighbors.

Beth looked over to see the children watching them. "Hi!" she said, and the little girl waved. The boy was about two, and, after staring for a moment, he started running toward the street. His sister followed, but the toddler had momentum working in his favor. Without stopping to think, Beth entered the security code and squeezed through the opening as soon as it was wide enough for her. She crossed the street and caught the baby before he stepped off the curb. No cars were coming, so danger wasn't imminent, but Beth's heart was beating fast just the same.

"That was so bad, Bud!" the sister reprimanded breathlessly as she reached them. "Mom is probably going to spank you!"

Bud didn't seem overly concerned by this possibility as he clutched Beth's shirt with one fist and gave her a slobbery grin. "It's really my fault," Beth accepted responsibility. "I shouldn't have called from across the street." Assured that the little boy was unharmed, she leaned over to put him down, but he clung to her. Beth shook him gently in an unsuccessful attempt to loosen his grip. Finally she stood back up, the baby still firmly attached.

Beth didn't know what to do. They couldn't stay where they were, Chloe couldn't come outside the gate, and Beth certainly couldn't take the neighbor's baby into the Gamble's yard without permission. "What's your name?" she asked the little blonde girl.

"Kristen," the child responded.

"Kristen, do you think your mother would let you and your brother come over and play?"

Kristen looked at the big fence. "I don't think so."

"Well, could you ask her to come talk to me?"

Kristen's eyes dropped to Bud's hand, which was still latched onto Beth's shirt, and nodded. "I'll be back in one minute," she promised, already running.

Beth watched Kristen climb the front stairs and disappear inside the house. In seconds, a very pregnant woman emerged and made cumbersome progress in their direction. "Kristen said that Bud almost ran into the road!" she exclaimed as she reached them. "I can't imagine what made him do that. He's terrified of cars!"

"It was my fault. I spoke to them through the gate," Beth explained. "But there wasn't any traffic," she added to reassure Bud's mother.

The other woman nodded, staring at the Gamble's house. "You live there?"

"I'm Chloe's babysitter." Beth extended her hand. "Beth Middleton."

"Ellen Northcutt," the woman provided. "When we moved in I rang the buzzer on the gate a few times, but nobody ever answered." Beth couldn't explain Jack Gamble's peculiar household, so she remained silent. "Come on, Bud," Ellen reached for her son. Her stomach was enormous, and Beth doubted there was room for Bud in her arms. The little boy shrank against Beth, apparently reaching the same conclusion. "Enough of this nonsense." Ellen sounded tired. "Come on inside and I'll give you a cookie." The child seemed unimpressed by this offer.

Beth glanced back at Chloe, who was still watching through the metal bars. "Would you let Bud and Kristen come over for a short visit?" she asked. The neighbor looked at the ground, obviously searching for an excuse. "We'll stay in the front yard and leave the gate open."

Kristen pulled on her mother's arm. "Please, Mom! You know it's not very fun to play with just Bud." She turned to Beth. "How old is your little girl?"

"She's five," Beth replied, her chest tightening. "And she'd be so glad to have company."

Whether it was out of compassion for Chloe or general exhaustion, Ellen finally nodded. "You'll leave the gate open?"

"And we'll stay in the front where you can see us," Beth reiterated.

Ellen looked at her watch. "Kristen, you bring Bud home in one hour."

"We won't even know that little girl good in one hour!" Kristen wailed.

"They are welcome to stay as long as you'll let them," Beth offered.

"If you're not home by four o'clock, I'm going to tell your father," Ellen threatened.

"I'll make sure," Beth promised, leading the way over to where Chloe was waiting. Ellen watched them cross the street, then turned and waddled up to her front porch and sat in a wicker chair.

Beth entered the security code and made introductions. The little girls exchanged shy smiles. "I told Kristen's mom that we'd leave the gate open. Do you know how to do that?" she asked Chloe.

"I don't think we ever wanted to before, but I can ask Hipolita." She started up the driveway. "Don't go home," she called to Kristen. "I'll be right back!"

Beth stood by the keypad, occasionally waving to Ellen and continually reentering the code to keep the gate open. Chloe returned soon with a life-size, plastic Barbie head. Hipolita was close behind her. "Mr. Jack never leave the gate open," the housekeeper reported. Beth explained about Mrs. Northcutt's conditional permission to allow her children to play with Chloe. Hipolita looked down at Chloe's hopeful face and sighed.

"Have to do that inside," Hipolita agreed reluctantly.

"Thanks," Beth said as the housekeeper turned toward the house.

"I'm going to get some toys for Bud," Chloe said over her shoulder as she followed Hipolita. Four trips later, the front lawn was littered with various items from Chloe's room. Beth stretched out on a quilt and read books to Bud while the girls applied makeup on the plastic Barbie. Then they decided to have a tea party, and Chloe made another trip inside. She returned with costumes and a tea set. Hipolita was behind her with cookies.

The girls put on the dress-up clothes, then arranged the dishes on the quilt. Bud was invited to join them, but they insisted that he wear a Goldilocks wig and ballerina outfit. Hipolita stood back, her attention divided between the children and the open gate.

"We need some milk to put in our teacups!" Chloe exclaimed around a mouthful of Oreo. Hipolita turned to go get it, but Beth stopped her.

"I'll go this time," Beth insisted as she began the hike across the lawn. She walked into the kitchen, took a jug of milk out of the refrigerator, and rushed back outside. She could hear the children giggling and smiled as she rounded the hedges. The smile froze on her face when she saw Jack Gamble sitting cross-legged on the quilt between his daughter and Bud Northcutt, the temporary ballerina. Mr. Gamble raised his eyebrows in an unspoken challenge.

"It's such a beautiful day," she began. "We wanted to enjoy the sunshine, but Hipolita said Chloe couldn't go to the park." Beth looked around for support, but the housekeeper had disappeared. "The baby," she waved at Bud, "ran into the road and I had to stop him. I knew Chloe would enjoy some company." He continued to stare. "And I thought you would be gone all afternoon," she admitted finally.

Chloe intervened. "This is Kristen, Daddy. She is six." Then she pointed to Bud, whose left eye was completely hidden by a yellow curl. "And this is Bud. They are my new friends." She took the milk and began pouring. To Beth's surprise, Mr. Gamble participated in the activity and didn't even seem to mind when Bud put a cookie-encrusted hand on his leg.

"I hope you are taking notes," he said pleasantly to Beth. "So you can tell the judge that the selfish, absentee father did make a gracious appearance at his daughter's tea party." He finished his cookie, then stood and shook the crumbs from his hands. After inviting the Northcutts to visit again, he told Chloe he would see her later. Then as he walked past Beth, he paused. "Leaving the gate open defeats the purpose of this expensive security fence, and I think I deserve extra points in your report for the cookie slime on my pants."

Beth watched her employer disappear around the corner of his house, then sat on the edge of the quilt while the girls sipped daintily from the little cups, and Bud dribbled milk down the front of his borrowed tutu. A few minutes later Roy joined them and accepted a half-eaten cookie from Bud. He leaned against the trunk of a nearby tree and studied the partial Oreo.

"Please don't eat that," Beth begged. "We have plenty that no one has chewed on."

Roy smiled and put the cookie in his pocket. "Guess I'll save it for later. Let me know when our visitors are ready to go home. Boss said to close the gate behind them."

Beth pursed her lips. "No one can sneak in here in broad daylight."

Roy shrugged. "Didn't say anyone would try. Just doing what the boss told me to."

Chloe and Kristen made a tent by draping the quilt over an expensive wrought-iron table, then played underneath. Bud fell asleep in the soft grass, still wearing his wig. At four o'clock Roy carried the little boy back across the street while Beth and the girls followed behind. It was a sad farewell, but Beth promised that the Northcutts could come over again soon.

Chloe was quiet during dinner and asleep before Beth could finish reading her bedtime story. Alone in her own room, Beth decided to work on her report for the family court judge. She listed Chloe's absolute adherence to bedtime, her father's obsession with safety, and his blasé attitude toward her school situation.

When she finished, the results were conflicting. Jack Gamble did not spend much time with his daughter, yet Chloe seemed well-adjusted and fond of him. Hipolita was an excellent housekeeper and filled in some of the parental gaps. Even Roy played a nurturing role, and Beth didn't feel that Chloe had been neglected before her arrival. What the child really needed was a mother, and the thought made her heart ache.

At ten o'clock Beth found Jack Gamble leaning against the garage wearing cut-off sweatpants and a tattered T-shirt. "You really don't have to do this," she tried once more.

"I know that."

Turning away from him, she started down the driveway at a slow jog, then increased her speed in increments until she reached a comfortable level. Her knees were a little sore, so she didn't push too hard, and Jack Gamble ran silently beside her for the first two miles. After three miles his breathing was ragged, and when they turned back onto his driveway he was struggling to remain upright.

Beth stopped on the patio and bent forward, palms against her thighs. Jack Gamble fell onto his hands and knees in front of her. Sweat was dripping from his face onto the stone pavement and with effort he raised his blue eyes to meet hers. Instead of feeling triumphant, she had an unreasonable urge to comfort him.

He dropped his head again. "You are a serious runner," he spoke to the ground, and she didn't have the heart to tell him she was way off her usual pace.

"And I made it back alive," she said with only a trace of sarcasm.

"Tomorrow night at ten," he said as he stood, and Beth gave him plenty of time to clear the kitchen before following him inside.

On Labor Day morning Beth saw Chloe and her father briefly in the kitchen before they left for his office in Albany. While Beth was eating a bowl of cereal, Hipolita handed her an envelope that contained her first paycheck. She stared at Jack Gamble's signature scrawled along the bottom of the check, amazed that she was actually being paid to spend time with Chloe.

The reunion with her family at the airport went better than she had expected. Her mother limited herself to one desperate hug, and her father was too busy taking pictures to give Beth more than a quick wave. Her brother Calvin, his wife, and their two beautiful children were on the way back to Memphis, which spared Beth the ordeal of having to watch a display of familial bliss.

Her sister Stephanie, who was studying entomology at the University of Georgia, said hello, then went back to reading a text-book on beetles. Melissa showed Beth every piece of new clothing she had on and wanted to open her carry-on bag to exhibit more, but their mother wouldn't allow it. Before Melissa could press the issue, her flight was called.

Nancy Middleton wept quietly as she gave her baby daughter final instructions. Stephanie put aside her bug book to wish her sister luck. Douglas Middleton caught Melissa in a big hug, then drew Beth into the embrace. Looking between them, he smiled. "The oldest and the youngest, the first and the last, the beginning and the end . . ."

"That's enough, Daddy!" Melissa protested, pulling away. "I'm going to miss my plane."

Her father gave Beth's shoulder one final squeeze, then bent down to pick up Melissa's bag. "Call us as soon as you get there." He passed the small suitcase to his daughter. "You know how your mother worries."

Melissa waved to everyone, then hurried away. Beth stood with the rest of her family until the plane was in the air, then they walked to the short-term parking lot. "We're going to get a sandwich before we head home," her father said. "Want to come with us?"

Beth shook her head. So far the visit had been pleasant, but time spent with them brought painful memories of David and the family she would have had with him close to the surface. Afraid that if they stayed together much longer she might dissolve into uncontrollable tears, she said good-bye and headed back to Haggerty.

Jack Gamble had guests when Beth returned, so she went straight to her room. Roy brought her a plate later and invited her to join them out by the pool, but she told him she wouldn't be comfortable. Then he said that he was going to put in an appearance at the Haggerty Methodist Church's annual Labor Day picnic and asked if she'd like to ride along.

"Don't worry about me, Roy," she said, shaking her head. "I'm used to solitude."

"Being used to something doesn't make it good."

"I enjoy peace and quiet," she assured him. "But thanks for dinner." She raised the plate, then closed the door.

At ten o'clock there were still people around the pool, so Beth didn't stop by the garage. She jogged down the driveway, entered the security code, and ran out into the street toward the park. Jack Gamble fell into step beside her before she reached the track. "You were sneaking off without me," he accused.

"After last night, it seemed like the compassionate thing to do," she replied with a smile.

"You took me by surprise yesterday. I'm ready for you now."

She took off fast, skipping about three intervals. Her knees were killing her by the time they stopped, and her running partner looked like he needed medical attention. Stooped on the front lawn, illuminated by the security floodlights, he struggled to catch his breath. She wouldn't have thought that a man dripping with sweat and gasping for air could be attractive, but he was. His loose shirt had fallen forward, revealing most of his chest and abdomen. Beth averted her eyes to conserve oxygen.

"Tomorrow you might want to let Roy protect me while I run," she teased.

"I work out," he responded with his limited air supply.

"Long distance running requires endurance and conditioning more than muscles," she answered charitably. "So I've got an advantage."

"I'll adjust."

"That's true." Beth knew her physical superiority was only temporary. "In fact, in a few weeks you'll enjoy running, and in a month . . ." He raised an eyebrow. "You won't be able to miss a day."

"And I thought I didn't have anything to look forward to," he said, then pushed himself into an upright position and staggered into the house.

On Tuesday morning Beth faced another day of boredom. Ignoring the television, she got out one of her library books and tried to develop an interest in the characters without success. Finally she put Monday's episode of *The Brave and Relentless* in the VCR. She was watching Tori cry when Roberta knocked on her open door. The secretary was carrying a briefcase, which she placed on the small coffee table.

"Good morning," she said cheerfully. Beth returned the greeting as Roberta looked at the television screen. "Don't you just love this show?" She sat down on the couch and they watched together for a few minutes. Finally she turned to Beth with moist eyes. "Poor Tori." Beth agreed that it would be awful if your husband's half brother had fathered your child, and Roberta pulled her eyes away from the television screen. "So, you want something to do during the day?"

"I'm going crazy," Beth admitted.

"You said you can type?"

"I'm not very fast, but I'm accurate."

Roberta pulled a file from her briefcase. "This new case of Jack's, the Ferris Burke trial?" she clarified, and Beth nodded. "We have all these depositions and police statements." Roberta waved at the folder. "Jack said you could summarize each one, then arrange them alphabetically so he can find what he needs quickly when he has to refer to something." This sounded almost interesting, and Beth reached for the file, but Roberta pulled the folder back. "You've heard of attorney-client privilege?"

Beth nodded again. "Anything a person tells his lawyer can't be used against him."

"As Jack's employee, what you read in this file falls into that same category. You can't tell anyone, even under oath."

The seriousness of Roberta's tone was daunting, but Beth was desperate for something—anything—to occupy her. "I understand."

Roberta exhaled, then stood up. "Good. I've got a laptop for you in my car. I'll be back in a minute." Beth opened the folder and glanced at a statement given by the arresting officer at the scene of the murder. She was completely engrossed by the time Roberta came back in with the laptop. "Where do you want me to put this?" she asked. Beth pointed to her little table. It only took a few minutes for Roberta to explain the basics of the word-processing system. "Just save what you type to these disks." Roberta held up a box. "Any questions?"

"Not yet." Beth just wanted Roberta to leave so she could get back to Ferris Burke's file.

"Well, call if you need me," Roberta said as she always did.

Beth waited until she heard the door close, then started reading the policeman's statement. By the time she stopped for lunch, she had the three page police report condensed into two informative paragraphs. She went into the kitchen for a piece of fruit, but found food from the Labor Day party spread out on the counter. So she fixed a plate and ate it while watching her soap opera until Roy came.

Chloe reported another good day at school. She had an invitation for the open house on Friday night, which Beth told her to be sure and give to her father. Kristen Northcutt was getting off the school bus in front of her house when Roy pulled up to the security gate. Beth rolled down her window and Chloe called out a greeting.

Kristen's backpack bounced as she ran over to the car. "My mom says we can come over and play again if you invite us," Kristen divulged, and Chloe immediately issued an invitation. "I'll go tell my mom," Kristen replied. "Can you wait for me?"

Roy watched while Beth and Chloe climbed out of the SUV. "Guess this means the gate will have to stay open again," he murmured, and Beth nodded.

Kristen returned shortly with her mother and Bud. The baby went straight to Beth, and she couldn't help but feel flattered as he grabbed her shirt and settled his chubby cheek into the crook of her neck. Beth promised to return them in two hours, then they walked past Roy, who was standing guard beside the open gate.

After Chloe was in bed that night Beth worked on the Ferris Burke file until ten o'clock. Jack Gamble was waiting for her by the garage when she arrived. "You're going to try again?" she asked as they started down the driveway.

"I'm not a quitter, and in the end, I always win," he replied without a trace of humor.

Beth took it easy on him, controlling her speed to accommodate his lack of conditioning. When they got back to the patio, he leaned against the house. "You don't have to give me a handicap," he gasped.

Beth couldn't control a little laugh. "I think I do." She had felt kindly toward him all day. "And thanks for letting me summarize the file on Mr. Burke," she added between deep breaths.

"I should thank you. Keep track of your hours and I'll pay you."

Beth shook her head. "I asked for the work. I won't charge you for it."

"How far did you get?" He pushed himself up and faced her.

"The policeman's statement that the murder was committed with 'unnecessary force' and the neighbors that reported continual fighting at the Burke house before and after the divorce," she recounted. "From the sound of it, the only ethical thing for you to do is recommend that Ferris Burke throw himself on the mercy of the court and plead stupidity."

He nodded slowly. "So you don't believe in due process, 'innocent until proven guilty,' and all that other nonsense in the Constitution."

This brought her up short. "Of course I believe in the Constitution, but Ferris Burke is so obviously guilty . . ."

He took a step toward the back door. "People are innocent under the law until *proven* guilty, Miss Middleton, and things are not always what they seem. Tomorrow night at ten."

On Wednesday morning Beth was standing outside the gate when Miss Eugenia Atkins pulled her Buick up to the curb. The old woman scanned Beth's attire quickly, then did an illegal U-turn in the middle of the street. "You don't spend much money on clothes, do you?"

Beth examined Miss Eugenia's snug-fitting, red polyester dress covered with large, royal blue polka dots that could not have been available in stores after 1970. Miss Eugenia followed the direction of her gaze. "It's okay for me to look like the back end of bad weather, but a pretty young woman like yourself should fix up a little."

The basement room that housed the library was cramped, and the furniture in it looked like rejects from other offices. "The furniture is all stuff that some city employee didn't want," Miss Eugenia confirmed as they walked in. "The books are old, and the card catalog is out-of-date. I'm not really sure why we even bother."

Beth wasn't sure either, but listened as Miss Eugenia explained the check-out process, which involved a battered spiral notebook with dates going back to 1998. "You might want to start by going through and throwing away any damaged books," Miss Eugenia suggested.

Beth began with the fiction section, examining each book and either reshelving it or putting it in the garbage can. Miss Eugenia spent her time on the phone discussing someone who was getting a divorce.

At ten o'clock a group of elderly ladies came into the room. Miss Eugenia hung up the phone and approached the other women. She pointed at Beth. "This is Beth Middleton. She is living with the hermit lawyer out on Highway 11 by Annabelle."

Miss Eugenia paused for a second to let this information sink in, then continued. "Beth, this is Miss George Ann. I'll go ahead and tell you that her grandfather donated the property that the Baptist Church is built on so she won't have to," said Miss Eugenia, pointing to a tall woman with a long neck and a deep frown. "You've met Miss Polly, who knows everything about everybody. If you've got any secrets, you might as well tell her now and get it over with." The small, plump woman in the floral print dress huffed. "And this is Miss Eva Nell. It's her goal in life to preside over every committee in the town of Haggerty, preferably at the same time." By now the women were all staring angrily at Miss Eugenia. "Beth wants to help three days a week in the library, and she has experience," Miss Eugenia added proudly.

The other ladies stopped glaring at Miss Eugenia to welcome Beth as the newest Friend of the Library. "What are you girls doing here?" Miss Eugenia asked when the hand shaking was completed. "You're supposed to be at Bridge Club."

Miss George Ann stiffened. "Bridge Club has been changed to Thursdays so we can attend the meetings of the Haggerty Genealogical Society."

"I don't know anything about a Haggerty Genealogical Society," Miss Eugenia said.

"That's because you don't know everything," Miss Polly was pleased to inform her.

Miss George Ann spoke again. "Rita Wilcox has been trying to start a group for years. She posted a note on the bulletin board at the library in Albany, and finally someone has volunteered to come on Wednesdays and help us."

"Rita Wilcox is dead," Miss Eugenia pointed out.

"Others of us are interested in our ancestors," Miss Eva Nell answered.

Miss Eugenia's response was lost when the door opened and Derrick Morgan stepped into the small room. "Derrick!" Beth exclaimed, dropping a mildewed edition of *Death on the Orient Express*. "What are you doing here?"

Derrick smiled. "I'm volunteering my services to help these ladies set up a genealogical society." He stepped closer and lowered his voice.

"And keeping an eye on you." He turned back to the old women and told them that it was time to begin their planning meeting.

"I'd like to nominate myself as president of this new society," Miss Eva Nell offered.

"You can't nominate yourself!" Miss Eugenia objected. "It's against parliamentary procedure."

Miss Polly nodded. "Besides, you're already the president of everything."

"We could probably get by without officers for now," Derrick suggested. "I'll conduct the meetings until we have enough members to hold an election." Mollified, the women settled themselves around a scarred table, and Derrick took a position at the front of the room. "First we'll need to designate an area of the library for our genealogical department." He looked at the crowded space, and Beth had to control a laugh.

"We could throw out the biographies," someone said.

"You can't have a library without biographies," another scoffed.

"How about those old encyclopedias?" Miss Polly proposed.

"If we throw them *all* out, we'll free up about four feet of space." Miss Eugenia muttered in disdain.

Derrick pointed toward the far side of the room. "What's behind that door?"

Everyone turned in unison. "I think it's the old cloak room," Miss Eva Nell said.

Derrick walked over and the ladies followed him. There were several cases of toilet paper stacked by the door and a large portrait of Jimmy Carter propped against one wall. Derrick found the light switch and bright fluorescence bathed the small space. "This would be perfect," he said.

"George Ann, you contributed some of your daddy's hard-earned money to Mayor Witherspoon's reelection campaign," Miss Eugenia reminded the other woman. "Why don't you go and ask him if we can have this closet for our genealogical department."

"I gave him fifteen dollars myself," Miss Polly announced proudly.

"Then go along with George Ann and be sure to mention you are a staunch supporter," Miss Eugenia encouraged. "And if he says yes, tell him we'll need some more ugly furniture," Miss Eugenia called after the old ladies as they disappeared down the hallway. Then she turned around to study Beth and Derrick. "You two know each other?"

"We worked together at the library in Albany," Beth replied.

Miss Eugenia examined Derrick for a few more seconds. "You're too old for her," she pronounced, and Derrick blushed crimson.

"We're just friends!" Beth cried.

"Humph," Miss Eugenia continued to look at them. The awkward moment ended when Kate Iverson and her daughter came through the door. Miss Eugenia took charge of Emily immediately. "Emily's overdressed." She stripped a tiny jacket off the baby.

"It's a matching outfit," Kate explained.

"She'll get a heat rash." Miss Eugenia handed Kate the jacket, then carried Emily over to the storage room. "Let me show you the new Haggerty Genealogical Department," she whispered to the baby.

Beth was introducing Derrick to Kate Iverson when the other members of the new genealogical society burst through the door. "Mayor Witherspoon said we can use the closet. I think he just wanted to get rid of us, and he says it's not official, but we can borrow it," Miss Polly reported.

Satisfied with their success, the ladies left the library promising to return the next Wednesday for another meeting. Kate took Emily home for her morning nap, and Derrick helped Beth transfer the toilet paper to a janitorial closet down the hall. He asked if he should move Mr. Carter as well, but Beth decided the former president should stay. "After all, he was here first," she pointed out. So they hung him on the wall.

"We can come back tomorrow and try to round up some furniture," Miss Eugenia said as she locked the library door at noon. Derrick said he would arrange his schedule at the downtown branch to accommodate another trip to Haggerty, and they agreed to meet the next morning at nine o'clock. Then he offered Beth a ride home and she accepted.

When they pulled up in front of the Gambles' house, Derrick stared at the gate. "You're still determined to keep this job?"

"More than ever." She considered telling him that she was now working on the Ferris Burke murder case, but decided that would only increase his anxiety. "And I'm dying for you to meet Chloe." Beth opened the passenger door and climbed out. "But I'm worried about this new project you've taken on. The Haggerty Genealogical Society looks like a big job."

Derrick smiled. "I've got plenty of time, and I can handle a bunch of old ladies."

Beth looked up to see Annabelle at her mailbox and waved to the neighbor. "We've just spent the morning with your sister at the library," she called over the top of Derrick's car.

"My condolences," Annabelle replied, crossing the street to stand beside Beth.

"This is Derrick Morgan. He's a researcher at the downtown library in Albany, and he's donating time each Wednesday to help your sister and her friends start a genealogical society."

Annabelle leaned into the car and shook hands with Derrick. "Nice to meet you," she said, then turned to Beth. "Eugenia is interested in genealogy?"

"She and several other ladies from town," Beth replied.

"Well, it was a pleasure. I'll see you tomorrow, Beth." Derrick restarted his car. "I've got to get back to my real job."

The women waved good-bye, and then Beth looked at Annabelle. "You're home early."

Annabelle looked surprised, as if she'd forgotten something. "Oh, yes. Excuse me."

Beth watched Annabelle cross the street and disappear into her house, then entered the security code and walked up the Gambles' driveway.

That night after Chloe was comfortably tucked into bed, Beth went downstairs and opened the Ferris Burke file. She summarized depositions from two magazine photographers who claimed that Mr. Burke had threatened them and was starting on a statement made by a disgruntled employee when she noticed that it was ten o'clock.

Jack was waiting by the garage. She started to apologize for being late, but he waved her words aside and held out a stack of photographs. She shuffled slowly through the pictures, discovering that they were all photos of Derrick. In the first one he was standing on the sidewalk in front of the Gamble's house, talking on his cell phone and looking at the security fence. The next two were taken as he drove by in his car, and in the last one, his face was pressed between the metal bars of the gate. This one was particularly endearing, and Beth separated it from the others.

"Did you take these pictures?" she asked.

He shook his head. "Roy did." Beth looked up in surprise. "Is this guy a friend of yours?"

She nodded, holding out the picture of Derrick peering toward the house, his cheeks pressed against the cold metal and his hands clasping bars on either side. "Can I keep this one?"

"You can keep them all, but tell your friend that standing on someone's property without their permission is called trespassing."

Beth looked back at Derrick's worried expression and smiled. "He thinks I'm in danger here. He said your house is scary enough for Dracula."

Jack raised an eyebrow. "He thinks I'm a vampire?"

"Maybe worse."

"But you're not worried?" he asked as she put the pictures in the backseat of her car. Beth shook her head. "Well, maybe you should be," he said as he started down the driveway.

On Thursday morning Beth joined Derrick, Miss Eugenia, and a few other Haggerty ladies at the library. There really wasn't room for everyone in the small closet, so Beth worked on the fiction section while an assortment of mismatched chairs were located and set up around the walls in preparation for the next meeting. Beth was home by eleven o'clock, and when Roy came to pick her up that afternoon, she had complete summaries of three police reports of spousal abuse against Ferris Burke.

That night Beth was standing by the garage at 10:15 when Jack pulled up. "I was afraid Ferris might have killed you too," she said as he climbed out of his black Jeep.

"It has yet to be established that Ferris killed anyone," he replied.

Beth laughed. "The man is incredibly violent, and you should be careful around him."

Jack considered this for a second, then shrugged. "Give me five minutes to change and we'll run." He returned a moment later wearing his cut-off sweatpants and the old T-shirt. They took off at a steady pace, and although she didn't run at full speed, she was fast enough to avoid insulting him. When they stopped, he surprised her by saying that he expected her to attend the open house with them on Friday.

She wanted to go badly, but shook her head. "It's just for parents."

"If I have to be there, I want you recording it for family court." His breathing settled into a seminormal pattern. "Tomorrow is Ferris's arraignment hearing. I'll get home as soon as I can, but I'll be cutting it close. Let's plan to leave at 6:30," he suggested, then held the door for her.

She walked quickly through the kitchen and into her room, unable to keep a smile off her face. She was going to the open house. She would get to see all of Chloe's work displayed around the classroom and witness the meeting between the evil Miss Hyde and Jack. As she climbed into bed she realized she hadn't looked forward to anything so much in years.

CHAPTER 5

After riding to school with Chloe on Friday morning, Beth faced her closet. She hadn't bought new clothes in a long time and couldn't imagine wearing anything she owned to an open house presided over by the glamorous Miss Hyde. Discouraged, she put her report to the family court judge in a postage-paid envelope provided by the court, then drove into Haggerty.

Miss Eugenia had a funeral to attend at eleven o'clock, so they closed the library early. Ellen Northcutt was backing down her driveway when Beth stopped in front of the Gamble's house to enter the security code. Beth reversed the Volkswagen and pulled up beside the neighbor.

"You haven't lost Bud, have you?" Beth asked, glancing into the empty car.

Ellen smiled. "No, I'm going to the doctor, so my husband came home to watch him."

"The new baby's coming soon?" Beth guessed based on the size of Ellen's midsection.

"About another week," Ellen reported with a sigh.

"I'd be glad to watch your kids when you go to the hospital," Beth offered.

"We might just take you up on that." Ellen smiled.

As Beth turned around in the Northcutt's driveway she saw Annabelle Grainger sitting on the front steps of her house. She parked the car along the curb and crossed the street. "Good morning!" she called from the sidewalk.

"Same to you," Annabelle returned.

"You're home from work early again."

Annabelle nodded morosely. "I guess I'd better start getting used to it."

Beth took a few steps closer. "Are you on vacation?"

"Come on out of the sun," she motioned for Beth to join her on the porch. "If the bank has their way, I'll be on permanent vacation." Annabelle stared at her front lawn as Beth sat beside her. "Mandatory retirement," the woman explained. "I didn't think they'd hold me to it."

"You don't want to retire?"

"I don't want to be old," Annabelle clarified. "My job is all that separates me from Eugenia and George Ann Simmons and Polly Kirby. If I retire, I won't have anything to do except attend useless club meetings and gossip about other people, waiting to die."

"You're sure the bank won't let you stay?"

Annabelle laughed harshly. "I thought they would beg me to stay, but yesterday the bank president gave me a retirement packet and said that they were planning a reception in my honor for the end of this month. When I told him I didn't want to retire right away, he informed me that they had already hired a promising young woman from Atlanta to replace me. She's starting on the first of October, and they want my office cleaned out before she arrives."

"He'll regret that."

"I haven't been able to bring myself to tell Eugenia yet."

"I won't say a word," Beth promised.

"So, what are your plans for the afternoon?"

Beth sighed. "There is an open house at Morrow Academy tonight, and Mr. Gamble is insisting that I attend. Since I don't have anything to wear, I was thinking about driving to that mall outside of Albany."

"I buy most of my clothes at a shop on the square called Corrine's," Annabelle said thoughtfully. "It's a little expensive, but they have some lovely things. I could take you by there, and since we've both got time on our hands, maybe we could get our hair trimmed too."

"Is that a nice way of saying my hair looks awful?" Beth smiled as she stood.

Annabelle hung her head. "I'm turning into Eugenia already."

Beth laughed. "Your sister told me that I look like the back end of bad weather."

"Be glad she said 'back end'," Annabelle muttered. "My car is at Grady's Garage having the tires rotated, so you'll have to drive us on this little excursion."

Beth pointed at the Volkswagen parked along the curb in front of the Gamble's house. "I'm ready when you are."

"Come inside while I get my purse," Annabelle invited as she stood and dusted the seat of her pants. Beth followed her into the incredibly beautiful home. The ceilings were high and lined with intricate crown molding. The walls were painted in pastels and covered with Monet prints. Instead of doors, large archways led from one room to another, and lush plants were arranged tastefully in corners and nooks. "This is the most magnificent house I have ever seen," Beth breathed.

"A local girl named Happy Goodwin decorated it for me," Annabelle replied with a satisfied smile. Then her eyes narrowed. "And praise from you means a lot."

"From me?" Beth was surprised.

"You've seen the inside of Jack Gamble's house," she explained. "None of us have been past that atrocious fence, but he hired an interior design firm from Nashville to decorate the inside. Everyone assumes it's incomparable."

"Mr. Gamble's house is beautiful." Beth looked around at the sunlight pouring through large windows. "But yours is so bright and cheerful."

Annabelle laughed, then led the way to the front door. Once they were settled in the Volkswagen, Annabelle gave directions to a house with a big sign nailed to the porch railing that proclaimed it to be Melba's Place. "We'll go in and see if she can take us now."

Beth followed Annabelle up the rickety steps and into the old house that had been converted into a beauty parlor. A huge woman with orange hair was talking on the phone behind a makeshift desk and waved them over when they cleared the small entryway. "Come in girls!" she boomed. "I've got customers, Eunice. Call me later." She hung up the phone and stood as her guests approached. "Who have we got here?"

"This is Beth Middleton," Annabelle supplied. "She's Jack Gamble's nanny."

The beautician raised an eyebrow. "Well, well."

Beth stepped forward. "Actually, I'm his daughter's nanny, and you must be Melba."

The woman almost doubled over with laughter. "I'm sorry," she gasped after a few seconds. "Just give me a minute to catch my breath." She dissolved into another fit of giggles.

Annabelle was smiling too. "This is Myrtle. Her sister Melba started the business but moved to Tampa. Myrtle is running the place for her."

"Melba weighs less than a hundred pounds, and she'd die if she found out anyone had mistaken me for her," Myrtle added as she wiped the tears from her eyes. Seeing Beth's discomfort, the big woman shook her head. "I'm not sensitive about being overweight. When I see skinny girls like you, it makes me sad thinking of all that good food you've missed out on!"

Myrtle appeared to be on the verge of another laughing spell, so Annabelle spoke quickly. "We would both like our hair cut. Do you have time now, or should we come back?"

Myrtle looked around the empty room. "I'll have to ask all these folks ahead of you . . ." she began, then clasped a hand to her ample stomach as giggles overcame her.

"In spite of her behavior so far today, Myrtle really isn't crazy, Beth," Annabelle's tone indicated that she was growing impatient. "And she is actually very good with hair."

"I'm sorry!" Myrtle did seem repentant. "You first, Annabelle," Myrtle commanded, and Annabelle sat in the swivel chair. "I'll need a minute to think about a style for Jack Gamble's nanny." Myrtle began dividing the short gray hair on Annabelle's head. "You need some bounce," she told Beth. "If I cut off a few inches and put in a subtle layer, that should be enough," Myrtle mused around a mouthful of hair clips. "Have a seat and make yourself comfortable. Or go on into the back and look around. I sell clothes as a little sideline, although that stuff would wrap around you twice. But my older sister, Mavis, is an Avon distributor, and she brought in some clearance stuff yesterday."

Anxious to escape the eccentric beautician, Beth walked through the hall and into another room. There was a rack of knit pantsuits and a folding table where various Avon items were arranged. She ignored the plus-size clothing and approached the cosmetic table timidly. It had been a long time since she had bothered with makeup, but she knew she would need plenty of fortification to face Miss Hyde at the open house.

When Beth returned to the main room and piled her things by the cash register, Myrtle whistled. "Now you are a girl who can't resist a bargain!"

Annabelle stood and removed the cape from around her neck. "It's your turn, Beth. And I think I'll go check on Mavis's table," she commented as she walked to the other room.

Myrtle settled Beth in the chair and began brushing. "Your hair is healthy and has a good texture," Myrtle praised as she worked. "And lots of women pay all kinds of money to get this platinum color, but if you let it get too long, it seems heavy and limp."

Beth promised to be more conscientious about haircuts in the future as Myrtle snipped happily. Annabelle returned with environment-friendly bug repellent and a discontinued beach hat. When Myrtle finished, they all studied Beth's new haircut in the mirror.

"You remind me of a line from *Breakfast at Tiffany's*." Annabelle closed her eyes and quoted. " 'For all her chic thinness, she had an almost breakfast-cereal air of health, a soap and lemon cleanness' . . ."

Beth stared at the older woman in confusion, and Myrtle laughed. "I think what she means is that you look nice in spite of being so skinny."

Annabelle frowned. "Well, that's not *exactly* what I meant."

The beautician gave Beth's hair another pat, then walked to the cash register. "You girls going to eat lunch at Haggerty Station?"

Annabelle shook her head. "No, we're headed to Corrine's to find Beth a dress to wear to an open house tonight."

"What's opening?" Myrtle asked.

"It's an open house at Chloe Gamble's school in Albany," Beth explained. "So the parents can come and meet the teachers." The older women exchanged a glance. "I'm just going . . ." Beth floundered, "in case Chloe needs me."

After leaving the beauty shop, Beth and Annabelle drove toward Corrine's. On the way they passed by Haggerty Savings and Loan, and Beth asked Annabelle how difficult it would be to open an account.

"It wouldn't be hard at all," Annabelle said with a shrug.

"It would just be a lot more convenient to have my account here instead of Albany," Beth explained. "Do you mind if I stop and set up an account real quick?" Annabelle shook her head.

Inside the bank Annabelle introduced Beth to Miss Sara Sue Larrabee, who processed the new checking account quickly. Then they walked down to Corrine's. Annabelle described the occasion, and Miss Corrine started flipping through the hangers. Finally she pulled out a light-green linen dress and held it up to Beth. "This should do. Try it on back there."

In the tiny fitting room, Beth smiled at her reflection. The gentle lines of the dress smoothed out her figure deficits, and her eyes picked up some of the soft color. It was a dress the sophisticated Miss Hyde could envy, and Beth was determined to buy it even when she caught a glimpse of the price tag. She walked out of the dressing room and gave her Visa card to the owner. Annabelle was talking into her cell phone and rolled her eyes when Beth joined her.

"This is Eugenia," she whispered, holding a hand over the tiny receiver. "She thinks that cellular phones cause cancer, so she won't buy one, but she doesn't have any problem with calling me on mine," Annabelle related as she hung up abruptly. "She's mad that we went shopping without her and wants me to ride with her out to the Wal-Mart so she can get some laundry detergent. Could you drop me by her house?"

Beth agreed as they walked out into the scorching afternoon sun. Beth placed her dress carefully in the backseat of her car, and then Annabelle directed her around the square and down Maple Street to a white house surrounded by flowers. Miss Eugenia was standing in the gravel driveway and approached the curb with purpose.

As Annabelle got out, Miss Eugenia leaned in and spoke to Beth. "Sara Sue at the bank said you opened a new account this morning." Beth barely had time to wonder how Miss Eugenia had obtained this information before the other woman continued. "They give you a toaster for referring a new customer. If you'd told me first, I could have been your referral and gotten a free gift," Miss Eugenia lamented.

"You've got a toaster!" Annabelle said in exasperation, but her sister continued to scowl.

"I'll stop by the bank on my way home and add your name to my application," Beth offered as the Volkswagen tried to stall. She gave it some extra gas, and Annabelle closed the passenger door. With a wave at the sisters, Beth pulled away and drove back into town.

She went straight to the bank and arranged for Miss Eugenia to be awarded a toaster. On the way back to her car she saw a shop called Edith's Shoe Emporium. The thought of wearing any of her old shoes with her lovely new dress was unbearable, so Beth walked inside. The small shop was very cool and smelled of leather and expensive perfume. A saleswoman met her immediately. "May I help you?" she asked.

Feeling a little intimidated, Beth nodded. "I need a pair of shoes."

"Then you've come to the right place," the woman replied with a pleasant smile.

Beth explained that she had just bought a dress from Corrine's and wanted shoes to match. "I guess I should have brought the dress in with me," she realized belatedly.

"Describe it," the lady requested. "I shop at Corrine's all the time." Beth only had to say a few words before the other woman nodded and walked over to a pair of pumps exactly the same shade as the new dress. "These will be perfect. What size do you wear?"

"Seven and a half," Beth said as she pulled out her Visa card again.

Very pleased with herself, Beth stowed the shoes in the backseat with her dress and climbed in behind the wheel. She was not nearly so pleased when she tried to start her car and couldn't. After the tenth try she knew there was no use, but she continued to turn the key, hoping for a miracle.

When the man parked next to her returned to his car, he offered assistance. Beth watched as he hooked up jumper cables and charged the battery, but the car still wouldn't start. Thirty wasted minutes later, she thanked the man and used her cell phone to call Roberta.

Beth explained the situation and asked Roberta to notify Roy and tell him to pick her up at the Haggerty Town Square instead of at the Gamble's house.

Discouraged, she sat down to wait for Roy. Car problems were a regular part of her life and shouldn't have upset her. But after spending a few days in the Gamble household, she had almost convinced herself that she was entitled to wear expensive clothes and drive cars that started. The old Volkswagen had brought her forcefully back to reality.

Ten minutes later she watched in horror as Jack's black Jeep pulled up behind her car. He leaned over and pushed open the passenger door from the driver's seat and then waved for her to join him. As if car problems were not enough, she was humiliated further by having to drag the new dress, the shoes, and the bag full of Avon products out of the backseat.

After sliding inside the Jeep, she closed the door and arranged her purchases on her lap, carefully ignoring her employer. She expected him to point out that he had warned her about the condition of her car, but he concentrated on the traffic until they were out of town. Then he asked what she wanted to do about the Volkswagen.

"I'll find a garage in the yellow pages and have it towed in."

"You might want to consider having it taken directly to the county dump," he suggested. "With what I'm paying you, you can afford a decent car."

"I don't want another car." She couldn't expect Jack to understand, but the Volkswagen was a lot like her—dented and damaged, but still trying.

"You can't possibly want *that* car," he challenged, glancing toward her briefly.

She didn't owe him any explanations, so she didn't respond.

Jack waited for a few seconds, then sighed. "Grady's is the only garage in town. I'll tell them to tow your car in and fix whatever is wrong."

"I . . ." she wanted to say she could handle things herself, but knew it would be foolish to refuse his help. "Thanks," she said finally. "For the ride too," she added. "I didn't mean for anyone to go out of their way. I thought Roy could just stop by town on his way to get Chloe."

"Roy's in Albany, and I didn't want you to have to wait in the heat until he could get here."

She couldn't bring herself to thank him again, so she asked about Roy instead. "Did he get the job at the Chamber of Commerce?" Jack gave her a blank look as he rolled down his window and entered the security code. "He told me he had applied with them," she added.

He drove through the gate and parked by the patio. "I don't know about that. Roy was taking care of some business for me today." Beth collected her purchases and he held the kitchen door open for her to walk inside.

Hipolita had a late lunch waiting on the table. Beth was starving and Jack didn't seem to expect her to make conversation, so they ate in silence. Beth was finishing a piece of pecan pie when Chloe ran through the door. She gave her father a hug, then embraced Beth as well. Roy followed closely behind and handed Chloe's backpack to Beth. Hipolita brought out more food for Roy while Chloe described her day in great detail—the highlight of which was Jeffrey throwing up in the lunchroom. Beth smiled, imagining Miss Hyde's reaction.

Chloe paused for a breath and saw Beth's new dress draped over the back of a chair. "Oh! This looks just like Miss Hyde." She reached under the thin plastic to touch the fabric.

Beth was pleased by this remark. "I bought it to wear to the open house tonight."

Chloe clapped her hands with delight. "I'm so happy you're coming! Our room is all decorated and I made you a name tag. One for you too, Daddy."

Jack gave his daughter a crooked smile. "That will come in handy if I forget who I am," he teased, and she giggled. He glanced at his watch, then lifted Chloe onto his lap. "I've got to go back to Albany for a little while." Her cheerful expression dimmed. "Mr. Burke had his arraignment today, and I need to talk to him."

"Are you still coming to my school?" Chloe asked.

"Absolutely," he assured her as his gaze met Beth's. "Can she stay with you for a while?"

Beth agreed and Roy accompanied his boss outside. They talked for a few minutes, then Roy walked to his apartment over the garage, and Jack got into the Jeep and drove away.

When it was time to get ready for the open house, Hipolita took Chloe upstairs. Beth went to her room and, keeping a mental picture of Miss Hyde as incentive, brushed her hair with a round brush and applied makeup liberally. She waited until the last minute to put on the dress in an effort avoid wrinkles. When she was finished, she faced herself in the bathroom mirror. Her hair did look fuller and maybe even bouncy. The makeup drew attention to her eyes and gave some color to her pale cheeks. And the dress was absolutely perfect. With a smile, she walked into the kitchen.

Hipolita was washing dishes and Chloe was sitting at the table, wearing a bright red sundress. "You're so pretty tonight!" the child told Beth.

Beth returned the compliment, then looked around the room. "Your father isn't here yet?" she asked, and Chloe shook her head. Then the door opened and they both turned, but it was Roy, not Jack, who walked through.

"Hey!" he greeted cheerfully. "Got anything to eat over there?" he called to Hipolita. "Just need a little something to tide me over." He took a chair beside Chloe. "Now, are you ladies famous movie stars or beauty queens?" Roy asked as Hipolita placed a plate of lasagna in front of him.

Chloe laughed and Beth glanced at her watch. It was twenty minutes after six o'clock. "We'll need to be leaving soon," she told Roy quietly.

He answered with his mouth full. "Boss said to wait for him until 6:30. Said if he wasn't here by then to go on and he'd meet us there."

"Daddy's not coming?" Chloe's voice rose in distress, and Beth pressed her lips together in a hard, unforgiving line.

Roy was still shoveling food into his mouth. "He's with Mr. Burke right now. They drew a bad judge who denied bail, and Ferris is fit to be tied. Boss has to calm him down."

Mildly surprised that Roy was so familiar with the details of Ferris Burke's case, Beth leaned forward. "Some things are important," she told him. "And some things," she looked quickly over to Chloe, "are more than important."

Roy nodded. "Nothing's more important to the boss than Chloe. He knew his day was going to be tight, but thought he had it worked out. Then something came up this afternoon that threw him way off schedule."

As the meaning of his words sunk in, Beth felt the heat rise in her cheeks. She had disrupted his schedule, and if Jack missed the open house and Chloe was disappointed, it was going to be her fault.

At 6:30 Roy stood and held out his hand to Chloe. "Let's head for Morrow Academy and see if your daddy's there." He took his time driving into Albany, and Beth knew he was stalling to give Jack a chance to get to the school before they arrived. The minute they passed through the front gates, Beth started scanning the parking lot. She had almost given up when she saw the black Jeep and Chloe's father leaning against it. Her relief was so profound that she smiled up at him when he opened the SUV door.

"I'm glad you made it!" she told him, then blushed.

His eyes widened slightly at her friendly greeting, then moved quickly from her fresh haircut to her new shoes. "I was afraid if I missed it, Chloe would be put in foster care," he said with a smile.

Beth rolled her eyes and led them into the building. Chloe described various features as they walked, and Beth was actually enjoying the tour until they crossed into the kindergarten building. Then a horrible thought occurred to her, and she stopped so suddenly that Jack almost ran into her.

"There's something I need to tell you," she confessed with extreme reluctance. "Miss Hyde doesn't understand . . . I've been meaning to correct her . . ." He raised both eyebrows, waiting expectantly. "Miss Hyde thinks I'm your wife."

He stared at her for a long moment. "Why would she think that?"

"When I brought Chloe to the school for the first time, she made that assumption."

He expelled a deep breath, then started forward again. "And just a few days ago, I thought my life couldn't get any more complicated."

Miss Hyde was standing by the classroom door when they walked in. She gave Beth a cool nod, visibly unimpressed by her improved appearance. Then, without acknowledging Chloe, she took Jack by the arm and thanked him again for the flowers.

Beth admired Chloe's work posted on the walls while the teacher flirted with Jack. Finally another parent demanded her attention, and

Miss Hyde released her hold on him. He joined Beth and Chloe by the art center, looking quickly around the room at Chloe's papers, and then suggested they make their escape while Miss Hyde was distracted.

"Where's Roy?" Beth asked as he hurried them down the hallway.

"You and Chloe are riding home with me," he responded as he unlocked the Jeep.

Beth stole glances at Jack's profile during the drive home. She knew she owed him an apology, but decided to wait until after their run. He was much more approachable when he couldn't breathe.

They met on the driveway at ten o'clock and ran at a steady pace. When they stopped on the patio afterward, Beth spoke. "I'm sorry for the inconvenience I caused you today with my car troubles, and I should have told Miss Hyde that I wasn't your wife." She took a deep breath, then pressed on. "I should have realized that sending the teacher flowers in your name might make her think you were . . . interested. But if you could have seen the way she treated Chloe before . . ."

"You're saying she's a bad teacher?" he asked.

"I'm saying she's selfish and lazy and vain . . ." Beth paused, unsure how far she should go. Then she remembered that first awful day. "I'm saying that she's the devil's spawn with a Boston accent. She has no business in a classroom, and if I hadn't sent her those flowers, she'd have labeled Chloe 'stupid' and stuck her in a remedial class just to save herself some trouble."

"Her credentials were impressive." His tone was noncommittal.

"She is overqualified to teach kindergarten, and I don't think she even likes children. She needs a nice office job so all she has to concentrate on is looking good."

Beth was prepared to defend this position, but he didn't challenge her. "The devil's spawn?" he repeated, and she nodded. "And you think the only reason she showed any interest in me was because you sent her flowers?"

Beth glanced up. The dim light softened his features, making him seem younger, and the bright blue eyes regarded her steadily. "I imagine you have to deal with interested women fairly often," she guessed.

"It happens. Miss Hyde liked me well enough to give me her phone number."

"Even though she thinks you're married?" Beth was shocked.

He laughed. "Miss Hyde must be open-minded about that sort of thing." He reached for the doorknob. "I usually throw unsolicited phone numbers away, but I guess I'll hold onto this one in case I ever get desperate enough to date a demon."

On Saturday morning Beth found Chloe in the kitchen eating cereal. The child pointed to the counter, where several more cereal boxes were arranged. Beth poured Cheerios and sat down at the table. Chloe informed her that Hipolita was out of town until Sunday night, so they were on their own for meals. Her father came in at that moment and amended this announcement.

"Hipolita is gone, but she left us plenty of food, so we won't starve." He opened a box of Froot Loops and dumped some into a bowl. He sat next to Chloe, which happened to be across from Beth. She watched the cereal disappear into his mouth, his white teeth crunching.

"Daddy says I can go to the office with him today, but he'll have to bring me back to you at night because he has a date," she disclosed with relish.

The thought of Miss Hyde danced across Beth's mind. "Anyone I know?"

"Miss Georgia," he muttered between multicolored bites.

"Her name is Amy, and Mr. Fuller wants my daddy to kiss her," Chloe provided.

"Chloe!"

She was not discouraged. "Well he does!"

Jack raised his eyes to meet Beth's. "Publicity pictures," he explained.

"For the state senate appointment?" Beth asked.

Jack shrugged. "Indirectly. Amy Phillips and I are cochairmen of the Albany chapter of the American Cancer Society, and they want a picture to put on posters."

"That's an honor," Beth said.

"It's a pain," he replied with a small smile. "I'll bring Chloe to you about five o'clock."

Beth watched them leave together, and the kitchen seemed depressingly quiet without them. Beth was glad when Roy walked in and poured a bowl of Frosted Mini-Wheats. She wasn't tempted to watch the cereal disappear into his mouth, so she looked out the window. "Maybe another pound," he said as he chewed.

Beth nodded. "I'll probably need to go on a diet before long."

Roy didn't smile. "You have to take care of yourself, Beth. Just because your life didn't work out the way you planned . . ."

Beth looked up in surprise. "What makes you think my life hasn't 'worked out'?"

"Chloe told me the boy you were going to marry died."

Beth never talked about David, but sitting in the lonely kitchen with Roy, she couldn't stop the words from slipping out. "He died on our wedding day. I used to have nightmares, but I don't anymore."

"That's because you feel safe here," Roy told her as if he were a practicing psychiatrist instead of a part-time chauffeur. "This has been a place for all of us to heal."

"All of us?"

"Would you call Roberta a confident, self-assured woman?" Roy asked, and Beth nodded. "Her husband and the boss were partners for a while. He and Roberta had been married for over twenty years when one day he ran off with an aerobics instructor younger than his own daughter. Before he left he cleaned out their bank accounts, got a second mortgage on their house—the creep even borrowed against their life insurance. Roberta had to sell her house and move in with her mother to keep their kids in college."

"That's so sad," Beth whispered.

"Roberta ended up in the mental ward of Memorial Hospital. As soon as they'd let him in, the boss went to see her. Told her he needed a secretary and to be in his office at eight o'clock on Monday morning."

"That was nice of him," Beth mused.

"Worked out pretty good for him too. Roberta's turned into the best secretary in the world." He shifted a little in his chair. "Then there's Hipolita. She paid a guy to help her immigrate from Mexico, but all he did was drive her across the border and dump her in Dallas. She had relatives in Atlanta, and made it as far as Albany before her money ran out. Didn't speak much English and had to live on the streets. She finally got a job as a dishwasher at Aristotle's. Boss was there the day they found out she didn't have papers and had to let her go. He hired her to cook for Chloe, took care of her legal problems, and earned her undying loyalty."

Beth smiled. "And Hipolita is *unquestionably* the best housekeeper in the world." Roy agreed with a nod. "What dragons did Jack Gamble slay for you, Roy?"

She was teasing, but Roy's expression changed drastically. He clasped his hands in front of him on the table and stared at them for a few seconds before responding. "I killed a man," he said slowly.

"Oh, Roy," Beth touched his freckled hands, horrified that she had forced him into such an awful admission.

"It was an accident and there were never any charges filed," his tone was hollow. "I turned into a worthless drunk, but the boss saved my life by giving me this job." He looked up and tried to smile. "And most of the time, I'm grateful."

"I'm so sorry." Beth knew that she would never look at Roy in quite the same way again, and her opinion of Jack Gamble had also been altered. Then her eyes narrowed. "Did you tell me all this so I would feel more lenient toward Mr. Gamble?"

Roy shrugged. "I owe the boss a lot, but I told you about us because I don't want you to waste your life. Can't settle for being somebody's nanny. You need children of your own."

Other children, not Chloe. She couldn't even bear to think about it. "I know I can't stay here forever."

"Haven't seen the boss kick anybody out yet," Roy said gently. "But the point is, just being safe ain't living."

Their conversation was interrupted by the arrival of Malcolm Schneckenberger with a memo for Jack. Beth greeted the little man with enthusiasm, glad for a chance to escape the uncomfortable topic. Roy was less friendly.

"He's at his office. You could have given it to him there."

"I must have just missed him," Malcolm said, taking a tentative step forward as if he might like to join them for breakfast.

Roy eyed the man's pudgy hand as he touched the back of a chair. "Just leave the memo on the table. I'll see he gets it." After Malcolm left, Beth asked Roy why he didn't like Mr. Fuller's assistant.

"Something about him grates on me," Roy replied. "And Hipolita absolutely hates him. That would be enough all by itself."

Beth almost mentioned that Hipolita didn't seem to really *like* many people, but decided against it. She left Roy eating his fourth bowl of cereal and worked on the Ferris Burke file until Chloe got home at five o'clock. Roy was with her, carrying two pizza boxes.

They ate on paper plates, completely ignoring table manners. Roy was demonstrating his ability to touch his nose with his tongue when Jack walked in dressed in a black tuxedo. His hair was still damp around the edges, and he'd cut his chin while shaving. But in spite of that, he was breathtakingly handsome, and Beth felt her heart pound.

"Can you do that, Daddy?" Chloe asked, pointing as Roy quickly retracted his tongue.

"I've never been tempted to try."

"Taking the Jeep, Boss?" Roy asked.

"Naw. Mr. Fuller is sending a limo," he muttered.

"Malcolm brought you a memo," Roy said with a gleam in his eye.

Jack scowled. "I'll look at it when I get back."

Chloe lifted her arms and he picked her up. "Tomorrow's Sunday, Daddy."

"I know that Chloe." He sounded tired.

"Remember you were thinking about if I could go with Beth to church."

"What about our lunch at Aristotle's?" He rubbed the soft curls around her face.

"I could bring her to the restaurant right after church," Roy suggested.

Jack looked at his driver. "You don't mind giving up your Sunday morning?"

"Haven't made any big plans," Roy said with a shrug.

Chloe's father turned to Beth. "This is just a visit, not a commitment of any kind," he warned, and she nodded. Then he spoke to Roy. "Bring her straight to Aristotle's. I'll be waiting. Now," he addressed his daughter, "give me a kiss."

"Boss didn't seem too excited about his date," Roy mused after Jack had gone.

"Mr. Fuller is making him do it," Chloe contributed. "But at least he's letting me go to church!" she pointed out honestly.

"Thanks for providing our transportation," Beth felt obligated to say. "I'd forgotten that my car is in the shop and hadn't even thought of trying to find a ride into Albany."

"No problem. After you read the comics on Sunday, what's left to do?" Roy smiled as he collected the pizza scraps and said he'd be back to pick them up at 8:30 the next morning.

They went to Chloe's room and selected a dress for church, then tried to decide on a way to spend the evening. Chloe didn't want to read or watch TV, and they discarded several other possibilities before Chloe suggested that they cook something.

"Like what?" Beth asked.

"Maybe cookies or a cake."

Nancy Middleton had offered many times to teach her oldest daughter the fundamentals of food preparation, but Beth had never been interested. The closest she had ever come to making a cookie was eating one. "I don't know how to make anything," she admitted with embarrassment.

Chloe was not discouraged. "Hipolita has books that tell you what to do."

"And I can read."

Chloe laughed, her eyes shining with mischief. "We could wear our matching pajamas," she said, running to her drawer.

"Meet you in the kitchen!" Beth headed downstairs as their evening began to take shape.

They found a recipe for oatmeal cookies in a book called *Cooking Made Easy*. Trusting the title, Beth collected ingredients on the counter. The oven was computerized, and it took Beth forever just to turn it on. The mixer was much more powerful than she expected, and as a result, the first bowl full of batter ended up slung all over the kitchen cupboards. Moving to a fresh section of the counter, Beth tried again. This time she mixed the ingredients with a wooden spoon, and the resulting batter looked thin.

"Sort of like brown cement," Chloe remarked as they watched the dough run together.

"We'll just have one real big cookie." Beth tried to sound optimistic. They put the cookie in the oven and sat down to wait.

"I'm glad Hipolita can't see the kitchen now." Chloe took in the flour on the hardwood floor, the gooey batter dripping off the cupboards into small blobs on the granite counter, and the miscellaneous ingredients scattered around. There was a devilish look in her eyes. "What if she came home early?"

Beth gave this some thought. "I'd tell her Roberta did it."

Chloe shook her head. "She wouldn't believe it. Roberta doesn't make this much mess."

"Well then," Beth paused for effect. "I'd tell her your father did it!"

A giggle bubbled out of the little mouth. "She'd never believe that!"

Beth pretended to reconsider. "I know, I'd tell her Roy did it!"

Chloe dissolved into a fit of laughter. "Roy wouldn't leave all this mess. He'd eat it!"

Beth laughed along with Chloe, happier than she'd been in forever. Then several things happened all at once. The timer sounded, and they looked up to see smoke pouring from around the oven door. Beth jumped to her feet, knocking over her chair. When she pulled open the oven, their cement cookie was black and smoldering. She found an oven mitt, grabbed the hot pan, and dropped it into the sink. Turning on the cold water seemed like a good idea, but the steam that rose from the pan combined with the smoke already billowing around the kitchen and set off the fire alarm.

All of this had Chloe laughing hysterically. Sinking to the floor, Beth pulled the child down into her lap. Chloe wrapped her arms around Beth's neck and pressed their flour-dusted noses together. About then, Jack walked through the back door.

He emerged from the cloud of smoke and stood before them, tendrils of steam dancing around his head. More concerned that he had caught her holding Chloe than she was about the condition of the kitchen, Beth transferred the child to the hardwood floor.

"What in the . . ." he started to say, then walked over to turn off the alarm.

"We made cookies, Daddy." Chloe tried unsuccessfully to stifle another giggle.

Jack surveyed the disaster area. "Chloe, go upstairs. I'll be there in a minute." Chloe scrambled to her feet and ran to the safety of her room.

Beth stood up and pulled the oven mitt from her hand. "Your date ended earlier than I expected."

He turned his piercing gaze to Beth. "I can't figure you out," he said slowly.

"What do you mean?"

"I expected you to be a perfect Mormon girl. I was prepared for a Cindy Crawford look-alike who could bake bread with one hand and knit quilts with the other. Instead, I got you."

She leaned back on the dirty counter for support.

"Before you'd been here an hour, you loaded Chloe in the worst vehicle I've ever seen and took her to eat junk food. Then you drove all over Albany pretending to be my wife." Beth opened her mouth to object to that outrageous remark, but he moved on quickly. "You have no concept of safety, evidenced by the fact that you leave the security gate open, invite strange children into my house, and leap in front of cars in the middle of the night. You antagonized Chloe's teacher, and you can't even boil water!" He waved toward the cookie smoldering in the sink. "And you don't look anything like Cindy Crawford."

Blood pulsed through Beth's veins with amazing force as she closed the distance between them, pointing a sticky finger at his black satin lapel. "I most certainly can boil water." It seemed wise to begin with her strengths. "I know you didn't mean that crack about Chloe's teacher, the she-devil. I didn't leap in front of your car, I ran across the street, and if you were a better driver I wouldn't have gotten hurt." He made a growling noise, and she knew she had better finish fast. "I should have asked you before inviting the Northcutt children over—" she lost a little momentum here, "but it *was* my day off. My car may be old, but I don't happen to be rich like you." She was pleased that he flinched at the reference to money. "I don't even want to look like Cindy Crawford," a bold-faced lie, "and just for your information—you don't *knit* quilts."

Their eyes held for a few seconds, then he turned and surveyed the chaos. "I guess it doesn't really matter anyway. When Hipolita sees this mess, she'll probably kill you."

He walked up the stairs, and Beth spent the next hour cleaning the kitchen. She propped open the back door and turned on the ceiling fan, hoping to blow out the smoke, then swept and wiped and scrubbed. The oven was still on, and she took perverse pleasure in knowing that she was increasing Jack's electric bill. She was basically finished at 9:45 but had no intention of going for a pleasant run with him after the things he'd said. So she stretched out the clean-up job, planning to run by herself later.

"It's now or never," he said from behind her, scaring years off her life. "I'm running, and when I get back, I'm going to change the security code on the gate."

Adrenaline pumping, she turned to face him. "Holding me prisoner will not impress the family court judge."

"That threat won't do you any good tonight." He didn't look concerned.

Beth searched for an appropriate response, but her mind was blank. Finally she stalked to her room, pulled on her running shoes, and jerked a sweatshirt over her head. Jack eyed her faux leopard-skin pajama pants as she walked past him, but didn't comment.

They ran around the track in hostile silence. Beth led at full speed, grateful for the cool air on her flushed face. After four miles she sailed through the gates and up to the house, feeling stronger than she had in a long time. He came up behind her a few minutes later, winded but better off than she had hoped. Beth moved toward the door, but he blocked her path.

"I lost my temper earlier," he gasped, then pointed at a patio chair. Too astonished to object, Beth sat down and he took the seat across from her. "My date was a disaster." He paused to breathe, and she shook her head, thinking that this man discussing his social life had to be a hallucination. "Miss Georgia kept kissing me." He shivered. "She wanted the media to assume that we were . . . involved, so I had to define our relationship."

"What did you do?" Beth leaned forward, all her animosity forgotten.

"I left her at the restaurant. I told the limo driver to take her home, and I called a cab."

"Was she mad?"

"Oh, yeah. She's mad, her agent will be mad, Mr. Fuller will be mad, everybody will be mad. If there wasn't already a rumor going around that I'm married, she'd probably start one that I'm gay."

"I'm sorry about that. I should have corrected Miss Hyde immediately."

He smiled. "That rumor might save my political career after tonight. But I wanted to explain my bad mood when I got home."

She couldn't resist him. "Anyone would have been upset to see that mess."

"I overreacted and I apologize. And you don't need to worry about Miss Hyde anymore. Friday was her last day at Morrow Academy."

"Her last day?" Beth repeated.

"You said she wasn't suited for the classroom, so I had her replaced."

Beth was amazed by his power, and even more surprised that he had accepted her judgement of the teacher. "You had someone fired based on my opinion?"

His blue eyes regarded her solemnly. "Your credentials were the main reason I hired you. In addition to that, I had a very extensive background check done on you." She gasped and he continued. "I wouldn't let anyone get close to Chloe without checking them out first."

Of course he wouldn't. She had assumed he'd accepted Bob Wells recommendation and the basics of her degrees on a résumé, but instead he had investigated her entire life. Her childhood, her family, David. "Then you know everything?" Beth whispered.

He shrugged. "Pretty much." Even in the darkness she felt exposed. His chair scraped the patio as he stood. "Don't feel guilty about getting the teacher fired. I bought out her contract, so she has a year's salary to live on until she finds a nice office job." He gave her another quick smile. "And I've never been all that crazy about Cindy Crawford," he added as he walked inside.

CHAPTER 6

When Beth walked into the kitchen on Sunday morning, she couldn't see any evidence of their oatmeal-cookie disaster. Chloe was sitting at the table wearing a bright yellow dress. Her hair was pulled into a French braid and tied at the bottom with a ribbon to match. The hair stood up on the back of Beth's neck. "Hipolita's not here," she gasped. "But your hair is braided."

"Hipolita doesn't braid my hair!" Chloe cried as if it were the most outrageous suggestion. The blood drained from Beth's face, and she knew the answer before Chloe said the words. "My daddy does."

He braids her hair. Beth pulled out a chair and sat down heavily, the words repeating themselves in her mind like a mantra. He was a single parent. Chloe's hair was long and needed to be fixed daily, so he had learned to braid. That was not such a huge feat. But the mental picture of his hands working patiently through his daughter's hair shook the foundation of everything she thought she knew about Jack Gamble.

Suddenly anxious to get out of the house, she told Chloe they would wait on the patio. Roy was already waiting in the Expedition, and they climbed inside. A "Happy Maids" van pulled up and parked by the patio as Roy started down the driveway. Beth realized that Jack had hired professionals to reclean the kitchen, and she spent the entire ride into Albany trying to decide whether to be grateful or insulted.

They walked into the chapel just as the meeting began and took seats behind Mark and Emily Iverson. Beth nodded to the Gospel Doctrine teacher as the baby handed a purple dinosaur to Chloe.

Soon Chloe had an extensive assortment of baby toys piled on the seat beside her. Beth suggested that she try to return some of them to Emily, and Chloe complied. Emily squealed happily, and Mark Iverson urged her to be quiet.

When Kate joined her family after the sacrament, she whispered a greeting over the back of the pew. Beth introduced Chloe as the baby threw a bottle of juice halfway across the room. Beth and Chloe spent the rest of the meeting watching the wrestling match in front of them.

Afterward, Beth exchanged a few awkward pleasantries with Mark Iverson, waiting for his wife to return. When Kate arrived, Beth offered to hold Emily during Primary again. "I hate to impose on you," Kate said as she collected the items Emily had distributed over an impressively large area.

"It's no imposition. I'll be going to Primary with Chloe anyway."

Kate stuffed a toy camera into the bulging diaper bag with a nod. "I'm sure Sister Sterling will be grateful for the reprieve." She hooked the strap of the bag over her shoulder and reached for a stack of books.

Beth extended her hands toward Emily and the baby went to her, then giggled down at Chloe. After Chloe was settled on the CTR row, Beth took Emily to a minichair at the back of the Primary room, and they watched the children practice for the sacrament meeting program. When it was time to dismiss for classes, Chloe followed her classmates out with a quick wave in Beth's direction.

Kate retrieved Emily and invited Beth to Relief Society. "I think I'd better sit outside Chloe's door in case she needs me." She looked at the CTR classroom.

Kate squeezed her arm. "I understand completely. In a few weeks Chloe will be comfortable here, and you can join me in Relief Society."

Beth watched her new friend walk down the hall and wondered if Jack would allow Chloe to attend church long enough for the little girl to get comfortable. Then she pulled a chair from the Primary room. She settled herself in front of Chloe's classroom and stared at the door until it opened forty minutes later. Chloe walked out wearing a CTR ring and a badge proclaiming she could "Make Right Choices."

"So, did you have fun?" Beth asked as they walked outside.

"I had so much fun," Chloe assured her with a smile. "My teacher is Sister Tipper, and she told everyone I was their new friend."

When they reached the SUV, Roy opened the door, then watched Chloe secure her seat belt. Once they were on their way he asked if the preacher had pounded on the pulpit, screaming about fire and brimstone. "No one screamed," Beth replied.

Roy glanced at her in the rearview mirror. "Don't see the point of going to church if the preacher doesn't yell at the sinners."

Beth smiled. "There is still plenty of talk about repentance, it's just presented calmly."

Roy shrugged. "Seems like that would take all the fun out of it."

When Roy turned into The Crossroads, Beth leaned forward. "I thought you were supposed to take Chloe to the Greek restaurant to meet her father."

"Boss called and said that Ferris got into a fight with another inmate and he would probably have to spend all day straightening out the mess. So he told me just to bring Chloe home. Said Hipolita left a bunch of sandwiches in the refrigerator we can eat for lunch."

Beth was not surprised that Ferris had been involved in a violent incident or that Jack was canceling a lunch date with his daughter. Roy paused at the front gate to enter the security code, and Chloe pointed to the Northcutts' house.

"Look! There's Kristen and Bud!" Beth turned and saw that, indeed, the Northcutt children were standing on the front porch of their house. "Can they come over again?" Chloe begged.

Beth glanced at Roy. "We can talk with them for a few minutes at least," she said as she opened the SUV door and waited for Chloe to slide out. Then they crossed the street and walked up to the Northcutts' house. Before they made it halfway across the lawn, Bud started running toward them. Kristen called stridently from the steps but Bud ignored her, and Beth hurried to intercept the little boy.

"Bud!" Kristen wailed. "You know Mama told us to stay right here on the steps until Mrs. Brantley comes to get us."

"Your mother isn't here?" Beth asked, shifting Bud to her hip and facing Kristen.

The little girl shook her head. "Daddy took her to the hospital to have the baby." Kristen reported as Chloe moved up beside her friend. "Mama was going to call you, but she couldn't find your number. So Mrs. Brantley is on her way to get us now." Kristen looked up with tears in her eyes. "Mrs. Brantley is old. She feeds us rice pudding, and she doesn't have any toys for Bud."

"You can come home with us instead," Beth decided. "I'll call the hospital and talk to your dad . . ." At that moment, a gray sedan pulled up the driveway and everyone watched an elderly lady emerge. She surveyed the scene before her, noting that Kristen and Bud were both alive and well, then turned her eyes to Beth.

"Who are you?" she asked, her tone barely within the polite range.

"My name is Beth Middleton, and I've just moved in across the street."

"You live in the hermit's house?" the woman demanded, and Beth nodded.

"This is Chloe Gamble, and I'm her nanny," Beth introduced as another car pulled into the driveway and several women in Sunday clothes climbed out.

"This is Beth Middleton," Mrs. Brantley said when the other ladies had joined them. "She lives with the hermit."

"I'm his daughter's nanny," Beth reiterated, although none of the women were listening. They were whispering amongst themselves, watching Beth suspiciously. "Well, come on Kristen, Bud." Mrs. Brantley reached for the baby, but he clung to Beth.

"Kristen and Bud can just go home with us," Beth said courageously. The women looked at her as if she had proposed selling the children to gypsies. "They spent last Sunday afternoon with us," she added. Kristen nodded, and Bud tightened his hold on Beth's blouse. "We'll leave the gate open." The women glanced at the security fence, then consulted with each other. "I'm a Friend of the Library," Beth tried desperately.

The miniconference ended and Mrs. Brantley stepped forward. "Ellen put me in charge of the children."

Beth stood her ground. "They want to go with me. Ellen couldn't find my number, that's why she called you in the first place." Mrs. Brantley looked offended, but Beth pressed on. "Call Mr. Northcutt at the hospital, and I'm sure he will approve this change of plans."

"I want to play with Chloe," Kristen added her endorsement. "And she has toys for Bud."

Mrs. Brantley studied the death grip Bud held on Beth's shirt and sighed. "If Mr. Northcutt has any objections, I'll come and collect the children at once!" her voice rose slightly. "You'll leave the gate open?"

Beth nodded. "And I'll give you my phone number in case you need to call."

The older woman wrote the number on the back of her church program, then all the women watched as Beth led the children back across the street. Roy had parked the SUV on the driveway and was standing by the gate.

"Mrs. Northcutt has gone to the hospital to have a baby," Beth explained to him. "I've invited Kristen and Bud to spend the afternoon with us, and I told those ladies that we'd leave the gates open." Beth pointed at Mrs. Brantley and her retinue gathered on the sidewalk across the street. Roy nodded without comment.

Beth started up to the house, away from the staring women. After about ten yards she realized that Roy was not following. She looked back to see the chauffeur stationed beside the open gate. "Aren't you going to eat lunch with us, Roy?" she asked.

"Better stay here," he replied.

Beth realized she had doomed him to an afternoon in the hot sun. "We'll bring you some sandwiches!" she promised, and he nodded.

Bud was getting heavy, so Beth hurried the children inside. She settled everyone around the table, then served milk with Hipolita's sandwiches. After they finished, Beth sent Chloe and Kristen down to take Roy some lunch while she straightened the kitchen. Beth tried not to think about Jack's reaction when he found out that she had invited children into his house again. The Northcutts couldn't strictly be considered strangers since he had met them the week before and had apologized for complaining about their previous visit. But Beth would accept the consequences for her decision, whatever they might be.

Mr. Northcutt called a couple of hours later to tell Bud and Kristen that they had a new baby sister named Megan. Ellen and the baby were both doing well, and he said he would pick up the kids in a few minutes.

Kristen was pleased with the news. "Bud is okay, but I really wanted a sister instead of two brothers," she said, and Chloe nodded her understanding.

"I would like to have a baby sister too," Chloe said.

"First you have to get a mom," Kristen told her, and Chloe frowned. "I'm glad my grandma is coming to take care of us while my mother rests," Kristen continued with a smile.

Chloe had no comment on grandmothers, but suggested that they wait outside for Kristen's father. Beth gathered Bud into her arms and followed the girls down the driveway. Roy looked hot, but greeted them cheerfully.

"Kristen has a new sister named Megan," Chloe told him.

Roy congratulated the Northcutts, then offered to hold Bud. Beth handed the heavy little boy to the chauffeur as Jack pulled into the driveway and parked the black Jeep behind the silver Expedition. He glanced at Roy, and Beth thought she saw a trace of amusement in his expression before he leaned down to pick up Chloe.

"Kristen has a new baby sister named Megan, and she said if I want a sister you'll have to get me a mom first."

"That's true," Jack agreed as they watched Mr. Northcutt drive slowly by and park in his own driveway. Then the neighbor walked across the street to collect his children. He took Bud from Roy, then held out a hand to Kristen.

Beth apologized to Mr. Northcutt for changing their child-care arrangements, but he shook his head. "Mrs. Brantley was a desperate decision. I know the kids were happier with you, and we appreciate your help."

"Our pleasure." Jack graciously took credit for Beth's hours of baby-sitting.

"Come back and play some more tomorrow!" Chloe cried. Once the Northcutts were out of sight, Jack turned and carried Chloe toward the house. Roy closed the gate, then got into the Expedition and drove it to the garage. Beth followed behind Chloe and her father.

"I know I should have checked with you before I invited the Northcutt children over again," she said to his back. "But it was kind of an emergency." Beth couldn't hear his response, so she quickened her pace until she was walking beside him. "They were going to have to go with Mrs. Brantley, who feeds them rice pudding."

"And she doesn't have toys," Chloe added solemnly. Jack gave her a smile as Roy trotted past them on his way to get the Jeep. "Can I ride with you?" Chloe asked, and Roy held out his hand to her. Chloe was transferred to Roy, leaving Beth uncomfortably alone with her employer. When they reached the patio she looked up and saw that one side of his jaw was swollen, and there was a small cut under his chin.

"You're hurt." She stared at his face.

"It's nothing." He touched the gash. "Ferris had a bad morning."

Beth's mouth fell open. "Ferris Burke hit you?"

Jack shook his head as he held open the kitchen door. "A policeman trying to subdue Ferris hit me by mistake."

"I guess that's one of the hazards of defending violent men."

"How far have you gotten with the summaries?"

"To the incredibly lengthy list of Ferris's juvenile crimes," she said, then blushed, embarrassed for him since his client was so obviously guilty.

At this moment, the door opened and Chloe rushed in. She was followed closely by Roy and Hipolita.

"Hipolita's home!" Chloe announced.

With resignation, Beth gave an account of her unsuccessful attempt at baking to the housekeeper. She left out the fact that they had made a terrible mess and set off the fire alarm, but still expected a cold reproach or maybe a string of Spanish obscenities. Instead, Hipolita shrugged and moved to the sink. Chloe followed the housekeeper, describing their exciting day.

Beth went to her room and called Derrick, then checked in with her mother. Nancy Middleton moaned about a project Stephanie was doing that required her to catch fifty different species of insects. She said that Melissa was doing well in Utah, Beth's father had a cold, and Calvin's wife was expecting another baby. Saddened by so much motherhood, Beth stretched out on her bed. She startled awake at 9:30 and was still groggy when she met Jack by his garage at exactly ten o'clock.

"You missed dinner," he said as they jogged down the driveway.

"I fell asleep," Beth admitted.

"You're too thin as it is. You shouldn't make a habit of skipping meals."

Beth scowled at his back, then sailed past him. After their regular four miles they slowed to a brisk walk. When they crossed the street in front of Annabelle Grainger's house, Jack reached out and halted Beth's progress. Following the direction of his gaze, Beth saw a dark-clad figure perched high on the metal spikes that topped the fence around the Gamble's home. She just had time to think that Derrick was obviously wrong about electrification before Jack leaned in close.

"Stay here," he whispered against her ear, then ran toward the gate.

Beth followed directly behind him. The intruder heard their approach and jumped off the fence, then fled into the darkness. Jack pursued and Beth kept pace. They were almost at the entrance to the subdivision when the man jumped into a nondescript car and sped away.

The Tom Clancy books she had read made Beth wonder if a government agency was watching Jack. Then she remembered the way Mark Iverson, whom Bishop Sterling had introduced as an FBI agent, had perked up when he found out who Beth worked for. While she considered these possibilities, she noticed Jack doubled over, gasping for breath. Once he recovered enough to walk, they turned back toward his house.

"Why did you follow me?"

"I figured if one of us had a chance of catching that guy, it was probably me," Beth explained, massaging a cramp in her side. She saw a muscle jump in Jack's jaw and wondered if he was controlling a smile or biting back a curse. "Could that have been a law enforcement person of some kind?" she asked.

"It could have been an undercover cop, someone from the district attorney's office, or even a television reporter. Heck, it could have been a private investigator hired by my parents to see if Chloe is eating all her vegetables. I don't know." He sounded discouraged.

"For a second I was afraid it might be Derrick, but he thinks your fence is electrified and would never have climbed on it." Beth looked over to catch his reaction and was rewarded with another jaw twitch.

"Well, until we find out who it was, maybe we can keep the gate closed," he suggested, then broke into a slow jog.

On Monday morning Beth ignored the rules and walked Chloe to her class at Morrow Academy. She knew the child was anxious about starting over with a new teacher. Mrs. Hoffeins was in her early thirties and well-groomed but not polished. She had a short, sensible haircut and friendly eyes. Chloe went into the classroom and sat next to Allison. Beth smiled as she watched the little girls confer. Chloe had friends now and was familiar with the school. It would be up to Mrs. Hoffeins to make adjustments.

Roy dropped Beth off at the city hall with a promise to return at noon. Beth thanked him, then went in to wait by the library door for Miss Eugenia.

"Here bright and early, I see," the older woman mumbled when she arrived. Today she was wearing a fairly modern denim dress, but her toes hung over the top of her bright green sandals by at least an inch. "Might as well get busy." As they entered the musty room, Beth could hear Miss Eugenia's overlapping toenails clicking against the old linoleum.

Beth continued her progression through the fiction section while Miss Eugenia made dozens of phone calls organizing a baby shower. They had two customers during the entire course of the morning. One was a teenager who needed Cliff Notes for *Moby Dick*, which they didn't have. Beth suggested that he could just read their copy of the actual book, but the boy looked at her as if she'd lost her mind. Their only other patron was an elderly man who had come to the city hall to pay his annual garbage-collection fee and gotten lost.

At noon Beth said good-bye to Miss Eugenia and went outside. Roy was parked in the spot reserved for the mayor. "I'm surprised you didn't get a ticket," Beth remarked as she climbed into the SUV.

"This is Jack Gamble's vehicle, and if he gets a ticket, I figured he can probably get out of paying it."

"Undoubtedly," Beth agreed.

After lunch Beth worked on the summary of Ferris Burke's childhood crimes until *The Brave and Relentless* came on. Elena was having more tests run on her vision, but the prognosis was not good. At 1:30 Beth set the VCR to record and rode into Albany with Roy.

According to Chloe, everyone liked the new teacher except Wesley, who said Miss Hyde had whiter teeth. Chloe's homework that afternoon was to draw a picture of her family. She carefully arranged her crayons on the small table in Beth's room, then began the project. Beth watched the last half of her soap opera as Chloe drew herself and her father in the middle of the paper. Then she asked how to spell "Roy," "Hipolita," and "Beth," adding three additional people in the corner. Beth knew she should be happy to be included at all, but the little picture made her sad.

When Chloe was finished with her homework, she asked Beth if they could go outside and walk around the yard for a while. The sky was gray and threatened rain, so after one lap around the fence, they sat on a patio bench and watched the wind blow through the trees. Thunderstorms always made Beth uneasy, and she couldn't repress a small shudder. Chloe snuggled up against her. "Are you sad, Beth?" she asked, her eyes wide with concern.

"I just don't like storms."

Chloe was silent for a few minutes, then she touched Beth's hand. "Are you thinking about the boy who died?"

Beth took a deep breath. "His name was David," she confided. Chloe pressed closer and they sat in companionable silence, watching the clouds roll in. Then Beth saw lightning in the distance, and they ran for the house as the first fat raindrops fell.

After dinner, they played Old Maid until it was time for Chloe to get ready for bed. Beth tucked her in, allowing herself a quick kiss on the child's forehead, then went downstairs to read. At 9:15 there was a knock on her door. Startled, she opened it to find both Jack and Roy standing in the hallway.

Roy was dressed in a blue and white striped shirt, a red tie, and khaki pants. Beth assumed he had been to another hopeless job interview and turned her attention to Chloe's father. Jack was wearing tattered blue jeans, a T-shirt with a motorcycle emblem on the front, and an old Braves cap.

"Came to ask a favor," Roy spoke first.

"I was going to approach it more as a money-making opportunity," Jack amended. Beth stared at them, unable to think of a response. "I've got to go to a bar out on Highway 76," he continued. "We are looking for a very important witness, and I've gotten a couple of reports that she's been seen at a place called Heads Up."

"Boss needs to go there, but if he shows up alone, he'll look suspicious," Roy contributed. "So he needs a date."

Jack gave Roy an irritated look. "I need a companion. I'll pay you overtime. Double your usual hourly wage."

Beth took a deep breath. "I don't know what my hourly wage is."

Jack shrugged. "Me either, but Roberta can figure it out."

Beth waved at Roy. "Why can't the two of you go together?"

A flush crept across Jack's cheeks, and Roy laughed. "If the boss and me was to show up together, they might think we're boyfriends." He paused for emphasis. "And in a place as rough as Heads Up, that could get us killed."

Beth couldn't keep from smiling, and "the boss's" scowl deepened. "I guess I'll go."

Jack eyed her blue jeans and shirt. "You'll have to look a little worse than that," he told her.

She stared at him incredulously. "Even I don't have any clothes worse than this."

"I don't mean that your clothes have to be worse, but you have to look less . . . ladylike and . . ." He searched again. "And not so . . . clean."

"What do you want me to do? Black-out a tooth?" she demanded.

He seemed to be seriously considering this suggestion, and Beth was already shaking her head when Roy intervened. "Wear your hair down and put on a lot of makeup. On your face, not your teeth!" he hastened to assure her.

"I'll see what I can do," Beth muttered, pushing the door closed.

"Hurry. I'm anxious to get this over with," Jack called.

Grateful for her new supply of Avon products, Beth applied cosmetics generously and pulled the ponytail holder from her hair. When she opened her door a few minutes later, both men were still standing in the hall. They studied her, exchanged a glance, then nodded.

"Keep an eye on Chloe. We'll be back before it gets too late," Jack told Roy.

Beth reached for her purse. "Don't take anything with you. It might get stolen," her "date" explained. Slightly alarmed, Beth followed him outside, where an old pickup was waiting. Beth looked at Jack in confusion. "This truck belongs to the guy who services the pool. I don't want anyone to recognize me . . ." he began.

"Or steal your car," Beth guessed.

"That too." He held the passenger door open for her.

Beth secured her seat belt, then clasped her hands in her lap as they drove along. The rain had cleared, exposing innumerable glittering stars in the cloudless sky. The clock in the truck was broken, but she guessed it was close to ten o'clock. "It's kind of late to be going out, isn't it?"

"I doubt Heads Up opens much before dark," Jack replied. "And I apologize for involving you in this, but it is very important that I find Ferris's sister-in-law. She was living with his ex-wife at the time of her death."

"And you think her testimony will help Mr. Burke?" Beth asked skeptically.

"Why else would he want me to find her?"

Beth considered this. "That would make sense," she admitted, then examined his face in the moonlight. "I don't see any new bruises, so I guess Mr. Burke didn't get into any more fights today."

"Not today," he agreed with a smile. "Ferris was raised to believe that violence is the answer to everything. That's why I'm going to introduce his juvenile arrest record as evidence."

This seemed like a mistake. "You're going to show the jury that he's always been a criminal?"

"I hope to prove that Ferris felt threatened and fought back. That's called self-defense. And if Amber Harper testifies in Ferris's behalf, my case is won."

Beth tried without success to imagine how practically pulverizing someone could be considered self-defense. "What about his wife?"

"Audrey Burke was a known addict and died of an overdose. Ferris was never charged in her death. He's only being tried for the murder of the boyfriend, Sean Ballard."

"Roy said that Mr. Burke was upset about not getting bail."

"Ferris has homes and bank accounts all over the world, making him an incredible flight risk. I knew the judge would deny it, just like he'll deny the change of venue I'm going to ask for tomorrow. But the more times I force him to say no, the better chance I have that he'll eventually say yes to something I really want, to keep from looking partial," Jack explained.

"So you're asking him for things you don't really want?"

He shrugged. "I'd be the happiest man alive if Judge Tate had set bail. Then Ferris would have left the country, saving all of us the trouble of a trial. But I knew we wouldn't get any kind of break from Judge Tate."

"He doesn't like you?" Beth guessed.

"None of the judges like me, but Judge Tate truly despises me." He sighed. "Judge Tate is old and notoriously forgetful. About a year ago I got him to overturn one of his own rulings. Unfortunately, he *has* managed to remember that."

"He'll block you at every turn," Beth realized.

"And then some." He pulled off Highway 76 onto a gravel road. Beth was shocked when he parked in front of a small cinder-block building with peeling paint and no windows. Several Harley Davidson motorcycles were assembled to one side, and Beth noted that the pool man's battered truck was the nicest vehicle on the lot.

Jack led the way up to the large piece of plywood that functioned as a front door and knocked. As the makeshift door opened, he reached for Beth's hand. She was vaguely aware of a small man with an impressive handlebar mustache who admitted them to the smoke-filled interior. Several people were crowded around a bar, and something crunched under their feet as they crossed the room to a booth in the corner, but Beth barely noticed. All she could think about was the feeling of Jack's fingers wrapped around hers.

She slid into the booth, and the sticky vinyl upholstery resisted the fabric of her pants. Once she was settled, Jack sat down close beside her. "Try not to touch anything. This place is filthy," he told her unnecessarily.

The room was ominously quiet, and Beth realized that their arrival had attracted attention. She peered over at the bar and saw a group of men dressed in black leather, staring. "Why are those men looking at us?" she whispered.

"I think the makeup was a mistake," Jack replied. "And wearing your hair down too." He glanced at the blonde tresses on her shoulders. "I should have realized that you were too pretty to be inconspicuous."

At this moment the Heads Up version of a waitress spoke from beside their table. "Ya want something?" the middle-age woman demanded in a deep, nicotine-altered voice.

"A couple of beers," Jack said.

"Strangers pay in advance, $9.50 plus tip."

He shifted closer to Beth and reached into his back pocket to pull out his wallet. He removed a twenty and handed it to the woman. "Keep the change."

She nodded, then shuffled off. Beth was trying not to think about her leg pressed against Jack's and didn't see the man until he was standing right beside their table. "Wanna dance?" he addressed Beth.

He was huge, wearing a vest but no shirt. His bare arms were covered with tattoos, and a grisly beard obscured his mouth. Beth couldn't repress a shudder as she stared at his matted chest hairs. Jack lifted his arm and put it around her shoulders, pulling her even closer to his side. "No thanks," he said to the man.

"Let her answer for herself," the man growled.

"My wife doesn't dance with other men," Jack stated flatly.

The big man looked at Beth's hands clasped together on the table. "Don't see no ring."

"I lost it," Beth forced the words past the lump of terror in her throat. "He said he'd buy me another one, but he hasn't—yet."

There was a brief pause, and then the man chuckled. "If you ever get tired of this cheapskate, come back and see me." He returned to his friends at the bar.

"Don't want no trouble with the bikers," the waitress warned them as she placed two overflowing mugs of beer onto the table in front of them.

"Me either," Jack assured the woman, putting another twenty into her hand. "I'm looking for a girl named Amber Harper. There's money for anyone who can help me."

"How much money?" the waitress asked, her voice low.

"A thousand dollars," Jack whispered back. "She's not in any kind of trouble. I just need to talk to her." He slipped a business card into the woman's calloused hand. The waitress nodded, then disappeared. "We'll wait a few more minutes, then get out of here." Jack picked up the mug of beer and brought it close to his mouth, but didn't drink.

With each minute that passed, Beth's feelings of uneasiness grew, and by the time he was ready to leave, she was trembling. Jack gripped her shoulders and shook her slightly. "It's okay. We'll be fine."

He slid out of the booth and took her hand. They walked to the entrance, where the man with the mustache pushed open the plywood door.

Beth sighed with relief when they stepped out into the fresh air. Then she heard gravel crunch to their left. They turned in unison to see the bikers, led by the hairy man, closing the scant distance that separated them. Jack pulled Beth into a trot as footsteps from behind approached rapidly. Just when she realized that they were never going to make it to the safety of the truck in time, a tall figure appeared in front of them.

"Whoa! What's the rush?" a deep voice asked, reaching out a hand to stop them. Beth glanced over her shoulder and saw the bikers fade into the shadows.

"It's been a long night, and we're in a hurry to get home," Jack replied.

The tall man swung his eyes back to Beth. "Heard you had a girl living with you, but don't usually pay much attention to town gossip." Beth blushed as Jack explained that she was Chloe's nanny. "This seems like a funny spot to bring any date, let alone your kid's nanny." In the moonlight Beth could see that the man was wearing a uniform. "Or maybe it wasn't a date. Maybe it was business." The big man removed his hat and rubbed his head. "Heard that Ferris's sister-in-law hangs around this place."

"I've never seen her here," Jack said cautiously.

"You wouldn't be planning anything illegal would you? Like maybe finding Amber Harper and then hiding her whereabouts from the district attorney's office?"

Beth saw Jack's jaw tense. "If I locate any witnesses, I'll notify Lance Kilgore." He strengthened his grip on Beth's hand and pulled her toward the truck. "Glad we ran into you, Winston," he called back to the officer. "Get in," he whispered to Beth.

She obeyed, sliding quickly under the steering wheel and over to the far window. Jack started the truck, then sped out of the parking lot and onto Highway 76. "You were great in there," he said once they were a safe distance from the beer joint.

"I think I'm going to faint," Beth answered. "Or throw up. Or both!" Jack put his foot on the brakes and steered the truck onto the shoulder. "Don't stop!" Beth screamed. "They might be following us!" He pulled back onto the road.

"Put your head between your knees," he instructed, "and take slow, deep breaths." Beth complied, and a minute later she was feeling moderately better. "I'm sorry," he said, his jaw clenched. "I didn't expect it to be quite that bad."

"If that policeman hadn't come . . ." she couldn't force herself to complete the thought. "Is he a friend of yours?"

"His name is Winston Jones, he's the police chief in Haggerty, and he's not my friend. His cousin was arrested for bootlegging a few months ago, and I got the charges dismissed, so he feels an obligation to be congenial."

Beth rested her elbows on her knees and supported her chin with her hands. "The cousin wasn't really bootlegging?"

Jack spared her a brief look. "I didn't say he was innocent. I said the charges were dismissed." Beth couldn't keep the disappointment from her eyes, and she saw his jaw tighten even more. "He's a creep, but he has a wife and three little kids to support."

When Jack parked the truck beside the garage, he turned to face her. "I wouldn't have taken you there if I'd known there was a real threat of danger," he said. "But you really surprised me with your bravery."

Beth frowned. "Did you think I was a coward?"

Jack laughed. "Not a coward, but you're even afraid of me!"

"I'm not afraid of you. I'm just a little uncomfortable."

"And there's the possibility that I'm a vampire."

"Or worse," Beth agreed with a smile.

"So, will you forgive me?"

Beth nodded. "Just don't forget that you owe me overtime."

He laughed again. "It's almost midnight now. Do you still want to run?"

"Give me a few minutes to wash my face, and I'll meet you by the garage." She climbed out of the car and headed toward the house, already pulling her hair up into a ponytail.

That night after she took a shower and got into bed, she closed her eyes and tried to remember the smell of his aftershave, the feel of his hand in hers, and the exact inflection in his voice when he said she was too pretty to be inconspicuous.

CHAPTER 7

On Tuesday morning Jack was sitting at the kitchen table when Beth walked in. She felt a little awkward, but relaxed when he gave her a big smile. "Hipolita made omelettes from Mexico with green and red things," Chloe informed her. "But she'll let you have Cheerios if you hate it."

Beth glanced over at Hipolita. "I'd love to try an authentic Mexican omelette." Hipolita began filling a plate. "Just be sure and save some for Roy."

"I make one special for him," the housekeeper replied.

"So, you must be about finished with the summaries," Jack said after Hipolita had served them both breakfast.

Beth lowered her fork. "I thought you said there was no rush."

His mouth was full, so he had to swallow before he could speak. "There isn't, but I have another project when you're ready for it."

Beth couldn't restrain a satisfied smile. "I'll have them done by tonight."

Chloe finished her cereal just as Roy arrived. He put ketchup and pickle relish all over his omelette and ate it in four bites. Then he drank two glasses of milk and said he was ready for the ride to Albany.

Beth worked furiously all morning to complete the Ferris Burke file. She didn't even pause to watch her soap opera, but recorded it for later. By the time she left to pick up Chloe, the summaries were done and neatly organized onto one of the disks Roberta had given her.

Chloe was supposed to bring a collection of fall leaves to school the next day, so Beth walked her around the yard, picking up likely candidates. Then Roy took them swimming until dinnertime. Jack drove up in a new, gray Lexus while they were drying off. Chloe wrapped her towel around her wet bathing suit and climbed into the front seat with her father.

"This is so pretty!" She rubbed her hand along the dashboard.

Beth approached the open car door with reserve. "You traded in your Jeep?"

He shook his head, looking almost sheepish. "Actually, this is your payment for going to Heads Up with me last night."

Beth's mouth fell open. "You bought me a car for two hours of work?"

"Would it make you feel any better if I told you it was leased?" Jack asked.

"Is it?" Beth demanded.

"No," he admitted.

"Then telling me so won't make me feel better." Beth eyed the beautiful car with anxiety.

"You should be glad my daddy got you a car that isn't broken," Chloe said.

"As my employee, what you drive reflects on me," Jack added.

"And your car is really ugly." Chloe had chosen sides on the issue.

Roy stepped up and admired the sleek finish. "Not that I mind taking you places, but seems like it would be nice to have dependable transportation of your own." His loyalties were not in question either.

Jack smiled. "Grady says the engine in your Volkswagen is shot and even a used one will be expensive. The radiator is about to go, and the hoses all need to be replaced . . ."

Beth held up a hand to stop him. "If I agree to drive this car, it will be with the understanding that when I leave, the car stays with you."

He slid over into the passenger seat. "Let's go for a test drive."

"I'm not dressed," Beth waved down at the T-shirt covering her swimsuit.

"We won't go far," Jack promised.

"Hipolita will help Chloe change." Roy was already steering the little girl inside.

Reluctantly Beth sat behind the wheel, tucking her T-shirt carefully around her bare legs. Jack reached over her to adjust the seat and the steering column. Once he was satisfied, he returned to his side of the car and nodded. "Put it in drive, and you're ready to go."

Beth pulled slowly down the driveway and turned toward the park. "It seems like a waste to spend so much money on a car for a temporary employee."

"I got a good deal on the car, and it's been convenient having you around, so I'm hoping you'll stay . . . indefinitely."

Beth's heart started beating faster and her mouth went dry. "The contract was for three months. After that I'll probably go on a mission," she said, even though she never really gave missionary work more than a passing thought anymore.

"You could just stay here and convert us," he suggested, and she almost hit a curb.

Once she had the car back under control, Beth pulled to a stop under a tree on the edge of the park and turned to face him. "The gospel is nothing to joke about."

"I'm not kidding. Chloe enjoyed Primary last week, and regular church attendance should impress my parents and the judge." He shot her a quick smile. "So she can keep going as long as you take her. And who knows, you might even soften my hard heart."

Beth stared at the road, unable to think of a reasonable response. He was presenting her with the chance to teach Chloe Primary songs, as well as help the girl learn about prophets, and, most importantly, help her gain a testimony of the Savior. When she looked up, she saw satisfaction in his eyes and knew that he had purposely offered her the one thing she couldn't refuse.

"I still have over two months left on my original contract. We'll wait until the end of that time and then decide about the future," she said slowly, then started the car. "How did things go with Judge Tate today?"

Jack's jaw tightened. "The old goat was a step ahead of me. He didn't deny my motion to change the venue outright, just said he didn't have enough information to make a 'fair and judicious' decision. So he told me to redo my motion in more detail and present it again on Thursday." He paused while she entered the security code. "He's making me waste more time on something we both know he's going to deny, and made it look like he's trying to be fair by taking an extra two days to consider it."

"Maybe he's not as senile as you thought," Beth suggested as she parked near the garage.

"Keep the keys," Jack told her when she started to leave them in the ignition. "That's your set."

Beth frowned at him, but before she could respond, Chloe stuck her head out the kitchen door. "Hipolita says come in and eat before the food is all soggy."

"I guess you could use the Volkswagen as a trade in on this," Beth waved at the new car. "I mean it *is* old, so the parts must be worth something."

"I wouldn't dismember your car for a few dollars," he said. "But thanks."

During dinner, Beth told Jack that she had finished summarizing the Ferris Burke file, and he nodded. "I'll come by your room and pick up the disk after we eat."

She waited for a few seconds, but when he didn't continue, she prompted him. "You said you had another project for me?"

"I do. We'll discuss it when I pick up the disk."

Roy left after his third plateful of red beans and rice, and Chloe went into Beth's room to watch *Wheel of Fortune*. Beth waited nervously until Jack finally joined them. He sat by his daughter on the small couch, seeming to take up more than his share of space. Beth got the disk and handed it to him, then waited expectantly.

"Rock around the clock." He solved the puzzle, then smiled down at Chloe.

With a sigh of impatience, Beth addressed him. "Do you have something else for me to do on Ferris Burke's case?"

He pulled his eyes away from the television screen and sat up straight. "I have a tape that I'd like you to listen to. It's Ferris's life story and his version of what happened on the night of the murder."

"You're having him practice for when he testifies in court?"

Jack shook his head. "Putting Ferris on the witness stand would be an absolute last resort. A good attorney can twist words and make even an innocent man look guilty."

"Or a guilty man look innocent," Beth said. "That's why you always win."

"Are you calling me a good lawyer?" He skipped over the insult to find the compliment.

Beth had to smile. "You are a very successful lawyer," she hedged her response. "So, you want me to type a transcript of the tape for you?"

"No. I don't want one word of that tape in writing, but I want you to listen to it and tell me what you think."

"Why?"

"Because like many of the potential jurors, you already think Ferris is guilty. Your reaction will help me decide on the most effective defense." Jack pulled a tiny Walkman from his pants pocket. "Give the tape back to me personally when you're finished, and don't tell anyone that you have it, not even Roy or Roberta." As he pressed the cassette player into her hand, his warm fingers wrapped around hers.

Beth eyed the tape and suppressed a shudder. "You trust me with this?"

"I trust you with Chloe. That tape is nothing in comparison." He pulled his daughter to her feet. "I'll put Chloe to bed tonight and meet you by the garage at ten."

Beth watched forlornly as the Gambles left, then stared at the cassette in her hand. Unable to stand the suspense, she locked her door and put it into the tape player.

＊ ＊ ＊

"My name is Ferris Earl Burke . . ." the country music singer's semifamiliar voice spoke from the cassette player. "My mother died right after I was born, so I never knew her. My daddy spent fourteen hours a day, six days a week, in the coal mines, and died when I was twelve. My oldest brother, Warren, was in the federal penitentiary by that time, but my next brother, Alfred, was twenty-one and had a job at the local Jiffy Lube. So the court gave him custody of me. I guess Alf tried his best. He sent me to school and even asked about my grades a few times.

"One night I was riding around with some older boys, and they robbed a convenience store. They got caught, and I was charged along with them. Since I was only sixteen, they sent me to a juvenile correctional facility in Nashville called the Speakeman School for Boys.

"The school was clean and the meals were regular, so I didn't really mind it. None of my family sent letters or came to see me, but I didn't hold it against them. I knew most of them couldn't write, and none of them had the money for a trip to Tennessee.

"I got my GED there, then started some college courses. I was due to be released when I turned twenty-one and a few months before my birthday, the headmaster introduced me to Claudia Wisenhaut. Claudia was a high-class do-gooder type and had volunteered to teach guitar lessons to the inmates. The headmaster knew I liked to write song lyrics and sing, so he asked me to be her student.

"Claudia taught me how to play basic chords, and we enjoyed singing together. She came every day until I was released, and after our last lesson she talked me into giving her some lyrics I'd written. When I left Speakeman I never expected to hear from Claudia Wisenhaut again.

"I got back to Georgia and found out that Warren had killed a guy in prison, so his sentence had been changed to life without parole. Alf was married and offered to let me sleep on his couch. I tried that for a few nights, but him and his wife fought all the time and I couldn't stand the racket. Then an old friend named AJ offered to let me stay at his place. He was out of town a lot and wanted somebody in the apartment while he was gone so he wouldn't get robbed.

"Alf got me a construction job, and I saved enough money to get a decent car. Then I heard that a little country band out at the Yellow Lantern needed a guitar player. They couldn't pay much, but they were pretty good, and after a few months they let me do some of my songs in the show. That's how I met Audrey.

"One night a group of kids came into the bar. Anyone could see they were underage, but the folks at the Lantern weren't too strict on rules. One of the girls in the group was the prettiest thing I'd ever seen, and I couldn't take my eyes off her. The next night she was back, and she waited for me when the Lantern closed. McDonald's was the only place open that late, so I took her there and sprung for hamburgers. Audrey was drunk on our first date, and I should have smelled trouble, but I didn't.

"We went together for the next year or so, then she got pregnant. Her folks were upset when we told them that we were getting married. They begged me to make sure she finished high school, and I promised them that she would, but I lied. One of the things I learned quick was that I couldn't make Audrey do anything.

"We got a little apartment, and while I was at work she'd watch TV and drink. I showed her all kinds of articles about how alcohol could hurt the baby, but she wouldn't stop. She said she couldn't help it, and maybe she couldn't. I don't know. Those were terrible months for me. I worried myself sick about the baby. Jasmine came a month early and she was small, but the doctor said she was okay.

"Audrey's drinking got worse after Jasmine was born. Since I couldn't trust Audrey with the baby, I dropped her off at Mrs. Harper's house on the way to work in the morning and picked her up at night. Jasmine gave me something to look forward to at the end of every day, and I really needed that, since most of the time Audrey was drunk or gone when I got home. Maybe there was something else I could have done to help Audrey, but if there was, I don't know what.

"One night the phone rang, and it was Claudia Wisenhaut calling me from Nashville. She'd been taking my lyrics around to different recording studios and finally found somebody who was interested. They wanted me to come and bring everything else I'd ever written. So I talked to the Harpers and they agreed to keep Jasmine. They even loaned me fifty dollars for gas. I left the next morning.

"Claudia took me to the studio and introduced me to a small-time producer. I showed him all my lyrics, and then he had me sing. After a little while he got up and left. I thought he didn't like my songs, but he came back later with a band, and we played for the rest of the afternoon.

"I didn't have any money, so Claudia let me stay at her apartment for the next couple of weeks while we worked out arrangements for two songs. I missed Jasmine and called the Harpers every night to check on her.

"I told Claudia all about Audrey and her drinking and our marriage. She wanted me to get a divorce and move to Nashville, but I was afraid that if I tried to divorce Audrey, I might lose Jasmine.

Finally the studio offered to buy two of my songs outright and let me record another one on a CD single that I would make royalties on.

"That next year I did two more single CDs and finally an album. People kept telling me how lucky I was to have Claudia. Most performers had to hire agents and split their money, but Claudia didn't charge me anything and looked out for me better than any agent.

"By then Audrey had moved on to hard drugs, and I had to go out of town a lot. Audrey's younger sister, Amber, loved to baby-sit Jasmine, so when I had to travel Amber would come over and take care of the baby. The two sisters were different as night and day. Audrey was as beautiful as an angel but mean as the devil. Amber was plain but sweet. She was always glad to help, and I think she had a crush on me."

* * *

Beth glanced up at the clock and was surprised to see that it was almost ten o'clock. She had gotten so involved in Ferris Burke's life that she'd forgotten about her own. She buried the tape player and cassette under a stack of her clothes, then changed into sweats and ran out to meet Jack.

He was waiting by the garage. "So, how far did you get?"

"He's cut his first album and Audrey's on drugs."

Jack started down the driveway. "What do you think?"

Beth considered this. "I hated to turn it off even to come run." Jack raised an eyebrow. "In spite of everything I know about Ferris Burke, on the tape he sounds . . . nice."

"I told you things aren't always as they seem." He headed toward the park.

"Like the way skinny girls can run faster than big, healthy men," Beth called over her shoulder as she passed him.

He caught up with her quickly and they ran at top speed. Afterward Beth was too tired to even take a shower. Collapsing on top of her bedspread, she thought of Wednesday stretching out before her, gloriously full of meaningful activity. Then she fell asleep with a smile on her face.

On Wednesday morning Chloe was beside herself with excitement. A nearby petting zoo was bringing baby animals to the kindergarten. She was particularly interested in rabbits, and described in detail the bunnies she hoped to hold. When Hipolita asked what type of cereal Chloe would like for breakfast, Chloe claimed she was too happy to eat. Beth was trying to think of a way to encourage her when the housekeeper spoke.

"No breakfast, no school." Her tone was calm, but it left no room for argument.

"Cheerios," Chloe surrendered.

When Roy came in, Beth suggested that she take Chloe to school in the new car. "Thanks, but if you start driving Chloe around, I'll be out of a job."

Beth immediately regretted her offer. "Still no luck finding anything permanent?"

Roy frowned. "Applied to be a receptionist at a big law firm downtown." The horror must have shown on Beth's face. "I know that kind of job is usually for women, but it's against the law to discriminate. And all I'd have to do is greet visitors and answer the phone."

"Have you ever considered trying something more . . ." she searched for the right word, "manly? Like installing television cable or reading electric meters?"

"Naw, I want to work inside and stay cool," Roy responded, then attacked his breakfast.

Jack walked in as they were leaving and accompanied them to the Expedition. He was dressed in an expensive business suit and looked every bit the part of a high-powered lawyer. He opened the door of the SUV and watched as Beth and Chloe climbed in.

"I've been meaning to ask you," Beth said from the backseat. "What will happen to my Volkswagen, since you don't want it for a trade-in?"

Jack smiled. "It seems like I heard about a Volkswagen museum up in Arkansas. I thought I'd tell Grady to send your car there."

All the way to Albany, Beth kept thinking about her tired, old car in a Beetle museum, getting the respect it deserved. When Roy dropped her back off at the Gamble's house, Beth transferred into the Lexus, then drove into Haggerty.

She was a little nervous about seeing Derrick again. For the past several days, she had purposely called at times when she knew he wouldn't be home so she could just leave messages assuring him of her safety. Her involvement in Ferris Burke's case, her attachment to Chloe, and her growing trust of Jack made discussing her life with Derrick difficult.

Self-conscious about being seen in the new car, she parked a block down from the city hall and walked back. Miss Eugenia was already sitting at the desk in the small library and glanced at the clock when Beth came in. "I declare, I thought you must be taking the day off," the older woman greeted her. "I've been getting everything ready for the genealogical society meeting." The room looked exactly as it had when they left on Monday. Beth's eyes came to rest on the telephone sitting in the middle of the desk and Miss Eugenia followed the direction of her gaze. "I did take a few minutes to make some calls about Rowena Crowe's baby shower."

Beth nodded. "One of the Gamble's neighbors had a baby on Sunday."

Miss Eugenia waved the news aside. "Ellen Northcutt. They only attend church on special occasions, and then they worship with the Baptists. So Miss Polly is hosting her shower. I'll tell her that you'd like an invitation," Miss Eugenia added as the door opened and Annabelle walked through. "What are you doing here?" her sister demanded.

"I took the day off so I could come and protect that nice library man from all you old women," Annabelle replied. "And I might like to find out who we have in our family tree."

Miss Eugenia looked less than pleased by her sister's unexpected presence, but didn't have time for another comment before more ladies arrived. Miss Eugenia directed them to their seats and pumped the ladies for local gossip, then reminded them of their food assignments for the shower on Sunday. Derrick arrived at nine o'clock, lugging a big cardboard box.

"It's a good thing you're here," he whispered to Beth as he placed the box on the floor in the former closet. "Because I had made up my mind to call the police if I didn't see you face-to-face."

"You've misjudged Mr. Gamble, Derrick. He wouldn't do anything to hurt me."

He studied her like a lab experiment gone awry. "You might want to read through those newspaper articles again. The man is charming. He confuses people, makes them think that wrong is right."

Miss Eugenia saved Beth from a reply by asking Derrick to begin the meeting. After a brief greeting, he explained the purposes and limitations of their group. "We will be able to make some simple inquires here. Then, if any of you want to pursue a serious investigation, you can come to the downtown library in Albany."

"So, where do we even start?" Annabelle asked.

Derrick smiled at her. "That's a good question. I have a basic pedigree chart for each of you. You write your name on this line." He held up a sample and pointed to the correct space. "Then you put your father here, your mother here, your grandparents here, and so on."

"What if you don't know the names of your grandparents?" someone wanted to know.

"Write down what you know and we'll go from there," Derrick replied as he began handing out the sheets.

"I don't have a pen." Annabelle was digging through her large leather purse.

"I'll get some," Beth offered and walked over to the desk as Kate Iverson came in carrying Emily. "You're sure you want to get involved in this?" Beth whispered.

"I wouldn't miss it for the world," Kate assured her with a smile. Kate took a seat beside Miss Eugenia, and the older woman reached for the baby.

"The downtown branch has agreed to donate some books on local history, and I've brought a few of them with me today," Derrick pointed at the box. "It would be wonderful if we could get some computers, so if you know a company who might be willing to donate some . . ."

"There's a whole closetful at my bank," Annabelle said thoughtfully. "I'll bet they'd give me a few."

Miss Eugenia made a sound in her throat. "You may be Miss High and Mighty at *your* bank, but it's not ladylike to brag."

"It's not ladylike to cheat at cards either!" Annabelle responded with spirit. "But that never stopped you!"

"Eugenia cheats at cards?" Miss Polly Kirby asked in a scandalized tone.

Derrick intervened. "Another good resource for finding information about your family tree is to talk to relatives."

"Before she died, my mother told me that we were descendants of Stonewall Jackson," Miss George Ann informed the group. "I'd like to trace my line back that far and have it framed to hang in my parlor."

"Right alongside the picture of the Baptist Church built on the land your daddy donated," Miss Eugenia muttered.

"Many families claim kinship to Civil War generals, and Stonewall Jackson is particularly popular," Derrick said with a smile.

Miss Polly leaned forward. "In Evelyn Campbell's *Complete History of Dougherty County*, there is a story about my great-great grandmother. William Tecumseh Sherman and his army destroyed her home, but when he tried to burn her Bible, she hit him with her broom."

"My great-great grandfather was an English nobleman who fought with the Confederacy and settled in Georgia after the War Between the States," another lady announced.

"Many families in the South have similar stories. In fact, the stories are so similar that professional genealogists refer to them as 'fables.' Most of the documentation of them, such as marriage and birth records, were lost during the war, especially here in Georgia, where Sherman made his march of destruction. And the stories have been retold so many times and mixed together until it's hard to find the truth," Derrick explained.

"What did he say?" an old woman hollered from the back of the small room.

"I think he just called our ancestors liars," Miss Eugenia informed her dourly.

The women reacted with predictable outrage, and Derrick was quick to appease them. "I most definitely did not! It's just that few things were written down, and inaccuracies occurred. But," he rubbed his hands together, "that is why we're here today. We don't want to depend on stories passed down through the generations. We want to find out the facts."

"Couldn't that be a little dangerous?" Miss Eva Nell asked. "Like what if one of us was to find out something unsavory about an ancestor?"

Miss Eugenia bounced Emily on her lap and laughed. "With our luck, Annabelle and I will find out that instead of whacking General

Sherman with a broom, one of our great-grandmas was meeting him in the peach orchard!"

"That is a risk we all take when we do genealogy. No family is perfect, and there are usually a few skeletons to be found," Derrick admitted.

"But you can't be a member of the Daughters of the Confederacy just because your great-grandma said she hit General Sherman with a broom," Miss George Ann said. "You've got to have proof that an ancestor contributed to the war effort."

"Well, sorry about that, Kate," Annabelle rolled her eyes at Miss Eugenia's neighbor. "Since you're not from the South, I guess there's no hope of you getting into the Daughters of the Confederacy."

Kate smiled. "That's okay. My family fought on the winning side."

"Everyone start working on your pedigree sheets right now!" Derrick commanded before another argument could break out.

Derrick spent the next hour helping the ladies with their pedigree charts. When someone noticed that Kate was not filling hers out, they asked why. "My genealogy is completed back for many generations. I just came today for the social interaction." She winked at Beth, who was safely in the fiction section.

"It's another odd thing that Mormons do," Miss Eugenia told the group. "They look up the names of their ancestors, then offer them the chance to join the Mormon Church after they're already dead."

"See 1 Corinthians 15:29," Kate said calmly.

"Paul wasn't really talking about doing baptisms for dead people," Miss Eugenia retorted.

"You're right. He was talking about the resurrection, and just used the practice of doing baptisms for the dead to illustrate his point," Kate answered with a smile.

"What?" the deaf woman from the corner yelled.

"She's talking about the scripture that asks why the people in Paul's time performed baptisms for their dead."

"I thought the preacher said to skip over that part!" the woman replied loudly, and Miss Eugenia grimaced.

"A friend gave me a *Bible for Modern Christians* that she bought in California, and it doesn't even have that scripture in it. She said they had left out several unexplainable passages."

Derrick stepped between the women. "If I can direct your attention to this book that contains the 1880 Georgia Census!" he pleaded.

When the meeting finally ended, Beth walked Derrick to the door. "I've missed the past several episodes of *The Brave and Relentless.* I'll have to call and get you to fill me in."

"Nothing much has happened. Parker still doesn't know that his brother is the father of his wife's baby. Elena has officially left the real-estate firm, she's ordered a Braille Library, and is looking into getting a seeing-eye puppy."

"That seems a little premature, since the doctor isn't even sure she's going blind yet."

"Can't wait until the last minute on something like that," Derrick said.

"Well, be careful on your way back to Albany." Beth opened the door for him.

Derrick looked up at the clock. "You get off in fifteen minutes. Why don't I just wait and drive you home?"

"Oh, don't do that!" Beth knew she had protested too strongly when she saw suspicion creep into Derrick's eyes.

"Grady at the garage told me that your Volkswagen was unfixable and that Jack Gamble bought you a new Lexus," Miss Eugenia contributed helpfully.

Derrick's face went pale as his eyes widened with fear. "You let him buy you a car?"

"He bought a car and I agreed to drive it," Beth answered. "But it's not mine, and when I leave, he'll just have an extra vehicle."

"I knew something like this was going to happen," Derrick moaned. Miss Eugenia took a step closer, listening to every word. "You're falling in love with him."

Beth laughed out loud. "Love has nothing to do with it! I just agreed to drive a safe car so that I won't be stranded all the time." With a glance at Miss Eugenia, Beth picked up her purse. "Since we don't have any customers, I think I'll leave a couple of minutes early," she told the other woman. "I'll see you on Friday."

Derrick was quiet on the way outside, and Beth knew he was worried, but couldn't think of a way to comfort him. "I'll call you tomorrow," she promised when they reached his car.

"You'd better," he said grimly.

Beth waited until he was out of sight, then walked down to the Lexus. She still felt awkward, but the comfortable interior and efficient air conditioner were luxuries she could get used to. On her way out of town, she saw Grady's Garage and pulled up to the curb. A man walked over and Beth lowered the automatic passenger window.

"Can I help you?" the man inquired.

"Are you Grady?" she asked, and he nodded.

Beth cleared her throat. "I'm Beth Middleton, and my Volkswagen was towed in here a few days ago."

The man wiped his greasy hands on a red cloth. "Worst vehicle I've ever seen. Every part needed to be replaced. I told Jack he'd be better off buying a new one than trying to repair that piece of junk." The man looked at the Lexus again, and Beth felt heat rise in her face. "Looks like he took my advice."

"I don't think there was anything valuable left in it, but if it's still here, I wanted to check . . ."

The man stepped aside. "It's around back. I'll show you."

She followed the mechanic into a field behind the garage. The Volkswagen was parked in a far corner under a shade tree, surrounded by wildflowers. "Have you ever heard of a Volkswagen museum in Arkansas?" she asked softly, and he shook his head. "I'll just be a minute," she told him, then waited until he left before approaching the old car.

There was nothing of any consequence in the trunk or the glove compartment, but she emptied them both. Then she slid in behind the wheel. Ignoring the stifling heat, she looked through the dusty windshield and thought of Chloe holding baby rabbits. There was still half of Ferris Burke's tape left to listen to, and for the first time in two years, the promise of the future was stronger than the pull of the past. With only one glance back, Beth left the old Volkswagen in its final resting place. Then she climbed into the new Lexus and drove home.

She was able to catch fifteen minutes of *The Brave and Relentless* before Roy came to get her for the drive into Albany. He seemed distracted on the way, and Beth asked if he'd heard from the receptionist job. He looked up and nodded. "Gave it to a pretty girl fresh out of college, so it's back to the want ads for me."

Chloe reported that she'd had a wonderful day with the baby animals. "I got to hold everything!" she exclaimed as Beth looked through her backpack. "Except the frog because I didn't want to."

As they approached the Gamble's security gate, they saw Kristen Northcutt standing on the sidewalk in front of her house. Roy pulled the SUV up to the curb and watched while Chloe and Beth walked over to talk to the little girl. Kristen reported that her mother was home from the hospital, and the baby was cute.

"Can I see her?" Chloe wanted to know.

"The baby is asleep today, but I'll tell my mom to keep her awake tomorrow," Kristen promised.

"We'll plan to come right after school, but if that's not convenient, tell your mom to call me," Beth said, pulling Chloe back across the street.

Jack made it home in time for dinner, and during dessert asked if she'd finished listening to the Ferris Burke tape. "I'm sorry." Beth put her fork down beside the partially eaten strawberry pie. "It's been a busy day . . ."

He waved a hand. "Just let me know when you're done and we'll talk."

Chloe went upstairs with her father after dinner, so Beth settled down on the couch in her room and started listening to Ferris's story again.

* * *

"Things started to go pretty well for me with my singing career. Claudia helped me get a contract with a bigger studio and even talked me into doing a music video. I was making good money and decided to buy a house. Claudia and the studio people wanted me to move to Nashville, but Jasmine was attached to the Harpers, so I bought some land not far from where they lived and built a house there.

"I offered to buy Audrey a condo if she wouldn't move with us, but she just laughed. I fixed up a room for Amber so that she could come and stay with Jasmine whenever I had to be gone. Audrey was drunk or high all the time, and we got into fights over it. The neighbors complained about the fighting and even called the police a couple of times, but I'd like to see what they would have done in my situation. Audrey just made me crazy.

"The more successful I got, the more I had to be away, and finally I bought another house in Nashville. Sometimes Amber and Jasmine would go there with me, but I didn't want Jasmine to miss school, so I mostly traveled alone. It was lonely, and I wanted a normal life for me and my baby. Finally I talked to the Harpers about getting a divorce from Audrey. They knew that it would be the best for Jasmine and even said they would testify in court against their daughter if it came to that. I got a lawyer, but Audrey put up a huge fuss, so I dropped it.

"I didn't think that things could get worse with Audrey, but just before Christmas that year, the Harpers were killed in a car accident, and she snapped. I knew it was only a matter of time before Audrey killed herself or me, so I found her an expensive drug-rehabilitation program. When she came out, she seemed better.

"The sisters had inherited the Harper's house and a little money, so when Audrey was released from the drug hospital she moved in with Amber. A few months later Audrey had a new boyfriend living there too. Then she got her own lawyer and sent *me* the papers for a divorce, and I really got my hopes up.

"Audrey got Jasmine two weekends a month, and I didn't like the idea of the boyfriend being around my daughter. I tried to get Audrey to send the guy away for at least those few days, but Audrey wouldn't listen. I talked to my lawyer about canceling Audrey's visitation rights since she had a man living in her house, but he said that would take time. Amber promised to keep an eye on Jasmine, but it wasn't enough."

Beth felt her body tense, waiting. "It was just a few days after Jasmine's birthday when she called me, crying so hard I could barely understand her." There was another brief pause and then Ferris continued. "I'm not the best person, but I've tried to be a good father and that little girl is everything in the world to me. Hearing her so upset on the phone almost ripped my heart out. I kept asking her what was wrong, and finally she said that Sean had kissed her on the mouth and touched her . . ." Ferris's voice trembled and he took a few deep breaths before continuing.

"She said her mother was asleep, which I figured meant drunk. Jasmine was locked in a bedroom with Amber, but Sean kept pushing on the door. The Harper's house was only two miles away, and I drove there fast. I didn't really plan to kill him, but I felt like what he'd done to an innocent child was enough to deserve dying.

"I found Audrey in the living room, passed out on the couch. I yelled at her, trying to get her to tell me what had been going on, but she wouldn't answer. Then the stupid boyfriend came in and threatened me with a tennis racket. I blocked the first few blows and finally managed to take it away from him. He ran up the stairs, and all I could think was that he was trying to get to Jasmine. I caught him in the hall and started hitting him. He fought back for a while.

"When I realized he wasn't moving, I told Amber to call the police. I knew she would be nervous talking to them, but I didn't realize how scared she really was until I found out she'd climbed out of the window in Jasmine's room and disappeared."

* * *

Beth listened to a few seconds of static, then turned off the tape player. Jack had said that things were not always as they seemed, and this was particularly true in Ferris Burke's case. If he could find a way to get Ferris's story across to the jury, his client would be acquitted. For the first time since she'd heard of the country singer's arrest, Beth didn't find this prospect disturbing.

She met Jack at ten, and they ran first, then sat on the patio and discussed Ferris Burke. "So, are you going to try for justifiable homicide or temporary insanity, something like that?" Beth asked, drawing on all her *Matlock* and *Perry Mason* knowledge.

He shook his head. "Temporary insanity is hard to prove and difficult to live with. I'm going for a straight not-guilty verdict, but I'll settle for involuntary manslaughter if we have to."

"And the demands of justice will be met," Beth said softly.

"Justice is not my responsibility," he answered. "My duty is to represent Ferris, to do everything in my power, within the bounds of the law, to get him acquitted. The district attorney's job is to collect evidence and prove that Ferris is guilty. The judge controls the proceedings, making sure that both attorneys stay within the law. Then the jury tries to find the truth. If we *all* do our part, justice should be served."

Beth watched a breeze move the curls at the base of his neck, then spoke. "Any luck finding your witness?"

"No." He shook his head.

"Why don't you just let Jasmine testify? She should know as much as Amber Harper."

"Jasmine's testimony would be valuable, but the experience might be psychologically damaging, and she's been through so much already. Ferris and I agree that we can't risk it."

"What's the next step?"

"Well, tomorrow Judge Tate will deny my motion for a change of venue . . ."

"After fair and judicious deliberation," Beth provided with a smile.

Jack grinned back. "Then he'll assemble a juror pool, and we'll begin the selection process."

"You'll want men," Beth predicted. "They will be able to identify with Ferris's fury."

Jack nodded. "But they might feel sympathy for Audrey. Mothers are probably my very best candidates. They will feel the same fury, and they won't give Audrey any slack."

"What kind of jurors will the district attorney be looking for?"

"Single, unemployed pedophiles who are attracted to drug addicts?" he suggested.

Beth considered this. "There can't be many in the Albany area."

"Then he'll go with liberal thinkers. People who abhor the death penalty and believe that Sean should have been rehabilitated instead of beaten with a tennis racket. Or candidates who don't have children and can't relate to Ferris's protective reaction."

Beth smiled. "Well, at least he's got his job cut out for him too."

Jack agreed with a nod. "And I'll find soft spots in some of the people he picks." He stood and stretched, pulling his T-shirt tightly across a well-defined chest. "I'd better finish up my desperate plea for a change of venue."

"Do you want me to type it?"

"Thanks, but I'll type it myself. Roberta will clean it up and print it in the morning. Judge Tate won't even glance at it, so I guess I could just write nonsense."

"But you won't." Beth was sure that he'd stay up well into the night working on the hopeless motion, and she was curiously touched by the thought. "Well, I still have plenty of free time, so if you think of anything else I can do . . ."

He held the kitchen door open and they walked inside. "Once the jury pool is assembled, I'll need help on the evaluations we will do of each potential juror. And then maybe you could type a motion asking Judge Tate to remove himself from the case because of conflict of interest."

"What's the conflict?" Beth asked.

"He hates me," Jack replied with a smile.

They paused awkwardly by the entrance to the hallway that led to Beth's suite. "Well, good night," she said finally.

"Good night." His voice was soft, but she couldn't see his eyes because of the dim light.

"And good luck on your motion."

"Thanks." He turned toward the front of the house. "I'll need it."

CHAPTER 8

On Thursday morning Beth came in from taking Chloe to school and called Derrick. He ended the call quickly, and Beth knew that his feelings were hurt, but she couldn't explain to him what she didn't understand herself. She scribbled out a hasty report for the family court judge, then drove to the post office in Haggerty and mailed it.

That afternoon they finished Chloe's homework, then walked over to the Northcutts. Kristen met them at the door, and Bud came flying as soon as he heard Beth's voice. She scooped him up, and they followed Kristen inside. Ellen Northcutt was relaxing in a large recliner in the den, her new daughter nestled in her arms. Chloe approached reverently, and Ellen pulled back the receiving blanket to reveal the tiny, pink face.

"Oh, she's cuter than a doll!" Chloe proclaimed, and Kristen nodded with pride. "Can she talk yet?"

Kristen shook her head. "Bud can't even talk yet."

"He can talk," Ellen corrected. "We just can't understand him."

At the mention of his name, the toddler beamed up at Beth. She was content to admire the tiny girl from a distance and hold Bud instead. Ellen thanked her again for her help on the day of Megan's birth, and Beth offered additional assistance anytime.

"Rick's been off this whole week, and my mother is coming tomorrow. Besides, the neighborhood ladies have brought in so much food we could open a restaurant! But I found your number if something comes up."

Chloe went upstairs with Kristen to see her room, and the baby started to fuss so Ellen began nursing. When Chloe came back she watched this process for a few minutes, then turned wide eyes to Beth. "Did I do that when I was a baby?" she whispered.

Beth smiled. "You'll have to ask your father."

Since they didn't want to tire the new mother or her baby, they left after a short visit. Roy was sitting at the kitchen table talking to Hipolita when they got home. Whatever the discussion was, it changed immediately to his futile job search once Beth and Chloe joined them. "Don't know why they wouldn't want me to do facials. I can slop goo on ladies' faces as well as a woman can," he lamented, then smiled at Chloe. "Did you meet any bunnies today?"

"Not today, but yesterday . . ." she began a review of the previous day's activities, and Beth listened with amusement. Jack didn't make it home in time for dinner, and afterward Chloe went to Beth's room and looked at a picture book while Beth watched the last half of her soap opera.

When the episode was over, Beth put in *Sleeping Beauty*. It started to rain, and she snuggled next to the child, grateful for the company. Jack knocked on the door just before eight. He was wearing a damp raincoat and looked tired. "How did your motion go?" Beth asked as they joined him by the door.

"About like we expected. Judge Tate did read the entire thing, though, and I could tell he was surprised that I had put so much effort into it."

"Well, maybe he'll start to like you better now," Beth suggested.

"There's not much chance of that, but at least I know he's paying attention. See you at ten." He took Chloe's hand and led her down the hallway.

It was still raining at ten o'clock, a steady downpour with no thunder or lightning. Beth pulled on a thin, water-resistant jacket and went out to the garage. Jack was already there, soaked to the skin. "I could skip tonight," Beth offered, although her muscles cramped in protest.

"Well, I couldn't." He turned into the rain and jogged down the driveway. Beth followed him, and they kept an easy pace the whole time. When they made it back to the house, they paused in the kitchen and Beth peeled off her wet coat. "I understand that I owe you for the opportunity I had to discuss breast-feeding with Chloe this evening," Jack said as they dripped on Hipolita's spotless floor.

"One of the advantages of parenthood." She smiled over her shoulder and headed toward her room.

On Friday morning Hipolita gave Beth her weekly check, and she made a deposit at the bank on the way into the library. This caused her to be a few minutes late, and she was pleased to see Miss Polly Kirby sitting at the front desk instead of Miss Eugenia. Miss Polly didn't mention her coworker's tardy arrival, but she announced that the Northcutt's baby shower had been planned for the next Wednesday and asked Beth to bring cocktail peanuts.

"We weren't sure that you had cooking privileges in Mr. Gamble's house, so we decided to give you something you could just buy already made."

Beth thought about her cookie-baking disaster and nodded. "I appreciate that."

"It will be at two o'clock at my house. I live down from Eugenia, on the other side of Kate Iverson," she provided. Then Miss Polly proceeded to tell her all the local gossip. She talked for a solid two hours, and her stories were all full of amazingly specific details. It was like a real live soap opera, and Beth enjoyed herself until she started to wonder what stories might be circulating around Haggerty about her and Jack.

They closed the library at 11:30 because Miss Polly had a dentist appointment. Beth picked up a Kids Meal at Burger King on her way home and ate it on the patio, wishing Chloe could share it with her. She made a point of watching that day's episode of *The Brave and Relentless* because Friday's programs were usually good, encouraging everyone to come back for more on Monday.

The first of the program was dedicated to Parker snooping through Tori's desk. He found an envelope with the doctor's return address, but no test results. So he stormed out, headed for the clinic and a confrontation. Beth had to leave before anything was resolved, so she set the VCR to record.

When they got back from Albany, Chloe ate some of Hipolita's homemade chocolate chip cookies while Beth watched her soap. Roy came and stood at the bedroom door as Parker reached the clinic and demanded to see a copy of the test results. "You can't keep the results from me! After all, I am the father!" the man on the screen claimed foolishly.

"Leave us alone," the doctor told the nurse, and after the door closed behind her, he reached into a file folder on his desk and removed one sheet of paper. Then the theme music came on, and the program ended for the day.

"Why is that man so mad all the time?" Chloe wanted to know. "And why didn't we get to see Elena play with her new puppy?"

Beth shrugged, then glanced up at Roy. "Did you need something?"

"Hipolita says you have a phone call," he reported.

The phone in her room had been silent, so Beth guessed the call must be from someone she had not given her number to. She left Roy eating the rest of their cookies and went into the kitchen. Hipolita was preparing dinner and motioned toward a cordless receiver with her head.

"Hello?" Beth said cautiously.

"Beth? This is Kate Iverson. Getting in touch with you is a major production! Mr. Gamble's number is so unlisted I finally had to get Mark to look him up on the FBI's mainframe," the other woman exclaimed.

Beth relaxed. "You've seen the fence. Everything is a production with Mr. Gamble."

"I just wanted to ask if you can go visiting teaching with me tomorrow. I think we will be officially assigned as companions on Sunday, but I don't want it to put it off until the last week." Beth agreed, and Kate said she'd pick her up at ten o'clock the next morning.

Back in her room, Beth found that Chloe had rewound the soap opera video to show Roy the black Labrador puppy being trained as Elena's seeing-eye dog. "Her vision seems pretty good to me." Roy squinted at the screen.

"The doctor told her there is a chance that she's going blind, so she wants to be prepared," Beth informed him as she opened Chloe's backpack and started looking through her papers. "Color all the balloons red and the kites blue," she told the child, extending a homework sheet. "And Hipolita said dinner will be ready in an hour."

Roy stood up and took a step toward the door. "Forgot to tell you that the boss might be a little late tonight. Told him I'd ask you to keep an eye on Chloe until he gets here."

Beth was pleased. Since it was Friday, Chloe's bedtime would be extended, which gave them hours together. During dinner they discussed how they should spend their evening. Roy suggested they try to cook something, drawing a glare from Beth and a giggle from Chloe. Hipolita made no comment. They had just decided to eat popcorn and watch *The Wizard of Oz* when Jack walked in. Hipolita hastily fixed him a plate, and he joined them at the table. Beth was torn between the pleasure of seeing him and the disappointment that he had just ruined her popcorn-and-video night with Chloe.

After dinner Chloe went upstairs with her father. Alone in her room, Beth called Derrick and then her mother. After balancing her checkbook, she put *The Wizard of Oz* in the VCR and thought that the movie had magically drawn Chloe down to her room when the little girl came running through the door without stopping to knock. She had taken a bath and was wearing her leopard pajamas. Beth invited her to watch the video, but she shook her head.

"It's almost nine." She pointed at the clock. "I just wanted to say good night." Beth walked with Chloe up to the yellow bedroom and after tucking her in, felt much better. The video was still playing when Beth got back to her room, so she curled up on the couch to watch.

She woke a few minutes before ten and quickly pulled on her sweat clothes. It had never occurred to her to check on Chloe before, but for some reason, that night she did. Walking quietly up the stairs, she paused by Chloe's door and pushed it open. The bed was empty, and it took a few seconds for that fact to sink into Beth's sleep-dulled brain. She remembered bringing the child upstairs at nine o'clock. She could even see the impression her small body had made in the soft mattress. But Chloe was gone.

Beth thought of Jack's obsessive concern for his daughter's safety, and her imagination ran wild. He was a wealthy man, one with powerful enemies, and he would pay any price for Chloe. Staggering with fear, Beth rushed down the forbidden hall toward his quarters. She had to tell him that his daughter, who strictly observed bedtime every night, was not in her bed. Gone, missing. Chloe!

She banged on the first door she came to, then turned the door-knob and went inside. It was neither a bedroom nor an office as she had expected, but a family room of some kind. There was a big-screen

TV, a couple of comfortable-looking couches, and a small table scattered with crayons. In a reclining chair facing the television sat Jack. Chloe was asleep in his arms.

Beth's immediate reaction was profound relief. Everything was okay. Chloe was safe. Then she glanced around again and realized that this room was different from the others in the house. It was a little cluttered, homey, lived-in. Hipolita obviously did not have jurisdiction here. She looked back to find her employer watching her. "Chloe doesn't go to bed at eight o'clock every night." It was as close as she could come to a sensible comment.

"She goes to bed. She just gets up again."

"It was a trick," Beth challenged, feeling very stupid.

"I'm not a neglectful parent," he said, his jaw tense. "I needed your presence here to avoid further problems with family court. But once you agreed to come, I had to think of a way to protect our privacy." He paused for a few seconds. "I didn't know you or if you'd be fair."

She walked into the room and sat down on the couch across from him. "You let me believe that you didn't spend much time with Chloe." He nodded. "But really she was here with you every night after I thought she was asleep."

"I would give up air before my time with Chloe." He pressed his daughter close.

She tried to keep the hurt from showing on her face. "What if you had convinced me that you were negligent? The judge could have insisted on the psychological testing, even awarded custody to your parents! You could have lost Chloe."

"There was never any danger of that. After I'm through with Ferris, I'll concentrate on my parents and their 'concerns.' A good report from you will help me," he added with a smile, "but before things ever reached the point of a custody change, I would take Chloe and leave the country."

Beth was surprised and impressed. He would give up his career, his home, everything to protect Chloe. And he really didn't leave anything to chance where his daughter was concerned. He stood then, adjusting Chloe in his arms.

"I lost track of the time." He glanced toward the clock, then walked into the hall and Beth followed him to Chloe's room. She pulled back the covers on the bed, and when he had the child settled, Beth tucked the comforter under Chloe's arms, just the way she liked it. Beth ran a hand over Chloe's hair to reassure herself, and when she glanced up, Jack was watching her.

"I'll meet you outside in five minutes," he said.

Beth walked downstairs and waited. He joined her in less than the promised five minutes, and they ran fast. Afterward she leaned down to catch her breath, and he dropped heavily onto a patio chair. "So, do you forgive me?" he asked. "About the bedtime thing?"

It was hard to hold good parenting against him, so she nodded.

"I didn't mean to hurt your feelings."

"I know."

"I thought I'd take Chloe with me into the office downtown in the morning. You could come along, and I'll show you around the courthouse."

Beth was grateful for the darkness to hide the heat that rose in her cheeks. "Thanks, but I've already got an appointment to go visiting teaching in the morning."

"Maybe another time, then." He opened the door and they went their separate ways.

On Saturday morning Kate Iverson was parked in a gray minivan outside the security gates when Beth walked down at 9:50. Kate greeted her warmly, then turned onto Highway 11 heading west. "So, what brought you to Haggerty anyway?"

"I was supposed to get married a few years ago, but it didn't work out. I moved to Albany to start a life of my own and was thinking about going on a mission, but then a friend convinced me to be Chloe's nanny for three months."

"I've only seen Mr. Gamble a couple of times. He's handsome and mysterious," she added with a smile. "Do you like living there?"

Beth nodded. "I love Chloe," she said the words casually, but their absolute accurateness stunned her for a second. "At the Genealogical Society Meeting, Miss Eugenia said you were from the north," Beth said in an effort to deflect attention from herself.

"I'm from the Salt Lake area. Mark and I moved here a little over a year ago. Oh, and we're going to have the same visiting teachers, Sister Baylor and Sister Armistead. You'll love them," Kate guaranteed.

"I wouldn't feel comfortable having visiting teachers come to the Gambles' house," Beth responded.

Kate considered this for a few seconds. "Well, when Sister Baylor and Sister Armistead make their appointment with me, I'll tell them that they can get both of us at my house." She paused, then glanced over at Beth. "Do you can?"

Beth stared back. "Can what?"

"Vegetables and fruits. I know some people can meat, but I just like the things that look pretty in jars. Peaches, tomatoes, green beans, squash . . ."

Beth felt she had to warn her. "I'm not sure I've ever heated up a home-canned vegetable, and I certainly don't know how to preserve them. In fact, Chloe and I tried to make oatmeal cookies a week ago and almost burned down the house."

"Well, when you come over to meet the visiting teachers, I'll teach you to can something. Miss Eugenia started me on tomatoes last year, and I'm almost addicted to it. Mark tried to fuss about the jars stacked everywhere, but it's food storage, so what can he say?"

Beth wasn't particularly interested in learning to can, but spending time with Kate sounded nice, so she nodded. Beth was relieved that Kate did most of the talking at all their stops, and on the drive back to Haggerty, she covertly checked her watch. It was getting close to noon, and she wondered if the Gambles were back from Albany. She couldn't stop thinking about Jack, a dedicated single father, spending quality time with his daughter each night.

"I'm sorry we ran a little late." Kate noticed Beth's interest in the time and apologized. "I talked too much."

"You did a great job with the lesson, and I enjoyed our visits," Beth assured her.

Kate smiled. "I like visiting teaching, but I hate leaving Emily." Kate glanced over at Beth. "Even with Mark. I know that probably sounds silly to you, but we almost lost Emily when she was a baby, and I'm still nervous about being away from her."

"My youngest sister, Melissa, was sick when she was born, and they weren't sure she would live," Beth remembered. "Melissa's eighteen now and very healthy, but Mama *still* worries about her."

Kate smiled as she turned into The Crossroads. "I'll see you tomorrow, and we'll plan our canning adventure."

Beth entered the security code and walked up the driveway. The kitchen was deserted, so she went to her room and called Derrick. He seemed to be a little distant, and Beth tried everything to get him into a better mood. Finally she asked him how he thought Parker was going to react to the blood test results, and he sighed.

"If Tori wasn't such a popular character, I'd say he'd kill her. As it is, there will be an awful fight, Parker may leave her for a while, but in the end they'll kiss and make up."

"Will all this happen on Monday's episode?" Beth was already calculating how much of the program she could see without making Roy late to pick up Chloe.

"Unless Marissa thinks of another inspirational reason to help Cedric stay sober."

Beth laughed, glad that Derrick had found his sense of humor, as Hipolita opened her door. "I've got company," she told Derrick. "I'll talk to you tomorrow."

Hipolita waited until Beth ended her call, then spoke. "Mrs. Grainger, she ring the gate and say to come see her."

Mildly alarmed, Beth hurried outside and over to Annabelle's house. Annabelle opened the door before Beth had reached the porch. "The bank sent out invitations to a retirement party they are holding in my honor next Saturday night. It's at The Club, heavy hors d'oeuvres, Sunday dress," she said in a rush. "I told the bank president that I didn't want a party," Annabelle whimpered as they passed through the spacious entryway and into the living room.

"But I met Nina Hocutt at the gas station, and she showed me her invitation. Now the whole town knows that I'm retiring. And what am I going to say when they ask why I didn't tell anyone? Eugenia's called four times, and I keep letting the answering machine pick up, but it's only a matter of time before she comes over, and I'll have to tell her something!"

The phone started to ring, emphasizing Annabelle's words. Beth took a deep breath. "You can say that the bank had no choice but to honor the mandatory retirement age," Beth said, thinking hard. "And that replacing you has been so difficult that they had to bring in someone from Atlanta. You told the bank that you wanted to slip away without unnecessary fanfare," Beth continued, and the older woman nodded. "But after all your years of faithful service, they just couldn't let you go quietly. You can admit to a little embarrassment over the fuss they are making and express some concern about the new girl's ability to handle your job."

"It might work," Annabelle whispered.

"And then encourage all your friends and family to come to the party so that it will cost the bank a fortune," Beth added with a smile as the phone started ringing again. "I need to check on Chloe . . ."

"I'll tell you how it goes," Annabelle nodded, walking bravely toward the phone. "And Beth?" The younger woman paused. "Thank you."

Beth smiled. "What are friends for?"

Annabelle smiled back, then picked up the receiver. Beth let herself out the front door and walked across the street. Chloe and her father were home and splashing in the swimming pool when Beth arrived. They invited her to join them, but she didn't want to put on a bathing suit. So she sat on the edge and tucked her skirt around her legs, then dangled her feet in the water. Jack asked if everything was okay with the neighbor, and Beth explained the situation. "I got an invitation at the office today," he said to Beth's amazement.

"You got an invitation to Annabelle's retirement party?"

"The Georgia Republican Party has accounts with the Albany Bank of Commerce, and Oscar Fuller was invited as a valued customer. He wrangled an invitation for me so that I could meet future voters." He rarely mentioned his interest in the state senate, and Beth hoped he'd say more on this subject, but he didn't. He did say that Chloe could go to church again the next day, as long as she made it to Aristotle's for lunch.

On Sunday morning Roy came in as Beth and Chloe were finishing breakfast and said he was planning to take them to church. "That's not necessary," Beth told him. "I'll drive the Lexus." Roy filled a bowl with Captain Crunch.

"You saying you don't want to ride with me, Beth?" he asked as he sat down.

"I don't mind riding with you, but I won't have to inconvenience you anymore," she replied with a trace of impatience.

"Sure does hurt my feelings that I got up early and came over here, thinking I'd get to take you two lovely ladies into Albany, then find out you don't want my company," he pressed.

Chloe looked up from her cereal, a little worry line forming between her bright, brown eyes. Beth sighed with exasperation. "You must have something better to do with your Sunday mornings than sit in my church parking lot! And Mr. Gamble trusts me with Chloe."

"Course he trusts you. It's other people he worries about." Beth was surprised by Roy's tenacity. "But if you really want to drive your own car, I can follow behind to make sure you get there okay."

Beth's eyes narrowed. "Did Mr. Gamble say that Chloe can't go to church with me unless you drive us?"

"It's not a matter of trust," he evaded the question, "it's just that he's . . ."

"Paranoid, obsessed!" Beth pushed back from the table, humiliated.

"Don't be too hard on him," Roy defended his employer. "It's a crazy world we live in. Maybe he worries about Chloe too much, but it's because he loves her."

Beth initially refused to be appeased, but as she helped Chloe to put on her dress, she remembered how frightened she'd been the night she thought Chloe was missing. Jack may have been overprotective as well, but she finally decided to forgive him. Then she offered to try to braid a ponytail herself so Chloe wouldn't have to wake her father up. The child smiled and said he wouldn't mind. Ten minutes later she returned with braided pigtails and Jack close behind her, looking adorably rumpled.

"Chloe says you're riding with Roy." He ran his fingers through his sleep-tousled hair.

"No point in taking two cars," Beth answered.

He winced. "I'm sorry, but I told you I can't take chances with Chloe."

"No," she agreed with resignation.

Emily was glad to see them as they took their seats behind the Iversons in the chapel. The baby held out her chubby little arms, and

Beth looked to Mark Iverson for permission. He nodded, so Beth pulled Emily into her lap. When Kate returned from the organ after the sacrament hymn, the baby gave her mother a hug and spent the rest of the meeting going back and forth over the bench.

Afterward, Kate led the way to Primary. Chloe sat down with her CTR class while Beth and Emily found a spot on the back row. Chloe tried to sing along with the other children and was so earnest in her efforts that Beth had to press her mouth against the back of Emily's head to keep from weeping. Maybe Jack was right. Maybe her missionary efforts could be better spent on Chloe than on anonymous strangers in a distant land.

When the meetings ended, Kate invited Beth to come over on Thursday morning to meet the visiting teachers. "Sister Baylor and Sister Armistead will be at my house at nine o'clock." Kate lowered her voice. "And after they leave we'll have our first canning session."

Beth agreed, and Kate continued, "Our home teacher is a precious little man named Elmer Stoops. He has a crush on Miss Eugenia, and vice versa." Beth raised her eyebrows at this declaration. "He had hip replacement surgery a few weeks ago, but he won't miss a home teaching visit, so this month we had to go to his house!" Kate said with a smile.

Beth collected Chloe and they walked out to Roy's parking spot under a shade tree. Chloe gave them a detailed description of her Primary lesson, her teacher, and her classmates as they drove. Then she showed Beth a slip of paper and a cassette tape the Primary president had given her. "What is this?" Beth asked, reading the first article of faith.

"There's a program next week, and they want me to say this," Chloe reported proudly. "And the songs are on this tape, and she said I could practice with my parents at home. I'm going to put it in my pink tape player and sing the songs every day."

Beth considered this as she watched Chloe clutch the tape to her chest. Jack had been friendly lately and didn't seem to mind that his daughter was going to church, but he might draw the line at actual participation. Beth closed her eyes, considering possible ways to approach him, and actually dozed off but startled awake when the car stopped. She glanced up, expecting to see the Gamble house, but instead saw a small restaurant on a crowded street.

"There's nowhere to park," Roy pointed out as they idled in the loading zone. Beth looked at him blankly. "This is Aristotle's, the restaurant where Chloe and the boss eat on Sunday. I'll drive around the block and see if I can find a parking place."

"You want me to take her inside?" The meaning of his words finally sank in to Beth's sleep-dulled brain.

"I'll be there in just a minute," he promised.

Beth looked up and down the street—not a parking space in sight. "Okay, but hurry," she answered irritably. Chloe yawned and then climbed out of the SUV after Beth. They walked into the small lobby and stood against the wall to wait for Roy. The man at the reservation desk recognized Chloe and welcomed her. Then he turned to Beth. "This way please." He took Chloe by the hand and started down a narrow hallway. Left with no choice, Beth followed him through a door. Jack and Roy were both seated at a large table.

"How did you get in here?" Beth demanded when she saw Roy.

"I found a parking place in the alley and came in the back way," he replied. Chloe hugged her father, then sat beside him.

"Well, Chloe is safely inside." Beth took a step toward the door.

"Why don't you stay?" Jack walked around Chloe and pulled out a chair for her.

"Oh, no, I couldn't." Beth shook her head.

"Roy always eats with us." He pointed at the driver.

"If Beth really wants to go home, I'll take her," Roy offered. "I'm not that hungry." Chloe giggled at this ridiculous remark.

"You're not really going to make Roy miss a meal, are you?" Jack came nearer, blocking Roy and Chloe from view. "Or miss a chance to spend time with Chloe?" This was the second time he had used Chloe to manipulate her, and she knew he had guessed the strength of her feelings for the child. However, the position he had placed her in was very awkward.

"I can't eat here," Beth whispered.

"Why not?" He moved a little closer so that no one else could hear.

"I can't buy on Sunday."

He smiled. "I'll pay for your lunch."

Beth shook her head. "It's still breaking the Sabbath." His closeness was unnerving, so Beth took a step back.

"I don't see how it could be breaking the Sabbath to watch other people eat." He turned and waved at the big table. "So just sit with us."

"Sit by me, Beth," Chloe offered, touching an extra chair. Jack moved aside, clearing the way for Beth. Chloe was smiling, and Roy was staring at Beth and Jack in open fascination. Beth took the chair by Chloe, and Jack slid into his seat as a large man with curly black hair rushed in. In heavily accented English, he demanded food preferences. Roy responded with a long, detailed order. The man took careful notes, then turned to Chloe.

"My guess is that Miss Chloe will have her regular," he boomed. Chloe laughed and said she wanted a hamburger and french fries. "Then you have come to the wrong place today!"

"The regular!" Chloe amended her order.

"Aristotle," Jack spoke from across the table. "I want to introduce you to our guest, Miss Beth Middleton."

Beth nodded to the restaurant owner as he rounded the table and took her hand in both of his. "Miss Middleton, it is truly an honor to have you here today. But I ask, what is a beautiful woman like yourself doing with these two?" He waved his hand toward Roy and Jack.

"Aristotle," Jack began again when the laughter died down. "We do have a small problem." The man tugged on his apron, looking pained. "Miss Middleton believes it's morally wrong to buy on Sundays, so she plans to sit here and watch the rest of us eat." Beth glared at him, but he continued to look steadfastly at the restaurant owner.

"No!" the man cried as if he had been shot. "It cannot happen. No one leaves Aristotle's hungry!" He looked Beth over again. "And she is so thin!"

"Isn't it your policy that all first-time customers who are blonde and very thin get to eat free?" Jack asked, ignoring Beth's furious gaze. Mr. Aristotle pulled up a chair and sat down at the table. Jack continued, "Then Miss Middleton can eat without compromising her standards."

"I'm not even hungry," Beth said between clenched teeth.

"But of course Miss Beth Middleton will not pay for her first meal at Aristotle's! What could you be thinking?" The man sent Jack an aggrieved look.

"Think I paid for my first meal here," Roy said with his mouth full of complimentary breadsticks.

"You aren't a blonde woman," Chloe pointed out logically.

"I think *I* paid for your first meal here," Jack disputed, and Mr. Aristotle stood.

"Sorry I leave you with these boorish fools," he apologized to Beth, then sailed out of the room.

After Mr. Aristotle was gone, Jack avoided the consequences of his actions by asking his daughter about church. "There's a program next week, and I have a part." She held out the crumpled paper with the first article of faith printed neatly. "I have a tape with all the songs so I can practice at home with my parents," she repeated the Primary president's instructions.

"If it's okay with you," Beth felt that she was required to insert. Jack gave her a little smile, then returned his attention to his daughter.

"And in my class today we talked about prayer. We are supposed to pray lots of times, Daddy." Her tone was reproachful, as if he had been keeping a big secret. "There's a prayer when you get up in the morning and at night before you go to bed. And you have to pray before you eat anything." She looked pointedly at Roy's latest bread stick, and he stopped chewing. "Can I say a prayer on our food now?" she asked.

Jack nodded and all heads bowed, waiting for Chloe to begin. After a few seconds of silence, Beth peeked sideways to see Chloe's face twisted with frustration. Feeling Beth's gaze, she looked over. "I forgot how to do it," she whispered.

Beth leaned forward. "I'll help you." She whispered a simple prayer and Chloe repeated each word carefully. Jack seemed a little shaken as Mr. Aristotle came in carrying a huge bowl of salad, which looked wonderful except for the anchovies draped across the top. Jack served Chloe and then offered to put some on Beth's plate as well. "You have to eat salad with anchovies to have an authentic Greek experience," he said.

"I'll settle for a pseudo-Greek experience," Beth responded, and he gave her a fishless portion. When their host left to get the next course, Beth directed her attention to Roy. "Have you been to any job interviews lately, Roy?"

He glanced up reluctantly. "Boss is keeping me pretty busy right now."

"I think you're more than a part-time driver. I think you're friends," Beth accused, watching the two men. Roy looked uncomfortable, but Jack gave her a charming smile. "Very good friends," Beth continued.

"Roy is even more than just a very good friend," Jack admitted shamelessly. "He's my head of security, my private investigator, my right hand man."

Beth let this information sink in. "But you let me think that he was a down-on-his-luck bum you hired to drive Chloe around."

Roy lowered his fork. "You told her I was a bum?"

Jack ignored this question. "I thought it would be to my advantage for you to consider him a short-term employee like yourself," he told Beth.

"He was spying on me?" Beth cried. She had come to think of Roy as her friend, and this thought hurt more than she could have imagined.

"I didn't know you when you first came on, Beth." Jack's expression turned serious. "And I don't take chances with Chloe."

"Roy was there to protect Chloe from me?"

"Only at first. Now you're one of us." His tone was warm, and Roy looked between them.

"Don't you like Roy, Beth?" Chloe asked.

She let out a deep breath. "I like Roy just fine, as long as I don't have to watch him eat."

Chloe laughed and everyone relaxed as the main course was served. Beth waited until Mr. Aristotle left to ask what it was. "That is blackened flounder, and this," Jack pointed to something that looked like a chicken nugget, "is a fried snapper throat."

"I don't want 'blackened' anything, and I absolutely refuse to eat a throat."

Jack shrugged. "Suit yourself, but you'll hurt Aristotle's feelings."

The restaurant owner had been kind, and she couldn't bear to think of offending him, so Beth picked up her fork and poked the throats, then put a small piece into her mouth. It wasn't bad, so she tried another one.

During the meal Roy asked about Sabbath-day observance. "I don't remember ever reading anything in the Bible about eating in a Greek restaurant on Sunday."

"There's nothing quite that specific," Beth had to smile. "But the Old Testament prophets were very strict about the Sabbath, and modern-day prophets have reiterated this."

"So Mormons have their own prophets and don't use the ones in the Bible?" Roy asked.

"We still use the ones in the Bible too, but we believe that there is a living prophet on the earth today who receives revelation for our time."

"The Dead Sea Scrolls contain the names of prophets not mentioned in the Bible," Jack contributed. "And hieroglyphics in South America indicate that the ancient people there had spiritual leaders that spoke to God. So a living prophet is not such an unusual concept."

Beth was staring at him in astonishment when the door opened, and Malcolm Schneckenberger walked in. "Good afternoon!" the little man greeted. "Oscar said you highly recommend this place, so I thought I'd give it a try. When the owner found out I knew you, he told me you were back here." Malcolm glanced at the empty chairs around the table, but Jack didn't offer him a seat. "What's good today?"

When no one responded, Beth took pity on him. "I had snapper throats. They sound awful, but they were actually pretty good."

"Thanks for the tip." Malcolm took a step in her direction. "And I guess it must be fascinating to live in the house with the world's greatest legal mind." He gave Jack a shy look.

"I don't know enough about the law to tell a brilliant lawyer from a mediocre one," Beth responded, also glancing at Jack.

"I have a book at home that I bought when I first started working for Mr. Fuller," Malcolm told her. "It's called *Law for Dummies*, and it helped me a lot with terminology. I'd be glad to loan it to you."

Beth had no great desire to learn legal lingo, but hated to refuse Malcolm's offer, so she nodded. "I'd appreciate that."

"We're just about finished," Jack said, and Roy pushed his chair back.

"Well, I'll find myself a seat out front. It was nice to see you all," Malcolm told everyone, then left with a wave over his shoulder.

"I thought Mr. Malcolm was going to stay forever and make me miss dessert," Chloe said after the door shut behind Mr. Fuller's assistant.

"If Beth had been any friendlier he probably would have," Roy remarked.

Beth forgave Chloe, but took exception to Roy's comment. "It wouldn't hurt you to be nicer to him. Any of you." She turned her head to include Jack in her censure.

Her employer raised an eyebrow as Mr. Aristotle came in with chocolate almond pie.

"I thought we were leaving," Beth reminded everyone when Mr. Aristotle was gone.

"I said we were just about finished," Jack corrected as he cut Chloe's pie into bite-size pieces. "And we will be after we eat dessert."

The pie was as good as everything else had been, and Beth was uncomfortably full when they left the restaurant. They stood under the awning at the back entrance while the men discussed plans for the afternoon. Finally it was decided that Jack would take the girls home while Roy handled some type of business for his boss. As they drove, Jack made Beth admit that the meal and the atmosphere at Aristotle's had been perfect. "From now on, you will eat there with us every Sunday," he decreed with a satisfied smile.

Beth didn't appreciate his dictatorial attitude or his suggestion that she do something in direct violation of her religious beliefs. "That won't be possible, Mr. Gamble. I won't buy on the Sabbath, and I can't expect Mr. Aristotle to give me a meal every week," she answered evenly.

"I'll buy your meal," he offered.

"No matter who buys my meal, I'll be breaking a commandment." Beth was adamant. He didn't respond, and Beth assumed that she had convinced him. At home he parked in front of the garage, and Chloe ran into the house. Beth followed at a slower pace and as she reached the door, Jack came up close behind her.

"Chloe can be in the Primary program if you'll eat with us at Aristotle's afterward."

Beth turned to face him. "That's blackmail," she said flatly, and he didn't deny it. Looking up into his amused eyes, she wanted to tell him that nothing would make her agree to his outrageous terms. But then she thought about Chloe learning Primary songs and the first article of faith. "It's wrong to put me in this position," she tried once more, but he just waited patiently. "If that's the only way you'll let Chloe be in the program, I accept."

He smiled without remorse. "I'll see you at ten," he said as he held the door open for her.

"I've been meaning to talk to you about that." Beth couldn't keep the satisfaction from her voice. "Running on Sunday is also breaking the Sabbath, so we'll have to skip tonight."

His eyebrows rose. "You've been running on Sunday."

"I've repented." It was a small victory, but it felt glorious.

"Okay, then we'll run at midnight. The Sabbath will be over at twelve o'clock." He was quick, she had to admit that.

"You need to be sharp if you're going to get Ferris out of a life sentence. Staying up late might dull your wits," she added, but he just shrugged.

Beth went to her room and changed clothes, then stretched out on the couch. She dozed off and was awakened a couple of hours later by a knock on her door. Before Beth could reach it, Chloe hurtled through, throwing her arms around Beth's waist.

"I wanted to say thanks for taking me to church and eating with us at Mr. Aristotle's today," she said all in one breath. Beth felt sure that her father had put her up to most of it, but the child was still irresistible.

"It was my pleasure," Beth told her with a smile.

"In fact, Beth had so much fun that she has promised to come next week too," Jack reported from the hallway. Chloe looked up at Beth for confirmation, and she nodded. Chloe smiled, then lifted a pink tape player.

"I've got my singing tape, and Daddy said you would help me learn the songs."

"I'd be happy to sing with you." Beth agreed as they walked over to the couch. Chloe pushed Play, and strains of "I'm Trying to Be Like Jesus" filled the room. Chloe started to sing along, and Jack moved closer to Beth.

"We've got a lead on our missing witness. Roy and I are going to check it out if Chloe can stay with you," he told her.

"Of course," Beth agreed. "But you aren't going back out to that awful place on Highway 76?" she asked, and he nodded. "Without me to distract the bikers?"

"Last time you attracted trouble rather than preventing it," he said with a little smile. "I think if Roy and I go in separately, we should be okay."

Beth couldn't control a shudder, and he leaned so close she could feel his breath on her cheek.

"But try not to worry about me too much," he whispered. "I'll be back as soon as I can." With a wave to Chloe, he left the room, closing the door behind him.

They sang with the tape until they were both hoarse, then watched a video until Chloe fell asleep. Beth was about to carry the child upstairs when the phone in her room rang.

"Beth?" Roy's voice sounded a little muffled. "I need you to meet me at Memorial Hospital in Albany as soon as possible. Leave Chloe with Hipolita." Roy didn't wait for a response, just disconnected. Beth's hand started to tremble as she grabbed her purse. She slipped her feet into her tennis shoes and walked across the hall to knock on Hipolita's door. She repeated exactly what Roy had said and the housekeeper nodded solemnly.

"I sit with Chloe."

Beth rushed to the garage and got into the Lexus, grateful that there was no question about whether or not it would start. Her mind raced with possibilities as she drove to Albany. Roy was the one who called, so Jack was the one in the hospital. Beth gripped the steering wheel and increased her speed, trying not to think.

CHAPTER 9

Beth parked on the street near the Emergency Entrance at Memorial Hospital and hurried inside. Roy was in the waiting room. "Is Mr. Gamble hurt?" she asked.

"Not real bad," Roy answered. "They think his shoulder is dislocated, and there may be a broken rib or two." Beth couldn't imagine what Roy would consider "real bad." "Doctor said he could go home as soon as the police are through questioning him."

"What in the world happened?" she demanded.

"Not exactly sure myself," Roy replied, but whether it was out of ignorance or loyalty, Beth couldn't tell. "Boss was jumped in the parking lot of Heads Up when he was getting back into the Jeep."

"I'll bet it was those bikers!" Beth exclaimed, furious with Jack for going back to the bar.

"Don't think it was. Winston said the bikers are all at some motorcycle convention in Tupelo this weekend. Said the guys who beat him up were strangers," Roy told her.

A set of big double doors swung open and Winston Jones walked through. "Ma'am," he tipped his hat toward Beth. "Mr. Gamble's ready to go."

The policeman left and Beth followed Roy back to a small cubicle, where they found Jack sitting on the edge of an examination table. His pants and shoes were muddy, and his shirt was gone. White medical tape crisscrossed his chest, and he gave them half a smile. "You should see the other guys." He tried to joke, then winced as a cut on his lip started to bleed.

Beth was not amused. "How bad is it?"

"A couple of cracked ribs for sure. I'll have to see a specialist about the shoulder," he replied.

"I'm going back to Heads Up with Winston to see what we can find out," Roy stepped into the conversation. "I called Beth to take you home," he told his boss.

With a nod, Jack slipped off the edge of the table. His lips formed a grim line as he put weight on his feet and grasped Roy's arm. Beth ran ahead and brought the car up to the entrance. Roy helped Jack into the passenger seat, then turned to Beth.

"Take it easy," he advised.

Beth drove slowly and tried to avoid bumps in the road. If the ride was painful for Jack, he didn't complain. Hipolita met them on the patio and helped Jack upstairs. Chloe was still asleep on the couch, so Beth carried her up to bed. Once Chloe was settled, Beth headed toward the stairs. Then she heard loud voices coming from down the hall.

Curious, she turned around and walked to Jack's quarters. The door to the family room was ajar, so Beth went in without knocking. The voices were coming from a room to the right, and Beth approached it quickly. Jack was propped up against several pillows on a large bed, and a well-dressed couple was standing beside him. The man had deep-blue eyes and the woman's jaw was clenched in a way Beth had come to recognize. They were obviously Jack's parents, and their presence in the room explained the explosive atmosphere. Hipolita was standing in a corner, watching the proceedings from a safe distance.

"I'll stay here for a few days . . ." Jack's mother was saying when Beth walked in.

"You certainly will not. I've got Hipolita and Roy," her son countered. When he saw Beth, he waved in her direction. "Heck, I've even got a child psychologist to make sure my injuries don't have an adverse effect on Chloe!"

"I'm not a child psychologist," Beth corrected, but he didn't amend his statement.

"At least let me call a nursing service," his mother begged, and Jack laughed, then grasped his ribs.

"You're killing me, Mother," he said through his teeth. "And it's too late to act like you care about me now."

She sighed. "Our concern for Chloe doesn't mean that we don't still care about you, Jack. However, I must say that a bar fight does not indicate much improvement."

"The judge gave me three months. Please just go away."

The Gambles conferred for a few seconds, then backed out of the room. Feeling sorry for them, Beth followed. When they reached the hallway, Jack's mother forced a smile and extended her hand. "You must be Beth. I'm Joyce Gamble, and this is my husband, Reed."

Beth shook their hands, then led them to the front door. "I'm sure they wouldn't have let him leave the hospital if there were any doubt about his condition," she offered as slim comfort. Reed Gamble patted her shoulder, then accompanied his wife out into the warm evening.

Beth knew she should mind her own business, but was drawn back upstairs. When she walked through the family room, she saw Hipolita standing beside the bed trying to convince Jack to take some tablets that the Emergency Room doctor had sent home with him. "I don't take drugs." He sounded as belligerent as a two-year-old.

"The doctor say yes." Hipolita stood her ground.

Beth watched them argue for a minute, then stepped into the room. "Chicken," she said.

"What?" He turned his menacing eyes to her, but she wasn't afraid.

"I said you're being a lily-livered, scaredy-cat, whiny crybaby." Beth drew on experience gained during childhood fights with her brother. "And the only way you can prove me wrong is to take your medicine like a big boy."

He blinked, and Beth could feel Hipolita holding her breath. Then his gaze became more speculative. "Only if you promise to sit here with me in case I choke on my own vomit."

"Why would you do that?" Beth asked, taking a reluctant step toward him.

"That kind of thing happens to people who take drugs." He took the tablets from Hipolita's hand and threw them into the back of his throat.

Beth laughed and pulled a chair up next to his bed. "How do you know I'd call for help?"

He raised an eyebrow. "You'd do it for Chloe, and besides," he paused, and Beth felt her heart pound, "deep down, I think you like me." With that remark he closed his eyes and collapsed against the pillows.

A little later Roy stuck his head through the door and asked how things were going. "As long as he stays asleep we'll be fine," Beth whispered.

"Call if you need me," he replied with a smile.

About one o'clock in the morning, Jack stirred slightly and then flinched. "Beth," he cried out, and she assured him that she was there. "I need more dangerous, habit-forming drugs."

Beth read the bottle to be sure enough time had elapsed since the last dose, then shook two pills into her hand. She extended the medicine in her palm, but instead of picking up the pills he pulled her hand against his lips. They were chapped but warm, and the heat seemed to transfer up her arm and settle in her cheeks.

He swallowed the pills dry, and he didn't relinquish his hold on her hand. When she started to struggle, he reminded her about his injuries and said that he knew she wouldn't want to be responsible for sending him back to the hospital. So she sat on the edge of her chair, waiting for the pills to take effect. Finally his grasp relaxed and she slipped her hand from his. Then she leaned back and watched the gentle rise and fall of his chest until dawn when Hipolita came to relieve her.

Beth took a quick shower, then met Chloe in the kitchen. The child looked up from her pancakes. "My daddy is sick," she announced.

"But he's going to be well soon," Beth comforted automatically.

Roy was eating a huge stack of pancakes topped with sausage, jelly, and syrup. He took in the circles under Beth's eyes with an amused glance. "Rough night?"

Beth selected a banana from the fruit bowl. "Only for me. He slept like a baby."

Roy laughed, then finished his breakfast in three gulps and herded them out to the SUV. When they got back from Albany, Beth called Miss Eugenia at the library and explained that she would not be able to come in that day. Miss Eugenia gave her a brief lecture on duty, then pumped her for information about Jack's fight, the news of which was apparently all over town.

After her conversation with Miss Eugenia, Beth went up to check on the invalid. A doctor was there, finishing his examination, and Beth stepped back from the bedroom door, mortified. "Come back, Beth," Jack waved her in. "This is Dr. Bynum, and he's a recreational medicine specialist. Apparently getting beat up by thugs falls into the 'sports' category," he explained.

Beth ignored the joke and spoke to the doctor. "Is his shoulder going to need surgery?"

"I don't think so," the man replied as he repacked his equipment in a small duffel bag. "What it needs now is plenty of rest."

Jack thanked the doctor, and then Hipolita materialized from nowhere to escort the physician to the door.

"I didn't know doctors made house calls anymore," Beth said once they were alone.

"He's a friend of my father's," Jack smirked. "But he's the best, so I let him examine me anyway. Besides, Judge Tate might throw me in jail if I don't get a doctor's excuse." Beth commiserated with a nod, then started to leave, but he insisted that she stay. "I can't be left alone! I might have an undetected head injury and go into a coma."

Beth's eyes dropped to his chest. "I thought they hit you in the ribs."

"I bumped my head when I fell." He touched the cut on his lip.

Unable to help herself, Beth agreed to stay. He was a terrible patient, but it was impossible for her to tell if he was actually in pain or just trying to manipulate her. He asked her to read him the newspaper, saying he wanted to keep up with world events, but his eyes were affected by the medication. Every few minutes he would interrupt her, saying he couldn't hear and she needed to move her chair closer. By the end of the obituaries section, she was so close he could probably have read the paper himself if he'd made an effort.

When Hipolita brought Jack his lunch, he tried to convince Beth to feed him, but she refused. "If you're feeling that weak, we need to hire one of those nursing services your mother was talking about," she suggested, and he managed to eat his entire meal without assistance.

When he was finished, Beth questioned him about the fight. "I really think I need to rest here quietly and let my food digest." He leaned back and closed his eyes.

"Your food can digest just fine while you tell me how you got beat up."

He opened one eye, then sighed. "When we got to Heads Up, Roy went in first and I followed a few minutes later. I was a little worried about those biker guys, but there weren't any motorcycles parked outside. Roy was at the bar, so I sat at our booth." He gave her a quick smile. "I waited around for a while, to see if anybody else would approach me, but finally gave up. I went out to the Jeep and two guys jumped me. One pinned my arms behind me while the other one worked on my ribs." He winced and Beth leaned forward.

"They could have killed you," she whispered.

"Easily," he agreed. "But they didn't, so they were probably just trying to scare me off." He looked over at her. "Which means I'm getting close."

"You think those guys were friends of Amber Harpers?"

Jack shrugged. "Something like that. Now, I need to make a few phone calls, but my fingers are numb." Beth knew he was lying, but she dialed the numbers and sat patiently while he talked to various people. Then she retrieved files, sharpened pencils, and fluffed his pillows, but drew the line when he said he needed help getting into the shower. She told him she'd find Roy and heard him laughing as she walked down the hall.

Beth was eating a sandwich in the kitchen when Roy came in to report that their boss was bathed, back in bed, and asking for her. She shook her head. "I'm through playing nursemaid."

"I think he really is in pain," Roy told her sincerely. "Some of that medicine would make him feel better, but he won't take it from anyone but you."

Beth gave him a doubtful look. "Whatever he's paying you, it's not enough," she said as she trudged upstairs.

Jack did look pale, and he took his pain medicine without complaint. He said the sun was in his eyes and asked her to adjust the blinds. He said his toenails needed to be cut, and she told him he could handle his own pedicure once his ribs healed. Finally, at almost one o'clock, he fell back against the pillows and closed his eyes. Beth waited for his breathing to regulate, then approached the television set. In a few minutes she had the theme music to *The Brave and Relentless* playing softly.

Parker had learned the awful truth and was headed toward the Chinese restaurant where his half brother Pierre worked. Tori was headed to the same location, desperate to avoid bloodshed. There had not been this much action on the program in weeks, and Beth was sitting on the edge of her chair when Jack spoke from his bed. "What are you watching?"

She hated to tell him the truth. "A soap opera."

Jack watched Parker screech to a halt in front of a restaurant. "Is this the show where a doctor has hypnotized everyone in town and has them doing all kinds of crazy stuff?" he asked.

"That was a year ago, but it's the same show."

"My mother watches this." He leaned forward as Parker rushed into the restaurant. "What's wrong with this guy?"

"He just found out that his half brother is the father of his wife's unborn child."

Jack raised an eyebrow. "That would be enough to make you mad."

"Shhh," she instructed as Parker got Pierre by the neck. Tori ran in, begging him to stop, and at this point, the scene switched to Cedric attending his first AA meeting. Beth moaned with frustration.

"What's wrong?"

"Nobody cares about Cedric!"

"But you do care about the woman who sleeps with brothers?" he asked.

"What she did was wrong," Beth conceded quickly. "But she was suffering from amnesia at the time . . ."

"Yeah, I'd stick to that story if it were me."

When Roy came to get her for the ride into Albany, she left without giving Jack a chance to object. Chloe had a homework sheet and instructions to collect five things beginning with the letter A. She was concerned about her father, and Beth gave her a good report on his condition.

Chloe was allowed to eat her after-school snack upstairs so she could visit with her father. She nibbled on apple wedges and completed her worksheet while sitting on the end of his bed. Beth was repacking Chloe's backpack when Malcolm Schneckenberger called from the family room. Jack groaned, and seconds later the little man appeared in the doorway.

"I brought this for you." Malcolm showed Jack a large fruit basket. "And this is for you," he handed Beth a book.

Beth thumbed through the first few pages. "*Law for Dummies.* Thanks."

"I never use it anymore," Malcolm told her, then turned to the injured lawyer. "Oscar says that Judge Tate is mad as heck that you're not in court. Any idea how long it will be before you can come back?"

Beth glanced at Jack. With a T-shirt covering his chest, the only visible injury was the small cut on his lip. "A specialist came by this morning and said he has to rest for a while before they can decide if he needs surgery on his shoulder," Beth answered, earning a grunt from her employer and a look of horror from Malcolm.

"That could take weeks, months even!" the little man gasped.

"You can tell Oscar that I'll be back in court in a couple of days—as soon as I can stand up without fainting."

Beth offered to escort Malcolm to the door, and Chloe came along. Beth put the big law book in her room, and then they circled the backyard looking for an acorn to put in Chloe's A collection. While they walked they practiced the first article of faith, and Beth was impressed by Chloe's quick progress. When she commented on it, Chloe admitted that her father had helped her the night before. Beth digested this unsettling information as they went in to dinner.

Hipolita took a tray up to Jack, but brought it back untouched saying the patient refused to eat a single bite. Roy looked over at Beth, and she knew he wanted her to go and spoon-feed their boss, but she went into her own room instead.

She left a message for Derrick on his answering machine, then checked in with her mother. As Beth hung up the phone, Hipolita came to her door and said that Mr. Jack was asking to see her. When Beth got upstairs Chloe had taken her bath and was snuggled under the covers beside her father. The sight of them together was heartwarming, and Beth paused in the doorway to enjoy the moment. After a few seconds, Chloe glanced up and smiled.

"Daddy says we can watch a video in here tonight. I picked *Old Yeller.*" Chloe pointed at the screen. Beth nodded and took a seat in the chair by the bed.

Once Chloe was asleep in her own bed, Beth administered Jack's pain medicine.

"I'm hungry," he said after he swallowed the pills.

"You should have eaten your dinner." Beth was not sympathetic.

"Medicine can make you sick if you take it without food. I need some ice cream to coat my stomach."

Beth didn't feel like arguing, so she got him two scoops of chocolate swirl. When she tried to hand him the bowl, he claimed that the medicine had made him too groggy to hold a spoon. It was an obvious trick, but she gave in, hoping he'd finish quickly and let her get some much-needed sleep. He ate most of the ice cream without a single spill, but concentrating on his mouth left Beth a little breathless.

She took the bowl back to the kitchen, and when she returned, he was asleep. She pulled his comforter up over him and then couldn't resist pushing the hair back from his forehead. Then she hurried down to her own room.

On Tuesday morning Chloe climbed into the SUV carrying her pink tape player, which was blaring Primary songs. Roy suggested they use the car stereo instead, since it would provide better sound quality. Roy's voice joined with theirs in an off-key tenor all the way to Morrow Academy. The singing put Beth into a good mood, but Hipolita changed that when Roy dropped her off at the Gambles' home. With a serious expression, the housekeeper informed her that Mr. Jack was asking for her presence.

The patient was eating his cereal just fine until Beth walked in, but his hand went limp when he saw her. She firmly refused to feed him again, so he grabbed her hand and pulled her close. "Last night I dreamed that I was being caressed by a beautiful angel." Beth felt herself blush as she assured him that this must have been a drug-induced hallucination. He laughed, then sent her into his office to get some notes on Ferris Burke's defense. "You can't miss the file," he called from the bedroom. "It's four inches thick and growing every day."

Beth shuffled through stacks of file folders, computer printouts, and newspapers until she found the conspicuously large Ferris Burke file. When she picked it up, she exposed an old copy of the Book of Mormon. She stared at the royal blue cover and the picture of a golden statue of Moroni for a few seconds, then took it with her to Jack's room.

When he saw the book in her hand, he looked almost guilty. "I thought I'd better brush up on the articles of faith in case Chloe needs to memorize any more of them," he offered as an explanation.

Beth opened the scriptures to the spot he had marked. Her eyes scanned the account of Alma the Younger's visit from the angel. "I guess that's why you're reading in Alma."

He was saved from a response by Roberta's arrival. "I'm here to earn my exorbitant salary," she told her boss as she breezed in.

Beth handed the file and the Book of Mormon to Jack, her mind racing. Jack had been reading the scriptures, and his choice of passages seemed significant. Confused, she backed toward the door. She had to put some distance between them so she could think clearly.

"You don't have to go," he called after her, but she shook her head and hurried down the hall. She passed Hipolita in the kitchen and told her she was going for a walk. Then she crossed the street to the Northcutt's house. The grandmother answered the door and said that Ellen was taking a nap. Beth spoke to Bud and admired the new baby again, then left assured that the little family was well taken care of. She wasn't ready to go back into the Gambles' house yet, so she headed toward Annabelle's.

"I've been wanting to talk to you, but after we heard the awful news about Mr. Gamble, I hated to disturb you," Annabelle said when she opened the front door. "Would you like something to drink? I know you don't drink tea or coffee, but I think I have some orange juice."

Beth declined the offer of refreshment and took a seat at the kitchen table. She knew that Annabelle wanted details on Jack's injuries, but she didn't intend to discuss her employer or any of his various problems. "How is everything with your retirement party?"

Annabelle smiled. "Eugenia was a little miffed that I didn't tell her first, but otherwise my explanations went smoothly. Then I called Mr. Hubbard at the bank and told him there were a few additional people I would like to invite. He foolishly agreed, so today I faxed him a list of one hundred names, and the bank is paying $18.50 per person for the party!"

"Wow." Beth was impressed by the scope of Annabelle's revenge.

"Your name is on the list," Annabelle added. "It will give you an excuse to dress up."

"I don't have an evening gown," Beth shook her head.

"A nice Sunday dress will do. Check at Corrine's. She's bound to have something."

Annabelle returned to the subject of Jack's injuries, so Beth stood to go. When she walked into the Gambles' kitchen, Hipolita said that Mr. Jack wanted to speak to her. "Tell him I've gone into town and you don't know when I'll be back," Beth replied. Then she got her purse and headed to Haggerty in Jack's Lexus.

Miss Corrine was delighted to see her again and said she had just the dress. "It was one of our spring arrivals from last year," she explained as she led the way to the clearance rack. "I've sold them all except one tiny size three." She ran her eyes along Beth's thin frame.

The dress was black and simple, yet elegant. It fit perfectly, and since the price had been reduced four times, its purchase was not terribly painful. While she waited for Miss Corrine to process her Visa card, Beth looked around at the beautiful clothes. She was staring longingly at a "burnished pumpkin" dress on the new arrivals rack when Miss Corrine handed her the ticket for her signature. "There are no refunds on sale items," she warned. "But if you change your mind, I'll let you exchange it."

"I won't change my mind," Beth assured her as she tucked the receipt in her purse. On the drive back to the Gambles' house, Beth thought of Chloe. Soon they would be riding home from school, looking through her backpack and making plans to do her homework. Then they would spend a pleasant evening with Chloe's father . . .

She was so lost in her happy thoughts that she didn't notice the bright red sports car parked outside the garage until she pulled up beside it. Wondering if Jack had bought yet another new car, Beth walked inside. The kitchen was empty, but she could hear voices coming from the front of the house.

She stopped at the entrance to the living room, and her eyes went straight to Jack, who was slouched in a wing chair near the fireplace. Since he had claimed to be too weak to hold a spoon earlier, she was understandably shocked to see him dressed and receiving company. He looked at Beth, then over to the couch.

Following his gaze, Beth found Chloe sitting beside the most beautiful woman she had ever seen. Her dark hair was cut short so that it curled around her face and brushed the collar of her green silk suit. Small and petite, she had flawless skin, and her big brown eyes were staring back with avid interest as a miniature poodle danced around her feet. Beth took a step forward, vaguely aware of a tall, tan man and a blonde woman in the background.

"You must be Beth." The voice was cultured and slightly accented.

Beth nodded. "You are even more beautiful than your picture."

The woman's dark, mauve-colored lips formed a smile, exposing perfect, white teeth. "You've seen my picture?" She was pleased.

"There's one in Chloe's room." Beth felt someone behind her and turned to see Roy.

"Monique," he said with a nod toward the woman.

"Ah, my old friend Roy." She scooted to the very edge of the couch and crossed her legs, exposing a great deal of smooth, nylon-covered skin. "Beth, maybe you can help me convince Jack to be reasonable." She looked back at her ex-husband as Beth glanced from one to the other, wondering why Jack was being unreasonable and why Chloe's mother thought she could change his mind. "I've planned a wonderful birthday party for Chloe tomorrow, and he says he won't let me have it."

Beth stared at her blankly. "Tomorrow is not Chloe's birthday." She was sure.

Monique laughed. "Of course it's not really her birthday." Beth heard Jack exhale loudly. "But who knows where I might be in April? So I want to have a party now. It's all planned. I've got a caterer, balloons, clowns, and even a pony. But Jack says they can't come."

"I said we can't invite kids from Chloe's class to a pretend birthday party," he amended. "Besides, I've only got superficial background checks on the children and their parents."

"You are as nervous as an old woman! For once, won't you just let Chloe have a good time?" Monique cried. Then she smoothed her skirt and continued more calmly. "If we can't invite her school friends, maybe we could rent some children from a casting agency."

"Rent some children? Do you ever listen to yourself?" Jack asked.

Chloe shifted uncomfortably, and Beth felt required to intervene for the child's sake. "I know some children we could probably borrow." All eyes turned to her, and she regretted her brave words. But the hopeful look on Chloe's face gave her the courage to continue. "The Northcutt children. They've been here before, and they aren't a security risk."

"They'd come on short notice?" Monique questioned Beth with enthusiasm.

Beth nodded. "I think so."

Everyone turned to Jack. "Okay," he relented. "But this will not turn into a publicity event for your movie. No press of any kind. No television, newspaper, radio, nothing."

"Nothing?" she asked.

"I mean it."

"But we can have the party?" she verified.

"Check out everything and everyone with Roy," he said with a nod.

"Wonderful!" Monique cooed. "Now where is Hipolita? I've invited a few guests for dinner, so I need to go over the menu. And we'll want to settle into our rooms."

Jack frowned. "You're staying here?"

"Why would I come all the way from France to visit my daughter and then stay somewhere else?" She arched a delicate brow. "Unless you'll let Chloe go with me to a hotel."

Hipolita walked in as if on cue. "Monique needs a room," Jack said, trying to rise from his chair. He fell back with a moan, his face white as a sheet.

"And give Eduard a room near mine," Monique told Hipolita with a wave toward the large man in the corner.

"We're not running a bed-and-breakfast," Jack said firmly. "Eduard *will* be staying at a hotel."

Monique's eyes narrowed. "He's my personal trainer."

"You can do sit-ups by yourself tonight," he returned.

"What about Dana? She's my masseuse."

Jack shook his head, and Roy stepped forward. "I'll help bring in your bags."

"What about that dog?" Jack wanted to know.

"Here Cleopatra," Monique called as the animal growled at Hipolita.

"Cleopatra had better go with Eduard and the masseuse," Roy reached down and grabbed the little ball of fur.

Beth worked her way over to stand beside Chloe, anxious to get her away from all the confusion. "Why don't you come to my room? We can go through your backpack and then watch a video during your mom's party tonight," she suggested.

Monique reached down beside the couch and picked up the backpack. "Chloe's not going to school tomorrow, so you won't need to worry about homework. And she's coming to the party." Monique turned from Beth and addressed her daughter. "I brought some new clothes from Paris for your daddy to buy. There is a gorgeous, white dress with handmade lace that will dazzle everyone."

Chloe smiled and Beth looked at Jack.

"She doesn't get to see Monique very often, so I thought she could miss one day of school." He grimaced, and Beth didn't know if it was from pain or annoyance.

Beth eyed the backpack longingly. She wanted to find out what kind of homework Chloe had and add another check mark to the neat row in her take-home folder. Beth glanced up and saw Monique watching her. "After all, it's only kindergarten," Monique said, taking the child by the hand. "Come on, Chloe honey."

Once the room was quiet, Jack managed to rise and walk over to stand beside Beth. "I hate to ask, but could you help me get upstairs?" he requested. "I don't want to humiliate myself by fainting in front of our uninvited company."

He leaned heavily on her shoulder and took the steps one at a time. When he laid back on his bed, he was pale and sweating, so Beth gave him his pain medication. He closed his eyes, and a few minutes later he fell fast asleep.

Beth ate a lonely dinner in the kitchen, watching Hipolita prepare food for Monique's dinner party. She wanted to see Chloe's new dress, but she wanted to avoid Monique even more, so she went to her room. When guests started arriving, she peeked out of her window.

Hipolita had food arranged on tables around the patio, and Beth watched Monique, dressed in a tropical print sarong, move through the crowd. She caught glimpses of Chloe in her white lace gown and occasionally saw Roy in the shadows, always on the lookout for danger. As the evening progressed, a small jazz combo started playing and some couples danced. Others changed into swimsuits and got into the pool.

About 9:30 it started to drizzle and the party moved inside. Beth shuddered to think of what the damp guests were doing to Hipolita's spotless floors. She could hear doors slamming and bursts of laughter coming from different parts of the house.

By eleven o'clock the rain had stopped, and most of the guests were gone. Wearily Beth prepared for bed and had just dozed off when she heard a knock on her door. Cracking it open, she peered into the dark hallway. Jack was there, holding Chloe's hand.

"Would you mind if Chloe sleeps with you tonight?" he whispered.

"Of course not." Beth led the way into her bedroom, and they watched together as Chloe curled into a pillow and fell back asleep.

Jack waited until they returned to the little living room before he spoke again. "I'm sorry to impose on you, but I don't know all of Monique's guests, and I don't trust any of them." His expression grew dark. "I'd let her sleep with me, but as a single father I have to be very careful. People might think or say . . ." he trailed off, unable to voice the unspeakable.

"I understand, and I'm glad for the company." Her eyes drifted toward the bedroom.

"If you want to run, I'll get Roy to go with you," he offered, slumping against the wall.

Beth shook her head. "It's too late. Can you make it back upstairs by yourself?"

Exhaustion was etched around his eyes, but he gave her a crooked smile. "Roy's in the kitchen, and he'll drag me up if necessary." He turned and walked slowly into the hallway. Beth listened until his shuffling footsteps faded, then got back into bed and snuggled against Chloe.

The next morning Chloe couldn't remember coming to Beth's room the night before, but didn't seem concerned to find herself there. However, Beth felt an explanation was advisable. "Your dad was nervous with all those people in the house last night, so he brought you down here."

"He worries about me a lot." Chloe nodded wisely as she stood and stretched. "And today's my extra birthday party," she added with a smile.

"That reminds me that I need to go call Mrs. Northcutt and ask if Kristen and Bud can come," Beth said as she reached for the telephone. "You sing these Primary songs." She pushed the Play button on the pink tape player and music filled the room.

Ellen's mother answered, and Beth apologized for calling so early, but the grandmother assured her they had been up for hours. Ellen came to the phone and Beth issued the invitation. "That sounds like fun," Ellen answered after a brief pause. "Strange, but fun."

"So, you'll let Bud and Kristen come?"

"As long as you'll be with them," Ellen agreed.

"I'll walk over and pick them up at three o'clock this afternoon," Beth replied.

"They're coming?" Chloe asked between verses of "Keep the Commandments."

"They are coming," Beth confirmed, turning off the tape. "Now let's get some breakfast."

Chloe ate cereal in her pajamas, then insisted that Beth accompany her upstairs. Beth was anxious about running into Monique, but Chloe assured her that her mother never woke up before lunchtime. Beth sat on Chloe's bed while the little girl took a shower, then helped her choose an outfit for the day. Beth was trying to comb through Chloe's tangled hair when Jack hobbled in. Beth looked up at his damp hair, and he followed the direction of her gaze, reaching up to run his fingers across his head.

"Mr. Fuller called and said that Amy Phillips has agreed to come over and have some publicity pictures made today," he reported glumly.

"Miss Georgia?" Beth confirmed, and Jack nodded.

"After today, the rest of our cochairman responsibilities can be handled by our secretaries."

"So, does this mean she has forgiven you for dumping her during your date?"

"I wouldn't go that far, but she's willing to suffer my presence briefly for the advancement of science." He rolled his eyes, then winked at Chloe. "Monique wants to take Chloe shopping before the party, which is okay as long as Roy drives them. Are you working at the library today?"

Beth nodded. "Until noon."

"That's when Amy is supposed to get here. After she leaves, maybe we could discuss how I'm going to convince a jury to acquit Ferris without my main witness."

Jack looked discouraged, and Beth agreed out of sympathy. She waved good-bye to Chloe and hurried to the library, anxious to avoid a lecture on tardiness. Miss Eugenia was so excited about Annabelle's retirement party that she seemed to have forgotten Beth's absence on Monday.

"I had my black suit dry-cleaned, and they must have used some new chemical on it because the whole thing shrunk about three sizes," the older woman told Beth. "I told Mr. Draper at the cleaners that he ought to pay for my new outfit, but he said I'd have to file a claim with his insurance, and I don't have time for that!"

Beth offered condolences as she put extra chairs in the Genealogical Department, anticipating new members after the Historical Society's successful meeting the week before.

"And I'm wondering about getting a blue rinse put on my hair. What do you think?"

Beth coughed to cover a laugh, and Miss Eugenia's eyes narrowed. "I've always been partial to the natural look myself," Beth finally managed. Miss Eugenia was still watching her suspiciously when Derrick and several society members arrived.

"We're going to need a larger room soon," Miss Eva Nell commented.

"The Methodist Church might let us use their Family Life Center," someone suggested.

"Or we could just change the day of our meeting and not tell anyone," was Miss Eugenia's solution to the overcrowding problem.

The meeting was a success, and afterward the members stood around to visit. Beth didn't want to miss Jack's photo session with Miss Georgia, so at noon she walked up behind Miss Eugenia and whispered that she was leaving. When Beth returned to the Gambles' house, she found Chloe sitting at the kitchen table, watching Hipolita pick pecans. "Baptism" was playing on the pink tape recorder. Beth turned down the volume, then pulled up a chair and took a handful of the cracked nuts from the bowl. "So, did you have a nice morning?"

"I helped Hipolita make three pies, and she didn't burn any of them!" Chloe reported.

"That oven likes her better than me." Beth risked a quick glance at the housekeeper as Monique walked in wearing black leather and looking just as good as she had in tailored silk.

"Hi, sweetie," Monique said to Chloe. "Good morning, Beth." She didn't acknowledge Hipolita. The housekeeper collected her pecans and moved to the counter by the sink. "Are you ready?" Monique asked, and Chloe nodded. "Well, go tell your daddy good-bye."

Chloe jumped off her chair and ran upstairs as instructed. Beth continued to separate the pecans from their shells. "Chloe likes you," Monique said abruptly.

Beth wasn't sure how to respond. "I like her too," she replied.

"And you're perfect for him," Monique smiled. "Jack, I mean. You're so pure."

Beth wasn't offended, but thought Monique probably meant for her to be. "I work for Mr. Gamble. He pays me to watch Chloe, and that is the extent of our relationship."

"Hmmm," Monique murmured. Then she startled Beth with a new revelation. "If it had been up to me, Jack and I would still be married. I thought we could pursue separate careers, but Jack has some antiquated ideas, and when you play with Jack, it always has to be by his rules. So . . ." She raised a shoulder as Chloe rushed back in.

"Daddy said that Roy is waiting by the patio!"

Chloe seemed happy to go, and Beth didn't know if that made her feel better or worse. Once they were gone she walked upstairs and into the family room. Jack's door was ajar, so she pushed it open and found him lying across his bed, fully dressed.

"Miss Georgia's late," he muttered.

"Are you sure you're up to this?"

"I have to be. I can't stand her up again."

While they waited Beth opened mail for him. She described the contents of each letter, and he told her whether to put it in the trash pile, the pay pile, or the look-at-it-later pile. They were about halfway through his accumulated mail when Hipolita walked in and said that Miss Georgia and the photographer had arrived.

Beth slipped out, hoping to catch a glimpse of the beauty queen, and almost ran into Miss Georgia. The woman was standing in the family room wearing a clingy white sheath that exposed a great deal of deeply tanned skin. She had the regulation satin sash across her shoulder proclaiming her title, and a lot of wispy, blonde hair. It was hard to imagine any man being able to resist her charms, and as Beth studied the young woman, her respect for Jack went up a notch.

Miss Georgia's gaze moved from Beth to Jack's bedroom door, then back. Beth knew the other woman had jumped to an erroneous conclusion, and this was confirmed when Miss Phillips spoke. "I didn't know Mr. Gamble was involved with someone else." Her bright red mouth formed a frown. "I think it was very inconsiderate of Mr. Fuller not to tell me before I agreed to go out with him on that 'date'."

Beth considered the situation. She could stick with the absolute truth and cause more trouble for Jack, or she could give a carefully edited version of the facts. Since she was at eye level with Amy Phillips's impressive bosom, which had almost surely been surgically enhanced, Beth decided the absolute truth was not compulsory. She leaned forward and lowered her voice.

"I'm insanely jealous, and he was afraid to be seen with someone as beautiful as you. He was right to be afraid . . ." Beth let her voice trail off. "My last boyfriend?" Miss Georgia nodded apprehensively. "Dead." The bright red mouth fell open.

At that moment, Malcolm Schneckenberger walked into the room. "Hello ladies!" he greeted, then turned to Miss Georgia, "What man wouldn't kill for the chance to have his picture with you?" Amy gave Beth a quick look to see her reaction to the word "kill." Then she grabbed Malcolm's hand and demanded that they get the pictures over with immediately. "I thought we'd take them here in the family room. It will give the photos a nice, homey touch," Malcolm suggested as Jack walked through his bedroom door.

"I don't care where we take them as long as we get them over with fast," she hissed.

Jack raised an eyebrow as he stepped up beside the woman. They beamed at each other for a few seconds while the photographer snapped pictures furiously. Then Jack moved away. "Hipolita will see you to the door," he said, walking back to his room.

The guests followed Hipolita down the hall, and Beth heard Malcolm reminding them that Mr. Gamble had suffered an injury on

Sunday and was not himself. She was waiting for the coast to clear before she went down to watch *The Brave and Relentless* when Hipolita walked in carrying a tray of soup.

"I bring you lunch too," she informed Beth.

Jack had taken off his dress shirt, and Beth suspected that he wanted her to see the awful discoloration visible around the white medical tape that supported his ribs. If he was trying to gain her compassion, it worked. He pulled on a T-shirt, then made fun of Miss Georgia while they ate lunch. Finally Beth told him that she was surprised he didn't *want* to date the woman.

He looked up. "She's not at all my type."

Beth laughed at this remark. "I thought she was every man's type."

"Maybe every sixteen-year-old's," he admitted. "But my tastes have matured." His gaze was warm, and she looked away.

After the meal, Beth removed his tray and gave him a pain pill. Then she turned on the television and they watched *The Brave and Relentless*. Pierre was in the hospital with neck injuries, Marissa encouraged Cedric to try oil painting instead of alcohol, Elena signed up for a Braille class, and Tori promised Parker that she would never sleep with his brother again. This caused Jack to laugh so hard that he hurt his ribs. Parker wasn't impressed either, and packed his bags.

By the time Monique and Chloe returned, the grounds were swarming with strangers preparing for the afternoon's festivities. Beth walked past the one-man band warming up on the patio, then weaved between a florist truck and a catering van to find Roy standing near a big-top tent. "This is amazing," she commented as she watched the people moving all over the backyard.

"This is a security nightmare," Roy said. "And it's costing the boss a fortune."

Beth frowned. "I thought Monique was hosting this party."

"Monique never pays for anything herself. She planned it, but all the bills have Jack's name on them."

Beth's opinion of Monique plummeted as she crossed the street to get the Northcutt children. Two hours later, Jack announced that the party was over. Chloe protested and Monique knelt in front of her daughter. "I have to catch a plane, but maybe your daddy will extend the party for a little while . . ."

Jack shook his head. "We told the Northcutts that we'd have their children home at five. It's time to say good-bye." Chloe started to cry, and her father carried her into the house.

Beth took their subdued guests home, and when she got back, the party had almost disappeared. Hipolita met her in the kitchen and said that Monique would be leaving in less than an hour. Beth expelled a sigh of relief as she continued on into her room. She was surprised to find Chloe sitting quietly on the couch.

"My daddy said for me to stay here while he talks to Monique," she said. Her voice was hoarse from crying, and Beth's dislike for Chloe's mother solidified. She sat down beside the child, and they waited until Jack knocked on the door.

"Monique is leaving now." He held his hand out to Chloe, and they walked outside. Beth followed behind them at a distance.

Monique was meeting Eduard and the masseuse at the airport, and she seemed smaller without her entourage. Beth stood on the patio as Roy loaded luggage into the sports car. Monique hugged Chloe, then tried to embrace Jack and laughed when he pushed her away. With a nod at Beth, she settled an expensive pair of sunglasses on her lovely nose and walked leisurely to her car. Jack picked up Chloe and held her against his injured ribs. Beth watched them wave good-bye, feeling like an outsider. Hipolita stuck her head out of the kitchen door and called everyone in for dinner. Roy took Chloe from her father's arms and put her up on his shoulders for a ride into the house. Jack and Beth followed behind them.

"Don't worry about Chloe," he said. "Monique is only a minor nuisance in our lives, and we probably won't see her again for months. But it's always a little hard for Chloe to say good-bye. I guess even a bad mother is better than no mother at all."

Hipolita had leftovers from the party spread out on the table. Roy piled his plate high and sat beside Chloe. Throughout the meal he concentrated on teasing the child into a better mood. Anxious to help, Beth mentioned Annabelle's party and the new dress she had bought for the occasion.

"I was thinking that you could wear your new dress from Paris." As the words left her mouth, Beth remembered Jack's injuries. "Unless your dad doesn't feel like going."

He lifted a shoulder. "I won't be the life of the party, but I can sit around there as good as I can sit around here. And Oscar might break my other ribs if I miss an opportunity to meet voters."

After dinner Chloe rearranged furniture in her playhouse while Jack practiced his approach to the jury on Beth. At nine o'clock they put Chloe to bed, and when they returned to the family room, Roy was waiting for them. He was dressed in a pair of tight purple bicycle shorts and an orange tank top.

"Roy's going to run with you tonight," Jack explained.

Running without Jack seemed disloyal somehow, but her muscles ached from the days of inactivity, and she couldn't think of a polite way to decline. So she changed clothes and met Roy on the driveway. Throughout their laps around the park he ran backward, sideways, and in circles. It was entertaining, but when they walked back into the kitchen she couldn't help but wonder how long it would be before Jack was well enough to accompany her again.

On Thursday morning Beth drove to Kate Iverson's house for their visiting teaching appointment and her first canning lesson. Kate already had a case of jars sterilized and sitting in the middle of her kitchen table when Beth arrived.

"I decided to start with tomatoes since we won't have to use a pressure cooker," Kate explained while Emily tugged on her leg.

Sister Baylor and Sister Armistead took turns holding the baby and giving the visiting teaching message. Then they made an appointment for the first Thursday of October before they left. Once they were gone, Kate pulled her hair into a ponytail and corralled Emily into a playpen in a corner of the kitchen. The baby protested until Kate handed her a graham cracker.

As they worked Kate explained that Annabelle had taken Miss Eugenia shopping for a dress to wear to the retirement party. "She tried the mall yesterday, convinced that she could buy something to fit without going into plus sizes," Kate said as she filled the jars with tomatoes. "Today I think Annabelle is going to take her to a specialty store."

They were taking the last batch of stewed tomatoes from the large pot when the back door slammed and they both looked up to see Miss Eugenia walk in. The older woman focused on the pile of tomato peels, the hot jars cooling on the table, and both young women dripping with sweat. Then her eyes swung back to Kate. "You didn't tell me you were canning today."

Kate removed the oven mitts from her hands and faced her neighbor. "Finding a dress for you to wear to the retirement party was much more important than canning tomatoes with us," she began as Annabelle entered the room. "So, did you have any luck?" Kate asked.

"We found a beautiful suit at Large and Lovely," Annabelle announced with a bright smile.

Miss Eugenia ignored the comments about clothing and ran her fingers along one of the shiny lids. "You sterilized the jars first and checked for knicks and chips?"

"Of course," Kate responded. "And you know I always use new jars."

Miss Eugenia turned to Beth. "I declare, I believe there have been more new jars purchased in the town of Haggerty during the past year than in the entire previous decade." Emily squealed, and Miss Eugenia dropped her purse to pick up the baby. "Poor, poor dear," Miss Eugenia cooed. "Your mama has gone crazy over canning and left you in this cage . . ."

Kate rolled her eyes as she removed two jars of baby food from the refrigerator. "Since you're the only one who cares about Emily, why don't you go feed her?"

Miss Eugenia took the food from Kate's hand and walked into the living room.

"I think her feelings are hurt that we didn't invite her," Beth whispered.

Annabelle winced. "I'm sorry, Kate. I know I was supposed to keep her busy all morning, but we found the dress so *quickly*. I tried to get her to let Myrtle put a blue rinse on her hair, but Eugenia said she'd decided to leave it natural. Then I suggested that we stop at a restaurant for lunch, but she said it was too early. I even offered to buy her a new purse to match her suit, but it was as if she has a sixth sense and knew that you were putting up tomatoes without her!"

Kate laughed at this. "She'll get over it by the time Emily finishes her lunch."

Beth hoped this was true, but couldn't invest the time to find out. She told the ladies good-bye and returned to the Gambles' house. Hipolita had Jack's lunch on a tray, and Beth offered to take it up to him. The housekeeper relinquished the food without comment.

Beth found her employer in the middle of his bed, surrounded by files and papers, talking on the phone. He waved her in, and she put the tray on his bedside table. He ended his call and offered her part of his lunch. She took half a sandwich and sat down in her regular chair. "What's all this?" She gestured at the documents that encircled him.

"Judge Tate has formed the jury pool, and Roberta got a list of the potential jurors. I've had them checked out by a private investigation firm."

"Is that legal?" Beth asked.

"Everybody does it." Jack reached for the stack closest to him. "These are the ones we have identified as people we will definitely strike."

Beth took the papers from his hand and started reading.

"These are people we want on the jury, which means they will be on Kilgore's strike list." He gave her another stack of papers.

"What about those?" Beth pointed to the large pile that remained on the bed.

"Unfortunately, that is the group that we can't positively classify. Like this one," he picked up the top page. "The guy is forty-two years old, loves country music, has two kids and one grandbaby. All of which sounds good." Beth nodded in agreement. "However, he is very active in an environmental group and hunts only with a bow and arrow."

"And that's bad?"

"As an environmental activist, he's in a general 'liberal thinking' group that I can't trust. So he's probably a no, but I hate it because I think he might vote our way."

"When do you have to pick the jury?"

"Selection begins on Monday."

"Any luck finding Amber Harper?"

Jack shook his head. "None."

"So, where do we start?" she asked, and he handed her the questionable stack. They worked right through *The Brave and Relentless*, and Beth didn't even realize how late it was until Roy came in and asked if she was going to ride with him to Albany. "Do you need me to stay?" she asked Jack.

He shook his head. "Chloe would be disappointed if you didn't come."

Beth helped him to organize his stacks, then left with Roy. Chloe was quiet when she got into the car, and Beth asked if she'd had a bad day. "The kids at my school think I didn't really have a pretend birthday party. They said we didn't have a pony and a man who could play a whole song all by himself and a striped tent." Tears sprang into her eyes as she spoke. "I told them I promise, but they still didn't believe me."

"Monique took some pictures. Maybe she'll send us some," Beth suggested.

"I'll ask my daddy," Chloe said more cheerfully. "And I want another party just like that when I really turn six."

Roy laughed as he glanced at them in the rearview mirror. "Good luck on that one."

After dinner Chloe asked her father if she could call Monique about the pictures. Jack considered this for a few seconds. "That might be difficult. I think she's in Los Angeles, but I don't know if she's staying in a hotel or with her friend Felix Hummer." Jack's tone changed when he said that name, and Beth got the impression that he didn't like the man. Or maybe he was jealous.

"Monique said Mr. Hummer is giving her lots of money to make her new movie in Hollywood," Chloe contributed. "And I think he's a friend of Mr. Burke's too."

Jack shook his head. "I doubt they even know each other."

Chloe nodded emphatically. "Mr. Hummer said 'my pal Ferris Burke' to Monique one time. I heard him."

Once Chloe was in bed, they settled in the family room. Beth asked if Jack thought there really was some kind of relationship between Monique's new boyfriend and Ferris Burke. "I thought it was odd that Chloe overheard them discussing your client."

"I don't know," he answered. "Ferris has risen to the top of the country music business pretty fast, and I guess that connections with someone like Felix Hummer could have helped his career along. But it's not a possibility that I really want to dwell on." He stretched out in the recliner, then smiled. "Now, where's my ice cream?"

That night in bed Beth stared at the ceiling, trying to picture David's face, but it wouldn't come to her. Panicked, she got up and dug through her box of memorabilia. She pushed aside old love letters, leftover wedding invitations, and a dried rose saved from her bridal bouquet until she found a snapshot of David. He was wearing his high school soccer uniform, smiling up into the camera with youthful enthusiasm, his green eyes shining with hope.

Beth clutched the picture to her chest and let the tears come. She cried for the years of loneliness and the happy future that had died along with David. But mostly she grieved because her memories were fading and she barely knew the boy in the picture anymore.

On Friday morning Beth arrived at the library five minutes early, and Miss Eugenia gave her an approving nod. Business was slow, and Miss Eugenia didn't have many phone calls to make, so finally she resorted to browbeating Beth. "You never did really explain why you aren't married," Miss Eugenia said as she cornered Beth by the large-print mysteries.

"I was engaged for a while, but he, my, I . . ." Beth searched for the right words. "He died."

"What was his name?" Miss Eugenia asked with unusual gentleness.

Beth took a deep breath. "David. He was killed in a car accident."

Miss Eugenia nodded. "My husband died of a stroke two years ago, and part of me died right along with him."

"At first I didn't know if I could go on," Beth admitted.

"Charles and I had been together for so long, we couldn't tell where my thoughts ended and his began. Without him I felt lost. I know you loved the boy who died, but you're too young to give up on romance."

"I'm not interested in having a love life." Beth didn't want to seem ungrateful, but she knew she couldn't discuss David with Miss Eugenia. So she picked up her purse and headed toward the door. "I've got some errands to run, so I think I'll leave a few minutes early." Without waiting for permission, she hurried outside.

After taking a few calming breaths, she walked to the bank to deposit her paycheck from Jack. Next she made a stop at the post office to mail her weekly report to the family court, then went into Edith's Shoe Emporium and bought a pair of black pumps to wear with her new dress. When she parked by the garage, she saw that Roy was already in the Expedition, ready to go get Chloe. Beth transferred directly from the Lexus into the SUV, and Roy raised an eyebrow. "Not going to check in on the boss before we go?" he asked.

"Why would I do that?"

Roy shrugged. "He might need medicine or something."

"I'm not his nurse," Beth replied more sharply than she meant to. Her conversation with Miss Eugenia had been unnerving, and the hour of shopping hadn't been enough to calm her.

"He expected you at 12:15, and he worries."

"My time while Chloe is in school is my own, and I can take care of myself."

"Boss has gotten used to having you around," Roy replied. "And you don't seem to mind his company too much either."

Beth had no intention of discussing Jack or their complex relationship, so she stared out the window until they reached Morrow Academy.

Just before dinner that night, Roberta called. "Is it true that you and Jack are going to Annabelle Grainger's retirement party tomorrow night?" the secretary asked.

"We are both going to the party."

"I can't believe it!" Roberta exclaimed. "I mean, Jack never dates."

"It's not a date!" Beth corrected. "We're just riding together."

"Riding together to a party is called a date."

"Chloe's going too . . ."

"It's a date Beth, whether you want to admit it or not," Roberta said, then disconnected without saying good-bye.

After replacing the receiver, Beth stared at the phone. Roberta was being ridiculous. Going to the party with Jack didn't constitute a date any more than her daily rides to Morrow Academy with Roy did. The fact that she had bought another new dress and matching shoes was incidental. And the anticipation she felt about the evening was a reflection of her otherwise dull life. Pushing the disturbing thoughts to the back of her mind, Beth went to join Chloe and her father for dinner.

CHAPTER 10

On Saturday morning Beth and Chloe walked up to check on Jack together. He was dressed and sitting at the chair in his office. Beth glanced at the newspaper lying on his desk. "Kilgore Accuses Gamble of Delay in Burke Trial," the headline screamed. "What does that mean?" She pointed to the paper.

Jack shrugged. "Kilgore's just making noise, trying to distract the press from his weak case. He's saying that I'm not really hurt, but stayed home with a doctor's excuse to give me more time to find my elusive witness."

Beth was offended by the idea of the district attorney printing lies to win a case and possibly a political appointment. "You could sue him for saying things like that!"

"And give him more publicity," Jack said as Roberta breezed in.

"Let's get to work, you big faker," she told her boss irreverently.

He scowled at his secretary, then spoke to Beth. "We'll need to leave at 6:30 tonight."

Beth nodded and headed for the door, but caught Roberta's speculative look before she could escape. Roberta left just before lunch, and when Chloe and Hipolita headed upstairs with Jack's tray, Beth followed behind them. Chloe's father was back on his bed, looking pale and uncomfortable. After they ate, Beth convinced him to take half a pain pill. Then she and Chloe went downstairs to watch *Anastasia.*

At 5:30 Hipolita came to get Chloe so she could change for the party. Beth showered, then tried to style her hair without much success. Finally she gave up, pushing the damp clumps behind her ears, and concentrated on applying some of her recently acquired cosmetics. Just as she slipped the new dress over her head, someone knocked on her door. Beth walked through the other room and found Chloe in the hallway wearing her French gown.

"You look like an angel," Beth exclaimed as the child walked in.

"That's what my daddy said too," Chloe confided, then her eyes clouded with concern. "But your dress is just plain . . . black."

"Miss Corrine said that black is chic," Beth told her with a smile.

"What's 'chic'?" Chloe asked.

"Beautiful," Jack said from the doorway. Startled, Beth looked up to see him staring at her.

She put a nervous hand to her head. "I couldn't do anything with my hair."

Jack stepped into the room. "Get me a brush, Chloe," he said as he circled behind Beth and gathered her hair into his hands. "I've been dying to do this since the first day I saw you." Chloe ran into Beth's room and returned seconds later with her brush. Jack worked quickly and soon he had an elegant braid at the back of Beth's head. "I need hairpins."

"There are some on the counter in the bathroom," Beth managed, then shivered as his fingers brushed her neck.

"Did a squirrel run across your grave?" he whispered, and she knew he was smiling.

"It's a rabbit that runs over your grave."

"Same general idea." He accepted a handful of hairpins from Chloe and secured Beth's braid. Then he pulled her in front of the mirror that hung over the couch.

She stared at herself in amazement. "If you ever decide to retire from law, maybe you could make a living braiding hair." She kept her tone light.

"I doubt there's much money in it."

She looked up to meet his eyes. "But I'll bet hair braiders almost never get beat up in the line of duty." He smiled at her reflection, and Beth felt the air desert her lungs.

Chloe wiggled her way in between them. "You fixed Beth's hair as nice as mine, Daddy," she told him approvingly.

Jack reached down and stroked his daughter's cheek. "Everybody's going to be jealous of me tonight, since I'll be accompanied by *two* beautiful ladies."

Chloe laughed as they walked into the kitchen. Roy was coming in through the back door and whistled. "Don't know which one of you is prettier."

"Well, you should be able to narrow it down to two," Jack responded on the way outside.

"Are you going with us, Roy?" Chloe asked.

"Roy is going to drive us so we don't have to find a parking place," her father explained. "Then he'll come back to get us."

Roy dropped them off in front of The Club saying he would return later. Inside, they were directed to the second-floor ballroom, where the retirement party was being held. Jack paused in the doorway to survey the room. There was a buffet set up along the far wall, and individual tables surrounded the dance floor. A small receiving line had formed to their left. Jack lifted Chloe, then held his hand out to Beth. After a brief hesitation, she allowed his fingers to close around hers, and by the time they reached the dignitaries, her heartbeat was irregular.

Beth was astounded to see Derrick standing beside Annabelle in the receiving line. "I asked him to come as my escort," Annabelle explained before Beth could ask. "If I didn't bring a date, I'd have saved the bank $18.50," she added quietly. Beth smiled as Jack pulled her down the line and introduced her to Oscar Fuller, who regarded her with interest.

"Ah, Miss Middleton, you are as lovely as I've heard." Then Mr. Fuller's expression became serious as he grasped Jack's elbow. "I need to discuss a few things with you." He glanced back at Beth. "If Miss Middleton doesn't mind."

Realizing that she had been dismissed, Beth took Chloe to the table where the Iversons were sitting with Miss Eugenia and Miss Polly Kirby. Kate and Mark were dressed conservatively in Sunday clothes. Emily was wearing a light blue dress with smocking across the bodice and tiny patent leather shoes. Miss Eugenia looked impressive in her new suit, and Miss Polly was impossible to miss in a hot pink muumuu.

"You all look so nice," Beth complimented the table as a whole.

"We were just going to say the same thing about you," Kate returned. "I love your hair."

Beth blushed, and Emily threw her arms around Chloe in a friendly hug.

"Emily!" Mark Iverson objected to the baby's enthusiastic mauling.

"It's okay," Chloe answered with a smile.

"They play together during church," Beth enlightened everyone.

"Tomorrow there's a program, and I'm going to say something," Chloe said with pride.

Mark Iverson smiled. "Emily and I were just about to make a second trip to the food table." He scooped up his daughter. "Would you like to come along with us, Chloe?"

Chloe accepted the invitation, but Beth looked at Jack. He seemed very intent on his conversation and she didn't want to interrupt, so she nodded. Keeping one eye on Chloe, she asked Miss Polly where she had found such an unusual dress.

"My niece sent it to me from Hawaii," Miss Polly explained, fingering the colorful material. "She said people there consider muumuus formalwear. I didn't know if I'd ever get another chance to wear it, and I hope it was suitable for tonight."

"It's very festive," Beth gave her approval.

"And we certainly won't lose you if the power goes out. You positively glow in the dark," Miss Eugenia added.

Beth turned her attention to Miss Eugenia. "I love your outfit too."

The older woman smiled, smoothing the tweed material. "Lorraine at Large and Lovely was very helpful, and they had a real size 16, not ones made for anorexic women." Kate choked on a cracker, and Annabelle walked up just in time to pound her on the back. "I declare, Kate, chew your food before you swallow it," Miss Eugenia recommended.

"Don't you have to sit at the VIP table?" Kate recovered enough to ask Annabelle.

The retiree made a face. "I guess we'll have to go up there eventually, but I'll put it off as long as I can. Derrick found some friends from his garden club, so I told him to meet me over here when he gets through visiting."

Mark Iverson returned with the girls, and after everyone was settled at the table, Miss Polly leaned forward and addressed Miss Eugenia. "Did you get confirmation of your reservation from the Bethany Arms in the mail today?" Miss Eugenia nodded and Miss Polly politely included the others in their conversation. "Some of us have a standing reservation for the first week of June at a small inn called the Bethany Arms on the Gulf coast."

"The Arms is an old antebellum house that was converted into a hotel during the forties. It has lovely antiques and amenities like 100 percent Egyptian-cotton sheets, a private beach . . ." Miss Eugenia itemized the features.

"And if you're going to put on a bathing suit at our age, believe me, an empty beach is an important consideration," Annabelle contributed.

Miss Polly continued as if Annabelle hadn't spoken. "It has an ambience that you don't find in the modern hotels. Although I must say, it hasn't been the same since Justin died."

"Poor Justin. His widow is trying to keep up the tradition without him, but . . ." Miss Eugenia shrugged.

Miss Polly smiled. "Mary Grace is such a sweet thing and absolutely beautiful. Like a fashion model."

"I've always thought she favored Julia Roberts with fewer teeth," Annabelle said.

Miss Polly shook her head. "She reminds me more of that girl from the Pepsi commercials, Cindy Crawford."

Beth thought about Jack's remark about the famous model and couldn't resist a smile.

"Whoever she looks like, and regardless of how sweet Mary Grace is, she doesn't have Justin's touch for the hotel business," Miss Eugenia summed up the situation.

"Last year my regular room was closed for repairs," Miss Polly added with regret. "And the breakfast buffet was far below Justin's standards. In the old days Justin would invite local politicians and visiting celebrities for dinner, and we'd have such lively conversations. Now it's just the guests."

"And who would want to talk to us?" Annabelle contributed with a smile. "But we don't have to go to the Arms next summer. There are other hotels."

"It's a tradition!" Miss Eugenia objected. "And we can't desert poor Mary Grace!"

"Or give up 100 percent cotton sheets and a private beach!" Miss Polly concurred. "Besides, you can't get a room like that for the price anywhere else," Miss Polly added, then blushed.

"It's only September," Annabelle reminded everyone. "We have months to work that out—" She was interrupted by a gasp from her sister.

"Is that Mavine Hobbs who just walked in wearing a red velvet dress with a black satin jacket?" Miss Eugenia whispered.

"It most definitely is," Miss Polly nodded, her lips pursed with disapproval.

Kate looked up from the cocktail sausage she was cutting. "You don't like her?"

"I like Mavine fine, but anyone knows it is in poor taste to wear velvet before Thanksgiving or after Valentine's Day," Miss Eugenia explained.

"I thought it was Mardi Gras that you couldn't wear velvet after," Annabelle said.

"I personally wouldn't wear it after New Year's Eve, and Protestants don't even celebrate Mardi Gras, Annabelle," Miss Eugenia replied with disdain. "You've been watching that little TV nun's show again, haven't you?"

"My mother said it's inappropriate to wear satin *any* time of the year, with or without velvet," Miss Polly contributed. "Unless, of course, you are a member of a wedding party."

"Who's having a wedding party?" a deep voice asked, and Beth looked over her shoulder to see Lance Kilgore, the Dougherty County district attorney, standing behind her. Beth was dumbfounded, but Annabelle stepped in smoothly.

"Nobody. We were just discussing the proper attire for various occasions. And it was nice of you to come to my party," she added.

"I had to pay my respects to the best loan officer in Georgia!" Mr. Kilgore oozed charm. "Aren't you going to introduce me to your friends?" he asked. "Their support could help get me appointed to state senate, you know."

Annabelle started with the Iversons and worked her way around to Beth. "Now you might have trouble with Miss Middleton. I think she is firmly committed to your opponent."

"Well, it's very nice to finally meet you," Mr. Kilgore said with a smile. "I've heard a lot about you."

"I can't imagine who you have been talking to," Beth responded. "Not Mr. Gamble, certainly."

Lance Kilgore laughed. "No, Jack and I don't do a lot of chatting," he admitted as the band began to play.

"Well, that's our cue," Kate said as she and Mark stood in unison. "It's Emily's bedtime. Good night everyone." She waved around the table. "See you tomorrow," she whispered to Beth.

"I guess I'd better rescue Derrick from the flower ladies and make an appearance at the head table," Annabelle excused herself as well. Then Miss Eugenia and Miss Polly decided to refill their plates and invited Chloe to go with them. Beth was surprised when the child accepted and was too flustered by Lance Kilgore's presence to protest. After everyone left, Mr. Kilgore took the empty seat beside Beth and pulled his chair close to hers. "So, what do you think of Jack?"

"I think you've got your work cut out for you on the Ferris Burke case."

Before the district attorney could respond, Jack spoke. "What are you doing here, Kilgore?" he demanded.

Beth was mildly alarmed by the tone of Jack's voice, but the other man smiled. "I haven't had a chance to do much of anything yet, but I was about to ask Miss Middleton to dance."

"Too bad you couldn't get a date, but I'm not sharing mine," Jack growled, extending his hand to Beth. "Let's dance."

He looked pale, and Beth was concerned about his ribs. "Are you sure this won't hurt?" she whispered as they moved away from his rival.

"We'll just kind of stand still and sway," he said with a half-smile.

"Chloe's with Miss Eugenia Atkins. She's Annabelle Grainger's sister, and I'm sure . . ."

"I can sway and keep and eye on Chloe at the same time," he said with confidence. "Besides, Roy's here."

Beth glanced to her left and saw Roy standing guard by the front door, then shook her head. "He may be the only person I've ever met who is more paranoid than you are."

"I don't want to talk about Roy or paranoia right now. Just listen to the music." He pulled her firmly up against his wounded ribs. At first she was afraid he might be in pain or that the dance would exhaust him, but the music was sweet, and after a while she forgot all her concerns and savored the close contact.

As the last strains of the song ended, they stared into each other's eyes and she thought he was going to kiss her, but Malcolm Schneckenberger rushed up and Jack released her instead. Beth grabbed the back of a nearby chair as if she were the one with broken ribs and a dislocated shoulder while Jack glared at Mr. Fuller's assistant.

"I've been looking for you," Malcolm told Jack. "Good evening, Beth."

"What do you want?" Jack asked, his jaw clenched.

"Oscar said to give you this rundown on the prospective jurors." He held out an envelope, which Jack slipped into his pocket. "And to remind you about the Fullers' costume party next Saturday!"

Jack nodded curtly, then led Beth back over to the table where Chloe was sitting.

"What costume party?" Beth asked.

"Oscar is hosting a pre-Halloween party to raise money for the Georgia Republican Party. The governor will be there, along with every other major or minor political figure in the state. Pure torture."

Beth introduced him to the ladies at the table, and he nodded.

Miss Eugenia leaned forward. "I see you made the papers again."

"I thought the picture of you was very flattering," Miss Polly said, then turned pink from her neck to her forehead. "Did Ferris Burke really kill his own wife?"

Jack smiled. "Regardless of what you read in the papers, I really do have broken ribs," he told Miss Eugenia. "And Mrs. Burke was not killed by anyone. She died of a drug overdose, and her boyfriend died as a result of Ferris's attempts to defend himself and his family."

"Humph!" Miss Eugenia was doubtful.

"Ohhh," Miss Polly breathed.

Annabelle returned to their table, this time with Derrick in tow. "We've escaped from the bigwigs. Sit there by Beth and I'll get us some food." She gave Derrick a smile over her shoulder as she went to the banquet table.

Derrick shot Jack a nervous look, then settled into a seat. "Did you see yesterday's episode of *The Brave and Relentless*?" he asked Beth.

She shook her head.

"Then you missed the program of the year!" Miss Polly exclaimed from across the table.

"Maybe of the century!" Miss Eugenia endorsed the remark.

Beth was immediately intrigued. "What in the world happened?"

"Well," Miss Eugenia began. "Tori was depressed after Parker left her, and Elena suggested they spend a day at an expensive health spa. So Elena and Tori are headed for the spa. Meanwhile, Pierre is released from the hospital, and he invites his nurse to spend the weekend at his mountain cabin."

Beth stifled a yawn, hoping the episode of the century got more interesting fast.

"Parker finally decides that he loves Tori, and it doesn't really matter who fathered her baby," Miss Polly said and Beth looked at Jack. "So Parker went home, but Tori wasn't there."

"She was on her way to the spa with Elena," Beth said to show she was paying attention.

"Elena's the real-estate agent who's going blind?" Jack clarified.

"And there's nothing Dr. Richards can do," Chloe contributed. All conversation stopped and the entire table turned to stare at the little girl.

"I don't really let her watch soap operas," Beth defended herself.

"Well, I should certainly hope not," Miss Eugenia said with disapproval. "They are only for mature audiences."

"I just let her watch the parts about Elena's seeing-eye puppy."

Miss Eugenia considered this, then shrugged. "I suppose that was educational."

"So anyway," Derrick picked up the story, "while Parker is looking for Tori, Marissa goes to check on Cedric."

Annabelle nodded. "It was no big surprise that he was gone."

"Where did he go?" Beth asked with interest.

"To a bar!" Miss Eugenia announced with relish.

"He fell off the wagon," Derrick said. "Way off."

"But you could tell that he was so sorry that he had broken his promise to Marissa," Miss Polly said in Cedric's behalf.

Miss Eugenia gave her an impatient look. "When she saw that Cedric was gone, Marrisa got into her car and started driving toward town. Cedric finished off his last drink and staggered to his car."

"Pierre and the nurse left for their trip to the mountains," Derrick added.

"Oh my gosh!" Beth exclaimed.

"What?" Jack asked, confused.

"They're all driving on the same road and Cedric is drunk. There's going to be a wreck!" Beth pointed out.

Jack looked skeptical, but Derrick nodded. "The camera switched from car to car while Cedric swerved all over the road."

"So who died?" Beth begged.

"I'll bet it was Pierre and the nurse," Jack suggested with a wide grin.

Miss Eugenia shook her head. "I knew it wouldn't be Pierre! He won the Daytime Emmy for best new actor in a supporting role."

"Okay, only the nurse died and Pierre would at least be injured!" Jack was warming to the subject.

"Unlikely," Beth said after brief consideration. "Pierre just got out of the hospital. Putting him back in would be redundant."

"Not to mention boring," Derrick concurred.

"Then I'll put my money on the drunk's wife," Jack made another prediction.

"You'd lose it!" Miss Eugenia replied with a loud cackle.

Derrick shook his head morosely. "That would have been too good to be true. They have to keep dull characters like Marissa on soaps to build suspense."

"Speaking of suspense, who was it?!" Beth asked in exasperation.

Derrick took up the story again. "They all converged on the same intersection at the same moment. Tires squealed, metal crunched, the tension was awful. The camera went out of focus for a few seconds, then zeroed in on Marissa kneeling beside Cedric's blood-covered body. Then they showed Tori and Parker as they ran beside an ambulance gurney, begging Elena to hold on!" Derrick finished with a flourish.

Beth processed this information. "So Cedric is dead and Elena is hurt but alive?"

Derrick shrugged. "We'll have to wait until Monday's show to be sure."

"Don't worry, dear," Miss Polly consoled Beth with a gentle pat on the hand. "They won't let Elena die. Not after she's finally accepted her blindness!"

The discussion was interrupted by a shout of laughter, and all eyes turned to Jack. "The injuries she sustained in the wreck will restore the blind lady's sight," he predicted smugly.

Beth wanted to deny even the possibility, but she had to admit that it did have a nice ring to it, and Miss Eugenia was nodding. "Several years ago Tori's biological mother was confined to a wheelchair. After a fall down an elevator shaft, she was able to walk again."

Jack leaned back with a big smile. "I rest my case."

Beth grimaced as two teenage girls rushed up to the table. Jack introduced them as student volunteers for the Georgia Republican Party. They begged him to dance with them, and he expressed deep regret but used his injuries as an excuse.

"You danced with her." One girl waved in Beth's direction.

"And it almost killed me!" He glanced over at Beth and gave her a covert wink. "You wouldn't want to make my injuries worse, would you?" The first girl stepped back, but the other was so insistent that he finally had to pull up his shirt and show her the bruises. The old ladies at the table were also impressed by the multicolored, well-muscled chest, and Beth hid a smile behind her hand as the young women left in disappointment.

A few minutes later Roy joined them, and Jack told Chloe that it was time to go. The child frowned, but Roy walked over and lifted her gently. "If we don't get you home soon you might turn into a pumpkin," he warned.

Chloe regarded him with wide eyes. "Why would I do that?"

Roy shrugged. "Thought that's what happened to beautiful women after midnight."

They had only been driving for a few minutes before Chloe fell sound asleep. The men spoke quietly in the front seat, and Beth enjoyed the warm weight of Chloe against her arm. Then she felt Jack watching her in the rearview mirror. "So, did you have fun tonight?" he asked.

"It was very nice," she responded. "What do you think about Annabelle and Derrick? I mean, was coming to the party together a real date?"

"It looked pretty real to me," he replied, then turned to Roy. "How did it look to you?"

"Didn't give it a thought, to be honest," the driver admitted.

"He's several years younger than she is," Beth pointed out.

Jack shrugged. "Once you reach a certain age, a few years doesn't matter."

"And why is Mr. Fuller helping you investigate jurors? It doesn't seem fair."

"I'm sure he's giving Kilgore pointers too, not that it really matters. I'd never trust anyone else's research, especially in a murder trial."

At home Roy carried the sleeping child to her bed, then said good night. Jack followed Beth to Chloe's room and watched her remove the child's beautiful French gown. Once the covers were tucked around Chloe, Beth pressed a quick kiss on the little forehead. Then she hung the dress in the closet and met Jack by the door.

"Who is going to tuck me into bed?" he asked.

"Try Roy or Hipolita. You hired me to take care of Chloe."

He smiled and she felt warm all over. Then he put his hands on her shoulders and drew her near. "I'm your date. You should be kissing me," he whispered softly as his lips lowered toward hers.

The kiss was soft and gentle, and afterward her eyes fluttered open. He studied her for a few seconds, then their lips met again. Finally she broke away and stepped back, leaning against the door frame for support.

"I don't understand what just happened," she told him breathlessly.

He smiled, but his expression lacked some of its usual cockiness. "We just shared a couple of incredible kisses." She continued to stare in confusion, but Jack persisted. "Surely the boy you almost married kissed you."

"Not like that!" Her protest burst out. "This," she waved between them, "is inappropriate. I'll have to leave here. Immediately." Just saying the words made her ill.

His jaw clenched. "You can't leave Chloe." It was a statement of fact, and Beth shrugged in despair. He ran his fingers through his hair. "Well, we can't settle it tonight. Go to bed for now, and we'll figure out something tomorrow."

She opened her mouth to speak, but the memory of their kiss was too fresh. So she nodded and walked to her room. She hung her new dress in the closet, then scrubbed the makeup off her face and pulled the pins from her hair. As she climbed into bed her eyes were drawn to the snapshot of David wearing his soccer uniform and smiling at her with perfect faith and confidence. She started to cry, and the weeping continued until she fell into a fitful sleep.

Beth was awakened a few hours later by the sound of someone screaming. Through the fog of sleep, she wondered what kind of agony could cause such an awful noise. Then the door to her room burst open and Jack ran in. She saw Hipolita standing behind him and realized the anguished scream was coming from her own mouth.

"I'll handle this," he said to the housekeeper as he reached a hand toward Beth. She shrank against the headboard, so he sat on a chair until she got her sobs under control. "Was it a bad dream?" he asked when she was calm.

Beth nodded in confusion. "It's a recurring nightmare. I haven't had one since I came here. Roy said it's because this is a safe place."

He smiled. "I'm glad you and Roy feel safe here. Can you tell me about the dream?"

"I don't want to," she answered, pulling herself up and resting her forehead on her knees.

"But I think you need to," he encouraged.

Beth hesitated for a few seconds then began. "It's my wedding day. I wake up and see my dress hanging on the closet door. My mother comes in to help me get ready, and I hear thunder. My mother says it's not raining, but the thunder keeps getting louder. Then I realize that the noise I hear is someone knocking. The door opens, and my father is there with tears on his face. I ask for David, but he shakes his head and I start to scream."

"Will you tell me about David?"

"You know all about me. About David too, I'm sure," Beth protested.

"I know the facts. I want you to tell me how you feel," he said.

Beth raised her head and looked at him. "You stay over there and don't touch me," she stipulated. He accepted her terms with a nod, and Beth closed her eyes and began to speak.

"David moved from California during our junior year of high school. He sat behind me in zoology class, and we got to be friends.

He spent a lot of time at my house, and after a few months he started asking questions about the Church. Finally my father suggested that he read the Book of Mormon." Beth looked up. "He did. Then he asked my dad to baptize him."

She put her head back down. "David's parents wouldn't let him join the Church until he turned eighteen and wouldn't give permission for him to serve a mission, so he had to wait until he was twenty-one. I finished graduate school while he was in Peru, then took a job with Bob Wells and the Department of Human Resources."

"That was quite a commute from Eureka," Jack interrupted her to comment.

"At that time my parents lived in Tifton. They sold their house about a year ago and bought some property on Lake Eureka. By then I already had my apartment in Albany."

He nodded that he understood, and she continued. "When David got home, he asked me to marry him. His parents disapproved until they found out the wedding would be in the temple. Then they *really* disapproved, and they hired an anti-Mormon specialist. So David packed his clothes and came to our house. My dad called the bishop, and we all talked. Our wedding was scheduled for June, but the bishop suggested that under the circumstances we go ahead and get married, then live with my parents for a few months until we could find a place of our own." Beth took a painful breath.

"David wanted to follow the bishop's advice. But," she hated to say the words and burrowed further into her knees. "I had waited so long for my wedding day, and I didn't want to give it up. And I didn't want to live with my parents after we were married. So David moved in with a family in our ward. We found a cute little apartment in Albany and spent hours cleaning and painting." Her voice quivered, but she forced herself to go on.

"Everything was busy for those few weeks. My mother worked frantically on dresses for my sisters and planned the reception. David started school, and my job at DHR was demanding. Finally we drove to Atlanta for the wedding. David's parents wouldn't come since they couldn't go inside the temple. My dad offered to let David ride with us to the temple, but he said it was bad luck for him to see me before the wedding." Another sob rose in her throat, but she controlled it.

"He was hit head-on by a truck driver who had fallen asleep. His parents' address was still on his driver's license, so the police contacted them. One of the ambulance drivers noticed the tuxedo and my bridal bouquet in the backseat. He searched through the wreckage until he found some extra copies of our wedding announcement and called the temple.

"I had no legal rights since we weren't married yet, so David's parents took his body back to California and buried him there. At that point, I thought I was going crazy. I cried all the time, awful, body-shaking sobs. I couldn't remember what day it was. I'd open my closet and stare at my clothes, but couldn't pick out anything to wear. My parents cancelled the lease on our apartment and put all the stuff in storage." She looked up again and he nodded.

"They thought I would get better with time, but I didn't. I couldn't face a future without David and rarely left my room. I didn't sleep or eat. I don't know what would have happened if my Aunt Jenna hadn't convinced me to start running." She stopped for a few deep breaths. "At one point I was running ten to fifteen miles a day. I'd get up every morning and think about running—where I would run and how far. The throbbing muscles helped numb the real pain.

"My parents didn't like my compulsive running. They wanted me to go back to work, to move on with my life. They encouraged and hovered until I knew I couldn't live at home anymore. So I took the money David and I had saved, found a cheap, furnished apartment in downtown Albany, bought a used car, and got a job at the library. I took life one day at a time, and I survived."

Jack waited until he was sure she was finished, then nodded. "I agree with every aspect of your survival plan except your choice of cars," he teased, forcing her to smile. "What David's parents did was wrong, cruel," he said. "They should have included you in his funeral, but their son was dead. I'm trying to imagine how I would feel if something happened to Chloe." Beth repressed a shudder as he continued. "But I probably wouldn't be considerate of other people's feelings."

"So what are you saying?" Beth asked.

"It's been two years. It's time to forgive them and accept David's death."

"I accept his death," Beth said with impatience.

"Then move on."

She made no comment, and finally he stood. "If you're still afraid, I can bring Chloe down to sleep with you."

Beth shook her head, looking up into his tired, beautiful eyes. "I'm okay. Thanks."

She waited until dawn, then took a shower and some ibuprofen. She covered the dark circles under her eyes with makeup and dressed for church. Hipolita was sipping coffee at the table and glanced up when Beth came in. The housekeeper didn't mention Beth's nightmare or her haggard appearance, but when Chloe joined them for breakfast, she said Beth looked sick.

"I'm not sick, Chloe. Hurry and eat your cereal. Roy will be here soon."

Chloe was too excited to eat and played with her Cheerios until Hipolita finally poured the soggy mess down the garbage disposal. Roy still hadn't come to get them by 8:35, and Beth was just starting to get worried when Jack walked into the room.

Her heart immediately started pounding, and she felt heat rise in her cheeks. He gave her a quick smile, then asked Chloe if she was ready to go. At this point Beth regained her senses enough to notice that he was dressed in a suit. "Go where?" she asked.

"To church," he returned.

"You don't go to church," she reminded him.

"I thought I might go today."

"He wants to hear how good I can say my part," Chloe explained, and Beth nodded. She should have realized that he would want to see his daughter perform.

Beth fidgeted during the entire drive to Albany and resisted Jack's efforts to draw her into conversation. They parked in Roy's regular spot under the shade tree and sat in their seats behind the Iversons. When Mark saw that Chloe's father had accompanied them, he reached back to shake Jack's hand. Emily leaned over the bench and extended a pink, polka-dot pony. Jack examined the toy, then returned it. Emily gave him a gap-toothed grin, then turned and threw it. They all watched the toy sail through the air until it hit the floor in front of the podium just as the bishop stood to open the meeting.

"She's got a pretty good arm," Jack whispered to Mark, and the other man smiled at his mischievous daughter. Then Jack settled back against the bench, looking perfectly comfortable. He bowed his head during the prayer, sang along during the songs, but refrained from partaking of the sacrament. Beth, on the other hand, was very ill at ease. She had trouble concentrating on anything except him, noticing every breath he took and each time he changed positions.

Finally the Primary presentation began, and Beth was able to drag her attention away from him. When it was Chloe's turn, she approached the podium with confidence. "We believe in God the Eternal Father and in His son, Jesus Christ and in the Holy Ghost." Her part successfully delivered, Chloe beamed at the congregation, and Beth thought her heart would burst. Jack took her hand in his, but she was too exhilarated to notice, much less object.

As soon as sacrament meeting ended, Chloe hurried down from the stand to accept her well-earned praise. Mark Iverson commended her and Emily gave her a congratulatory hug. When Kate came down from the organ, she was complimentary as well. "I personally thought you were the very best," she whispered as she rescued Chloe from the death grip Emily had around her neck. "And today in Primary we won't have to practice for the program during sharing time, so Sister Harless has a game for us to play!"

Pleased, Chloe turned toward the chapel doors. Beth started to follow, then remembered about Jack. She couldn't very well leave him sitting in the chapel by himself, and the thought of him perched on one of the minichairs in the Primary room was too ridiculous. With a defeated sigh, she sat back down.

"I guess I'll stay here with Mr. Gamble," she said, and Jack raised an eyebrow.

Kate gave her an encouraging smile. "Mark's a pretty good teacher. He practices his lessons on me every week, and I don't think this one will put you to sleep."

Beth was embarrassed. "Oh, I'm not worried about that. It's just that I like being in Primary with Chloe and Emily . . ."

"I could go out and wait in the car," Jack suggested.

"That won't be necessary."

The lesson may have been good, but Beth was too busy trying to ignore Jack to listen. Mark called on her once and she stared back, completely at a loss for words. Jack gave her the correct answer, which she delivered nervously. The lesson moved on, and she turned to her uninvited guest.

"How did you know that, Mr. Gamble?" she whispered.

"I went to church all my life. I didn't lose interest until college."

"You got too smart for the Lord?" Beth asked.

"No, just too busy," he replied with a crooked smile. "And since we've kissed, maybe you could call me Jack."

Beth felt cold and then hot as she glanced around to make sure no one had heard him. "Last night was an isolated incident. It will never happen again and does not affect our relationship at all, *Mr. Gamble*," she assured him.

He reached over and put his arm along the back of the bench behind her and scooted close. Warmth enveloped her, and her lips parted involuntarily. "I am very much looking forward to another 'isolated incident' and our relationship *has* changed, whether you like it or not, Beth."

She tore her eyes away from his and looked back at Mark just as he asked Jack to read a verse in Galatians. Since Jack didn't have scriptures, he borrowed hers. Then he spent the rest of the class trying to decipher comments she had written in the margins as a seminary student and laughing at her adolescent insights.

After Sunday School ended Beth was wondering what to do with Jack when the bishop stepped up. "It's good to have you with us today, Brother Gamble." Bishop Sterling punctuated his words with a firm handshake.

Jack smiled. "I enjoyed the Primary program, and everyone has made me feel so . . . welcome." He looked at Beth.

The bishop glanced at Beth as well, and she turned away from the speculation in his eyes. "Follow me and I'll show you the way to Priesthood meeting," the bishop offered, and Beth watched them leave with a mixture of relief and regret. Then she went to the Relief Society room and slipped into a chair beside Kate as Sister Gibbons stood to greet everyone. After the opening song the Relief Society president said she had a special announcement to make.

"The bishop has asked me to remind you all that discussing soap operas is inappropriate during Relief Society. So please remember to keep Elena and her problems out of any comments you make during the lesson."

Beth glanced at Kate. "She acts like Elena is a real person."

Kate shrugged. "Everyone takes that show pretty seriously. Do you watch it?"

"Do you?" Beth asked and Kate laughed.

"I don't have to. Miss Eugenia keeps me up-to-date."

"Shhhh," someone behind them insisted as Sister Gibbons introduced the lesson.

When Relief Society ended, Beth said good-bye to Kate, then picked up Chloe at her CTR classroom. They met Jack in the foyer, then they all walked out to the Jeep together. At Aristotle's, Jack parked in back, right next to the Expedition.

"Roy's here," Beth said unnecessarily.

"I've never known him to miss a free meal," Jack replied as he opened the door for Beth and helped her out. He led them into the restaurant without releasing Beth's hand.

Roy stood when they walked into the private dining room, and then his eyes dropped to their clasped hands. Beth pulled away and took a seat beside Chloe.

"So, did you get a dispensation from your prophet to eat out on Sunday?" Roy asked, taking a breadstick from the basket.

"That hasn't been blessed," Beth said. "And you get dispensations from the pope."

Roy swallowed quickly. "The pope said you could eat at Aristotle's on Sunday?"

"Of course not," Beth replied. "It was the Lord who gave the commandment to keep the Sabbath day holy, and it would be hard to go over His head. And besides, getting permission from anyone would have taken the fun out of it for Mr. Gamble."

"Jack," Chloe's father corrected.

Roy looked back and forth at them, then addressed Beth. "Why would it take the fun out of lunch for," he glanced at his employer, "Jack, if you got permission?"

"Because the only reason he wants me to come is to make me compromise my religious beliefs," she replied.

Roy's eyebrows shot up. "That true, Boss?"

Jack gave them both a lazy grin. "Naw, I just wanted some female companionship, and you know how hard it is for me to get a date."

Both men thought this was extremely funny, but when their laughter died down, Roy spoke with surprising seriousness. "My mama always took me to church when I was little."

"And look how you turned out," Jack said as Mr. Aristotle came in. Chloe ordered her regular, Roy selected two entrees with trimmings, and Jack ordered a Greek-style steak. Beth asked for a salad, but Jack shook his head. "Bring her a steak too." After the restaurant owner left Beth was going to object, but Roy spoke to Chloe first.

"So, how was your recitation?" She gave him a condensed version of the Primary program, including her article of faith and one rousing verse of "Follow the Prophet." The food arrived and Chloe blessed it. Beth was so proud of Chloe's progress that she almost forgot to feel guilty about breaking the Sabbath.

When they got home Hipolita was in the kitchen making cookies, and Chloe begged to help. Jack gave his permission, then turned to Beth. "My ribs are killing me. I'm going to go and lie down, but we need to discuss a couple of things. Will you come up for a while?"

She nodded. "I'll be there soon." She didn't wait for his response, just walked down the hall to her room. Inside she closed the door and leaned against it. She allowed herself a few moments to regain her equilibrium, then changed out of her Sunday clothes and climbed the stairs to face him.

Jack was stretched out on the recliner in the family room with his eyes closed. She approached quietly, hoping he was asleep, but as she stopped beside him his hand reached out and caught hers. "Sit right here on the arm of my chair."

She shook her head. "There are plenty of other seats."

"But you'll be so far away," he murmured. Thinking that if she resisted she might wake him completely and destroy any hope of a quick escape, she perched stiffly beside him. "Thanks for missing Primary to sit by me today," he surprised her by saying. "And I'm sorry that I made you eat at Aristotle's. Next Sunday we'll eat it at home." This statement shocked her speechless. "Now, on to a more serious subject. What are we going to do about our feelings for each other?" He pulled her fingers against his lips.

"Mr. Gamble," she began as warmth spread through her hand and up her arm.

"Jack," he insisted.

"Jack," she forced herself to say the word. "We don't have to deal with our feelings. We'll just ignore them."

"Are you sure we can?" he asked, and she nodded without much confidence.

"We won't touch each other." She tried to pull her hand away, but he held tight.

"You think that if we avoid physical contact, this heart-pounding, overwhelming feeling will be eliminated?"

With her heart pounding, Beth nodded.

"But just thinking about you takes my breath away. What are we going to do about that?"

"I don't know," Beth admitted, feeling a little breathless herself.

"We could just get married," he said, and Beth recoiled.

"I promised David forever."

"You didn't actually marry him," Jack pointed out. "And an LDS woman living outside the state of Utah has an average life expectancy of eighty-nine years. That's a long time to spend alone, and David doesn't need you anymore, Beth. We do."

She stood and moved toward the door. "I'm sorry, Jack," she said as tears filled her eyes, "But I can't have this conversation."

He ran his fingers through his hair. "At least say you won't leave us."

"I can't stay here as an observer for the court since my opinion is no longer impartial."

"Just keep turning in your reports to the judge until this trial is over. Then we'll settle things with my parents." He didn't sound very optimistic as Chloe burst in and announced that warm cookies and milk were available in the kitchen. "We're on our way," Jack told her.

"Better hurry before I eat them all!" Chloe cried over her shoulder.

Beth's eyes followed the child longingly, and she looked up to see Jack watching her. "So, you'll stay?"

"For a while," she agreed.

"Let's go eat cookies." He stood and walked slowly to the door. "That statistic about the life expectancy of LDS women?" he asked, and she nodded. "I made it up."

"Why would you do that?"

"To prove my point," he replied. "And the next time I ask you to marry me, I won't be half kidding." She glanced up sharply, and he gave her an easy smile. Then he turned and led the way to the kitchen.

CHAPTER 11

Jack was already gone when Beth and Chloe met in the kitchen for breakfast on Monday morning. "Do you think he's up to a day in court?" Beth asked Roy as she watched him desecrate his scrambled eggs with hot sauce, pickle relish, and strawberry jam.

"Boss'll be fine. How about you?"

"Me?" Beth looked up and saw the concern in his eyes. "I don't know," she admitted honestly.

When they got back from taking Chloe to school, Beth changed cars and drove to the library, where Miss Eugenia gave her a tour of the updated Genealogical Department. There were three computers set up along one wall and a nice rug in the middle of the room. "George Ann donated it so she can tell people how generous she is," Miss Eugenia explained.

Beth picked a far corner to work in, hoping to discourage conversation with Miss Eugenia, but her plan failed. "So, did you have fun at the party Saturday night?"

"I . . . yes . . . it was nice," Beth stammered.

Miss Eugenia's eyes narrowed. "Jack Gamble couldn't keep his eyes off you."

Beth dropped a heavy book on her toe and then took several deep breaths as the pain pulsated up her leg. "Mr. Gamble and I are just friends," she managed finally.

"He's in love with you." Miss Eugenia pressed closer. "I'd say you're in love with him too, and I can't understand why you keep pretending otherwise. I declare, it seems like a perfect solution to everybody's problems. If he marries a respectable girl, Chloe will have a mother, his parents won't have a case against him, and you won't be alone anymore."

"I can't marry Jack. I can't marry anyone!"

"Why not?" Miss Eugenia demanded.

"I told you about David, the boy who died?" Miss Eugenia nodded. "In our church we believe in eternal marriage, and I plan to be sealed to David after I die."

Miss Eugenia frowned. "I can understand you feeling that way right after his death, but you must have realized by now that living your whole life alone is not reasonable."

"If you really love someone, you don't just forget him after a couple of years," Beth claimed, causing Miss Eugenia's eyes to narrow.

"Charles and I were together for fifty wonderful years, but I'd marry again if the right person came along. Are you saying that means I'm not loyal to Charles?"

"No, of course not."

"Charles would want me to be happy, and if this boy of yours really loved you, he'd want you to get married and have a family."

Beth turned away and stared at the cinder-block wall. "I'm so confused."

Miss Eugenia studied her, then took a step closer. "Nephi said if you read the scriptures they will tell you 'all things that you should do'," the older woman whispered.

Beth turned around in surprise. "You've read the Book of Mormon?"

"Several times. It's quite entertaining," Miss Eugenia's tone became more casual. "And it's got some good sayings in it, like that one." At this point, the door opened and Miss Eugenia walked over to greet a rare customer. Beth tried to concentrate on the old books, but Miss Eugenia's words kept replaying themselves in her mind. Finally the patron left with a dusty copy of *Quilting for Beginners* and Miss Eugenia picked up the subject again. "Maybe we could get a message to the other boy."

Beth couldn't control a burst of laughter. "You mean like have a séance?"

Miss Eugenia shook her head. "No, I don't believe in that sort of thing. But there are plenty of old folks in this town. I could spread the word that if anybody passes over they need to find David and ask if he minds about you and Jack Gamble."

"Oh, please don't do that!" Beth begged. "I'll work things out in my own way."

"Well, don't take too long. That little girl of his needs a mother, and a man like Mr. Gamble won't wait around forever," Miss Eugenia continued as they stepped out into the hall. "Are you coming to Ellen's baby shower on Wednesday afternoon?"

Beth nodded. "I'm assigned to bring peanuts."

"Polly is notoriously disorganized. Try to get there early in case she needs your help," Miss Eugenia instructed in parting.

Beth hurried back to the Gambles' house and turned on her soap, anxious to find out Elena's fate. The former real-estate agent was lying comatose in a hospital bed, her head swathed in bandages, while Marissa planned a tasteful funeral for Cedric. Beth left for Albany with Roy at 1:30, and when she got back, Hipolita told her that Mr. Jack wanted to see her immediately.

"He's home?" Beth asked, moving toward the stairs.

The housekeeper nodded. "I give Chloe her snack."

Jack was sitting in the recliner in the family room, looking pale. "I knew it was too soon for you to go back to work!" Beth put a hand on his forehead, forgetting her vow not to touch him. "Do you want me to call the doctor?"

Instead of answering, he held out a letter and she glanced over the contents. It was from Mr. Fuller, asking that Jack get another doctor to examine him and clear up any doubts about his medical condition. "He believes Lance Kilgore?" Beth asked in astonishment. "He thinks you have been using your injuries to delay the trial?"

"You read the letter," he replied.

"There has been some kind of a mistake."

Before he could respond, Hipolita spoke from the door. "Malcolm here."

"I'll go talk to him," Beth offered, but Jack reached out and grabbed her hand.

"Send him up," he told Hipolita.

Malcolm rushed in a few seconds later. "I'm sorry to bother you," he said to them both. "I know this has been a big day." He saw the letter in Beth's hand, and his face turned red. "I tried to convince

Oscar that wasn't necessary, but Lance has been after him and he doesn't want to look biased."

"We realize that you aren't responsible, Malcolm," Beth stepped into the conversation. "But this letter is insulting. Jack has already seen two doctors and signed a release making his hospital records public. That should be enough."

"Of course," Malcolm agreed. "And you'd be within your rights to refuse, but the best way to settle the issue is to go see the other doctor." There was an awkward silence, then he waved a card. "The reason for my visit is to bring you this official invitation to the party on Saturday night. We added Beth's name." He smiled in her direction.

"Why would Oscar want me to come to his party when he thinks I'm a liar?" Jack asked.

"Come on, Jack! Oscar was just trying to protect the Georgia Republican Party. He knows you're telling the truth." Jack was staring stubbornly ahead, and Malcolm turned to Beth. "You have to convince him to come. A lot of important people will be there."

Beth nodded, then led Malcolm out. "I can't make any promises, but I'll do what I can."

"It could mean the difference between winning and losing the state senate seat," Malcolm said earnestly, then hurried down the stairs.

"So, what were you and Malcolm whispering about?" Jack asked when she returned.

"I told him I'd try to convince you to go to the party, since he thinks it's so important."

Jack leaned his head back against the chair. "The only way I'll even consider it is if you agree to come with me. So my political future is in your hands," he said with a wan smile.

Beth cleared her throat. "I'll go."

"It's a costume party, you know. We'll have to think of something to wear."

"We could go as Jane Eyre and Mr. Rochester," Beth proposed.

"No one would recognize us." He either missed the irony of her suggestion or ignored it. "Think of a famous liar . . ."

"Jack," she began, but he held up his hand to stop her. "What?" she asked in confusion.

"Say my name again."

"Oh, Jack." She shook her head in despair, and he smiled.

"Don't worry about the costumes. I'll come up with something."

The next morning after she got home from taking Chloe to school, Beth drove to Wal-Mart to buy her peanuts and a gift for Ellen Northcutt's baby shower. She met Myrtle by the frozen foods, and the big woman gave her a hug.

"Tell me about Annabelle's party!" Myrtle commanded, and Beth recounted what she could remember, including the woman who wore velvet and satin in September. Myrtle shook her orange head. "Some people have no taste. So, how is life in the fast lane?"

"Terrifying," Beth admitted. "And on Saturday we have to go to a costume party to raise money for the Georgia Republican Party."

"You got costumes?" the hairdresser asked thoughtfully.

Beth shook her head. "Jack said he'd take care of that, but I don't know how. He's in court all day."

"My sister Melba was in a community production of *The Wizard of Oz* a couple of years ago, and she bought a beautiful dress for her role as Glinda, the Good Witch of the North. She spent more than half of the entire budget on that gown, and it's a wonder her fellow cast members didn't kill her!"

Beth smiled in appreciation. "That must be some dress."

"And just like new. The old Methodist preacher said the play was full of sorcery and magic. He told his congregation only sinners would attend, and nobody was brave enough to go. It closed after the second night, so the costumes were barely used at all."

"Do you think your sister would mind if I wore her dress?"

"She wouldn't care a bit, and there might be something for Mr. Gamble and his daughter too. Come by the shop when you're done here, and I'll give you the whole box." Myrtle leaned into the cooler of popsicles and Beth went to find the peanuts.

Thirty minutes later she was walking into Melba's. Myrtle waved her in and led the way to the back of the old house. "Here they are." She pointed at a large cardboard box. "I'll help you lug it to your car." Myrtle hefted one side of the big box. Beth took the opposite position and they dragged it out to the Lexus.

"I can't thank you enough," Beth said breathlessly as she pulled her keys from her purse.

Myrtle laughed. "Don't thank me yet. That stuff may be full of moths for all I know!"

Beth got back to the Gambles just in time to ride with Roy into Albany to pick up Chloe. When the little girl climbed into the car, Beth told her there was a surprise waiting at home. Chloe guessed everything from a family of rabbits to Santa Claus before they parked by the garage. "Where is it?" she demanded as she jumped from the car. "Where is the surprise?"

"Roy will bring it inside," Beth replied.

When Roy came through the door with the huge box, Chloe screamed and Hipolita left her dinner preparations to come over and watch. Beth opened the flaps and lifted out a pair of ruby red slippers. "I think these will fit Chloe."

"I can wear these?" Chloe accepted the little shoes with reverence.

"For Halloween and to the costume party at Mr. Fuller's on Saturday," Beth told her, then reached in and extracted a blue gingham dress and a picnic basket.

"Only thing missing is Toto!" Roy declared.

"They don't look so clean," Hipolita remarked, fingering the little dress.

"Once we pick out the costumes we want, we'll have them dry cleaned," Beth said.

"The shoes fit and I want to try on my dress," Chloe cried, and Beth looked around to see that the child had stripped down to her underwear.

Beth pulled the dress over Chloe's head and squeezed the toes of the red shoes. "They are a little big, but they'll do." Beth buttoned the dress, then Chloe modeled the outfit for them. "You're perfect," she pronounced.

"I wish my daddy was here to fix my hair just like Dorothy."

"He'll be home to help you get ready on Saturday. Right now you need to find a stuffed animal to be Toto." Beth handed the picnic basket to Chloe.

"I'll be back," the little girl promised, running toward the stairs.

As she disappeared, the door opened and Jack walked in. "Home early again," Roy commented with a glance over at Beth.

Beth felt her face turn warm as Jack smiled at her, then took a seat at the table. "We settled on five more jurors today, so the judge let us leave. We'll finish the jury selection tomorrow and then start opening statements on Friday."

"So soon?" Beth gasped, and Jack grimaced.

"He says we've wasted enough time already."

"And still no sign of Amber Harper?" Beth asked.

"Not one." Jack confirmed as Chloe ran back in with a stuffed Dalmatian puppy hanging out of her picnic basket.

"Look Daddy!" she cried. "Beth got us costumes for the party. I'm going to be Dorothy from *The Wizard of Oz*!"

Beth's embarrassment increased. "Actually, they are community theatre costumes that Myrtle gave to me. We don't have to wear them if you've already found something else."

"I haven't even looked, and I appreciate the help." He waved at the box. "So, if we go with the Oz theme, what will you wear?"

"Myrtle's sister was Glinda, the Good Witch, and her costume is supposed to be in here somewhere," Beth told him. When she lifted the lid, she exposed a mountain of soft peach gauze. "Isn't this gorgeous?" Beth cried as she held the wrinkled fabric against her.

"Gorgeous," Jack concurred, and Beth knew her face was as pink as the dress. "Chloe is Dorothy and you are Glinda, but what will I be?"

"You could be the Scarecrow, Daddy," Chloe suggested lifting a straw hat from the box.

"The Scarecrow is stupid!" Jack exclaimed.

"He's not stupid! He just can't find his brain," Chloe corrected him, settling the straw hat on Roy's head.

"Well, I don't want to be anyone without a brain." Her father's tone was final.

"Roy can be the Scarecrow and you can be the Lion." Chloe showed him a pile of fur.

Jack eyed the lion costume with suspicion. "The Lion is a coward and he has a tail! Besides, that thing looks like it has fleas."

"Guess you could be the Wizard, since he's kind of the boss," Roy contributed.

"He's old and fat and not too smart either," Jack rejected this idea as well. "Why can't I be someone with a little dignity?"

"The only one left is the Tin Man," Chloe told him.

"Isn't he the one without a heart?" her father asked.

"Sounds perfect to me." Roy's smile broadened.

"I'll just give all the costumes back to Myrtle and we can think of something else," Beth offered, causing Chloe's jaw to clench with belligerence.

"I want to be Dorothy!"

"I guess I can be a heartless Tin Man," Jack relented.

"Thank you, Daddy!" Chloe cried, victorious. "And you even get to wear a pointy hat and carry a real oil can." Chloe pulled these items out of the box and Jack closed his eyes briefly.

Roberta walked in and asked what was going on. "Picking out costumes for Saturday, and you got here just in time," Roy told her. "There's still a Wicked Witch costume available."

Roberta made a face at him. "Thanks, but I wouldn't go to that party with those self-serving, hypocritical blowhards for a million dollars." Roberta turned to her boss. "Ready to go over your notes for tomorrow?"

Jack stood with a weary sigh. "I'll meet you in my office in just a minute."

Roberta went upstairs, and Hipolita told Roy to bring the box of costumes to the laundry room. "I call dry cleaners," she told Beth.

Chloe followed them down the hall and once they were alone, Beth looked at Jack. "Chloe will get over it if she can't be Dorothy."

He smiled. "I'd wear worse than tinfoil to make her happy and see you in that pink dress."

Beth fingered the fabric. "Myrtle said her sister spent more than half of the whole costume budget on it."

He touched her cheek. "Now I'm actually looking forward to Saturday."

* * *

On Wednesday during the Genealogical Society meeting, Derrick and Annabelle worked together, showing the ladies how to use the donated computers. As Beth watched Annabelle and Derrick confer on various questions, she wondered if something more than friendship was developing there. Kate and Emily arrived about fifteen minutes late and stopped to speak to Beth.

"I couldn't get Emily dressed this morning," Kate told her. "She's figured out how to take her clothes off, so she was working against me."

Beth smiled as Miss Eugenia charged in. "I thought I heard your voice. Good morning, my little angel." She plucked the baby out of Kate's arms.

"If you entertain Emily, you'll miss your meeting." Kate looked into the small room where all the old ladies were clustered around computer terminals.

"I never cared for computers," Miss Eugenia scoffed. "You'll never convince me that they don't send off dangerous radiation."

"She won't buy a microwave either, but she'll use mine," Kate said to Beth, who remembered Annabelle's remarks about Miss Eugenia's fear of cell phones.

"You can't be too careful," Miss Eugenia defended herself, then smiled down at Emily. "Let's go talk to all the overworked, underpaid city employees," she cooed.

Kate waited until Miss Eugenia went out the door, then whispered to Beth. "We need to pick a day to go visiting teaching again."

"Any Tuesday or Thursday is good for me," Beth replied.

"I don't guess you have a copy of the latest *Ensign*?" Kate asked, and Beth shook her head. "Miss Eugenia takes mine out of the mailbox every month. I offered to buy her a subscription, but she refused, saying she just likes the pictures."

"I never realized there were that many pictures in the *Ensign*," Beth said.

"The pictures are just an excuse. She reads it from cover to cover but she doesn't want to own a copy. Just like she'll go with me to any meeting during the week, but not on Sunday. It's as if the Sunday services are more real."

"Why does she need an excuse to read the *Ensign* or go with you on Sunday?"

"She doesn't want to admit that she's seriously interested in the Church. And I can understand why it's so hard for her. She's done things a particular way for seventy-four years, and besides, she doesn't want to offend any of her old friends."

"Miss Eugenia?" Beth asked, and Kate smiled.

"And religion is such a part of the social infrastructure here. They assign bridal teas and baby showers and even funeral food based on whether you are Methodist or Baptist."

Beth considered this. "They can add a category for the Mormons."

"Yes they can," Kate agreed. "But it's a big step, and if you want to know the truth, it will probably be her romance with our home teacher, Elmer Stoops, that settles the issue."

"Why are you talking about Elmer?" Miss Eugenia demanded, walking up beside them. "I said he was our home teacher," Kate provided an edited version of her comment. "And now we are headed to the grocery store. We'll see you this afternoon." Kate retrieved the baby and left.

Except for a fight between two ladies who wanted to look at a disk of the 1890 Georgia Census at the same time, the Genealogical Society meeting went well. Afterward, Derrick and Annabelle announced that they were going to lunch at Haggerty Station and invited Beth and Miss Eugenia to come.

"We don't have time for such foolishness," Miss Eugenia declined for both of them. "We have a social obligation this afternoon."

"I'm going to the baby shower too," Annabelle defended herself. "I just thought I could eat a salad first."

"Humph!" Miss Eugenia eyed Derrick with suspicion. After the happy couple left, Miss Eugenia turned to Beth. "I'm doing the punch for the shower and it takes forever to make, so I thought we'd close a little early. I could use some help if you're not too busy . . ."

Beth nodded and followed Miss Eugenia to her house. Then Beth spent the next two hours walking back and forth between Miss Polly's house and Miss Eugenia's carrying pineapple juice, ginger ale, and various other punch ingredients. By the time the shower actually started, she was sweaty and exhausted. She stayed long enough to watch Ellen open her gifts, then excused herself and drove back to the Gambles' house.

It was after eight o'clock when Jack came in that night. Beth and Chloe sat with him at the table while Hipolita served a rewarmed dinner. Chloe described her day in detail and Beth even contributed a few highlights from the baby shower. Then Chloe played checkers with her father until her bedtime. Once Chloe was settled, Jack invited Beth into the family room. She was hesitant, but he insisted.

"I'll behave," he promised, sitting down in the recliner.

"So," Beth began nervously. "Did you get a good jury?"

"It's one I can live with," he replied with a tired smile.

"Still no luck finding Amber Harper?" she asked, and he shook his head. "Don't you think it's a little strange that she's still hiding? I mean, she knows Ferris needs her testimony."

"Ferris says she's afraid of testifying."

Beth nodded, acknowledging this. "If I had a sister like Audrey, I'd hate to have to get on a witness stand and tell the world. And maybe she's heard what a good lawyer you are and thinks that you don't need her to win the case."

"Then again, she might not be hiding at all," Jack said, and Beth looked up sharply. "Somebody could be hiding her from me."

"What makes you say that?"

"I knew when I took this case that it was going to be tough, but I like a challenge. Even though Amber was missing, I felt sure Roy could find her before the trial began. The fact that he hasn't makes me wonder if somebody else has."

Jack ran his fingers through his hair. "There have just been so many strange things that have happened all at once. First Oscar comes up with the idea that the trial can be the deciding factor in his nomination for state senate, which put me under extreme pressure to win. Then a private conversation my parents had with a family court judge about Chloe is splashed all over the newspapers."

"Creating even more pressure."

Jack nodded. "We drew the worst possible judge, and then I thought we had finally gotten a break when I got that phone call saying Amber was at Heads Up."

"But instead you got a dislocated shoulder and broken ribs."

"And there was something funny about those guys who beat me up."

Beth's forehead creased with concern. "Funny?"

"They caught me by the Jeep and one held my arms tight enough to dislocate my shoulder while the other one punched me in the ribs. Then they just left without saying a word. They didn't even seem mad, and it makes me wonder if they were professionals."

"You think someone hired them to beat you up?" Beth demanded, and he shrugged. "Who would do that?"

"Lance Kilgore is a possibility. Maybe he told them to make sure none of my injuries showed so that when he accused me of delaying the trial, his rumor would take off. And it's possible that he found Amber first and is hiding her."

"If you really think the district attorney is breaking the law, you have to tell the judge."

Jack laughed harshly. "Judge Tate would laugh me out of town."

"If Mr. Kilgore wants to win that badly, he may not stop at breaking your ribs."

"I can take care of myself," he assured her.

Unconvinced, she looked at the clock and stood. "It's time for me to run with Roy."

Jack caught her hand. "How about just one little kiss before you go?"

"We agreed not to touch," she reminded him, staring at their joined hands.

"That was your idea, not mine."

"Please, Jack. It's the only way."

Reluctantly he released her, and she walked down to her room.

On Thursday morning Beth was surprised to find Jack at the kitchen table when she got back from riding with Roy to Morrow Academy. "I thought you'd be in Albany getting ready for the trial," she told him as she filled her bowl with cereal.

"I can prepare just as well here and conserve strength for tomorrow. Are you busy this morning?" he asked her.

Beth had planned to look around at Corrine's, but decided she could do that later. "I'm free."

"Good. I could use your help until Roberta gets here." They had just settled in his office at home when the phone rang. "Would you catch that for me?" he asked without looking up from his computer screen.

She stared at the phone for a few seconds, then picked up the receiver. "Hello?"

"Beth?" Monique responded. "Is Jack nearby?"

Beth covered the receiver and whispered, "It's Monique."

He made a face. "Put her on speaker phone."

Beth looked at the numerous options on his phone and finally picked one labeled Speaker. "Jack!" Monique's voice vibrated through the room.

"I've got a trial starting tomorrow, Monique, and I'm kind of busy."

"I won't waste much of your valuable time. I just wanted to see if you could arrange for me and my friend Felix to attend that party at Mr. Fuller's house on Saturday night," his ex-wife cajoled.

Jack gave the phone his full attention. "Are you in town?"

She laughed. "No, but Felix has a plane, and we can be there in a matter of hours."

"How do you even know about Oscar's party, and why would you want to socialize with a bunch of stuffy politicians?" Jack wanted to know.

"Felix has business interests in Georgia, so he wants to get involved in local politics. A friend told him about the party, and he thinks Saturday night would be a perfect time for him to meet the right folks," Monique explained.

"You know you'll have to wear costumes?" Jack verified.

"Of course. I thought I might come as Lady Godiva."

"Chloe will be there too, so don't wear anything that will embarrass her."

"We can come then?" Monique asked.

"The tickets are a thousand dollars each."

"That's pocket change to Felix," Monique assured him. "See you on Saturday."

After he ended the call, Jack told Beth to ignore the phone if it rang again. She made copies, looked up phone numbers, and handed him files until lunchtime when Roberta arrived. "So, did everyone find costumes for Saturday?" the secretary asked.

Beth nodded. "Chloe will be Dorothy, I'm Glinda, Roy's the Scarecrow, and Jack's the Tin Man. He has a pointy hat and gets to carry an oil can."

Roberta regarded her boss. "This I've got to see." He scowled and she laughed. "So what about makeup and your hair?" she asked Beth.

The future Good Witch looked back blankly. "What about it?"

Roberta frowned. "A political fund-raiser isn't like a friendly church social. Guests pay a thousand bucks just to walk in the door, and they'll be dressed to the nines. You can't pull your hair into a ponytail and slap on some Chapstick. You've got to make an effort!"

"Beth looks fine just the way she is," Jack said from his desk.

Beth gave him a smile, but Roberta waved his words aside. "Never listen to a man about things like this. Trust me, you need professional help."

Beth promised to give this some thought, then left Jack in Roberta's capable hands and drove to Corrine's. The dress she had admired previously had been reduced by ten percent, and Beth pretended that this made the price reasonable. Beth stopped by Melba's on the way home and Myrtle left a permanent in progress to greet her. "I came to thank you for the costumes," Beth told her friend.

"No moth holes?" Myrtle asked with a smile.

"Hipolita told me that the dry cleaner said they're in good shape." Beth glanced at the woman emitting the ammonia fumes. "I won't keep you, but I was wondering if you had an appointment available on Saturday afternoon to fix my hair and help with my makeup."

Myrtle checked the appointment book, then shook her head regretfully. "I'm booked on Saturday. I've even got my sister Mavis coming in to help because it's going to be so busy."

Beth looked down to hide her disappointment. "That's okay." She tried not to think about Roberta's warning or her dismal attempts at hair styling before Annabelle's party.

"Myrtle! You'd better not burn my hair!" the customer yelled from behind them.

"You've got another seven minutes!" Myrtle called over her shoulder. "Not that burned hair would hurt her appearance," the hairdresser whispered to Beth. "I've got an idea!" A smile creased Myrtle's plump face. "My last appointment on Saturday is at 4:30. When I'm done, I'll just come over on my way home and fix you up. Unless you don't think Mr. Gamble will let me in," Myrtle added as an afterthought.

"He'll let you in," Beth assured her. "But I'd hate for you to go to so much trouble."

"No trouble at all. And that way I'll get to see how you look in Melba's dress."

* * *

Once Chloe was at school on Friday morning, Beth drove to the library. She kept wondering what Jack was saying, what Lance Kilgore was answering, and how the judge was treating them both. The hours dragged by, and she thought noon would never arrive.

Back at the Gambles, Beth paced while she waited for Roy. The minute he pulled up, she climbed into the SUV and demanded a synopsis of the day at court. Roy smiled. "Better let the boss give you the details, but I think it went okay."

"Jack's opening statement was good?"

"Made Ferris sound like an angel," Roy affirmed.

"What about Mr. Kilgore?"

"Lance was well prepared, got to give him that, but I think the boss can take him."

"Jack always wins," Beth agreed with confidence, and Roy laughed.

It was almost bedtime when Jack got home that night. Chloe ran to greet her father at the door, and Beth had to restrain herself from doing the same. "I heat you some dinner," Hipolita offered, but Jack shook his head.

"Roberta brought me a sandwich, but thanks."

"So . . ." Beth prompted and he smiled.

"Come on upstairs, and I'll tell you all about it." They went to Chloe's room and sat on the bed while Jack read her a bedtime story. Then he left to change clothes while Beth tucked Chloe in. When she met him in the family room, he was wearing the cut-off sweatpants and tattered T-shirt he always ran in. "I thought I'd at least watch you tonight," he explained.

Beth nodded as she led the way into the hall and reminded him that she was waiting to hear about his day in court. "Lance was good, but I was better," he said without a trace of humility. "First he called one of the officers from the crime scene, and it was child's play to compromise him. Then he had an expert witness who was so boring he put the jury to sleep. Lance's strategy is painfully predictable, all the evidence is circumstantial, and most of the testimony is hearsay, so I think an acquittal is within my grasp."

"You're not even trying to find Amber Harper anymore?"

"Oh yes, we're still looking for Amber. Partly because Ferris is so determined to find her and partly because I never leave anything to chance." Jack waited in the kitchen while Beth changed clothes, and then they walked slowly to the park. "I've missed our runs," he said when they reached the track.

Beth bent down to do a few stretches. "I told you it could be addictive."

He collapsed on the bench, his eyes following every move she made. "I'm hooked all right." He gave her a warm smile, and she felt a blush rise in her cheeks. After her regular four miles, Beth told him she was ready to go. He claimed to be light-headed and said he would need to lean on her shoulder.

"You made it through the trial today," she pointed out.

"I was weakened by the strain." He draped his arm around her.

"I'm all sweaty," Beth objected, but he held tight.

"I don't mind." After a few seconds of deliberation, Beth settled her arm around his waist and they walked slowly home.

At breakfast on Saturday morning, Chloe reported that her father and Roberta were already hard at work in his office, getting ready for Monday. Beth explained to Chloe that she was going into Albany to watch a satellite broadcast of general conference. Chloe asked if she could go, and Beth felt that she had to warn the little girl. "It's kind of long and it might not seem like much fun to you, but I want to hear President Hinckley give his talk."

"The prophet is going to be there?" Chloe asked reverently.

"He's in Salt Lake, but we'll get to see him on a big television screen."

Chloe considered this for a few seconds, then said she believed she'd wear her yellow dress with the daisies. On the way upstairs, Beth told Chloe that they would have to get permission from her father. Ignoring Beth's plea to wait until he was through with his work, Chloe ran straight into his office. "He might not get through with his work until President Hinckley is through talking," Chloe called back with unarguable logic.

Jack didn't seem upset by the interruption and gave Chloe permission to attend the conference session. "What time does it start?" he asked Beth.

"Twelve," she answered.

He checked his watch. "We're almost through. I'll meet you in the kitchen at 11:30."

"You're going with us?" Beth was surprised.

"Unless you want me to find Roy and have him follow you," Jack replied with a smile.

"We could just call the National Guard and see if they could escort you," Roberta said smartly, but Jack ignored her.

When Beth got back downstairs, Hipolita told her the dry cleaners had delivered the costumes. "I put them on your bed."

Beth thanked the housekeeper, then rushed to her room. Her eyes skimmed over the Dorothy outfit and the silver suit and settled on Glinda's dress. It was beautiful beyond any dress she'd ever seen, and she blinked back tears of appreciation.

Beth changed into her new Sunday dress and returned to the kitchen. Hipolita had Chloe dressed, and Jack met them there at 11:35. He put his hand on Beth's back as they walked out to the car and told her that orange was his new favorite color.

All the way to Albany, Chloe talked about how she wished she could have worn her ruby slippers to church. Mark and Kate Iverson were in the foyer with Emily when they arrived, and Miss Eugenia was standing beside them. Jack spoke to the Iversons while Beth approached her library coworker.

"Well, it's a nice surprise to see you here."

Miss Eugenia had an excuse ready. "I came along to help Kate with the baby."

"Emily is a handful," Beth agreed. "Mark has a terrible time when Kate's at the organ on Sundays."

"Really?" Miss Eugenia asked.

"She screams and throws toys," Beth itemized Emily's crimes. "I try to help, but I'm sure your presence would be more effective. Emily seems so fond of you."

"I declare, I wish they had told me that they needed help on Sundays. I hate to miss my own church meetings . . ."

"But if you explain how much Kate needs you," Beth provided as a small man in a wheelchair rolled over.

"Elmer!" Miss Eugenia cried with delight. "Have you met Beth Middleton?" Jack and Chloe joined them and introductions were made, then they walked into the chapel.

The choir for the first session was made up of Primary children, and during the opening song, Chloe looked up at Beth in wonder and whispered, "They know 'I'm a Child of God,' just like me."

Beth swallowed the lump in her throat, then pointed to the screen. "There's the prophet."

Chloe listened to President Hinckley's talk, then drew pictures and finally fell asleep. Afterward, Miss Eugenia invited them to her house where she was hosting a between-the-sessions dinner for the Iversons and Brother Stoops, but they declined.

Hipolita had lunch ready for them when they got home, and Chloe offered her father the opportunity to bless the food. He hesitated for just a second, then bowed his head and said a short prayer. Afterward, Beth looked across the table at Jack, and he gave her a crooked smile. "I guess it's like riding a bike. You never really forget how." She smiled back and hoped he couldn't see the tears shining in her eyes.

As soon as she finished eating, Chloe put on her Dorothy costume, complete with red slippers and the Dalmatian puppy. "Don't you think it's a little early to be getting ready?" Jack asked mildly.

"I don't want to be late," Chloe replied.

Roy came in later carrying a big, gift-wrapped package. Chloe begged to know the contents and he handed it to her. "Guess you'll have to open it and find out," he said as he took a slightly stale sandwich off a plate on the table.

Chloe put the box on the floor and began tearing the paper. The unexpected gift turned out to be a *Wizard of Oz* collection of Barbie dolls. Chloe squealed with delight as she pulled out the miniature Dorothy. "She looks just like me! And here's you, Daddy." She handed Jack the Tin Man, complete with pointy hat.

"Thought it might inspire you," Roy said with a smile at his employer.

Chloe continued to distribute dolls. "Here's you, Roy," she handed him the Scarecrow. "And this is you, Beth." Beth accepted the doll wearing a tall crown and holding a magic wand. "Who's the Lion and the Wicked Witch?" Chloe waved the remaining dolls.

"I wonder if Monique and her friend ever came up with costumes," Jack pondered aloud. "They'd be perfect for our leftovers."

Everyone smiled as Hipolita came in and announced that Jack had a phone call. "I'll be right back," he promised and moved toward the stairs.

"You want new sandwiches?" Hipolita asked Roy.

"Naw, these are fine."

Hipolita shrugged, then told Chloe to help her get some towels out of the dryer. Beth picked up the scattered wrapping paper while Roy played absently with the Scarecrow doll.

"If you think about it, we really are like the characters of this movie," he said after a few minutes. "Chloe is the central character—all our lives revolve around her. There's Jack, the Tin Man who pretends that he doesn't have a heart," Roy continued, and Beth felt heat rise in her cheeks. "Then there's Beth." He took the Glinda doll from her hand. "The Good Witch who has the power to help us all." Beth raised an eyebrow. "A mother for Chloe, true love for Jack."

"What can Glinda give you, Roy?" she asked, watching him study the Scarecrow.

"Hope," he said as Jack walked back in. "Think I'll see if Hipolita has any pie-making plans." He gave the dolls to Beth and headed toward the laundry room.

"Do you think Roy's acting funny?" Beth whispered when Jack sat by her at the table.

"Not really. Why?"

"He just seemed kind of sad." She kept her voice low.

Jack looked at the dolls in her hands. "Don't worry about Roy, worry about me. Do I look a little sad? Maybe you should give me a big hug to cheer me up."

Beth stood in disgust. "I'm going find a good movie to watch until it's time to get ready. Don't forget that Chloe wants her hair to look exactly like Dorothy's tonight." She turned to leave, but he was quicker. "Jack!" she whispered as he pulled her onto his lap. "Let me up!"

"Kiss me and you can go," he murmured with a smile. She wanted to struggle, but couldn't make herself move as she watched his lips descend toward hers. The wonderful kiss was interrupted a few seconds later by Chloe's squeal.

"Daddy! Why are you kissing Beth?"

Beth jumped to her feet and her humiliation was complete when she saw Hipolita and Roy staring as well. Jack, on the other hand, didn't seem at all concerned.

"I like Beth and she likes me," he said with a broad grin in her direction. "Besides, we're practicing for tonight when she's Glinda and I'm the Tin Man." Now everyone was regarding him blankly. "I always thought the Good Witch had a thing for the Tin Man, didn't you?" he addressed the room in general, but no one responded. "You folks need to pay more attention to the subtleties when you watch movies." He gave Beth one last smile, then walked over to Chloe. "What can we do until it's time to go? Play Oz Barbies? Paint our fingernails?"

Chloe's mouth fell open. "Can I really put polish on you?"

"As long as you've got a silver color to match my suit," he said. Then with a wink over his shoulder he allowed Chloe to pull him out of the room.

CHAPTER 12

Myrtle arrived at 5:30 carrying a huge Avon satchel. She dried Beth's hair and put hot curlers in, then applied makeup with a generous hand. Beth expressed concern, but Myrtle waved her objections aside.

"We've got to turn you into the glamorous Glinda! The more the better."

Beth refused to put on the foot-high crown that Melba had worn in the ill-fated Oz production and would have objected to the aerosol body-glitter if she had seen it before Myrtle sprayed. She felt foolish until Myrtle made her look in the mirror. Then she could barely restrain tears of gratitude. "You're a miracle worker."

Myrtle gave her a quick hug and repacked the Avon satchel. Beth followed her into the kitchen, but Myrtle held up her hand at the door. "Don't come outside. It's about to rain and I don't want you to get messed up."

After Myrtle was gone Beth asked Hipolita where Chloe was. "Roberta fixing Mr. Jack," the housekeeper explained. "She say for Chloe to stay so Mr. Jack don't say bad words."

Beth smiled, imagining the scene upstairs, then hurried to her own room and put on the shimmery shoes that completed her costume. She was trying to get up the courage to go back to the kitchen when Chloe ran into the room. Jack was right behind her.

"You look beautiful," he said softly. "Magical even."

He should have looked ridiculous in the Tin Man suit, but he didn't. "So do you."

"It's time to go or we'll be very late!" Chloe prompted.

Jack smiled down at her. "We wouldn't want Beth to turn into a pumpkin!"

"Why do people keep saying that?" Chloe asked as they walked out into the kitchen. Roberta was sitting at the table eating one of Hipolita's homemade cinnamon rolls.

"I hope you appreciate what I went through to get him into that garb," she told Beth.

"You did a wonderful job," Beth said as her eyes strayed back to Jack and her heart pounded. "Where's Roy?" she asked, grateful that her voice sounded almost normal.

"He said he would meet us there," Jack answered as he opened the door. Beth saw a streak of lightning and shrank back. "What's the matter?" Concern creased Jack's forehead.

Beth took a deep breath. "I'm afraid of storms."

"It's just rain, no tornado warnings or anything like that," Jack tried to reassure her.

"Hipolita's getting an umbrella for you," Roberta said, then turned to Jack. "And you'd better not get messed up before all those snobs see my handiwork."

As Hipolita handed the umbrella to Jack, her lips curled up ever so slightly at the corners in what Beth realized was a smile. She didn't know if Hipolita was amused by their appearance or offering encouragement, but she smiled back.

Once they were settled in the Jeep, Beth watched the rain while Chloe chattered. She wanted to know if there was really oil in Jack's can and why Beth didn't wear her crown. Finally Jack turned onto a private road, then stopped at the gates to a large estate. A security guard stepped up to the car and checked their invitation, then gave them parking instructions. Men in raincoats directed cars under large tents with flashlights. An awning led from the parking area into the house so the visitors would be protected from the rain.

Jack carried Chloe inside, in spite of protests that Dorothy was supposed to walk. The house looked like an expensive hotel and was elaborately decorated for Halloween. The hosts were standing near the door dressed as George and Martha Washington. Beth had been afraid that she might be overdressed, but when she saw the powdered wigs and Martha's huge hoop skirt, she quit worrying.

Jack and Mr. Fuller exchanged cool nods, but Mrs. Fuller was enthusiastic in her greeting. "Don't you all look wonderful!"

"I'm Dorothy," Chloe provided.

"I recognized you right away," Mrs. Fuller nodded with delight. "And you've brought the Tin Man and the Good Witch with you."

"Roy is the Scarecrow and he's coming in a little while," Chloe replied. "But we don't have a Lion, and Roberta said she didn't want to be the Wicked Witch because—"

"We're blocking other people," Jack interrupted.

"And it's damp here by the door. Go on in and get something to eat," Mrs. Fuller invited graciously. Jack nodded, then led Beth into the massive living room. He found a couch in a corner and put Chloe down. Beth sat gingerly, anxious not to wrinkle her Glinda dress.

From their vantage point, they watched other guests arrive. Beth recognized a few city officials and local celebrities. Eventually Monique and Felix Hummer made a grand entrance, dressed as Bonnie and Clyde. "I hope somebody thought to check those guns to be sure they're not loaded," Jack whispered as they watched the couple talking to the Fullers.

Before Beth could respond, Malcolm rushed up. He was wearing a flowing toga, which exposed a good deal of pudgy white skin, and ivy circled his head, drawing attention to his lack of hair. Beth winced at the unfortunate choice of a costume as he greeted them.

"We're going to keep everything informal tonight. We'll give the guests some time to get settled, then Mr. Fuller will say a few words."

"Oscar can say anything he wants as long as he doesn't make me give a speech dressed in tinfoil," Jack replied.

"He promised no speeches. Just have a good time!" Malcolm said as he hurried off. Then Lance Kilgore walked into the room looking very macho in an Atlanta Falcons football uniform. Jack made a growling sound in his throat and Beth stood.

"Come on, Chloe," she extended her hand. "Let's get something to eat."

Chloe went happily to the dining room, where chefs in huge white hats were serving foods from flaming dishes. Beth was searching for something she recognized when Lance Kilgore spoke from behind her. "Do you have any idea what this stuff is?" he asked, pointing to a greenish paste formed into a flower and surrounded by wheat crackers.

"I haven't seen anything familiar except the fruit, and *it* seems to be just for decoration." She waved at the elaborate stack of produce in the middle of the table.

"I guess I'll be making a stop at McDonald's on my way home." He frowned and Beth would have been tempted to like him if he wasn't Jack's competition.

"Are you trying to trick Beth into admitting that I faked my injuries?" Jack's voice spoke from behind them.

"Actually, I didn't think of that," Lance Kilgore replied with a grin. "We were just trying to figure out what that stuff is." He indicated toward the green flower.

Jack scowled. "It's liver pâté, and you're holding up the line."

"Well, that settles our little mystery," Lance murmured as he scooped some on a cracker.

"You boys eat up," Mrs. Fuller commanded as she walked by.

"Everything looks delicious," Lance lied outrageously with a wink at Beth.

"I left Roy on our couch, but he won't be able to save it forever," Jack said after the district attorney had gone. Chloe helped herself to some of the wheat crackers, and Beth pulled a few grapes off the centerpiece and added them to the child's plate. A man intercepted Jack on the way back to their corner, but Beth and Chloe proceeded to the couch and sat down by Roy. His only concession to the event was the straw hat on his head.

"You're supposed to have straw coming out of your wrists and your neck, and the Scarecrow has a rope belt," Beth itemized the deficiencies of his costume.

Roy just smiled. "Everybody gets the general idea." They watched the crowd while Chloe ate crackers and grapes. Beth's eyes kept straying to Jack, and finally Roy laughed. "I think Jack was right."

"About what?" Beth asked.

"I think Glinda *does* have a thing for the Tin Man."

Beth blushed, then shook her head. "Jack and I can never be more than friends."

"Why not?"

Beth took a deep breath. She had told the story too many times lately and it sounded less sensible with each repetition. "I promised David that I would be his wife, so I can't marry Jack."

"Even though the other guy is dead?" Roy asked in surprise.

"I believe that David and I can be married to each other . . . later . . . after . . ." Beth stammered into silence. The only thing more hopeless than her romance with Jack was trying to explain something so complicated to Roy.

"You think that people can get married in heaven?" he confirmed and Beth nodded, pleased that he had gleaned that much. "Got another question for you." Beth waited in resignation for him to ask about the doctrines of eternity. "Mormons believe in the same God as Baptists, right?" Beth nodded again, more warily this time. "Well, from what I can remember of my days in Sunday School, God can do anything."

"I believe that," Beth agreed.

"And He don't make mistakes."

"He *doesn't* make mistakes," Beth acknowledged this as well.

"So David was meant to die two years ago."

Beth was shaken by the unlikely wisdom of his words. "Miss Eugenia said that David would release me from my promise if he could. She even offered to spread the word to all the old people in town so that the next person who dies could ask him for me."

Roy grinned. "Hey, that's a pretty good idea."

"It's not funny," Beth said primly. "I'm very serious about this."

"God sent you to us, Beth. And He *doesn't* make mistakes."

Beth was still trying to think of a response when Jack returned. He looked between Beth and Roy, but before he could say a word Monique and her date rushed up. Monique squealed when she saw Chloe. "Isn't she just so adorable?" she asked Felix, who nodded vaguely. "And Jack, I love your hat."

"What about mine?" Roy touched the straw, and Monique laughed.

"Your costume is a perfect example of understatement," she told Roy. "How about me?"

"Stunning as always," the chauffeur said.

Monique laughed again, then spotted someone across the room. "Oh look, Felix, there's the governor. Let's go meet him."

"Can I come with you?" Chloe asked, putting her plate on the couch.

"Oh, cutie pie, you don't match us so I think you'd better stay with your daddy." Monique blew a kiss to Chloe, then rushed off, leaving the child staring after her.

While Beth was fuming over Monique's insensitivity, Mr. Fuller stepped in front of the fireplace and asked for everyone's attention. The crowd quieted as he enumerated his personal contributions toward keeping America free. Then he encouraged everyone to have a good time. Jack looked at his watch.

"We can leave in about an hour without seeming rude."

"Mind if I go ahead now?" Roy asked. "I've got a date."

"Fine with me," Jack responded, then looked down at Chloe. The child was watching every move Monique made. "But would you mind taking Chloe to the house first?"

Roy hesitated for just a second, then nodded. "I had to use some creative parking to get the SUV under the tent outside. It's kind of blocked in, so I might take the Jeep, if you don't care."

Jack stood and lifted his daughter. "It doesn't matter to me, just look after my girl." He pressed a kiss to Chloe's cheek, then passed her on to Roy.

"You know I will," his friend replied.

"And be careful in this weather," Beth pleaded.

"Good night, Glinda," Roy said with a smile at Beth, then carried Chloe through the crowd and out the front door.

Beth had Jack to herself for a few seconds before a group of people from the Albany City Council came over to talk to him. While he was embroiled in a political discussion, Beth nibbled Chloe's abandoned crackers. After thirty minutes of half-listening to the conversation, Beth panned the room and she saw Roberta step through the door.

The secretary had said she wouldn't be caught dead at this party, yet there she was. The pallor of her skin, the tension around her mouth, and her clenched fists were indications of disaster. Beth's hands started to shake, and the wheat cracker she'd been eating fell to the floor. She stood, a low moan breaking from her lips. Jack turned to Beth and then, following the direction of her gaze, to Roberta as she worked her way toward them.

Jack raised a hand, silencing the man beside him, and took a few steps back so that he was standing with Beth when Roberta finally reached them. Unshed tears shone in her eyes, and Beth's heart constricted.

"There's been an accident."

As Roberta said those awful words, Jack drew Beth into the comfort of his arms. The room became ominously quiet. "Chloe," he managed to say.

"She was wearing her seat belt, and the policeman said that probably saved her life. But she's bleeding internally and they may have to operate. You need to get to the hospital." Roberta was weeping openly now. Jack took Beth's hand and headed for the door, but Roberta reached out to stop him. "Jack," she said quietly. "Roy's trapped in the Jeep. They're not even sure that he's still alive."

Beth felt Jack tremble, and then he pulled her across the room and outside. He enlisted the aid of the car-parkers to find the Expedition. "Which hospital?" he asked Roberta once they were in the SUV.

"Memorial," she replied.

Beth used a Halloween napkin to staunch the flow of tears from her eyes as Jack asked Roberta for details. "A car forced them off the road and into a concrete embankment." She took a deep breath.

"You said Chloe's bleeding internally." Jack glanced at Roberta in the rearview mirror.

The secretary nodded. "The Jeep is mangled. They've had to call in a special team to cut Roy out . . ."

Numbly, Beth listened to Roberta's ragged breathing, and Roy's name kept echoing through her mind. He had to be okay because anything else was unthinkable.

"Did they get the driver of the other car?" Jack broke the silence.

"No. It was hit-and-run."

Beth fumbled through her purse and got out her cell phone. "I need to call my parents," she explained to Jack as her trembling fingers dialed the familiar number. Her father answered after two rings. "Daddy," she whispered.

"Beth?" The concern in his voice was instant.

"Daddy, can you and Mama come to Memorial Hospital in Albany?"

"Are you hurt?" her father asked.

"No, it's Chloe, the little girl I've been taking care of and," she swallowed, fighting for control, "I want you to give her a blessing."

"We'll be there as quickly as possible," he promised.

Jack parked near the Emergency Room entrance at the hospital and stepped out of the SUV. He pulled off his hat and the top of his Tin Man costume and threw them into the backseat. Pushing his hair out of his eyes with one hand, he tucked his T-shirt into the silver pants with the other. Then he closed his door and they hurried toward the hospital.

A doctor met them by the admissions desk and said that Chloe was in serious but stable condition. There was significant internal bleeding, and x-rays indicated kidney damage. "We are waiting for our kidney trauma expert to examine her."

"Will this expert be here soon?" Jack asked.

The doctor nodded. "We can go ahead and get a few pints of blood while we wait. And some tissue samples to identify possible transplant donors."

Jack blanched. "Who needs to be tested?"

"Her parents and siblings will be the most likely matches."

"I'm her father," Jack told him. "Her mother is at a party nearby."

The doctor glanced at Beth. "Extended family and even close friends can be tested if necessary, but we'll wait for Dr. Long's opinion before we go that far." His pager went off and he paused to check the number.

Jack reached for his cell phone, then turned haunted eyes to Beth. "I was going to call Roy," he whispered.

Beth's hands folded around his shaking fingers. "Roberta," Beth looked at the other woman. "Please call the Fullers and tell Monique to come here immediately." Roberta nodded and walked down the hall, pulling out her cell phone as she went.

"What about Roy Hankins? Any word on him yet?" Jack asked, and the doctor nodded.

"They are bringing him in. There was extensive damage to his brain, but he's still breathing." The doctor glanced back at his beeper. "I need to get this call, but I'll send a nurse to take you to the lab for blood tests and tissue samples. Dr. Long will be in to talk to you as soon as he examines your daughter."

Roberta rushed up as the doctor left. "Monique is coming," she told them.

They stood against the wall, trying to stay out of the way, until a nurse finally came for Jack. Beth hated to be excluded, but she fell firmly into the "nonrelative" category. Before Jack had gone more than a few feet, the big doors behind them burst open and Monique came through, followed closely by Malcolm Schneckenberger.

Beth knew she should have been glad to see Monique since Chloe might need her, but felt ill as she watched them embrace. At that moment she realized that no matter what he thought of his ex-wife, they shared a bond that no divorce papers could sever.

"How's Chloe?" Monique fingered the neck of Jack's T-shirt.

"She's serious but stable. We've got to go up to the lab for tests," he told her. "This is Chloe's mother," he explained to the nurse.

"What kind of tests?" Beth heard Monique ask as they left with the nurse.

After they were gone Malcolm shook his head. "I can't believe this! I need to let Mr. Fuller know the details." With that, the little man walked down the hall.

"I'm going to find us a better place to wait," Roberta muttered, then followed Malcolm without waiting for Beth to reply.

Deserted, wearing a Good Witch costume and too much makeup, Beth was tempted to run out the big doors and never look back. But Chloe needed her. So did Jack and even Roy. With a sigh she rummaged in her purse for her cell phone again.

First she called Derrick and after a brief explanation she asked him to bring her a change of clothes. Then she looked in her checkbook where she had written the Iversons' number and dialed. Kate answered, sounding sleepy. "Chloe's been hurt in a car accident and needs a blessing. My father's on his way . . ."

"Mark will be there soon," Kate promised. "Do you want me to come? Miss Eugenia can keep Emily."

Beth knew that Kate hated leaving the baby, and waking Miss Eugenia at this hour would be a terrible imposition. "There's nothing you can do here tonight. Just send Mark."

After ending the call she walked to the nurses' station and asked if she could see Chloe. The nurse said that only parents were allowed in the ICU, so Beth resumed her place by the wall. Roberta returned a few minutes later and led the way to a small waiting room.

"Any news?" Beth asked, rubbing her arms for warmth.

"Dr. Long has arrived. He's with Chloe now." Roberta's cell phone rang and she answered it, then looked at Beth. "That was Malcolm calling from the Emergency Entrance. He said they've just brought Roy in." Beth moved toward the door, but Roberta put out a hand to stop her. "Let me go. You stay here and wait for Jack."

Beth watched Roberta leave, feeling like the most useless person in the world. She caught a glimpse of herself in the mirror that hung over the vinyl couch and shuddered, hating the fear and despair she saw in her own eyes. She turned away from her reflection as a nurse walked in.

"I thought I heard a cell phone ringing in here," the woman said looking around. "Cell phones interfere with some of the hospital equipment and have to be turned off." Beth nodded dully as Derrick walked through the door carrying a stack of blankets, two pillows, and a five-pound bag of oranges. Annabelle was right behind him.

"I thought you might be hungry, and I know you're exhausted," Derrick explained. "I wish I'd had time to make a proper fruit basket," he lamented as he put the oranges on a table.

Annabelle embraced Beth. "How is Chloe?"

"They might have to operate, but it sounds like she's going to be okay. It's Roy that . . ." Beth was unable to continue.

"I brought you some clothes." Annabelle held up a neatly folded pair of sweatpants and a pink T-shirt. "I hope you don't mind wearing my things, but we didn't want to take the time to stop by a store." Beth assured her that anything would be fine. "I saw a ladies' room down the hall. I think you'll feel much better once we get you out of that dress."

In the restroom, Annabelle helped Beth remove the bulky costume, then took it out to her car. Beth put on Annabelle's clothes and washed her face with the antibacterial hand soap provided by the hospital. She pulled her hair back into a curly ponytail with a rubber band she found on the side of the sink and hurried back to check on Chloe.

When Beth rushed into the little waiting room she saw Hipolita standing in a corner away from the others. Beth walked over and touched the housekeeper's arm. "Chloe's going to be okay," she promised. Hipolita nodded, but her eyes were desolate.

Then Beth's parents arrived.

"I'm so sorry about your friends, Lora Beth," her mother said.

"Thanks for coming, Mom," Beth responded, then stepped into her father's strong arms. She was tempted to dissolve into hopeless tears, but she pushed them back bravely. "Have we heard anything about Roy or Chloe?"

Derrick spoke. "Mr. Hankins is still being evaluated in the Emergency Room, and Chloe is being prepared for surgery."

"Now?" Beth cried.

Derrick spread his hands. "The nurse said her father's tissues match."

Beth felt the room spin around her. Jack and Chloe, both at risk. There was a sound by the door, and Beth caught a speculative glance pass between her parents just as Jack walked in. Then everything and everyone else faded from her consciousness, and she allowed him to draw her into his arms. "Chloe?" she asked, a small sob escaping from her lips.

He held her close, stroking her hair. "They're taking some more x-rays now, but based on the swelling of her abdomen, the doctor thinks they are going to have to operate."

"Will they do a transplant?"

"Only if both kidneys are damaged beyond repair."

Beth took a ragged breath. "The nurse told me about the tissue match."

Jack nodded. "It's a serious surgery for the donor, and there will be a scar," he exhaled. "So it's a big decision."

Beth stared up at him. "What do you mean it's a big decision, and why would you care if you have a scar on your stomach? This is for Chloe!" Beth felt her voice rising out of control.

"Beth," he called to her, but she could barely hear him. "Beth!" he took her face in his hands and forced her to look at him. "I would let them cut me into one-inch pieces if it would help Chloe, but Monique is the donor they want."

Beth's frightened brain processed this information. "The nurse said your tissues match."

"They do, but Monique's match too, and her size makes her kidney more suitable for a five-year-old. However, Monique is terrified of hospitals, hates pain, and displays her stomach often, so for her it will be a big decision."

"Monique." The thought of Chloe's fate being in the hands of that vain, selfish woman was worse than anything Beth could imagine. "How will you get her to do it?"

"I've offered to help with the financing of her new movie and told her that she can describe her ordeal to the press for publicity." He frowned, and Beth knew he hated this last part, but it was brilliant.

"What did she say?"

"She's agreed, but if the time actually comes . . ." Jack replied, his jaw clenched with tension. "She's still in the lab. Just giving a pint of blood made her faint."

Beth slipped out of his embrace, but kept his hand clutched in hers. She turned around and saw her parents staring, white faced and wide-eyed. "Daddy, Mama, this is Jack Gamble. Jack, my parents, Douglas and Nancy Middleton."

Jack extended his free hand and after the briefest hesitation, Beth's father accepted it. "It's nice to meet you," Douglas Middleton said.

Jack reciprocated, and then Beth stepped between them. "We'll get to know each other later. Right now Chloe needs a blessing," she told her father.

A young man with wire-rimmed glasses and a mass of curling dark hair stepped into the room and Beth turned to him. "We need to get permission to see Chloe Gamble for a few minutes. Could you tell someone?"

"I might be able to help you," the young man said, rubbing his hands up and down on the sides of his scrub pants. "Why do you need to see her?"

"We'd like for her to have a blessing. It's a special prayer," Beth elaborated.

"Can't you just pray for her in here?" He waved around the waiting room.

Beth shook her head. "For this kind of prayer we have to be able to touch her."

The young man pushed a clump of black hair behind one ear, considering. "I'll see what I can do," he said finally, then turned and left the room.

Beth made more introductions, and when she was finished, Derrick came up beside her. "Hospitals seem like much friendlier places on the soaps," he commented, and Beth smiled for the first time in what seemed like forever. Then Brother and Sister Gamble walked in.

"I guess I shouldn't be surprised to see you here," Jack said with resignation.

"I called them," Roberta admitted bravely.

Jack nodded. "So, are you going to have me arrested for gross negligence?"

"Oh, Jack," his mother replied. "At times like this, families should be together."

"I thought you had a nice reunion planned for family court."

Beth stepped forward, unwilling to allow the situation to deteriorate further. "Chloe's kidneys were damaged in the accident. An orderly has gone to arrange for her to have a blessing."

Sister Gamble approached her son tentatively. "Will Chloe have to have surgery?"

Jack sighed. "Her abdomen is swelling, and the x-rays show internal bleeding. They will probably have to do exploratory surgery to determine the seriousness of her injuries. If the kidneys are badly damaged, they'll do the transplant now to avoid another operation." As he finished this sentence, the long-haired orderly walked back into the room.

"Were you able to find anyone who can give us permission to see Chloe?" Beth asked.

"I had to pull a few strings, call in a few favors, even twist a few arms, but I convinced the nursing staff to let you come in for a short prayer."

Beth stared back at the young man in surprise. "You convinced the nurses?"

The curly hair bobbed as the man nodded and extended his hand. "Timothy Long," the surgeon introduced himself.

Beth blushed. "I'm sorry that I assumed that you were . . . well, not a doctor. You just look so young."

"No offense taken," he assured her with a crooked smile. "But we'd better hurry before the nurses change their minds."

"I'll stay here," Malcolm said. "I'm waiting for Mr. Fuller to call me back." He ducked his head, apparently embarrassed that his boss wasn't showing any concern for Chloe. "I'm sure he'll be calling any minute."

"Well, you can't use your cell phone. The nurse said it would interfere with hospital equipment," Beth told him, and Malcolm nodded.

"We'll wait here too," Annabelle spoke for herself and Derrick.

"There's no reason for us to go now that the grandfather has arrived," Nancy Middleton said, but Beth shook her head.

"I want Daddy to help with the blessing."

"And I get so nervous," Brother Gamble entered the conversation. "I'd appreciate it if you'd administer." Douglas Middleton considered this for a second, then nodded.

"Since you don't need me, I'll go see what the police can tell us about the accident," Mark Iverson told Beth.

She thanked Mark for his understanding, then caught up with the doctor. "So, now that you've examined Chloe, what will you do?"

"Your husband explained it pretty well," Dr. Long began, but Beth interrupted.

"We're not married." She waved at Jack.

"Not yet," Jack said, and the doctor looked at them.

"Chloe's losing a lot of blood into her abdominal cavity. Surgery will help us identify the source, and we've got a donor if it comes to that." They followed him into a little cubicle partitioned off from the rest of the large room with moveable screens. Chloe was lying in the middle of a narrow bed, still as a corpse. "She's sedated," the doctor explained as Jack and Beth moved beside the bed.

Chloe's dark hair was fanned across the green hospital pillow, and Jack reached out to stroke it. Beth touched a pale cheek, shuddering at the purple bruise forming on Chloe's forehead. Beth was conscious of the others crowding around the bed, and maintained control by taking slow, deep breaths.

Brother Gamble and Douglas Middleton reached around the equipment to put their hands on Chloe's head, and Beth saw Dr.

Long step into the doorway. Space was limited, so he remained there. After Brother Gamble sealed the anointing, Beth's father spoke. He used Chloe's full name and stated the purpose for the blessing. Then the timbre of his voice changed. "Chloe, you are fortunate to be at a modern medical facility in the care of well-trained nurses and physicians. You are surrounded by people who love you and pray for your recovery. The Lord has heard their prayers and He knows of your perfect faith. Because of this, there will be no need for surgery." As he spoke these words Brother Middleton's voice shook slightly, but he continued, promising Chloe that her body would heal itself, and she would enjoy a long life with the people she loved.

Beth opened her eyes as her father closed the prayer and saw the stunned look on his face. The small room was deadly quiet except for the hum made by the equipment that monitored Chloe's vital signs. Finally Dr. Long spoke quietly from the door and broke the tension.

"Well, I guess I'd better arrange for some new x-rays before we operate unnecessarily." They watched him disappear from view, and then the nurses descended, telling them to leave.

Beth was reluctant to abandon Chloe, but the nurses insisted, so she followed the others out. Once they were in the hallway, she approached her father, feeling optimistic for the first time since they had arrived at the hospital. "Daddy, I'd like you to give Roy a blessing too. One just like Chloe's."

"I doubt I'll ever give another blessing quite like Chloe's," Douglas told his daughter. "I meant to give a standard blessing." He looked at Jack. "Those were not my words."

Jack nodded. "I understand, sir."

"But if you can give Chloe a blessing to keep her from having surgery, surely you can give Roy one so he won't die," Beth persisted.

"It's the Lord's decision, Beth, not mine," her father said as they reached the waiting room.

"Roberta!" Beth called to the other woman. "How's Roy?"

"They've put him in a room on the critical care floor. All of his organs are heavily damaged, so machines are breathing for him, keeping his heart beating, everything. The nurse said he has a living will, and as soon as all brain activity ceases, they'll unhook the machines . . ."

Beth was trying to recover from the blow of these words when Monique walked in. She went straight up to Jack and put her arm through his. "The nurses told me they are doing some new x-rays of Chloe's kidneys. I'm supposed to wait here, and they'll call if they need me."

Jack nodded. "We're on our way to see Roy."

Monique glanced around. "I think I'll wait here."

"She's Chloe's mother," Beth explained to her parents as they walked to the elevator.

"The resemblance is striking," Nancy Middleton whispered back.

The Critical Care ward was a semidarkened room with a nurses' station in the middle encircled by patient beds. A nurse met them at the door and said that only two people could visit Roy at a time. Jack and Beth went first.

When they reached Roy, Jack grasped his friend's limp hand, and Beth wiped tears on the sleeve of Annabelle's pink T-shirt. Roy's red hair had been partially shaved, and the freckles that weren't covered by gauze and tape stood out against his pale skin. They watched him silently until a nurse tapped Jack's shoulder, indicating that their time was up.

"Hurry, Daddy," Beth said to her father when they joined the group at the door. Nancy put an arm around her daughter, and they watched as Douglas Middleton and Brother Gamble approached Roy's bed. Everyone bowed their heads while the blessing was given.

"Well?" Beth asked anxiously when they returned.

Douglas exchanged a quick look with his wife. "We blessed him with peace and freedom from pain . . ."

"That's all?" Beth cried. "You didn't bless him to get well or at least to regain consciousness so we could say good-bye?" Tears fell onto her cheeks.

"I'm sorry Beth. I felt that a comfort blessing was what he needed."

She started to protest again, but Jack put his hand on her arm. "Let's go check on Chloe."

Malcolm met them by the waiting room door. "Is Roy showing improvement?" he asked.

Jack shook his head. "He's the same. Has Dr. Long been back?"

"Not yet," Malcolm answered. "I still haven't heard from Oscar. I'm going to go to the pay phone down the hall."

Jack barely acknowledged Malcolm's remark as he led Beth to a couch in the corner. The Middletons sat beside them, and the waiting continued. "It's good that you've decided to date someone," Nancy said finally, looking between her daughter and Jack.

"Jack and I didn't exactly date. We just sort of . . ." Beth attempted to explain.

"Fell in love with each other in spite of our best efforts not to," Jack provided.

"You've grieved for David long enough. I'm sure he would want for you to marry someone else, eventually," Douglas said.

Beth was surprised by this remark. "Do you really think so? If I had been the one who died, I would expect him to wait for me . . ."

Beth looked up and saw Mark Iverson standing in the doorway. "Jack, Winston needs to talk to you and Beth."

Beth saw the Haggerty police chief standing in the hallway and realized that the conversation would be official. Jack pulled Beth to her feet. "Sure."

Winston led them to a small lounge at the end of the hall. The combined smells of strong coffee and industrial-strength disinfectants made Beth's stomach roll as Mark sat beside her.

"I thought I'd sit in, if you don't mind," he said.

"I'm sorry about Hankins," Winston began awkwardly. "The accident took place outside of the Haggerty city limits, but the sheriff asked me to handle the initial questions since I know you folks," the police chief continued, and Jack nodded. "We're still trying to determine exactly what happened last night. According to witnesses, your Jeep was forced off the road by a large, dark, all-terrain vehicle. Know anyone who drives a car like that?"

Jack concentrated on the question. "Not that I can think of."

"Do you have any disgruntled ex-employees? Received any threatening mail lately?"

"I don't have much employee turnover, and can't think of anyone who left unhappy, but Roberta has the personnel records. Threatening mail went to Roy."

Neither Mark nor Winston seemed surprised by the fact that Jack received threatening mail, but Beth certainly was. She stared at Jack as Winston continued. "We'll need to see both."

"I'll tell Roberta to show you her files and give you the key to Roy's apartment. He has a small office there."

Winston cleared his throat, then spoke with obvious reluctance. "In addition to the injuries Hankins sustained in the wreck itself, the doctors found a bullet in the base of his neck."

"A bullet?" Jack repeated. "You mean Roy was shot?"

Winston nodded. "The bullet went through the driver's side window and severed his spinal cord. That should have caused him to lose the ability to control his lower body immediately, but we've got a witness who swears Hankins applied the brakes hard for almost a hundred yards, then swerved to the right before he hit that embankment."

"His body probably fell forward against the brake pedal," Mark suggested.

Beth shook her head. "Somehow he managed to protect Chloe, even after he was hurt." Roy had sacrificed himself for Chloe, she was sure.

"But who would want to shoot Roy?" Jack's tone was bewildered.

The Haggerty police chief shrugged. "We don't know that anyone was trying to shoot him. It could have been a random drive-by shooting. That type of thing is common in larger cities, but there has been an increase of gang activity in rural areas over the past few years."

"Or the gunman could have mistaken Roy for someone else," Mark said.

"Like you, Mr. Gamble," Winston interjected. Beth looked at Jack in alarm as the policeman leaned forward. "Why was Hankins driving your car?"

"The SUV was blocked in at the Fuller's party," Jack responded.

Winston seemed satisfied with this. "It's still very early in the investigation, and we've taken enough of your time for now." He stood and opened the door, then waited for everyone to file out. Just before they reached the waiting room Winston turned to Jack. "Any idea why Hankins would have been headed north toward Macon instead of west into Haggerty?"

Jack considered this for a second, then shook his head. "He said he had a date, but I asked him to take Chloe home first."

Winston made a note of this before he proceeded down the hallway. Mark waved, then followed the Haggerty police chief. Beth pressed a hand to her throbbing temples as they walked into the waiting area and found Roberta there alone.

"They put Monique in a room for what's left of the night, Hipolita went to get you some clothes, and I sent everyone else home," she explained. "I promised to call them as soon as we know something. You two make yourselves comfortable." She pointed to the vinyl couches and the pillows and blankets that Derrick had left. "I'll go stay with Roy for awhile."

Jack waited until Roberta was gone, then pulled Beth to his chest. "It was bad enough when we just thought Roy had been in a car accident. But shot too! And possibly by someone who was trying to kill me!"

"I wonder why was he going the wrong way?" she whispered, confused and suddenly afraid.

"And why is the FBI interested?" Jack's voice echoed her concern.

"Maybe Mark was just there as our friend," Beth suggested, but Jack didn't look convinced as he picked the cleanest-looking couch and they sat down. "How are your ribs?"

"Killing me," he admitted. "Did Roy ever tell you how we met?"

The question took Beth by surprise. "He said he killed a man by mistake and turned into a drunk, and that you saved his life by hiring him."

"Roy was a detective for the Albany Police Department. We first met in the courtroom. I was defending a robbery suspect, and he was a witness for the prosecution."

"Did you win the case?" Beth asked.

"Of course." Jack gave her a little smile. "Roy's partner was killed a few months later and he felt responsible, so he quit the force. I needed someone to run down leads for me and looked him up. He laughed when I offered him a job, but I could see a glimmer of interest in his eyes. I told him I'd hire him on an hour-to-hour basis. Every hour that he didn't drink, I'd pay him. As far as I know, he never touched another drop of alcohol. I don't know what I'll do if . . ."

"We're not going to consider that," she insisted as footsteps sounded in the hall. "Someone is coming."

They both stood and faced the doorway. Seconds later Dr. Long appeared, looking tired but triumphant. "Chloe's on her way to a room."

"Then there won't be an operation?" Beth whispered.

"Not tonight anyway," Dr. Long conceded. "I took three sets of x-rays and couldn't see any sign of fresh bleeding. The swelling in her abdomen is no worse than it was two hours ago, and both kidneys are working at about thirty percent of normal capacity. So we're going to sit back and see if her body really can heal itself."

Beth swiped at tears again. "Where is her room?"

"I'll show you," Roberta said as she walked in, followed closely by Malcolm. "I'm headed home. Hipolita will be back soon to sit in the Critical Care waiting room near Roy, and I've tried to get rid of Malcolm, but he won't leave," the secretary reported with a grimace.

"I just want to make sure Chloe is settled before I go," Malcolm defended himself.

"Well, I'm going to get some rest, and I'd advise all of you to do the same," Dr. Long said.

"Go home, Malcolm," Roberta said on their way into the hall. "Jack, Beth, follow me." Roberta led the way to the elevator, and Beth gave Malcolm a little wave over her shoulder.

"It seems mean to leave Malcolm standing there," Beth whispered from the elevator.

Roberta huffed. "I'm not taking him home with me, so unless you want him to spend the night with you . . ."

Beth held up a hand. "You're right. Malcolm's on his own."

When they got to Chloe's suite, a nurse was arranging various pieces of equipment around the hospital bed. "The IV is just giving her fluids right now," she told them. "There's a fracture in her left wrist." She touched the small pink cast. "And she'll probably be catheterized for a few days, but all in all, she's doing very well."

Beth waited until the nurse left, then walked up beside Chloe. "It sounds like she's going to be okay," Beth whispered, and Jack nodded.

"I knew she would be." He touched a pale cheek. "I knew the Lord wouldn't take Chloe away from you. Not after David."

Beth took a trembling breath. "You had faith."

"I guess."

There was a sound at the door and they looked up to see Hipolita, clutching a small overnight bag to her chest. "I bring you clothes," she said to Jack. "And toothbrushes," she included Beth in her solemn gaze.

Jack stepped over to take the suitcase. "Thanks."

The housekeeper nodded, then looked over Jack's shoulder at the sleeping child.

"She's doing better, but go over and see for yourself," Jack invited.

Hipolita approached the bed tentatively, murmuring in Spanish. Jack opened the suitcase, and Beth had forgotten that he was still wearing part of his Tin Man Suit until she saw him remove a clean T-shirt and pair of jeans. Chloe's Dorothy dress now lay shredded on the Emergency Room floor, and their days in Oz seemed very far away.

Hipolita left when Jack came out of the bathroom a few minutes later, drying his hair with a towel. Beth got one of the toothbrushes Hipolita brought and went into the bathroom. It was full of steam, as if the very air belonged to him. Breathing deeply, she stared at herself in the foggy mirror. She loved Jack and Chloe. These were facts that didn't require discussion, even with herself. The question was, could they build a future on a foundation of broken promises? Miss Eugenia said David would want her to be happy. Roy said that God had sent her to the Gambles' home. Her father said that David would expect her to move on, but she was very much afraid that her betrayal of David would haunt her all the days of her life.

After brushing her teeth, Beth returned to find Jack in a large recliner by the bed. Beth tucked the covers around Chloe, then sat on the arm of his chair. "Will you still have to help finance Monique's movie now that she won't have a scar?" Beth asked.

"Monique's a very good actress, so I'm sure I'll end up making money on her movie. The part I wish I could renege on is the publicity."

"If she had a speck of decency, she wouldn't hold you to any of it," Beth muttered.

"Decency is a foreign concept to Monique. But she never even wanted to have children, so this is the second time she's put her life and career on the line for Chloe."

Beth snuggled against the soft fabric of his T-shirt, and soon the regular rise and fall of his chest told her that he was asleep. A few minutes later, Dr. Long walked in. He approached the bed with exaggerated tiptoes, a finger to his lips, and examined Chloe. "Swelling's down a little more, and her vitals are good. So far everything's just what the doctor ordered."

"I thought you were going to sleep," Beth reminded him as she eased away from Jack.

He shrugged. "I'll get around to that soon. And I was supposed to tell Mr. Gamble that his friend's moving into a room, but I guess it can wait."

Beth sat up straight. "Roy's better then?"

"No," Dr. Long shook his head. "Ten minutes without oxygen, incredible blood loss, the severed spinal column—to tell you the truth, I don't know how he's got any brain activity."

Beth spoke around the lump in her throat. "So why are they moving him to a room?"

"They need his spot in Critical Care for someone who might recover," the doctor replied.

Beth swallowed her tears. "I hate to wake Jack."

"It's okay. The ex-wife is there with Mr. Hankins."

That settled things for Beth. There was no way she would leave Roy in Monique's care. "Could a nurse come in and watch Chloe for a little while?" she asked, and he nodded. "Thanks," she said grimly, then walked through the door and toward the elevator.

CHAPTER 13

A nurse from the Critical Care Unit directed Beth to Roy's new location. A lamp by the bed threw a soft light on Roy's still face, but most of the sophisticated medical equipment was gone, indicating that the doctors had given up hope. Monique was sitting in a chair and lifted a hand to her hair in an automatic gesture as Beth walked in.

"Where's Hipolita?" Beth asked.

"She left the minute I got here," Monique replied. "She hates me." Beth was thinking that the housekeeper was a good judge of character when Monique continued. "Chloe's still improving?" Beth nodded, and they were quiet for a while, then Monique spoke again. "How old do you think I am?" Before Beth could answer, she supplied the information, "I'm thirty-four. That's about eighty in Hollywood years," she laughed bitterly.

"You are very beautiful," Beth said. "Just like Jack. You two were a perfect match."

"Jack and I might have made a pretty picture, but we're as different as night and day. I guess he hasn't told you much about our brief marriage."

"He said you didn't want to have children," Beth replied.

"Always the southern gentleman." Monique sighed. "Well, Beth, we've got lots of time so I'm going to tell you the whole sordid story. Six years ago Jack went to France as a consultant for his law firm. I was living in Paris, working at a burlesque, and waiting for my big break. Do you know what a burlesque is?" she asked, and Beth had to shake her head. "It's a musical variety show, but it's risqué, at least by American standards. Most people would consider it a bad job, but the pay was good, and I worked at night, which left my days free for auditions.

"Jack came to the club with some of the French guys he was working with. He had a freshness about him that was irresistible, so after my set I put on some clothes and went to his table. We talked for a while, and then he invited me to dinner. Struggling actresses never pass up a free meal, so I suggested an expensive place I'd only seen from the outside.

"We spent a lot of time together during the next few weeks, and when it was time for him to go back to the States, he begged me to marry him. I'd been looking for a way to get to Hollywood, so I said yes."

"You didn't love him?"

Monique shrugged. "Yes, no, maybe. He was gorgeous, he had money, he promised to help me with my career, and I didn't know how far Georgia was from Hollywood," she added with a wry smile. "His lawyer friends used their influence to get us a special license, and we were married the next day. Once we were settled in Georgia, Jack arranged for me to take acting lessons. I couldn't have been happier until I started feeling sick.

"I ignored it for a few weeks, but finally I went to the doctor, afraid I might have cancer or something. But it was even worse than I expected. I was pregnant." She said the word like it was a death sentence. "An abortion was the obvious solution." Beth couldn't control a shudder. "Then it wasn't Chloe, just a complication," Monique offered as a defense. They sat for a few minutes, listening to the machine breathe for Roy, and then Monique continued. "My father was an American soldier. Did you know that?"

Beth shook her head. "No, but that explains your excellent English."

"He went AWOL and eloped with my mother when she was fifteen. The Army quietly discharged him, and they moved in with my grandparents. They still live in that same little house in a small town where tuna is the major industry." She said the words as if this was the saddest fate she could imagine. "I'll bet you've never seen a tuna plant."

"I haven't," Beth had to confess.

Monique wrinkled her nose. "The whole town stinks. I don't mean that you get a little whiff of the tuna every once in a while. I mean that everything, every day smells like fish. It's taken me years to get rid of the stench, and even now I feel driven to keep putting distance between myself and that tuna plant.

"I thought Jack understood how important my career was to me. I thought he would realize that ending the pregnancy was the only logical choice, but he didn't. First he talked, then he negotiated, then he threatened. Jack is a bundle of contradictions. He married an exotic dancer, then tried to turn me into Susie Homemaker. Only Jack Gamble is arrogant enough to think that marriage to him would change me so completely. Finally I had to tell him that I couldn't even guarantee that the baby was his." Beth was shocked but controlled her expression. "I felt a little sorry for him then. Poor Jack. Raised by Puritans—"

"Mormons," Beth corrected.

"Same philosophy—monogamy and such. Anyway, I couldn't surrender my life, my dreams." She paused, and the women looked at each other. "Not to Jack or anyone."

"So what did he do?"

"He asked me to give him twenty-four hours and I agreed, although I thought nothing could change my mind. And I've got to hand it to him. He worked out a deal that even I couldn't refuse. He drew up a contract that gave me a lot of money and a movie deal with a well-known producer in France. All I had to do was live in a house he'd rented in the Everglades until the baby was born, then give him an uncontested divorce and full custody."

"And you agreed?" Beth asked, trying to hide her horror.

Monique shrugged. "He was offering much more than I could have accomplished myself in the same six months, so of course I signed. Roy and I left for Florida the next morning, and at first I thought I would die of boredom, but Roy made the time pass quickly. He let me win at cards, took me for long walks on the beach, and made delicious meals."

Beth glanced at the man lying on the hospital bed. "I didn't know Roy could cook."

Monique's eyes followed the direction of her gaze. "He is a wonderful cook and a good friend. We've stayed in touch," she admitted.

"You and Roy?"

Monique nodded as a nurse came in to change Roy's position.

Beth and Monique walked out. "Roberta said you had a hospital room for the night."

"Yes. I'm going to try to get some rest. I'll be by to see Chloe later."

Beth watched Monique disappear down the hall, then returned to Chloe's room. Jack's eyes opened when she walked in. "Where were you?" he asked, his voice heavy with sleep.

"Roy's been moved . . ." She saw the hope in his eyes and extinguished it quickly. "He's no better, but Monique was with him and she wanted to talk."

His expression became guarded. "About what?"

"A lot of different things," Beth tried to be vague, but he was still holding her with his gaze. "Roy, Chloe, France."

"She told you everything." It was a statement.

"Maybe not everything, but enough," Beth hedged.

His fingers sifted through his hair. "I didn't want you to know how stupid I was . . ."

"I'd met Monique before, so I already knew you weren't wise to marry her," Beth replied.

"Or that there was any question about Chloe's parentage," he continued.

"Did you ever have blood tests done to be sure?" Beth forced herself to ask.

"No," Jack shook his head. "I meant to, but after the first moment I held Chloe in my arms, I knew tests were unnecessary."

Beth smiled. "You knew instinctively that she was your child."

He dragged his eyes up to meet hers. "I knew it didn't matter who her biological father was. Chloe was mine, and nobody was ever going to take her away from me."

Beth touched his chin. "Even though she looks like Monique, she has your jaw. When she's being stubborn it sticks out just like yours. And your mother's."

"Daddy? Beth?" the child whispered from behind them. "Am I sick?"

They both rushed to opposite sides of the bed, and Beth took the little hand in hers while Jack stroked the silky hair. "You and Roy had a wreck," he told her. "You're in a hospital, but the doctor said you can go home soon and you've got a pink cast."

Chloe was pleased by this and asked if her friends could sign it. Once she was assured that this would be allowed, her eyes became serious. "Daddy, when we had the wreck, Roy got blood on his shirt. Did the doctor say Roy can go home soon too?"

"Roy was hurt very badly," Jack began. "The doctors are trying to fix him, but . . ."

Jack was interrupted by Dr. Long's appearance. He started running at the doorway and hopped up onto the foot of Chloe's bed, startling a giggle from the child. "Hi," he extended a hand. "I'm your doctor."

"You're too funny to be a doctor," Chloe pronounced.

"I am funny, but I'm still your doctor," Dr. Long insisted, and Chloe looked to Jack for confirmation. When her father nodded, Chloe turned back to the man seated at the end of her bed. "So, how do you feel?" he asked.

"I'm thirsty," she said. "My head feels bad and I hate all these things by me." She looked at the equipment that surrounded her bed.

"You can have something to drink," he said, making a note on her chart. "Your head will start feeling better soon, and we'll get rid of some of that stuff right now."

Chloe smiled, then studied Dr. Long carefully. "Are you a good doctor?"

"I am an excellent doctor."

"Then could you fix Roy?"

Jack stepped forward to intervene, but Dr. Long spoke first. "Roy's spine was broken and his brain went without air for a very long time. If he stays alive he might not ever be able to walk again or even talk. Sometimes when a person dies, it's the best thing for them."

Chloe accepted the words bravely, and Dr. Long said he had to check on other patients, but promised to send Chloe some water. After the doctor was gone, Chloe looked at her father. "If Roy dies, do you think he will go to heaven?" she asked, tears clinging to her dark lashes.

"I think they'll have to make a whole new room in heaven so they'll have a place good enough for Roy," he answered.

Chloe leaned back against her pillow, and Beth thought her heart would break. A nurse came in with a pitcher of ice water and told them that the police were waiting to talk to Chloe. Beth looked at Jack. "I don't really think she's up to that yet."

He shrugged. "We might as well get it over with." He walked through the door and returned a few minutes later with Mark Iverson and a stranger.

"I regret the necessity of this, but the longer we wait the more Chloe will forget," Mark said. "We'll be quick," he promised, stepping up beside the bed.

Chloe smiled at him. "Hey, Brother Iverson. Is Emily at home with her mom?"

Mark nodded. "Yes, she is. Chloe, I'd like you to meet Agent Gray. He lives in Atlanta, and he's come down here to help us figure out what happened last night."

"It's nice to meet you, Chloe." Agent Gray was tall and thin, almost gaunt, with dark, sad eyes. "What can you tell us about the accident?"

The child's expression dimmed. "I wanted to stay at the party, but Roy told me if I'd be good, he'd buy me some ice cream, so I put on my seat belt. Then Roy said we had a 'tail' and I thought that was funny, but he didn't laugh." She looked over at her father and he nodded for her to continue. "Roy started driving fast and his window broke and then a car crashed into us." Tears welled up in her eyes. "Roy got blood on his shirt."

"Was Roy taking you home?" Mark asked gently.

"After the ice cream," Chloe affirmed. "He said Hipolita would help me hang up my Dorothy dress." She looked around the room. "Where is my Dorothy dress?"

Jack moved closer to the bed. "It got torn, but I'll buy you a new one."

Agent Gray addressed Jack. "I might have more questions for her later, but that's all for now." Then he turned to Chloe. "It was nice to meet you, and I hope you get feeling better soon. I'm going to talk to your dad for a minute." He pointed into the sitting room and Jack nodded.

Even though Beth had not been specifically included in the invitation, she followed the men into the adjoining room. "Where's Winston Jones?" she asked.

"We took this case away from the local boys," Agent Gray said as he pulled a black-and-white photograph of a dark-colored van from his pocket and showed it to Jack. "This is the car that was used to force your Jeep off the road. Do you recognize it?" They examined the picture, then both shook their heads.

"It's a rental. Somebody reserved it in a false name and paid cash. It was found behind a busy truck stop a few miles down from the crash site. We're interviewing people at the truck stop, but the chances of finding anyone who remembers the driver are slim."

"There are a couple of things we need to make you aware of," Mark said slowly. His eyes were serious, and Beth grew uneasy. "We checked Roy's phone records for the past six months. He received phone calls on several different occasions from numbers associated with a known Mafia man named Felix Hummer."

"Which is where I come in," Agent Gray explained. "I'm with the FBI's organized crime unit in Atlanta, and any time Hummer's name shows up, I get a call."

"Felix Hummer is my ex-wife's new boyfriend," Jack said with a frown. "But I don't know why he'd be calling Roy."

"Roy wasn't talking to Felix, but to your ex-wife, Monique Rouleau," Mark said and Jack looked up in surprise.

Agent Gray explained. "All of Hummer's phones are tapped, and we were able to get transcripts of the conversations. They seem innocent enough, but it's possible that Roy Hankins was working for Hummer and that Miss Rouleau was a relay point."

"The middle man, so to speak," Mark added.

"Why would Roy be working for Monique's boyfriend?" Jack asked in obvious confusion.

"It could have been a long-standing relationship. Felix Hummer has 'employees' everywhere," Agent Gray told them.

"Or it could be a recent development related to the Ferris Burke trial," Mark said.

"You think Hummer hired Roy to spy on me?" Jack was incredulous.

Beth put a hand on Jack's arm. "Monique told me that she and Roy have stayed in touch." She turned to the agents. "I'm sure the calls were just conversations between old friends."

Agent Gray shrugged. "Maybe so." He cleared his throat. "But there are also five calls to Hankins over the past two weeks from a cell phone registered to your missing witness, Amber Harper."

Beth saw Jack's jaw clench. "Are you sure the calls were from Amber Harper?"

Agent Gray shook his head. "Anyone could have placed the calls using Amber Harper's phone, but it hasn't been reported as stolen. The last call was just a few hours before the Fuller's party." The agent paused. "Which leads me to believe that Hankins was headed to a meeting with Amber Harper when he was shot."

"Roy said he had a date," Beth whispered. "Maybe it was Amber."

Jack shook his head. "If his date was Amber Harper, he would have told me."

Beth tried to think. "What if Amber made him promise not to?"

"Roy knew I could keep a secret."

There was an awkward silence before Agent Gray spoke again. "We've got a team going over the apartment with a fine-tooth comb. They found these." He pulled a few sheets of paper from his coat pocket.

The first page contained lines from the nursery rhyme *Mary Had a Little Lamb*. Several words were underlined, and there was a big X at the bottom of the page. The second looked similar, except that it quoted *Little Bo Peep*.

Jack looked up at the agents. "This is just nonsense."

"They could be coded instructions to Hankins from Felix Hummer," Agent Gray said.

"Or they could be totally unrelated to the case," Mark admitted.

"I don't think Hankins would have saved them in a neat little file on his desk if they were unimportant," Agent Gray pointed out. "And the X on the bottom looks like a signature. Hummer is known in the underworld as 'Mr. X'."

Jack ran his fingers through his hair. "So, you think that Roy was working for Felix Hummer and that he found Amber, but didn't tell me."

Mark shifted his feet. "That's the way it looks."

"But why?" Jack asked.

"Maybe Hummer wants your witness and was working out a deal with Roy to turn her over," Agent Gray suggested.

"Why would Hummer want my witness and why would Roy even consider giving her to him?" There was a desperate tone in Jack's voice. "Roy knew I needed her to win my case."

Mark began hesitantly. "Felix Hummer is one of the richest men in the world."

Jack shook his head. "Roy couldn't be bought. I'll never believe that."

"Or, it could have been blackmail. The fact that those messages use nursery rhymes makes me wonder if Hummer was threatening Chloe." Jack looked up sharply as Mark continued. "But we don't have any proof of that."

Agent Gray leaned forward. "Our working theory for the time being is that Hankins knew where Amber Harper was, and Hummer was either paying him or blackmailing him to hand her over. Hankins tried a double-cross and got shot."

Before Jack could respond, a technician came to take Chloe for more x-rays. The FBI men excused themselves, promising to return when they had more information. Once they were alone, Beth waited for Jack to initiate a conversation, but he just kept staring at the copy of Roy's phone bill. When they wheeled Chloe back into the room, Dr. Long followed with a smile. "Everything looks good. If her rate of improvement continues, she can go home by the end of the week."

After the doctor left, Hipolita arrived with fresh clothes, and Beth gratefully took a shower. When she came out Roberta was sitting in a chair by the bed, talking to Jack while Chloe slept. "You look marginally better than a corpse," Roberta told her.

"Thanks," Beth returned.

"You won't do Chloe any good by killing yourself. Get some rest and eat occasionally. But right now the two of you had better go down and speak to all those people in the lobby."

"What people in the lobby?" Beth asked.

Roberta shrugged. "I'd say half of Georgia has come to check on Chloe."

Beth's heart swelled with gratitude. "People are so kind," she reached out to grasp Jack's hand.

"Do we really have to go down there?" he asked, pushing a hand through his hair.

"They took the time to come. The least we can do is thank them."

"Go on!" Roberta commanded. "I'll watch Chloe!"

Jack frowned but allowed Beth to lead him into the hall. They ran into Malcolm Schneckenberger by the elevator. He asked about Chloe and said that Mr. Fuller sent his best wishes. Beth could tell by the way he shifted his eyes that Mr. Fuller had sent nothing of the kind. Malcolm said he'd wait in the room with Roberta, and Jack nodded, then they proceeded on to the lobby.

"Why is Mr. Fuller acting so strange?" Beth asked when Malcolm was beyond hearing.

"Maybe he thinks Chloe's injuries are as fake as mine were," Jack said.

Beth was trying to think of a response when they walked into the crowded lobby. Bishop Sterling and his wife were there. Myrtle was standing by Miss Corrine, who was talking to Grady from the garage. Ellen Northcutt and Kate Iverson were right in front. Miss Eugenia was nearby, along with the other members of the Haggerty Genealogical Society. Brother Stoops was parked beside her in his wheelchair.

"I barely know these people," Jack whispered. "Why would they come?"

"Because they are good Christians," Beth told him softly.

"We came as soon as we heard," Miss Eugenia said, rushing forward. "I can't believe that Annabelle didn't call me last night to let me know." This with a venomous glance at her sister, who was again accompanied by Derrick Morgan.

"There was nothing anyone could do last night," Beth responded. "And I'm sorry that I won't be able to work at the library for a while."

"We'll manage," Miss Eugenia assured her.

"You could lock the doors and nobody would even notice," Annabelle said as she elbowed her way over. "Is Chloe still improving?" Beth nodded. "What about Roy?"

"No change," Jack answered, and Annabelle gave him a sympathetic look.

Beth took his hand and started around the room, speaking to everyone. When they reached Myrtle, Beth explained about the

Dorothy dress. "Jack will replace it," she promised, but Myrtle waved this offer aside.

"You just take care of Chloe, and I'm so sorry about Roy. Everybody's praying for him."

Tears collected in Beth's eyes as she gave the big woman a quick hug. Then they moved on to greet Bishop Sterling and Beth's visiting teachers. "We'd like to bring in some meals when Chloe comes home from the hospital," Sister Baylor offered.

"If I know Haggerty, you'll have more casseroles than you can eat in a year," Kate said.

"People in Haggerty have a strong sense of duty." Miss Eugenia nodded approvingly.

Jack smiled, but shook his head. "We appreciate your offer," he included the visiting teachers and Miss Eugenia in his comments. "But if people start bringing in food, our housekeeper will get worried about her job security."

"You'll never talk them out of it," Kate murmured as they moved down the line.

"Are you sure that's the real Jack Gamble?" Derrick whispered to Beth. "Maybe it's his nonevil twin," he suggested outrageously, and she laughed.

Brother Stoops wheeled over and handed Beth a Wal-Mart sack full of ripe tomatoes. "I just picked these last evening."

"I can't thank you enough, all of you," Beth raised her voice so that everyone could hear. "We'll tell Chloe how many wonderful friends she has."

It took them quite a while to accept good wishes and encouragement from all their visitors, and when they got back to Chloe's room, they found Malcolm reading the paper, Roberta watching *Mr. Ed* on Nickelodeon, and Monique standing by Chloe's bed promising to bring all kinds of gifts during her next visit. Beth put the tomatoes from Brother Stoops on the table with Derrick's oranges, and stared at the actress.

"So you're leaving?" Jack asked as he crossed the room. "Before Chloe goes home? Before Roy takes a turn for better or worse?"

"Chloe's going to be fine and Roy, well, you know I never was one to hang around to the bitter end," Monique quipped. "So I'm off to

L.A. unless you think you'll be needing any of my body parts," she added with a brilliant smile.

Jack shook his head. "It looks like you can keep everything for now, but remember that one kidney is bought and paid for. You should use the money to buy yourself a house and get away from Felix Hummer," Jack advised, and Monique got a petulant look on her face. "I'm serious. The FBI thinks your boyfriend had something to do with Roy's accident."

"That's ridiculous," Monique denied, but Beth noticed that her face paled. Beth followed Monique out into the hall and caught her by the arm. "The FBI knows that you were calling Roy regularly and he got a couple of coded letters signed with an X . . ."

"Mr. X? You mean Felix?" Monique hissed back, and Beth nodded. "I can't imagine why Felix would hurt Roy."

"Maybe he was jealous."

"No, not Felix." Monique sounded certain.

"Well, they think Roy was going to give Jack's witness to Mr. Hummer, and I figure it has to have something to do with you," Beth insisted.

"Roy choose me over Jack?" Monique asked with a laugh. "Not in a million years."

"Well, Felix Hummer is dangerous, and you need to stay away from him."

"Felix is my ticket to success, and you tell Jack that he'd better not help the FBI collect evidence against him. I've never tried to get back any of my parental rights, but all that can change in a heartbeat." With that, Monique tossed her head and turned away.

Beth watched Monique disappear down the hall, racked by true hatred for the first time in her life. Malcolm was still reading his paper in the sitting room and mumbled something when she walked by, but Beth was intent on speaking to Jack and ignored him. Jack looked up when Beth came through the door. "What did Monique have to say?"

"That regardless of Felix Hummer's criminal activities, she plans to stay with him, and if you help the FBI collect evidence against him, she might sue for parental rights," she whispered.

Jack sighed. "That's what I need. Another custody suit." He went into the other room to make some phone calls, and Beth watched cartoons with Chloe. When the child fell asleep, she went to find Jack as Roberta arrived with hamburgers from Wendy's.

"Sorry I didn't get you one, Malcolm," the secretary said as she distributed lunch. "I thought you'd be gone by now."

Beth couldn't tell if it was truly an oversight or Roberta's way of suggesting that Malcolm leave, but she refused to eat in front of the little man. "You can have mine, Malcolm."

"Oh, no!" Malcolm was horrified by the suggestion. "I'll grab something later."

Beth ignored him and used a plastic knife from Chloe's lunch tray to cut her sandwich. She gave him half, then settled down beside Jack. While they ate Roberta told them that she had searched exhaustively for Roy's relatives without success. "Both parents are dead, same for an uncle. I found a few cousins, but none of them knew him well. I'll keep trying."

"I'll help," Malcolm offered, but Jack shook his head.

"Just let Roberta handle it. Did you talk to Judge Tate?" Jack asked his secretary.

Roberta sighed. "He said he'll give you a few days, but he wasn't happy."

Jack nodded. "Ferris won't be happy either. We'd better get over there." Roberta stood and put her purse on her shoulder. "Will you be okay here?" he nodded toward Beth.

"We'll be fine," Beth assured him.

She dozed after they left and woke an hour later with her head pounding. Malcolm got her some aspirin from one of the nurses and suggested that she try to go back to sleep.

"Mr. Fuller doesn't mind that you're up here?" Beth asked, curling up on the couch.

Malcolm shrugged. "I took a few days of vacation, so he can't fire me."

Beth closed her eyes against the pain. "I can't understand why you don't just quit."

"Working for Oscar has advantages," Malcolm replied. "After a few years of dealing with politicians, I could run for office myself!" They laughed together at the absurdity of this suggestion. Then Beth slept for a while.

When she opened her eyes, she saw Jack's parents walking through the door. They had a Dr. Barbie for Chloe, and Beth promised to give it to her the minute she woke up. Then she offered to call Jack at his office, but Sister Gamble shook her head.

"It's probably just as well that we missed him. It will take some time for us to mend hurt feelings, but I'm determined to work at it." Sister Gamble reached into her purse. "I don't know how he'll feel about this, since it's coming from me, but I heard he's been going back to church . . ."

Beth accepted the set of scriptures with Jack's name on the front. "I'm sure he'll be very pleased."

After the Gambles left, Beth's parents called. "We were trying to decide if we should come back to the hospital or if we would just be in the way," her mother said.

Beth assured them that they were welcome to visit anytime. Just as she hung up the phone, Mark Iverson walked into the room, followed closely by the agent from Atlanta. "Is Mr. Gamble here?" he asked.

"He had to go visit his client," Beth explained.

"We've got some information for him." Agent Gray looked at Malcolm.

Malcolm stood. "I'll step into the other room while you talk," he offered, and the agents nodded in unison. With rising anxiety Beth faced them, knowing what they had to say couldn't be good.

Agent Gray spoke first. "The vehicle we found has been thoroughly examined, and it was perfectly clean. Not a print, a hair sample, or a foreign fiber."

"What does that mean?" Beth asked.

"Professionals," Mark said.

The other agent nodded. "I'm more convinced than ever that Felix Hummer is involved," Agent Gray agreed.

"But why?"

Agent Gray rubbed the stubble on his cheeks. "Burke is building a big dinner theater in Las Vegas, and my sources say that Hummer thinks it will cut into his casino business. So maybe he wants Burke to go to jail."

"Or there could be a political reason for Hummer to interfere with the outcome of the trial," Mark offered.

"Monique told us that Mr. Hummer wants to become more involved in local politics," Beth provided. "That's why they wanted to go to Mr. Fuller's party on Saturday night."

This didn't seem to surprise Mark. "Oscar Fuller has made it known that whoever wins that trial will get his nomination for the state senate seat, so if Hummer had a deal worked out with Kilgore, he'd want to make sure that Jack loses."

Beth thought about the fresh-faced district attorney and shook her head. "I can't believe that Mr. Kilgore would be involved with organized crime."

"Greed and power do strange things to people," Mark said slowly.

Agent Gray nodded. "We'll start looking for a connection between Kilgore and Hummer, but in the meantime you all need to be careful."

"Jack is extremely security conscious," Beth said.

"I've seen the fence," Mark agreed with a smile. "But Felix Hummer is very dangerous."

Agent Gray extended a business card with several phone numbers written on the back. "I'm going to be staying in Albany for a few days. Call if you need me."

"And I'm sorry about Roy," Mark said as they left. "He was a good man." Beth didn't realize he had used the past tense until they were halfway down the hall.

Malcolm stayed with Beth until Jack returned, then said he'd give them some time alone. Once he was gone, Beth told Jack about her visit from the FBI, and Jack ran his fingers through his hair. "I can't believe that Roy was in with Felix Hummer. Or Lance either, for that matter."

"All I know is that Roy loves you, Jack." Beth felt the words needed to be said.

"I know," Jack agreed, then glanced at the end table and saw his new scriptures. "Did you order them for me?" His voice grew soft, making her wish that she had.

"Your mother brought them by this afternoon." She didn't know what to expect in the way of reaction, but Jack just continued to stare at the burgundy leather.

"I'll miss those little words of wisdom you scribbled all over yours," he said finally, then put an arm around her.

"How did Ferris take the news that the trial is going to be delayed?" she asked.

"He's tired of being in jail, so he wasn't pleased," Jack responded. "But I don't want to talk about Ferris right now. I'd rather talk about us. You and me." Beth nodded, accepting the inevitable. "After Monique, I swore I'd never trust another woman. Don't you think it's ironic that now I've lost my heart to a girl who's already promised hers to someone else?"

She took a ragged breath. "I can't remember the sound of David's voice, and I have to keep his picture on the table by my bed to keep from forgetting what he looked like. You have filled my mind until there's no room for David anymore."

He tilted her head up with his hand, and she saw triumph in his eyes. "Do you expect me to feel bad about that?"

"How can you trust me, Jack? I promised David forever, and I've already forgotten him."

"I'll take my chances," he said.

"Why did you start coming back to church?"

"I wanted to see Chloe in the Primary program," he began slowly.

"You came to conference too," Beth reminded him. "Then you taught Chloe the first article of faith and started reading the scriptures."

"I wanted to impress you."

"I'm impressed. So what now?"

He sighed. "I'm not sure where I stand with the Lord. But I do know that I want Chloe to have a father like yours." He reached down to stroke her cheek. "And I want to be the man of your dreams."

Beth bit her lip to stop it from trembling and picked up his new scriptures. She turned to Alma 32:27. After clearing her throat, she began to read. " 'But behold, if ye will awake and arouse your faculties, even to an experiment upon my words, and exercise a particle of faith, yea, even if ye can no more than desire to believe, let this desire work in you, even until ye believe in a manner that ye can give place for a portion of my words'." She looked up into his blue eyes.

He nodded. "I do *want* to believe."

"And you've already exercised a particle of faith."

"But I've wasted so much time, and I've done things that I shouldn't have. Nothing terrible," he assured her. "I never took drugs, so you don't have to worry about my chromosomes."

She had to laugh. "Chloe proves the quality of your chromosomes, and recognizing that you've made mistakes is the first step in the repentance process. Remorse is the second."

"I want us to be a family, Beth." He nuzzled her forehead. "I'll do whatever I have to, but it may take some time. Maybe by Christmas . . ."

"So soon?" Beth interrupted.

"You think it will take longer to get me straightened out?" He gave her a beautiful smile, and she was powerless to resist him.

"It still doesn't seem right to make a decision that affects someone else without asking him first."

"I don't see that you have an option there," Jack said reasonably. "David is dead."

"Miss Eugenia offered to tell all her elderly friends that if they 'pass over' anytime soon to find him and explain the situation. Roy and I were laughing about that at the Fuller's party . . ." Beth's throat clogged with tears and she couldn't continue.

"Maybe Roy will work things out with David and write you a message in the clouds." Beth pressed her eyes closed. Jack didn't have any hope for Roy either. "But you will, won't you, Beth?" he asked.

"Will what?"

"Marry me."

She took a deep breath, then nodded. "Yes."

For the next few days their lives fell into a predictable routine. Hipolita delivered fresh clothes every morning, then spent the day with Roy. Roberta and Malcolm made regular visits, usually bringing fast food. The Gambles and Middletons came by, frequently bearing toys. Jack always seemed to miss these visits, and Beth wondered if he had some kind of internal radar.

Beth invested all her energies into entertaining Chloe and coaxing the child to eat. Jack divided his time between his daughter, Roy, and Ferris Burke. On Thursday morning Chloe woke up feeling much better. "I wish I could eat some Captain Crunch," she said around a mouthful of the Cream of Wheat the hospital had provided.

"We'll ask Dr. Long about that when he comes to see you," Beth suggested.

The doctor came by an hour later and promised to arrange Captain Crunch for lunch. "The x-rays still look good," he told Beth while Chloe watched cartoons. "We've put her on a strong antibiotic as a precaution, but I'm very optimistic. I don't want to get your hopes up, but there's a good chance we'll let her go home tomorrow."

After calling Jack on his cell phone to tell him this wonderful news, the morning passed slowly for Beth. Malcolm brought her a taco salad for lunch and apologized to Chloe. "I asked the nurse if I could bring you a Happy Meal, and she said your diet was restricted. But as soon as the doctor says it's okay, I'll buy you whatever you want to eat."

"How about a banana split from Fifty-Five Flavors?" Chloe asked.

"It's yours," Malcolm promised.

Annabelle and Derrick arrived as Malcolm was leaving. Beth offered them oranges, tomatoes, or her leftover salad, but they declined. "We worked your shift at the library with Eugenia this morning," Annabelle said with a sigh. "She had Derrick rearranging furniture and made me alphabetize the periodicals while she talked on the phone."

With a smile Beth asked if they wanted to watch *The Brave and Relentless*, but Derrick waved a hand. "No, we listened to the first half on the radio and nothing's happening."

Annabelle and Derrick left when Mrs. Hoffeins from Morrow Academy came in with Get Well Soon cards from all the students in Chloe's class. Then Malcolm called at 4:30 to see if Beth wanted him to bring dinner. She expressed appreciation, but said that Hipolita had brought them a Tupperware container full of sandwiches.

Roberta and Jack arrived at the hospital just as Dr. Long stopped by. Roberta volunteered to entertain Chloe while they talked. Once they were settled in the sitting room, the doctor gave them a big smile. "I've never seen a patient of any age recuperate from a trauma so severe this quickly. I'm going to let her go home, but you'll have to keep her quiet, and I'll see her in my office next Thursday."

"We can't begin to thank you for all you've done," Jack tried to express his gratitude.

"Hey, if I ever get sued, you can defend me!"

Jack smiled. "I'll even give you a discount on my fee."

"That's okay," the doctor shook his head. "I'll pay full price so I know I'm getting your best effort." Then with a wave over his shoulder, he left the room.

"That works out well, since Judge Tate is resuming the trial on Monday," Jack said, and Beth barely had time to digest this before Mark Iverson and Agent Gray walked in. Beth offered them a seat on the couch and Jack sat across from them. "Any news?" he asked.

Agent Gray nodded. "We've been checking into the Kilgore angle. We found out from his secretary that Kilgore's computer password is X-Man."

"So now you think Lance Kilgore is X?" Beth asked in confusion.

Agent Gray shrugged. "He had the most to gain by keeping Amber Harper from testifying. Also, the search of Roy's apartment turned up one set of fingerprints we can't identify and some pictures of your ex-wife," Mark told Jack.

Mark Iverson stepped forward. "Some look like surveillance shots. Others were taken with special cameras and are quite . . . embarrassing." Color rose in Mark's cheeks.

"Makes us wonder if the X guy was blackmailing Hankins with these pictures."

"I don't see how pictures of Monique, compromising or otherwise, would convince Roy to throw my case out the window."

"Unless he thought they would hurt your chances for the state senate," Mark suggested.

Jack shook his head. "Monique has done any number of embarrassing things over the years, but we're divorced, and I don't think her actions would reflect on me significantly."

Agent Gray and Mark both stood. "We have to be suspicious of everyone for a while." Jack remained seated, but Beth followed them to the door.

"Chloe's going home tomorrow," she told them.

Mark smiled for the first time since they arrived. "Now that's good news. Kate's dying to see you, but she's funny about leaving Emily."

Beth nodded. "She told me about almost losing her as a baby."

Mark looked at Beth in surprise. "She told you about that?"

"When we went visiting teaching. Is it a secret?" Beth lowered her voice.

"Not really. Kate just never talks about it, even to me. But in addition to her anxiety about being away from Emily, I've asked her not to come."

"That's understandable," Jack contributed from across the room. "Since we're surrounded by criminals and murderers."

"It's not that." Mark looked a little uncomfortable. "Kate is expecting another baby, and I hate for her to be around so many germs. But I'd appreciate it if you wouldn't mention that to Miss Eugenia. She'll kill me if she finds out I told someone else before her."

"We won't tell a soul," Beth promised as the men walked into the hall.

CHAPTER 14

On Friday morning everyone had mixed emotions. They were glad to take Chloe home, but hated leaving Roy. "The doctor said if there's no improvement soon they'll have to transfer him to a long-term care facility." Jack's distress was obvious. "Hipolita will stay with him during the day until after the trial, then we'll face decisions about the future."

They drove slowly to Haggerty, and the sight of Jack's controversial security fence gave Beth a tender sense of coming home. He parked by the patio, then lifted Chloe from the backseat. "You've gotten heavy. I think you've eaten too many bowls of Captain Crunch lately," he teased.

"Dr. Long said I can walk," Chloe told her father, their identical jaws touching.

"I know, but it makes me feel better to carry you," he answered.

Beth walked ahead of them on the way upstairs, opening doors and turning on lights. The house was quiet and a little eerie without Hipolita. And Roy.

That night they ordered pizza, then watched *Escape to Witch Mountain* and carefully avoided painful subjects. After the video was over, Jack told Chloe that he had something important to discuss with her. He draped his arm around Beth's shoulders. "Beth and I are planning to get married," he announced.

Chloe studied their cozy position on the couch for a second. "To each other?"

Jack laughed. "Yes, to each other. That would make Beth your mother."

Chloe's eyes were solemn. "And then she can't ever leave?"

The question was directed to Jack, but Beth answered. "Never."

Chloe nodded. "That would be good, then. Would I call you Mama or still Beth?"

"You choose," Beth suggested.

"You wouldn't be sad if people thought you were old because you had a girl that's five?"

Beth swallowed the sob that rose in her throat. "I'd be so glad to be your mother, I wouldn't care if people think I'm a hundred!"

Chloe laughed with delight. "I can count to a hundred!"

"I know!" Beth gathered the child into her arms and held her close.

"And now I can have a sister!" Chloe cried.

Beth felt herself blush and Jack laughed. "You can have two or three," he promised outrageously.

When it was bedtime they discussed where Chloe should sleep. "She should probably stay with me," Beth said, and he nodded.

"Which leaves me up here all alone." He lifted the child and carried her downstairs. "But not for long." He grinned back at Beth.

On Saturday they moved Chloe into the den downstairs and let her receive guests like a queen. The Northcutts came with crayon drawings, and Kate brought Emily, who squealed with delight when she saw Chloe. The Friends of the Library sent a potted plant and a note promising casseroles the next week. The Middletons spent an awkward couple of hours getting to know Jack, and the Gambles spent an even more uncomfortable thirty minutes trying to make conversation with their uncooperative son.

Beth had assumed that they would skip church that week, but when she walked into the kitchen on Sunday morning, Jack was dressed and ready. "You're not going?" He pointed at her sweatpants and T-shirt.

"I thought I should stay here with Chloe."

"But my daddy might be scared at church by himself," Chloe voiced concern.

Jack raised an eyebrow and Beth looked at them, trying to decide what to do. Finally Hipolita solved the problem for her. "I stay with Chloe and she help me make enchiladas for a good dinner. You and Mr. Jack go to church."

Beth turned to Chloe. "You're sure that's okay with you?"

The little girl nodded. "I'll help you find a dress." She took Beth's hand and led the way down the hall, then sat on the bed while Beth changed. "I'd like to go to Primary," she admitted. "But I'll be glad to make dinner with Hipolita."

"And once you learn how you can show me," Beth proposed. "I'll bet we could really make a mess with tortillas and refried beans!"

On Monday morning, Beth met Jack in the kitchen and watched him eat a bowl of cereal before he left for the courtroom. "I wish I could be there to see you in action," she told him with a smile. "Are you nervous?"

"Just a little. A big kiss would go a long way toward calming me, though."

Beth gave him two, then waved good-bye as he climbed into the SUV and drove to Albany. She served Chloe breakfast in bed, and they had just started watching *Gilligan's Island* when the phone rang. It was Malcolm.

"How is everybody today?" the little man asked.

"I'm fine, Chloe's fine," Beth told him. "Are you going to the courtroom?"

"On my way now," Malcolm confirmed. "I have my cell phone, so call if you need me."

The morning passed slowly, and at noon Beth heated up soup Hipolita had left in the refrigerator for them. "Will my daddy come and eat with us?" Chloe wanted to know.

"No, he's busy with Mr. Burke today."

While Chloe took a nap Beth tried to watch *The Brave and Relentless*, but couldn't concentrate. When the buzzer on the gate finally rang about three o'clock, she ran downstairs and pushed the intercom button. It was Malcolm, so she entered the code and waited anxiously for him by the kitchen door.

"I brought Chloe the banana split I promised her." He handed Beth the sticky container and she put it in the freezer.

"How did things go today?"

"Lance had the medical examiner describe in detail the viciousness of the attack on Sean Ballard," was Malcolm's less-than-comforting reply. "But Jack handled him well on cross."

"You think Jack's winning?"

"I think he held his own."

Beth sighed. "I'll just be glad when it's all over."

"We all will," Malcolm assured her. "Is there anything you need for me to do here?"

"I think what Jack will need most tonight is peace and quiet," Beth discouraged his company as gently as possible.

Malcolm took the hint and left soon afterward. When Jack and Roberta got home, they collapsed into chairs at the kitchen table and Beth distributed more of Hipolita's soup. Roberta ate hers hungrily, but Jack just swirled his spoon around the bowl.

"So?" Beth prompted when she sat across from him.

"I think I made some points with the jury on cross. Mostly I just hammered at the fact that the entire case is circumstantial. Lance will finish up tomorrow, and I'll probably present my first witness on Wednesday. By the time I get through painting Sean Ballard as the slimeball he was, the jury will be glad he's dead. And with no concrete evidence against Ferris, they should acquit on reasonable doubt." His spoon paused. "We stopped by the hospital on our way home. Roy's condition is unchanged."

Beth nodded. "I know. I called a little while ago."

"Well." Roberta put her spoon in her empty bowl and stood. "I'm going to go wake up Chloe, and I think Jack could benefit from a nice, brisk walk around the park."

"Sounds good to me." He gave Beth half a smile.

"Me too," she agreed. "Let me put on my tennis shoes."

Jack pushed his uneaten soup away. "I'll go see Chloe for a few minutes, then meet you by the garage." He leaned closer. "Just like old times."

Their walk was more strolling than brisk, and they didn't discuss Roy's tenuous hold on life or his questionable loyalties. They didn't mention the accident or the outcome of Ferris Burke's trial. They just walked and enjoyed the crisp autumn air.

On Tuesday, Jack was gone before Beth got a chance to wish him luck. With Hipolita spending so much time at the hospital, there was actually laundry to be done. Feeling very domestic, Beth arranged Chloe on the couch in the den, then started washing towels and sheets.

Kate dropped by with a chicken casserole and said the visiting teachers and ladies of Haggerty were all desperate to bring in food. She was holding them off for the moment, but didn't know how long she could last. Beth laughed and told her to keep up the good work, but was secretly pleased to have the casserole so they wouldn't have to eat soup two nights in a row.

Beth and Chloe were both waiting anxiously when Jack got home that evening. Roberta wasn't with him, and his grim expression told her that he'd been by the hospital again. He ate a little of Kate's casserole while he described his day.

"Lance finished up with neighbors who testified about the constant fighting between Ferris and Audrey. Ferris is suing one of them over a piece of adjoining property, and the other guy owes him money, so I was able to discredit them both."

"And the jury will ignore their testimony?"

Jack shrugged. "Part of it at least."

"Are you ready for tomorrow?" Beth asked, reaching out to touch his hand.

Jack wove his fingers through hers. "I'm *anxious* for tomorrow."

After Jack left on Wednesday, Beth found the vacuum and suctioned every carpeted surface in the house. Then she mopped the kitchen floor, expecting Hipolita to come in and catch her at any moment. Chloe felt so good that it was a struggle to keep her quiet, and Beth was grateful when Ellen brought Bud and the baby over to entertain her for a while.

"Where's Kristen?" Chloe asked in disappointment.

"She's in school," Ellen apologized. Beth brought down an armful of Barbies, and Chloe instructed Bud on the proper playing procedures while the women talked. When it was time for Ellen to meet Kristen's bus, Beth entered the code to open the gate, then lifted Chloe and followed them out onto the patio.

They watched the Northcutts cross the street, then Beth turned back to the house. Her eyes were drawn to Roy's apartment, and tears threatened to overcome her. She saw a little flicker near a window and blinked, then squinted but could see nothing else. Convinced that her eyes were playing tricks on her, but unnerved just the same, she rushed Chloe inside and locked the door.

Jack seemed a little more relaxed when he came home that night, and Beth mentioned this as they ate the rest of Kate's casserole. "I prefer being on the offensive," he agreed with a smile.

"Who testified today?" Beth asked.

"This morning friends described Ferris as father of the year and Audrey as a hopeless drug addict. Then this afternoon I put Ferris's minister on the stand. He told the jury that Ferris brought little Jasmine to church, but Audrey never came. Lance tried to twist it to look like the minister was testifying for Ferris because he donated money for a new administrative wing at the church, but it's hard to discredit the clergy without looking petty."

"How are you going to convince the jury that Sean Ballard was a lowlife?"

Jack sighed. "Since we haven't been able to find Amber Harper, I guess I'm going to have to put Ferris on the stand."

Chloe finished her dinner and moved to the corner where her Barbies where gathered. Once she was settled, Beth turned to Jack. "Do you think Roy's spirit is still in his body?"

Jack looked up. "You're asking a religious delinquent like me a deep question like that?"

Beth smiled. "Well, I don't know if there is a *real* answer. I just wanted your opinion."

"Even though machines are doing most of the work, technically Roy is still alive, so I think his spirit is still in his body where it belongs."

She nodded. "I'm sure that's right, but sometimes I get the feeling that he's watching us, just like always." She almost mentioned the movement by the window in Roy's apartment, but decided against it. It was probably her imagination, and Jack already had enough to worry about.

After Jack left on Thursday morning, Beth resumed her house-cleaning. She started in Chloe's room, and the child played happily while she worked. Then they moved to Jack's room. She had just finished remaking his bed when the buzzer on the gate rang insistently.

With Chloe on her hip Beth went into the kitchen and pushed the intercom button. "Dry cleaners," the male voice identified himself.

"We don't have anything for you today," Beth responded. Vacuuming and mopping was one thing, but she had no intention of trying to figure out Hipolita's dry-cleaning procedures.

"I got to deliver the stuff from last week," the man replied.

Beth entered the code, then adjusted Chloe onto her other hip and stepped outside. Together they watched the van drive up and park near the garage. A big man emerged from the front seat carrying several articles of clothing wrapped in thin plastic. Beth expected questions about Hipolita since the housekeeper always handled the dry-cleaning deliveries, but the man didn't mention her.

He handed the dry cleaning to Beth and she studied the pink dress and bright red sweater. The outfits weren't hers, and certainly didn't belong to Jack or Roy. Hipolita's wardrobe consisted of an assortment of sweat suits, so it was unlikely they belonged to her either.

"I don't think these are our clothes."

"No kiddin'? Let me check the tags." He stepped forward and Beth saw another movement in the window of Roy's apartment. This time she was certain it wasn't her imagination, and a little cry escaped her lips. "What?" He was uncomfortably close now.

Beth twisted away from him and pressed the strange clothes back into his hands. But before she could insist that he leave, she heard the sound of a car engine. She turned to see a Haggerty Police car pulling up the driveway.

"Hey!" Winston Jones called to them as he climbed from the patrol car. "I saw the gate standing open and thought I'd better check on you."

The deliveryman muttered something under his breath and hurried to his van. Seconds later he was headed down the driveway.

"You know that guy?" Winston asked as the van reached the street.

"He's from the dry cleaner, but he brought us the wrong clothes."

"I know pretty much everybody on this side of the county and I've never seen him before." Winston removed his hat to scratch his head. "Mr. Gamble around?"

"He's at court." Beth's eyes drifted back to Roy's apartment. "Winston, look up at that window." She pointed to the one overlooking the driveway. "I keep seeing something move."

Winston shaded his eyes and studied the window. "Tree limb's casting a shadow," he said slowly. "Might look like something moving if the light hit it right." He turned to Beth. "Or it could just be wishful thinking. We all wish Roy was at home instead of lying in that hospital."

"I guess you're right." Beth forced herself to look away. "And thanks for stopping to check on us." Winston left and Beth turned to Roy's apartment again. "I was thinking we might go up into Roy's house for a minute," she told Chloe.

The child considered this. "I was thinking you could make me a peanut butter sandwich and close the gate before my daddy gets home."

Beth laughed and carried Chloe inside. Then she entered the code into the keypad to close the gate and tried to forget about Roy's haunted apartment. Chloe ate her sandwich and fell asleep. Beth sat in the quiet house, wishing that someone had thought to televise the trial. She asked Malcolm about it when he called later.

"Bringing the courtroom into all the homes in Georgia would have been great free publicity for Jack," Malcolm said with a laugh.

"For Lance too, I guess."

"Just depends on who wins," Malcolm agreed.

Jack called at two o'clock and said that he and Roberta were at the hospital.

"Court is finished already?" Beth tapped her watch to be sure it was working.

"Yeah," Jack answered with a sigh. "Lance is playing some kind of game with us. Ferris testified this morning and Lance was supposed to do his cross this afternoon, but he didn't show up after the lunch break, so the judge adjourned until morning."

"Mr. Kilgore just didn't come back after lunch?" Beth repeated Jack's words. "Why would he do that?"

"He's probably trying to rattle Ferris, but the judge said if Lance isn't in the courtroom by eight o'clock in the morning, the assistant DA will have to take over."

"How did Mr. Burke's testimony go today?" Beth asked, anxious to keep him talking.

"As well as can be expected considering that Lance was jumping up with an objection every thirty seconds."

Beth twisted the phone cord around her finger. "Well, maybe we should hope that Mr. Kilgore doesn't find his way back to the courtroom by eight o'clock tomorrow morning."

"He'll be there," Jack predicted. "Nothing short of death would keep Lance from his moment of glory. I've got to stop by the office, but I'll be home soon, and I thought I'd pick up dinner from Aristotle's."

"Does this mean you're tired of soup and reheated casseroles?"

"I refuse to answer on the grounds that it might incriminate me."

Beth hung up the phone feeling more hopeful than she had since the accident. Hipolita came in from the hospital a couple of hours later. After a brief tour of the house, she found Beth and Chloe in the den. "You clean up," she said.

Beth nodded. "A little, but I still can't cook, so Jack is bringing dinner from Aristotle's tonight." The corners of the Hipolita's mouth turned up, and Beth smiled back.

They had a pleasant dinner, but Beth knew that everyone was reminded of Roy's absence. Chloe watched Hipolita wash dishes while Jack and Beth went for a walk, then they settled in the family room to watch a video. Chloe was asleep by the time it ended, and as Beth stood to take her to her bed, the phone rang. Jack was staring at the blank television screen when she returned, his expression bleak.

"What?" Beth demanded.

"That was Agent Gray. The unidentified fingerprints they found in Roy's apartment belong to Amber Harper."

Beth sat beside him and considered the implications of this news. "So what does that mean?" she asked finally.

"I guess it means that in addition to having telephone conversations with my missing witness, Roy actually had the girl in his apartment at least once, but never said a word to me."

"There has to be an explanation," Beth insisted.

"Up until now, I really thought there was." Jack's tone was desolate. "But this . . ."

"Maybe there was an old warrant for her arrest, and she was afraid to testify," Beth suggested desperately. "Roy might have been trying to talk her into it."

Jack shook his head. "If she didn't want to testify we could have taken a deposition, but Roy didn't make decisions like that on his own. He would have come to me."

Finally Beth sighed in defeat. "I don't know."

"Me either." Jack stood and pulled her up, then they walked together as far as the kitchen.

"I wish I could come to court tomorrow," she told him as he drew her into an embrace.

"I could certainly use the moral support, but I don't think Chloe's up to it."

"You'll call me as soon as the jury reaches a verdict?"

"If I didn't know better, I'd say you doubt my ability to win." She smiled into the warm hollow of his neck, then said good night and went to her room.

Jack and Hipolita were both gone by the time Beth and Chloe got up on Friday morning. Beth fixed Chloe a bowl of cereal, then started discarding the assortment of expired and ruined food that had accumulated in the refrigerator during Hipolita's absence. Chloe finished her breakfast, then begged Beth to let her go upstairs and play Barbies.

"I've kind of got a mess here. Maybe you could just play with those." Beth pointed to the pile of dolls in the corner of the kitchen left over from Bud's visit.

"But I wanted my *Wizard of Oz* ones," Chloe said pitifully.

Beth caved. "I'll go get them."

"And Bath Time Barbie and Skateboard Barbie and Dr. Barbie!" Chloe called after her.

Beth had to make three trips to transfer the requested dolls and their various equipment downstairs. Then Chloe arranged them in a row. "All my Barbies are sick and have to go to the hospital," she explained. "The Scarecrow is real sick." She separated this doll from the rest. "But Dr. Barbie can fix him!" Beth was worried about the wisdom of letting her play such a morbid game, but then the phone rang. And once she heard Jack's voice, she forgot her concerns.

"Did Mr. Kilgore show up?" she asked, glancing at the clock.

"No, and Judge Tate is about to blow a blood vessel. Is Chloe okay?" Beth assured him that she was, then there was a disturbance in the background and Jack said he needed to go. "The Assistant DA is about to start Ferris's cross. I'll call you back later."

Beth barely had a chance to hang up before the phone rang again. This time it was Malcolm. "Beth!" he called over the static in the cellular line. "How's Chloe today?"

"She's fine, Malcolm. Are you going to the courthouse?"

"No, I'm bringing you a surprise instead. I couldn't arrange for the trial to be televised, but a friend loaned me a powerful little transmitter. He's wearing the microphone, and after I drop him off at the courtroom, I'll bring the transmitter to Jack's house so you can hear every word."

"Is that legal?"

"Don't ask," Malcolm laughed. "I meant to have it there first thing this morning, but I've been delayed." There was irritation in his voice, and Beth smiled. Even the unflappable Malcolm got his feathers ruffled occasionally. "But at least you'll get to hear the closing arguments."

Beth was pleased as she hung up the phone. Then she heard thunder rumble outside and walked to the window. Dark clouds were gathering on the horizon, and she shivered. "Is it going to rain?" Chloe asked from her makeshift hospital in the corner.

"I think so." Beth turned on the small television that Hipolita kept on the kitchen counter. It was already tuned to the Weather Channel, and Beth watched the radar for a few seconds.

Thunder rumbled again and the hair stood up on the back of her neck. Something was not right, but she couldn't put her finger on it. Her eyes were drawn to Chloe. Dr. Barbie's black bag was open and all her medical instruments were lying around the prone patients. The Scarecrow seemed to beckon her, and Beth knelt down beside him.

"Is the Scarecrow feeling better?" she asked the child.

Chloe shook her head. "Dr. Barbie's going to have to give him a big operation as soon as she finds her knife."

Beth stroked the Scarecrow's straw hat, and a feeling of peace came over her. Roy was their friend, loyal and true. He would not work against Jack or purposely take Chloe into danger, so it was a waste of time to try and figure out why he might have betrayed them. She put the Scarecrow back down, then stood, using a kitchen chair for balance. Her fingers left prints on the glossy surface, and an idea occurred to her.

"I'll be right back," she told Chloe, then went into her room and picked up her purse. After a little digging she found the card Agent Gray had given her. She dialed his temporary number at the Bureau office in Albany, and the answering machine picked up on the second ring. "This is Beth Middleton, and I was wondering if it's possible to tell how fresh a fingerprint is. Call me if you get this message." She gave him Jack's unlisted number, then hung up, her feeling growing stronger by the minute. Distant thunder sounded again and she walked to the door. She ignored the dark clouds and stared at Roy's apartment.

"Chloe, I'm going to walk over to the garage. You can watch me through the window if you want, but don't come outside or you'll get wet."

Chloe nodded as Beth pushed open the door and hurried out into the wind. She ran across to the garage, past the shiny new Lexus, and up the stairs to Roy's door. With a trembling hand she clasped the knob and turned. The apartment was dark and she wanted to retreat, but she forced herself to go inside. A movement to her left startled a scream.

"I guess you're looking for me," a voice said from the corner of the room.

Beth pressed a hand to her chest. "You're Amber Harper," she whispered, and the girl nodded. "You're not going to try to run away, are you?"

"Naw."

Beth's eyes adjusted to the dim light enough for her to see the young woman. Amber's hair was a dirty blonde color, worn long and tucked behind her ears. She had large features and could have benefited from braces as an adolescent. "How long have you been here?"

"Since the wreck."

"That long?" Beth couldn't hide her surprise.

"I figured this was the last place anyone would look for me."

"You've been watching us."

Amber nodded.

"If I take you to the courthouse right now, will you testify?" Beth asked, and Amber shrugged. "They've had a small delay, so we should get there in time." Beth led the way down the stairs, half-expecting the girl to take off running when they stepped outside. But Amber walked calmly into the Gambles' kitchen.

Chloe looked up from the corner as they came through the door. "Chloe, this is Amber Harper," Beth explained. "We've got to take her to Albany right away, so please go get your shoes on." Chloe didn't look happy about leaving her dolls, but stood and headed toward the door. "How did you keep the FBI from finding you when they searched the apartment?"

"Climbed into the trees by the fence."

The girl was certainly resourceful—Beth had to give her that. Chloe ran back in with her shoes on, and Beth turned to Amber. "I need to change my clothes. You'll still be here when I get back, won't you?"

Amber nodded and with that meager assurance, Beth took Chloe's hand and hurried into her room. Chloe watched from the bed while Beth pulled a jumper over her head. "Who can fix my hair since my daddy's not here?" the child wanted to know.

"Your hair looks fine," Beth replied absently as she reached down to get her shoes. Lightning flashed and illuminated the *Law for Dummies* book Malcolm had loaned her. It reminded her that Malcolm was coming with the transmitter. She frowned, realizing that he was going to be disappointed when he found out that all his efforts had been unnecessary. She picked up the book, thinking that she could return it to him so that his trip wouldn't be a total waste. Then thunder crashed so loudly that it seemed to shake the whole house. Beth screamed and dropped the book.

"What's the matter?" Chloe asked with concern.

"It's okay," Beth assured the child. "The thunder just made me clumsy." She looked down and saw that the book had fallen open. Malcolm had written his name on the inside cover, but instead of taking the time to spell out *Schneckenberger*, he had made a big X. Beth's heart started to pound. She tried to tell herself that the X was just a reflection of Malcolm's hatred for his long last name. But as she stared at the large, angry X, lightning and thunder occurred almost simultaneously.

Beth stepped back from the book, her mind racing. Malcolm knew all about Jack and Roy and the Ferris Burke trial. He had access to the house, Jack's office, the courthouse, everything. It would have been easy for him to blackmail Roy and hinder Jack. The question was, why?

"Beth?" Chloe whispered, and she looked up to see the child watching her. Beth's hands began to shake as she realized that if Malcolm was Mr. X, then he was responsible for Roy's accident. And now he was on his way to the house, which put them all in possible danger.

With as much composure as possible, Beth led Chloe into the kitchen. She was reaching for the phone to try Agent Gray again when the buzzer on the security gate sounded. Beth stared at the intercom as a familiar voice came through the speaker.

"Excuse me. My name is Derrick Morgan . . ."

Beth pushed the talk button frantically. "Derrick!"

"Oh, Beth! I'm glad you're home! I know Jack Gamble said he didn't want any food, but the ladies of Haggerty just wouldn't take no for an answer. The backseat of my car is full of casseroles that Annabelle's making me deliver. If you'll open the gate I'll bring them in and you won't get wet."

Beth was already punching in numbers. Then she turned to Chloe. "You're going with Mr. Derrick for a while." Amber's expression was anxious, but Beth didn't have time for explanations. "Does that sound like fun?" she asked in what she hoped was a cheerful tone.

"Not very much," Chloe responded. "I want to go to court and see my daddy."

"You can see your daddy later. Right now you're going with Derrick." She lifted the child, then pulled open the door. Rain was falling heavily, and a streak of lightning lit the sky.

"If we go outside, the storm will get me wet." Chloe's arms tightened around Beth's neck.

Beth took a deep breath, then looked around the room. The starched linen tablecloth caught her eye and she crossed over to the kitchen table. "Excuse me," she said to Amber as she yanked off the cloth, sending Hipolita's fruit bowl flying. Then she wrapped the stiff fabric around Chloe and ran out into the storm.

"I told you I'd bring the casseroles in," Derrick said as she reached his car.

"Forget the casseroles." Beth opened the passenger door and put Chloe inside. "Take Chloe away from here," she told him, holding a hand up to protect her eyes from the rain. "Someplace unusual where no one would think to look for you."

"What's wrong?" Derrick demanded, his forehead creased with concern.

"I can't explain now, just go. Fast."

Derrick studied her for a second, then started the ignition. Beth ran around the corner of the house and watched as he drove down the driveway and out onto the street. Limp with relief, she hurried back inside.

"What was that all about?" Amber asked when Beth closed the door behind her.

"A man named Malcolm Schneckenberger called before I found you. He knew I wanted to hear the trial, so he said he was bringing a little transmitter here."

Amber nodded.

"But I just realized he might be the person responsible for Roy's accident."

"So why didn't we go with the little girl?" Amber whispered.

"I'm sorry, but her safety is more important than ours and if we'd gone with her, Malcolm might have followed us."

"What will we do now?"

"First I'll call the FBI again." Beth dialed Agent Gray's number and hung up in frustration when she heard the answering machine. "Don't worry," she told Amber. "Nobody can get inside this fence unless I open the gate." Rather than waste time, Beth dialed 911, but before an operator could answer, Malcolm's big truck pulled up next to the patio. Beth hung up the receiver, staring at the vehicle in horror.

"I thought you said nobody could get in!" Amber cried.

"I must have entered the code that keeps the gate open," Beth whispered in disbelief. "Now our only hope is to bluff him. Let me do the talking." Through the glass panes they watched Malcolm approach, his sparse hair damp and windblown.

"Thanks for leaving the gate open for me. Who's this?" he asked when he saw Amber.

Beth cleared her throat. "Malcolm, I'd like for you to meet Amber Harper."

Malcolm's head swiveled back around. "The Amber Harper?" The girl nodded with a nervous glance at Beth. "How did you find her?"

"She's been hiding in Roy's apartment since his accident, but I've talked her into testifying. We're just about to leave," she added, hoping to speed their departure.

Malcolm frowned. "I don't think it's a good idea for you to try and take her into Albany. What if someone is watching your house and sees the two of you leaving?"

"You mean like Mr. X?" Beth couldn't make herself look him in the eye.

"Exactly," Malcolm confirmed.

"I have to try, for Jack's sake," Beth insisted.

"I guess I can take you," Malcolm said, and Amber took a step backward.

"Amber is understandably nervous," Beth explained. "I'm sure she'd feel more comfortable if I drove her to Albany. You can follow along behind us as a safety precaution."

Malcolm studied Beth's rain-soaked hair and clothes. "Why did you stand in the rain if you were planning to go to the courthouse?" he asked, reaching out to touch her wet arm. She shrank away involuntarily, and his eyes narrowed. "Are you afraid of me too, Beth?"

"Of course not," she replied. "And my clothes will dry." She picked up her purse and looked over at Amber. "Let's go."

Malcolm glanced around the room, taking in the overturned bowl and the fruit scattered on the floor. "Where's Chloe?"

Beth's mouth went dry. "She's with a friend."

Malcolm considered this. "I'm surprised that you would let her go off with friends so soon after being released from the hospital," he said, causing Beth to drop her purse. "I didn't mean to scare you." He reached down to retrieve the bag. "And I've never known you to be so nervous."

Beth accepted the purse and pulled out her keys. "I'm just anxious to get to Albany. And I probably should call Jack to let him know we're coming." She reached for the phone, but Malcolm covered her hand with his.

"Don't do that. I talked to Roberta earlier, and she said Judge Tate was furious that phones kept ringing in the courtroom. He threatened to have the next person who answered a cell call during the trial arrested for contempt. And there's no sense in taking two cars. Miss Harper can see that I'm harmless." He smiled at Amber, and the girl actually shuddered.

"I'd rather have my own car in case I need to leave early," Beth tried again.

Malcolm nodded, as if accepting defeat. "Which friend did you say Chloe was with?"

"You don't know them," Beth replied, her nerves stretched to the limit.

Malcolm gave her a speculative glance as the phone rang. Beth stared as he reached for the receiver. His eyes never left her face. "Hello?" he said. "Yes, Agent Gray, this is Malcolm Schneckenberger. I work for the Georgia Republican Party and we met at the hospital after Chloe's accident." There was another pause. "We're on our way out the door. Beth's going to watch the last day of the Ferris Burke trial," Malcolm said pleasantly. "I don't know what she wanted, but hold on just a second and I'll ask her." He covered the phone and lifted an eyebrow in Beth's direction. "Do you have anything to tell the FBI, Beth?"

"No." She shook her head.

Malcolm smiled. "She said it wasn't important and that she'll call you later." After hanging up the phone, Malcolm stared at the Barbies scattered in the corner of the room. "Looks like Chloe left in a hurry," he observed, reaching down to pick up the Scarecrow. He fingered the doll for a few seconds, then abruptly popped its head off. "Uh-oh," he said with a laugh.

Beth stared at the headless doll as the phone rang again, and Malcolm picked it up slowly. "Hello? No, there's no emergency here. It must have been a mistake." Malcolm replaced the receiver and Beth's eyes dropped to the floor. "You called 911."

"I . . ." Beth couldn't think of a plausible excuse, so she let her voice trail off.

"Somehow you know."

"Know what?" Beth forced her eyes up as far as his pudgy midsection, clinging to the hope that he would let them get to the safety of the Lexus.

"That I am your enemy," he said, and she knew that all hope was gone.

"I don't know what you're talking about." Beth couldn't give up.

"Oh, I think you do." Malcolm placed himself between her and the door.

"What do you want from us?" she asked desperately.

"What do I want?" Malcolm seemed to consider the question. "What *do* I want? How about a little respect? Some common courtesy?" His usually meek expression disappeared. "To bring Jack Gamble to his knees!"

"I thought you liked Jack," Beth whispered.

"Jack had his chance to be my friend, but he was too good for me. So I found other friends, powerful people who reward loyalty." Malcolm glanced at his watch. "Well, I guess I'll bring Lance inside. Then I'll set up the transmitter and we can enjoy the grand finale together."

"You have Lance Kilgore?" Beth tried to keep her voice from trembling.

Malcolm's expression darkened. "Unfortunately. That's the only drawback to my association with Mr. Hummer. He loaned me a couple of imbeciles!"

"You're working for Felix Hummer?" Beth gasped.

"Yes, *I'm* working for Felix Hummer," he mimicked her. "I gave the goons the simple assignment to follow Kilgore. We didn't want to actually kidnap him until *after* he won the Ferris Burke case, but before he could get Oscar's nomination for the state senate vacancy. But the idiots were so obvious Lance realized he was being followed and he jumped *them*!" Malcolm shook his head in despair. "So he's been riding around in the back of my truck since yesterday."

Beth processed this information. "You aren't going to take Amber to Albany to testify?"

"You're catching on." He held the door open. "Why don't you ladies come with me? And I have a gun, just in case you're planning to make a run for it." He pulled a small handgun from his pocket to emphasize his words. Outside the rain had faded into a light drizzle. "Don't make any sudden movements," Malcolm instructed as he climbed into the truckbed.

They watched as he retracted a black tarp to reveal Lance Kilgore. He was lying on his side facing them. Several pieces of duct tape covered his mouth, his hands were handcuffed in front, and his feet were shackled. He was soaked to the skin and filthy. Beth glanced at Amber as Malcolm grabbed the district attorney's elbow and pulled him into a semistanding position. The handcuffs were attached to the shackles, causing Mr. Kilgore to lean forward and walk in tiny, shuffling steps. Beth caught a cruel smile on Malcolm's face as he followed the other man's slow progress toward the tailgate of the truck.

"Oh, how the mighty have fallen!" he crowed.

Mr. Kilgore negotiated the end of the truck and staggered as he hit the ground. Beth reached a hand out to steady him, and Malcolm stepped between them. He had a small, gray toolbox in one hand and the gun in the other. His eyes were cold as he pushed Mr. Kilgore into the house. After closing the door he told Beth and Amber to sit in kitchen chairs.

Malcolm kicked an apple out of his way and shoved Mr. Kilgore into the far corner, destroying Chloe's Barbie hospital. Then he removed two large, U-shaped nails and a hammer from the box. He used the nails to secure the chains around Mr. Kilgore's feet to Hipolita's shiny hardwood floor.

"There, that should keep you out of trouble," Malcolm said as he stood. He returned the hammer to his toolbox and removed a roll of duct tape. "Now let's make sure that you stay nice and still," he told Amber as he taped her arms and feet to her chair. Then he looked at Beth. "I'm just going to trust you," he said.

"Why are you doing this?" Beth asked.

"Felix has invested in some local industries and needed a friend in state government. A new senator starting his career was perfect, but both Jack and Lance were unimpeachable. So he started looking for other alternatives, and his search led him to me."

"You want to be the state senator?" Beth asked in amazement.

"I had never really considered it until Felix came to me with his proposal, although I am immensely qualified," Malcolm assured her. "But in order for me to have a chance, Jack had to lose the Ferris Burke trial. So I bribed a clerk and got Judge Tate assigned to the case. Next I told a friend of mine at the *Chronicle* that Jack's parents were taking him to family court because he neglected his daughter."

"You did that?" Beth whispered.

"It was brilliant, I know. A bad judge, all the negative publicity, and no witness." He waved toward the taped-up girl. "Jack's case seemed doomed. But they kept searching, and I was afraid they might actually find her. So I arranged the beating at the sleazy bar."

Beth felt tears fill her eyes.

"Don't cry!" he commanded. "You've always been nice to me, so I had them keep his injuries mild for your sake. However, I did suggest to Lance that Jack might be faking to delay the trial so he could find his missing witness." Beth gasped, and Malcolm held out his hands. "Sorry, but the opportunity was too good to miss! And of course, I told Mr. Fuller that he had to ask Jack for a second opinion."

"You made them distrust each other."

"As easy as one, two, three," Malcolm admitted.

"Did you hire that man who tried to climb the fence a few weeks ago too?"

Malcolm frowned. "I won't take credit for the clumsy would-be intruder. The fence around this house presented almost as big an obstacle to us as Roy did when it came to gathering information. I thought that playing friendly was the best approach, but Felix wanted to disable the gate. You and Jack foiled his plan, and Roy was too 'ever-present' afterward. I did send the fake dry cleaner yesterday, though. He was supposed to grab Chloe."

Beth couldn't control a moan. "Oh, why?"

"So that I could control Jack, of course." He gave her a disappointed look as though he thought she hadn't been paying attention.

"You were going to blackmail Jack like you did Roy."

Malcolm shook his head. "I wasn't blackmailing Roy. I didn't even know he'd found Miss Harper."

"Then why did you send the nursery rhyme notes that the FBI found in Roy's apartment?"

Malcolm shrugged. "I sent Roy menacing letters about once a month, just to keep him on his toes. Those notes the FBI found were meaningless."

"If you weren't blackmailing Roy, why did you shoot him?"

Malcolm sighed. "The plan was so simple and so brilliant. Lance would win the trial, and Jack would be out of the picture. Then

Lance would leave town unexpectedly and never return. But in spite of my best-laid plans, it looked like Jack might actually win, so Felix decided to take him out."

"You mean kill him?"

"Yeah," Malcolm responded. "But Roy took the wrong car after the party and caught Jack's bullet for him." He looked up a Beth. "Isn't that just like Roy?" With a sigh, Malcolm continued. "Since we couldn't seem to kill Jack, we decided to manipulate him instead."

"Jack would do anything to protect Chloe," Beth acknowledged.

"Yeah, but his luck was holding, and the policeman showed up just in time. We wanted to have all this taken care of before the trial began today, but there's a certain drama in waiting to the last minute, don't you think?"

Malcolm studied the phone. "It's time to make our little phone call. Let's put it on speaker so we can all enjoy it. Even though Judge Tate has threatened to throw him in jail for answering his cell phone, somehow I doubt Jack will be able to resist a call from this number." Malcolm gave Beth another cruel smile.

"But you don't have Chloe," Beth said as he dialed.

"Something tells me you'll do just as well."

At that moment Jack's voice vibrated through the room. "Hello!"

"Jack!" Malcolm greeted cheerfully.

"What do you want, Malcolm?" Jack demanded. "I'm in the middle of a trial here!"

Malcolm looked at Beth and shook his head. "See what I have to put up with?" Then he turned back to the phone. "I'm about to simplify things for you, Jack. From now on, all you have to do is make sure that Ferris gets a guilty verdict. I don't want it to be too obvious, so object every once in a while. Just don't get carried away."

"What are you talking about?" Jack's tone was menacing now.

"I'm talking about Beth's life," Malcolm said, his voice full of hatred.

"Beth?" Jack repeated, and they could hear the tremor in his voice. "What are you doing in my house, Schneckenberger? Beth!"

"I'm okay, Jack," she answered without permission and earned a scowl from Malcolm.

"She's okay for now, but that can change if you don't do exactly as I say."

"Chloe's safe!" Beth added, anxious to alleviate as much of his anxiety as possible.

"Shut up!" Malcolm put his hand over her mouth. Then he spoke toward the phone. "It's not complicated really. Ferris goes to prison and Beth lives. I've got a microphone in the courtroom, and if I get even the slightest suspicion that you're not cooperating, I'll put a bullet through Beth's head." He stroked her cheek with the muzzle of the gun. "So work your magic, Jack. We'll be listening."

Malcolm disconnected the call and turned on his little transmitter. They heard someone talking in the background, and then Beth recognized Ferris Burke's voice. "Sounds like we're in time to catch part of the assistant DA's brilliant cross-examination" Malcolm gloated.

Beth glanced over at Mr. Kilgore and saw the look of despair on his face.

"I got this little toy from Felix," Malcolm continued as he adjusted the volume. "We can hear them but they can't hear us, so don't be tempted to scream for help." He grinned at Beth. "Just settle back and enjoy." Lance Kilgore actually moaned from his corner.

Through the transmitter they heard the low rumble of conversation and a few coughs. Then a voice asked a question and Ferris Burke answered. This continued for several minutes, and throughout the proceedings Jack remained ominously silent. Finally the judge asked if the defense was going to object to anything the assistant district attorney asked.

"Not at this time, Your Honor." Jack's voice sounded hollow, and Beth ached for him.

After several more minutes of one-sided questioning, the assistant DA rested the prosecution's case. "Do you have any redirect, counselor?" the judge asked.

"No sir," Jack responded.

"In that case we'll adjourn for one hour. At that time I want both sides to be prepared to present closing arguments." The gavel sounded and clamor enveloped the courtroom.

Malcolm turned off his transmitter. "I think that went exceptionally well."

Beth was getting tired of his smug attitude. "How can you expect Mr. Fuller to nominate you for the senate seat after all this?" She waved around the room to include Lance Kilgore.

"That's the real beauty of my plan. No one will ever know. I'm going to put Lance in Roy's apartment, then give him a nasty little shot to speed dehydration and he'll be dead in twenty-four hours. Amber will disappear again, permanently this time, and you, well, I don't want to think about that right now." Beth felt the blood drain from her face. "Like I said, you've been nice to me, and I hate to just kill you, so I'll face that decision later."

Beth wanted to cry, but she refused to give Malcolm the satisfaction. "Jack will look for me."

"Of course! Jack will search frantically, but to no avail!" Malcolm said in a dramatic tone. "Then the police will find Lance's body in Roy's old apartment, and Jack will have more legal problems than even he ever dreamed of. And at that point, his searching days will be over!"

Beth refused to give up hope. "Mr. Fuller will be suspicious."

"Oscar is going to have his hands full with other matters. I've been siphoning money from party accounts to fund my future political career. The national auditors are due to arrive on Monday, and all paper trails lead straight back to Oscar. There are also some irregularities on his personal tax return, and I felt it was my duty to report this. So the IRS will visit tomorrow morning. I'll be rushing everywhere, doing my best to help him." Malcolm put a hand to his head in false exhaustion. "And why would anyone ever suspect me? You never did."

Beth shrugged, then glanced at the district attorney and saw the prisoner watching her, his eyes angry and determined. The expression was so different from the one she had seen a few minutes before that she was immediately on guard. Something had changed. Mr. Kilgore tapped his index finger on the floor silently. Beth followed the movement with her eyes. Then the DA raised the finger and pointed at Malcolm, who was playing with his borrowed transmitter. She gave him a tiny nod and Mr. Kilgore hooked his thumb back at himself. Beth blinked in comprehension. Lance Kilgore wanted her to get Malcolm to come closer to him.

Malcolm stepped away from the transmitter and saw Beth and Lance looking at each other. "What?" he swung a suspicious gaze toward Mr. Kilgore.

Beth searched for a response. "I think he's thirsty. Can I get him a drink of water?"

Malcolm threw back his head and laughed. "Apparently you weren't paying attention when I said he was going to be found dead from dehydration. Giving him water now would just slow that process." Their captor took a seat, and Beth was trying to think of a way to get Malcolm into the corner when the buzzer on the security gate rang. Malcolm put a finger to his lips as he walked over to the talk button. "Yes?"

"Haggerty Police, sir."

Malcolm gave Beth an exaggerated look of shock. "Is there a problem, officer?"

"We check out all our 911 calls, sir. The gate is open, but I wanted to notify you that I'm coming up to look around."

"That's very efficient of you! I'm glad to see that my tax dollars are being put to such good use. I'll meet you by the back door." He turned to Beth. "You stand here with me." When she reached him he pulled her out of sight. They were only a few feet from Lance Kilgore, and Beth glanced over at the man in the corner, but he shook his head. They were still too far away.

A Haggerty Police car pulled up and parked beside Malcolm's truck, then they heard footsteps on the stone patio. Through the glass Beth could see the policeman approach, and he looked terribly young. "Tell him the door is unlocked," Malcolm whispered into her ear.

Beth looked back at the youth in uniform and shook her head. Inviting him into this situation would be as good as killing him. "I won't do it," she said firmly.

Malcolm brought the gun up and put it against her temple. "I said tell him to come in!" Beth trembled, but remained silent. With a growl of frustration, Malcolm swung the gun around and pointed it at Lance Kilgore. "Tell him to come in or the district attorney dies."

Left with no other option, Beth screamed. Malcolm cursed and shoved her down. She aimed her fall toward Lance Kilgore and landed at his feet as the door crashed open. The young officer paused in the doorway, his face anxious and his gun drawn. Malcolm fired and the policeman took the bullet in his chest, then fell backward onto the patio behind him.

"That was your fault!" Malcolm rounded furiously on Beth as she cowered beside Mr. Kilgore. "Get up!" he demanded, but she shook her head. He leaned down and Beth expected him to grab her, but he struck her across the face instead. "I said get up!" he hissed. Beth moved farther away, scrambling into the small space between Lance Kilgore and the wall. Malcolm advanced on her with a determined expression. "If you don't learn to obey me, the rest of your life will be calculated in minutes, maybe seconds . . ." He raised his hand to strike her again.

Beth awaited the blow, but a sound at the door distracted Malcolm. He turned as Mr. Kilgore pulled a small kitchen knife from under his leg and lunged. Derrick's slight form stepped into the doorway, straddling the policeman's inert body. As Malcolm raised his gun to shoot, Lance Kilgore buried the knife in Malcolm's back. The sound of a gunshot echoed in the room, and Beth covered her eyes. Seconds later she felt a gentle hand on her face.

"Beth."

"Derrick." She opened her eyes and smiled at her friend. Then she looked behind him at Malcolm's body, crumpled on the floor. "You shot him?"

Derrick nodded. "The policeman's gun was lying on the patio and I picked it up. I wonder if it's against the law to use a police revolver."

"I think the police will understand under the circumstances," Beth comforted him. "Is Malcolm dead?" she asked with a shudder.

"The chubby guy? Oh yes. He's very dead."

"What about the policeman?" Beth forced herself to inquire.

"He's still breathing," Derrick reported, and she sighed with relief. Derrick went back over and checked the injured man's pulse. "He's losing blood and I'm afraid he'll go into shock. Where can I find a blanket?"

Beth directed him to her room as Lance Kilgore made a frantic motion with his head, and she realized that he wanted her to take the duct tape off his mouth. "This is going to hurt," she cautioned, then grasped a corner of the tape and jerked quickly.

"Ahhhhh!" the district attorney screamed.

"I'm sorry!" Beth cried in distress.

He gave her a numb smile. "There was no way around it. Somebody needs to call an ambulance for the policeman." Derrick returned with a blanket and spread it over the bleeding man, then pulled out his cell phone and dialed 911. Beth started unraveling the duct tape that bound Amber to her chair. "Get me the hammer out of the toolbox," Lance requested once Amber's hands were free to untie her own feet. Beth handed him the hammer, then watched as he wriggled each of the U-shaped nails until they pulled out of the hardwood.

"Ambulance is on its way," Derrick informed them, closing his cell phone and kneeling beside the wounded officer.

"Now I need to get these handcuffs off. He probably has the keys." Lance lifted his shoulder toward the dead man.

Beth saw the knife protruding from Malcolm's back and knew the bullet wound on the other side was probably worse. "I don't think I can touch him," she admitted.

Derrick scrambled over. "I'll do it," he volunteered, and Beth looked away as he searched. "All he's got are these car keys." Derrick dangled them in the air.

Lance cursed under his breath. "One of his goons probably has them." Lance shook the chains that bound him. "I've got to get to that courtroom." He motioned toward the transmitter. "If we can't find a key, someone is going to have to shoot these handcuffs off."

Derrick left his patient again and picked up the police revolver, then got into position behind Lance. "Beth, get some towels to protect his hands from powder burns," he instructed. When Beth looked at him in amazement, he reminded her of a storyline from *The Brave and Relentless* a couple of years before. "The policeman who rescued Marrisa from that deranged psychiatrist forgot to protect her hands, and she got powder burns."

"What?" Lance asked in confusion.

"Never mind," Beth told the DA as she grabbed a handful of neatly folded dishtowels from a kitchen drawer and tucked them carefully around his hands. Then she stepped away and covered her ears as Derrick fired the gun. When she turned, Lance had his hands free and there was another hole in Hipolita's floor.

Lance reached for the gun. "I'll do the leg chain myself. If I'm going to lose a foot, I'd rather be the one responsible."

Slightly nauseous, Beth moved over to stand by Amber while Lance shot repeatedly at the chain between his feet. "Where's Chloe?" she asked Derrick over the deafening noise.

"At Mr. Termite's Insect Museum with Annabelle," he replied. Beth raised an eyebrow and he shrugged. "You said to take her somewhere unusual, and that was the strangest place I could think of. Then I came back to check on you, and when I saw that gate standing open . . ."

Beth clutched his arm. "You saved our lives." She looked around the room and her eyes came to rest on the fallen policeman. "I guess we need to call the police. Again."

"He'll call the police." Lance waved at Derrick. "I've got to get to the courtroom before the assistant DA gets credit for my closing argument. Do you think I could borrow one of Jack's suits?" he asked, gesturing vaguely at his wet, dirty clothes.

Beth led the way up to Jack's bedroom and Lance disappeared inside the walk-in closet. He rejoined her a few seconds later carrying a navy blue suit, a crisp white shirt, and a yellow tie. "How do you know they'll fit?" Beth asked as they returned to the kitchen.

"Nothing could look worse than what I've got on," he pointed out reasonably.

"Amber and I are coming with you," Beth told him, hoping the other girl wouldn't contradict her.

Lance shook his head. "It isn't fair for you to expect me to bring in a defense witness."

"It isn't fair that you'll be wearing Jack's suit without his permission," Beth countered. "And I know that you want to see justice served." Lance made a face and Beth turned to Derrick. "Try to reach Agent Gray or Mark Iverson . . ."

"That won't be necessary," Agent Gray spoke for both men as they came through the open door. The sound of a siren filled the air. "I kept getting a busy signal when I tried to return your call, so we decided to drive over and check things out."

Beth crossed the room and grasped Mark's forearms. "I found Amber Harper." She tipped her head toward the young woman. "She was staying in Roy's apartment."

Agent Gray studied the girl. "That's why you wanted to know about fresh fingerprints."

Beth nodded, then pointed in the general direction of Malcolm's body. "Malcolm was Mr. X, but he *was* working for Felix Hummer."

"Schneckenberger?" Mark asked in surprise.

"He was going to kill Amber and Lance and me too, eventually." Beth took a deep breath and continued. "He hoped Jack would be arrested for Lance's death and then he could just waltz into the state senate seat."

Mark shook his head. "I never would have figured him to be the criminal type."

"Nobody did. That was the secret to his success," Beth murmured.

Lance sighed impatiently. "We can discuss Malcolm's crime spree later. Right now I need to get to Albany, and I'll take Malcolm's truck if I have to."

"That truck is evidence, and it's not going anywhere," Winston Jones said from the door as ambulance attendants relieved Derrick from his position beside the fallen policeman. "Everybody in here okay?"

"Everybody except the dead guy," Mark replied without smiling. "We're on our way to the courthouse in Albany." Mark tipped his head toward Derrick. "He can fill you in on most of what happened, and Beth will give you a complete report when the trial ends."

Winston agreed, and Mark led the way to his government sedan. Beth paused on her way out to speak to Derrick. "After Malcolm is . . . removed, could you bring Chloe home?"

He nodded and Beth joined the others outside as Mark pointed to the handcuffs and shackles that still hung from Lance Kilgore's arms and ankles. "Are you going like that?"

"I don't see that I have a choice," Lance answered with a grimace.

"Maybe Chief Jones has a handcuff key," Beth suggested.

Winston was summoned and tried his key, but the handcuffs remained tightly locked. "Must be a custom set," he told them. "Probably have to get a locksmith to take them off."

"My luck just keeps getting better," Lance muttered as they climbed into the car.

CHAPTER 15

Lance got in the front seat with Mark. Agent Gray sat with the women in the back, and they started toward Albany. Mark used his cell phone to call the courthouse and have word delivered to Jack that Beth was safe. While they drove, Beth and the district attorney took turns describing Malcolm's deeds of destruction. As he talked, Lance pulled off his filthy clothes and shoved an arm into Jack's white dress shirt.

"You girls aren't trying to peek at me, are you?" Lance glanced over his shoulder as he pulled on the suit pants. Beth assured him that they weren't tempted, and he laughed. Then his eyes rested on Amber and his expression dimmed.

Traffic was heavy, and the trip to the courthouse seemed endless. Finally Mark parked in a loading zone and they rushed inside. They entered the courtroom just as the judge was calling the proceedings to order. Jack was standing in front of the judge's bench and turned when they walked in. He examined the bruises on Beth's face and her soggy clothes. Then his eyes moved to Lance. He took in the familiar suit and the handcuffs exposed by the ill-fitting jacket. Finally his gaze dropped to the shackles and tennis shoes that completed the ensemble.

"Glad you could join us finally, Mr. Kilgore," the man wearing the black robe and sour expression said with heavy sarcasm. Jack took a step toward Beth, but the judge stopped him. "And where do you think you're going, counselor?"

"I need to talk with my . . . nanny," Jack finished lamely.

The judge gave him a ferocious look. "Mr. Gamble, approach the bench *now!*" he commanded. "You too, Mr. Kilgore!"

Lance walked quickly down the aisle, and Jack gave Beth one last look, then joined his opponent in front of the bench. Roberta was sitting on the row behind the defense table and waved Beth down. Then she scooted over to make room for the new arrivals.

"Who are these people?" the judge asked in a whisper loud enough to be heard in the next county. "Besides your nanny," he added with a disparaging glance at Jack.

Lance answered first. "It's Amber Harper, sir, and a couple of FBI agents."

The judge studied the DA for a few seconds. "You've brought in the missing defense witness?"

"Against my better judgment," Lance acknowledged.

"And just what do you have to say for yourself, Mr. Kilgore? You disappeared from my courtroom without explanation or permission, then returned wearing jewelry more appropriate for the World Wrestling Federation than a court of law. And that suit is atrocious!"

Beth saw Jack's eyes widen, and she leaned forward, struggling to hear what was said.

"I didn't dress like this on purpose, sir," Lance responded humbly. "I was kidnapped." He waved his hands and the chains rattled. "And Malcolm Schneckenberger was going to kill me, but the soap opera guy saved my life!" The audience murmured loudly in response to this announcement and the judge reached for his gavel. "Then I knew I had to get to court, but I'd been in the back of a truck for almost twenty-four hours, and my clothes were filthy. So I borrowed this suit and, well, everyone doesn't have your fine sense of taste, Your Honor." Lance glanced at Jack.

The judge worked to restore order as the doors of the courtroom slammed open and a man ran down the center aisle. "I'm getting sick and tired of all these theatrics! Who in the heck is this?" the judge demanded, looking at Jack.

"I don't know who he is, Your Honor," Jack defended himself.

"Name is Horace Looney, sir," the man said as he came to a stop in front of the bench. "I'm a locksmith, and I got a call that some-body here needed some fancy handcuffs removed."

The judge waved toward the prosecutor. "Work quickly so this trial can proceed."

The people in the courtroom watched in fascination as Mr. Looney unpacked a wide array of tools from a small bag. Jack walked to the row where Beth was sitting and knelt beside her, his hand clutching hers. "You're really okay?"

"I'm fine," she assured him. "And Chloe's with Annabelle Grainger." She decided to keep their odd location a secret for the moment.

"What happened to your face?" He touched the swollen skin on her cheek.

"Malcolm hit me," she said and saw the instant rage in his eyes.

"He won't get away with this," Jack vowed.

"He didn't. Derrick killed him. Shot him with a wounded policeman's gun."

"Malcolm is dead? And your soap opera–watching librarian friend killed him?"

"After Lance stabbed him with a knife," Beth confirmed, and Jack's eyes swung back to the district attorney, whose hands were now free.

Mr. Looney pulled out a tiny electric saw for the shackles. "Been awhile since I saw a pair of these," he commented as the first shackle fell to the floor with a clang.

"Ferris is calling me." Jack gave her hand one more squeeze, then returned to the defense table to confer with his client.

Once all of Lance Kilgore's hardware was removed, Mr. Looney packed up his bag and left the courtroom. The judged pounded his gavel until he regained control of the crowd. "Let's get this over with," he said wearily. "Mr. Gamble, even though you have already rested your case, I'm going to allow you to call Miss Harper to the stand." The judge turned to Lance. "Then you will have a chance to cross-examine before we begin closing arguments. Proceed, gentlemen."

"Your Honor," Jack said without rising. "The defense waives the right to call Miss Harper as a witness."

The judge stared at Jack for a few seconds, then stood, his black robes billowing. "Approach the bench this instant! You too, Mr. Kilgore!" Once the men were in place, he turned to Jack. "What is the meaning of this?" he yelled.

"My client thinks our case is strong enough without Miss Harper's testimony. In the interest of time he requests that we go directly to closing arguments." Jack's jaw was clenched tightly, and he wouldn't meet the DA's startled gaze. Lance's eyes shifted from Jack to Ferris Burke and finally to Amber Harper.

"Mr. Burke must have some mighty big plans for the weekend if he's willing to risk the outcome of this trial for a speedy finish," Lance commented thoughtfully.

Jack stared ahead. "I have no idea what Mr. Burke's plans for the weekend are."

Lance considered this for a few seconds, then nodded. "Your honor, since Mr. Burke is willing to take a gamble, so am I. I think it's time that we all found out exactly what happened the night Sean Ballard died." He waved his hand toward the jury.

"You're not presenting an argument, Mr. Kilgore," the judge reminded him. "Direct your comments to me."

"Yes, Sir." Lance turned and faced the bench. "I'd like to call Amber Harper as a prosecution witness."

A universal gasp moved across the courtroom as Beth leaned toward Mark. "What's going on? Jack's whole case depends on Amber's testimony."

Mark shrugged as Jack spoke. "You've already rested your case."

Lance raised a shoulder. "Her testimony will be in rebuttal of previous defense witnesses. It would be judicial error to refuse a material witness the chance to take the stand."

"I object," Jack said without conviction.

Judge Tate ignored Jack and spoke to Lance. "I'll decide what constitutes judicial error in this courtroom. And I will allow you to call Miss Harper, but make it quick."

"I object," Jack said again, more firmly.

"I heard you the first time," the judge told him. "But I'm real touchy about 'judicial error.' I've been burned before and won't risk making a decision that I might have to overturn at some point in the future."

Jack nodded. "Just remember that we're dealing with a man's life here."

"I haven't forgotten that for a minute," Judge Tate assured him, then turned to the jury. "The prosecution is going to call one final witness, then Mr. Gamble will cross-examine. After that we will hear closing arguments." He looked at the district attorney. "Mr. Kilgore."

"I'd like a moment to speak with my witness," Lance requested.

"Make it quick," the judge agreed with a nod. The district attorney conferred with Amber, then faced the bench with a smile. "The prosecution calls Miss Amber Harper."

"I object, Your Honor," Jack said. "This witness is being called out of order."

"Your objection is noted. The witness will take the stand," Judge Tate replied.

Beth watched as Amber was sworn in, then sat on the front edge of the chair in the witness box. Lance approached her slowly.

"My name is Lance Kilgore, Amber. In all the confusion this morning, I don't know if I've even introduced myself."

"Objection!" Jack said from his seat at the defense table. "Any confusion Mr. Kilgore may have been involved in recently is not pertinent or admissible."

"I'll decide what is admissible," Judge Tate growled at Jack. "Proceed Mr. Kilgore."

The district attorney nodded, then addressed Amber. "Ordinarily I have a chance to get to know my witnesses before I put them on the stand," he said. "But this is not an ordinary trial . . ."

"Objection!"

"Rephrase, Mr. Kilgore," the judge instructed.

"In the interest of time," Mr. Kilgore glanced at Ferris "why don't you just tell us your story, in your own words. If I think something needs clarification, I'll interrupt you."

Amber took a deep breath, then began. "After our parents died, me and Audrey inherited their house. We lived there alone for about a year, then Sean moved in a few weeks after Christmas. He was lazy but sweet, and he wouldn't have hurt a fly."

Lance gave the jury a look of surprise. "You say that Sean Ballard wouldn't hurt a fly, but Mr. Burke here has testified that the deceased was molesting Jasmine."

"That's a lie. When Jasmine was at our house, I never let her out of my sight. She even slept with me."

"So to the best of your knowledge, did Sean Ballard ever mistreat your niece?"

"Never," Amber answered promptly, and Lance smiled at the jury.

"Thank you for clarifying that. Now tell us about your sister's relationship with her ex-husband," Lance suggested.

"Objection!" Jack called out. "Hearsay!"

"Your Honor," Lance approached the bench. "The entire defense case has been a series of people giving their opinions on the character of Audrey Burke and Sean Ballard. I should be allowed to rebut in kind."

"Overruled," the judge told Jack. "You may answer the question, Miss Harper."

"My sister was a good person. She drank too much, but it never made her mean. And Ferris seemed like a good father, so when Audrey told me bad things about him, I didn't believe her. But now I do."

"What kind of things did she say about Ferris?" Lance asked.

"Objection!" Jack interrupted again.

The judge nodded. "I'm giving you some leeway, Mr. Kilgore, since you didn't have a chance to depose your witness, but you'd better make your point fast."

"Go ahead, Amber," Lance encouraged.

"Audrey found out that Ferris had this girlfriend up in Nashville named Claudia. He wouldn't stop seeing her, so Audrey begged him for a divorce, but Ferris wouldn't sign the papers."

Beth inhaled sharply and Mark Iverson leaned toward her. "Are you okay?"

She nodded, thinking of the way Ferris had twisted the truth on the tape he made for Jack. He'd said that *he* wanted the divorce and never mentioned that he was romantically involved with Claudia Wisenhaut.

Mark settled back in his seat and Amber continued. "The fights with Ferris made Audrey's drinking worse, and she had to be put in a rehabilitation place. When she got out, our parents said if she'd stay away from drugs and alcohol that they'd help her get a divorce." Amber's voice trembled. "Then Audrey told me Ferris said if she went through with the divorce he'd kill our parents."

Murmuring was heard around the courtroom.

"Your Honor," Jack complained from the defense table.

"Hurry, Mr. Kilgore," the judge admonished.

"Was your sister able to stay sober?" Lance asked.

Amber cleared her throat. "Yes, the clinic counselors were real proud of her."

"Then your parents helped her to get the divorce from Ferris?"

"Yes, and our parents were killed a few weeks later."

"Objection! Mr. Burke is not on trial for the accidental deaths of his in-laws!"

"Your Honor, a few more questions will clarify the issue," Lance appealed to the judge.

"My patience is wearing very thin, Mr. Kilgore."

Lance turned back to Amber. "What makes you think that Ferris was responsible for your parents' car wreck?"

"Well, when my parents died Audrey went crazy. She said Ferris told her he hired someone to do it." Amber glanced at the defendant. "I didn't believe it. I mean, Ferris looks like such a normal person. Who would think he could kill people?"

Lance smiled broadly at this remark, and Jack started to stand, but the judged waved him down. "Let's move along, Miss Harper."

"One day I was baby-sitting Jasmine at Ferris's house and I went in his office." Color rose in Amber's cheeks. "He never had told me to stay out of there or anything," she explained.

"We understand," Lance assured her. "What did you find?"

"He has a calendar where he writes appointments. He knows a lot of famous people, and I was reading it to see if I recognized any names. Then I saw that on the day my parents were killed he had written their names, their car license number, and the word *Memphis*."

"Why was Memphis significant?" Lance asked.

"Because that's where my parents had their wreck. When I saw that, I knew right away that Audrey had been telling the truth. Ferris did kill them."

"Objection!" Jack said. "We've established that Ferris is not on trial for the Harpers' deaths, and besides, a few words written on a calendar is not evidence. He might have been planning to send them a fruit basket for all we know."

"In Memphis?" Lance challenged, jubilation written all over his face.

"Sustained," the judge said reluctantly. "Stick with Sean Ballard's murder, Mr. Kilgore, and the jury will ignore Miss Harper's comments relating to the deaths of her parents."

Lance nodded. "Tell us about the night your sister died."

Amber took a deep breath. "Sean and Audrey were planning a trip to California. Audrey was real excited, and I thought it would be good for her. The only bad part was that she knew Ferris wouldn't let her take Jasmine. That night, Audrey talked to Jasmine and told her that she would be gone for a while. Jasmine didn't understand and called her father, crying."

"But she was crying because her mother was going on a trip, not because Sean Ballard had harmed her in any way," Lance clarified.

"Yes," Amber affirmed.

"Then Ferris came over to your house?"

"I was in the kitchen with Jasmine when Ferris got there, and he was mad as anything."

"Why?" Lance asked. "Because Jasmine's feelings were hurt?"

"No!" Amber said emphatically. "He was mad because there was no way he was going to let Audrey out of his sight."

"Objection!" Jack stood again. "Miss Harper can't possibly know Mr. Burke's thoughts."

"Sustained. The jury is instructed to ignore Miss Harper's remarks regarding what Mr. Burke was thinking," the judge said, then waited for Amber to continue.

Jack gave the judge an exasperated look and sat back down.

Lance resumed his questions. "Why would Ferris care if your sister and her boyfriend went to California?"

"Ferris didn't believe in divorce. He still considered Audrey his wife, and he hated Sean, but he put up with it until he found out they were talking about going to California." Amber pushed a clump of stringy hair behind her ear. "Anyway, when he got there that night, he told me to take Jasmine upstairs so he could talk to Audrey."

"Where was Sean Ballard?"

Amber sighed. "He was in Audrey's room, hiding from Ferris."

"So you took Jasmine upstairs, and Ferris went into the living room with your sister?"

"Yes. We could hear them fighting, but they always yelled a lot so at first I wasn't worried. Then it got quiet, and I decided to go down to check on them. At the bottom of the stairs, I could hear Audrey crying, and Ferris was talking real soft."

Amber's voice shook as she spoke. "I walked in and saw him pouring pills into Audrey's hand. He didn't even look up, just told me to go back upstairs." Amber leaned toward the prosecutor. "She was putting the first pill in her mouth when I ran out. I shouldn't have left, but I didn't know he was going to make her take them all!"

"Objection!" Jack yelled from the defense table. "Mr. Burke is not on trial for the death of his ex-wife either."

"Sustained. The jury will disregard again, and Miss Harper, please limit your comments to Sean Ballard."

Amber looked at the ecstatic DA, who nodded. "I met Sean on the stairs. He had a tennis racket in his hand and said he was going down to tell Ferris to get out of the house. I went up to wait with Jasmine and a few minutes later we heard some furniture crash downstairs. I wanted to call the police, but the last time they came they said if there were any more fights, they were going to put Jasmine in foster care. So I waited," Amber said, her voice rising with anxiety.

"We heard footsteps running up the stairs and then Sean was right outside my door, begging Ferris not to hurt him. Ferris was calling him awful names, and I heard a sickening sound, then Sean screamed. Jasmine was scared so I took her into the bathroom. There's a wicker couch there, and I told her to sit down, and I covered her ears with headphones. When I got back to my door Sean wasn't making any noise, but there were still those terrible sounds, like something hard hitting something soft. Ferris wouldn't answer me, so I called the police." The courtroom was silent as a tomb.

"Objection!" Jack called, rising to his feet again.

"Sustained," the judge replied. "Miss Harper, you can only testify about things you actually witnessed."

Amber nodded and Lance gave her a quick smile. "Then what did you do?"

"I climbed out the window," Amber replied, looking down at her lap. "You probably think I was a coward to leave Jasmine, but I knew

Ferris wouldn't hurt her, and after what he did to Sean, I was afraid he'd kill me too . . ."

A rumbling was heard around the courtroom, and the judge had to use his gavel repeatedly as Jack rose again. "Since Miss Harper is very much alive, I fail to see how Mr. Burke can be held responsible for *her* death. Miss Harper obviously has a vivid imagination and I'm going to have to object to this entire line of questioning."

"I'm finished, Your Honor," Lance said cheerfully.

"Your witness, Mr. Gamble," the judge told Jack.

Jack moved over to the witness box, and Beth could see the tension in his face.

"How can he defend Ferris now that he knows he's guilty?" Beth whispered to Mark.

"He doesn't know anything," Mark replied. "Neither do we. Two witnesses have given contradictory testimonies. That's true in every trial. Jack still has a duty to defend Ferris, and it's up to the jury to decide who is telling the truth and who isn't."

"But why would Amber lie?"

Mark shrugged as Jack addressed the witness. "Miss Harper, how old are you?"

"Twenty-two," Amber replied nervously.

"How old were you when Mr. Burke married your sister?"

"Eleven or twelve."

"He's a nice-looking man." Jack waved over at the defendant and Amber's eyes followed the direction of his hand. "Rich and famous. I'll bet sometimes you wished that Ferris had married you instead of Audrey."

Color stained Amber's cheeks. "I guess I did, at first, before I knew he was mean."

"Or until you realized that a man like Ferris Burke was never going to pay any attention to a plain girl like you."

The judge made a choking noise, and Beth flinched as Lance jumped to his feet. "Objection!"

"I'm just stating the facts, Your Honor," Jack said reasonably. "I'm sure that even Miss Harper will agree that she is no beauty."

Judge Tate's complexion darkened dangerously, but Amber spoke before he could. "It's okay, sir. I know I'm not pretty, but I was never jealous of Audrey. And I might have had a crush on Ferris when they first got married, but not anytime lately."

The judge nodded, then rounded on Jack. "You had better watch your step, Mr. Gamble."

Jack addressed the judge. "After the incredible latitude you afforded Mr. Kilgore, I know you'll be patient with me, Your Honor." Without waiting for a reply, Jack turned back to Amber. "You have testified that Sean Ballard never touched Jasmine Burke in an inappropriate way. You've stated that she was 'never out of your sight.' Is that correct?" Jack asked.

"Yes."

"Jasmine is nine years old?" he clarified, and Amber nodded. "Yet she didn't object to you watching her bathe?" There was a long silence. "Do I need to repeat the question?"

Amber was obviously flustered. "It's just that I . . ."

"In the interest of time, why don't you give me a yes or no answer," Jack suggested.

"I'll worry about the time," the judge growled at Jack, then turned to Amber. "Please just answer Mr. Gamble's question."

"I did not watch Jasmine take baths," Amber said, her lips stiff.

"Did Jasmine ever go to sleep before you did?"

"Sometimes," Amber admitted.

"So even though Jasmine slept with you, there were times when she was upstairs in a bedroom by herself. Is this correct?" Jack pressed.

"I guess so."

"Yes or no," Jack insisted.

Amber hung her head. "Yes."

"So you cannot be absolutely certain that Sean Ballard never laid a hand on Jasmine Burke. Isn't that correct?"

"I . . ." Amber glanced up at the judge, "No, I can't say for certain."

"On the night of Sean Ballard's death, did you listen to Jasmine's telephone conversation with her father?"

"No, I was in the other room—"

"Then you can't be sure what was said?" Jack interrupted.

"I heard Audrey tell Jasmine that she couldn't go with them to California. I saw Jasmine start to cry, and then she ran in and called her father."

"But you don't actually know what Jasmine told her father. Ferris could have come over to your house that night thinking that his daughter had been abused by Sean Ballard, even if it wasn't true."

"I guess, maybe."

"Now, you said that you saw Mr. Burke pour pills into your sister's hand, and she put one in her mouth. Could you see what kind of pills they were?"

"No. I think they were pink."

"Pink pills," Jack looked at the jury with skepticism. "So they could have been antihistamines or appetite suppressants or Maalox, for all you know."

"They were drugs, the bad kind," Amber insisted.

"You said that your sister picked one up and put it in her mouth. Mr. Burke didn't force her in any way?"

"No, but . . ."

"And you only saw your sister take one of the pills Ferris supposedly gave her. She could have taken a hundred before he got there."

"She had been clean for months!" Amber answered angrily. "She didn't take any drugs before Ferris got there!"

"You were in the kitchen with Jasmine. You don't know what she was doing in the living room!" Jack countered.

"Objection!" Lance yelled. "He's browbeating my witness!"

"Where are you going with this, Mr. Gamble?" Judge Tate asked.

"I'm trying to point out all the holes in her testimony," Jack replied. "Okay, Miss Harper. Let's try something else. You met Sean Ballard on the stairs, and he was carrying a tennis racket. You know that that was the murder weapon?"

"Yes."

"You have now confirmed that it was Mr. Ballard, not Mr. Burke, who initiated the violence." Jack glanced at the jury. "Sean Ballard brought the tennis racket downstairs with the intention of doing bodily damage to Mr. Burke."

"Sean wasn't really going to hurt Ferris. He just brought the racket to scare him."

"I think you are exactly right about that, Miss Harper. I think Sean Ballard came into the living room and threatened Ferris Burke with the tennis racket in an attempt to scare him. Mr. Burke was afraid for his life and protected himself."

"Ferris was a lot bigger than Sean! And when they came upstairs Sean was crying and begging Ferris to stop, but he didn't."

"But you weren't downstairs when the fight began, were you?" Jack asked.

"No."

"So you couldn't see who threatened who, could you?"

"No."

"You don't know how many times Sean Ballard hit Mr. Burke before the defendant was able to take the tennis racket away and protect himself, do you?" Jack pressed.

Amber shook her head. "No."

"In fact, you never saw anything that transpired between the defendant and Mr. Ballard, did you Miss Harper?"

"No."

"And while you were putting Jasmine into the bathroom, you couldn't even hear what was happening in the hallway. Is that true?"

"Yes."

Jack turned to the jury, including them in the conversation. "Okay, let's recap. You didn't see anything and you didn't hear everything. If that qualifies you as a witness, everyone in this courtroom could testify."

"Your Honor!" Lance objected.

"If you are through with the witness, dismiss her," the judge said in a flat tone.

"Thank you, Miss Harper. I think you have done an excellent job of proving that the prosecution has absolutely no case against Ferris Burke."

Beth felt sick as the judge told Amber she could step down from the witness stand. The girl was trembling by the time she reached her seat, and Beth put a steadying arm around her shoulders.

"I just want Ferris to pay for what he did," Amber whispered.

"It will be okay," Beth promised, hoping that was true.

Judge Tate told Lance to present his closing arguments, and the district attorney stood. He walked to the jury box and began with a description of the crime. He reminded the jury of all the horrible things various witnesses had said about Ferris Burke. Then he moved closer and put his hands on the railing. Beth stared at the discolored skin around his wrists as he spoke.

"The defense counsel is a well-known trickster and has done a good job of blowing smoke into this trial. Mr. Gamble has brought witnesses who say that Sean Ballard was a bad man, I guess insinuating that he deserved to die. But in our country one man can't make that decision for another. We have laws and policemen and courts to protect the innocent and prosecute the guilty. If Mr. Burke really thought that his daughter was being abused, there were legal steps he should have taken. Instead, he beat Sean Ballard until long after he was dead, with a viciousness that surprised even the coroner, who sees violent deaths regularly.

"Mr. Burke is a wealthy man and has worked hard to suppress evidence, threaten witnesses . . ." Lance's eyes strayed to the row where Amber was sitting, then turned back to the jury. "Amber Harper had nothing to gain by testifying against Ferris Burke today. So why would she lie? Mr. Gamble says that Ferris protected himself against Sean Ballard," Lance added with disdain. "The deceased was a small man, and Mr. Burke was never in any physical danger. He killed Sean Ballard because Ballard was planning to take Audrey to California. The motive was jealousy, pure and simple."

Lance took a deep breath. "But even if we discount Amber Harper's testimony and accept that Ferris Burke thought Sean Ballard had mistreated his daughter, then what? If we say that it's okay for one man to kill another for any reason, we have nullified the Constitution, divested the law, and invited anarchy.

"So I ask you, as a jury of not only Ferris Burke's peers but also Sean Ballard's, to ignore the smoke. You must uphold the law, and if you do that, you will have no choice but to return a verdict of guilty. Because Ferris Burke did, with malice, murder Sean Ballard. In everything else that the defense has presented, not one time has Mr. Gamble disputed this fact."

Jack waited until Lance had taken a seat at the prosecution table, then stood. He walked casually to stand beside the jury, leaning forward to place his elbows on the rail that separated the jurors from the rest of the courtroom.

"Mr. Kilgore said that you are responsible to uphold the law, and that is true. He says that you shouldn't consider anything except evidence, which I will mention is almost nonexistent in this case. Basically you will have to use rumor and hearsay and circumstance and what a questionable witness thinks she heard through a door to make your decision. It will be up to you to determine if, based on evidence, you can find Ferris Burke guilty of first-degree murder beyond any reasonable doubt.

"I am a rational, level-headed man, but I also have a five-year-old daughter," his voice wavered, and Beth watched the jury bond with him. "If I got a call from her, saying that a man had been putting his hands on her, trying to kiss her . . ." his voice trailed off as he shuddered. "Who can say what anyone would do in that situation?

"Obviously Mr. Kilgore is not a parent, because no one who loves a child would call defending their innocence 'smoke.' Mr. Kilgore said that I have not disputed his allegation that Mr. Burke ended Sean Ballard's life and implied that my failure to do so constituted an admission of Mr. Burke's guilt. He says that if we allow people to defend themselves and their children from monsters, we invite anarchy. I say that the day in which a father would allow a man to molest his nine-year-old daughter without consequence is the day when all hope for our society is gone."

Jack gripped the railing. "So, I'm leaving the future of humanity in your hands," he concluded. The courtroom was silent as everyone watched Jack return to the defense table. Beth noticed that he took the chair as far from Ferris as possible and didn't look at his client. Judge Tate cleared his throat and faced the twelve people who would decide Ferris Burke's fate.

"Now it is time for you to reach a verdict. Both the prosecution and defense attorney spent most of their closing arguments doing my job of charging the jury." He looked from Jack to Lance. "So I can be brief. You must consider the charge that has been filed against Mr. Burke. You must consider the evidence and testimony that has been presented and decide on either 'guilty' or 'not guilty.' I won't rush you, but if we can wrap this up today, all of you will be home for the weekend." Both attorneys stood to object, but the judge waved them aside. "Bailiff, get the jury settled. Court is adjourned until a verdict is reached."

As the gavel sounded, individual conversations erupted around the room. Beth watched the jury file out, then a sheriff's deputy came

BETSY BRANNON GREEN

for Ferris. Jack ignored his client and continued to pack his briefcase. Lance left with the assistant district attorney and the courtroom was mostly clear before Jack walked around and took a seat beside Beth. "I'll understand if none of you want to speak to me."

Amber gave him a cool nod. "You didn't have a choice about helping Ferris," Amber told him. "I knew that."

Jack gave her a tired smile. "I appreciate your words, but they don't make me feel any better about the way I treated you on the stand."

"Since I'm going to marry you, I guess I have to speak to you no matter how awful you treat your witnesses," Beth told him with a smile.

Jack pulled her to his side. "Now that makes me feel just a little better. You said Chloe is with Annabelle Grainger?" Beth nodded. "Okay, tell me what in the world happened."

Beth took a deep breath and began. "Malcolm called this morning and said he was bringing over a transmitter so I could hear the trial. Chloe had set up a Barbie hospital in the corner of the kitchen, and I watched her play for a few minutes. I touched the back of a chair when I stood up and left fingerprints on the wood." She gripped his hands. "I told you how I've been feeling like Roy was still watching over us?"

Jack nodded. "I remember."

"Well, I wondered if Amber's fingerprints might have gotten in Roy's apartment *after* the accident and if she, not Roy's spirit, was watching me."

Jack looked at Amber Harper. "How?"

"Because she's been living there since the wreck," Beth told him

"But you never went there before the accident?" he asked the girl.

"No, I talked to him on the phone, but we never actually met."

Jack returned his attention to Beth. "Roy would have died before he betrayed you or put Chloe at risk. I went up to the apartment, and Amber was there. I was planning to bring her in to testify for you." Beth looked up with misery in her eyes. "You've done so much for me, and I thought I was finally going to have a chance to help you."

Jack shrugged. "I appreciate the thought anyway."

"I went to change clothes, and I saw that *Law for Dummies* book Malcolm loaned me. I thought I could give it back to him when he got there, but the storm made me nervous and I dropped the book. It fell open and on the inside cover Malcolm had written his name. But instead of spelling out Schneckenberger, he'd made a big X. Just like the ones on the papers Agent Gray showed us."

Jack raised an eyebrow. "So Malcolm was Mr. X?"

Beth nodded. "Malcolm knew a lot about you and Roy and your case," Beth itemized the evidence. "All of the sudden it just made sense."

"So how did you get Chloe to Annabelle?" Jack asked.

"Derrick came by with a carful of casseroles, and I told him to take her away from the house. I was afraid if we tried to leave with him, we might endanger Chloe, and I knew I couldn't take chances with her safety." Jack raised her fingers to his lips. "I felt pretty safe since I knew Malcolm couldn't get past the gate, but I was so nervous I entered the wrong code. The one that keeps the gate open."

"It was an understandable mistake," Jack assured her. "What I can't fathom is why Malcolm would be willing to kill people over the outcome of this trial."

"Malcolm said that Felix Hummer wanted the new state senator to be his 'friend.' Malcolm was willing to accept the appointment under those conditions, but they had to get rid of you and Lance first. The plan was for Lance to win, but 'disappear' before he could be appointed to office. Then when it started to look like you might get Ferris acquitted, even without Amber, they decided to kill you."

"Malcolm and Felix Hummer?"

Beth hated to continue, but nodded. "Malcolm said Mr. Hummer's men were watching for you to leave the Fuller's party. When Roy took the Jeep, he got shot instead of you."

Jack ran a trembling hand through his hair. "Poor Roy."

"But even though he's not any better physically, it's like we have him back again," Beth whispered. "Don't you feel it?"

Jack pressed a kiss to her forehead. "The irony in all of this is that if Malcolm wanted me to lose the trial, he should have been trying to find Amber and let her testify against Ferris."

"But no one knew how Amber was going to testify," Beth pointed out.

"Except Roy," Amber corrected, and all eyes turned to her. "I told him what happened the night Sean and Audrey died, but he didn't want Mr. Gamble to lose the trial. So he said he was going to put me somewhere safe until afterward. We were supposed to meet at a truck stop on Saturday night, but he never showed. Then I heard about the wreck and figured Ferris had gotten to him. The best place I could think of to hide was Roy's apartment."

Jack leaned forward. "How did you know where Roy lived?"

"That first time you came looking for me at Heads Up, I followed you home. I wanted to trust you, but I wasn't sure," she told him. "Your home felt like it would be a nice, safe place, and I came there a lot after that. Roy was always walking around, checking for trouble. It made me wonder how it would feel to have someone care about me so much," Amber said wistfully. "So finally I decided to call him."

Beth blinked back tears as Jack cleared his throat. "How were you able to get past the security fence?"

"I climbed a tree in your neighbor's yard then crawled over into one of yours."

Beth had to smile at the shocked look on Jack's face. "So much for security." He turned to the FBI agents. "But if Malcolm and Felix Hummer wanted Ferris to be convicted, why did they kidnap Lance before the end of the trial?"

"Apparently that was kind of a mistake," Beth answered first. "The kidnapping wasn't supposed to take place until after the trial, but Lance realized he was being followed, and they had to change their plans. That's when they decided to blackmail you."

"And we're not sure if Hummer cared one way or the other about Ferris Burke's conviction," Agent Gray told them. "Apparently it was just a matter of wanting you to lose."

Jack rubbed the back of his neck. "Thereby forfeiting Oscar's nomination for the senate seat so that Malcolm could waltz right in?"

"Then do whatever Felix Hummer told him," Beth confirmed.

"Well." Jack stretched his arms over his head. "Regardless of Malcolm's deranged motivations, this has been one of the worst days of my life."

"The rest of us haven't had a lot of fun either," Lance Kilgore commented, coming up behind him.

"It's probably illegal for you to talk to us until the trial is over," Jack said.

"And goodness knows you don't want to risk a mistrial." Lance smiled, then walked back out of the courtroom.

"Smart aleck," Jack spoke to the district attorney's back.

"I kind of like him," Beth admitted and drew a scowl from her future husband.

Mark laughed. "I wouldn't worry about it, Jack. It's probably just a cohostage thing. People who survive life-threatening circumstances together often bond with each other."

"Well, let's just hope it's temporary because I don't plan to be friends with Lance Kilgore," Jack's tone was final.

"He probably won't have time for you anyway once he gets the appointment to the state senate," Roberta contributed to the conversation for the first time, and Jack gave her a sour look.

"Mr. Fuller isn't the only politically powerful man in Georgia. Just because he nominates someone doesn't guarantee they'll be appointed," Mark pointed out.

"And with all his financial problems, he might not have time to worry about the state senate anymore," Beth agreed.

"What financial problems?" Jack asked.

"Malcolm stole money from some party accounts and made it look like Mr. Fuller did it. He said that National Party auditors and the IRS would be checking into Mr. Fuller's finances. We might need to warn him."

"I'll think about it," Jack responded.

Agent Gray stood. "I need to get a statement from Miss Harper and you too, Miss Middleton. Is there someplace we can go where it will be quiet?"

"There's a snack room upstairs," Jack reported. "Second door on your right."

"I'm going to call Kate," Mark said, taking his cell phone from his pocket. "Then I'll meet you there," he told his fellow agent.

After Amber followed the agents out of the room, Jack sent Roberta to check on Roy and pick up some lunch. Once they were alone, Jack drew Beth into an embrace. "I have never been so scared in my life," he told her. "And I still can't believe that Malcolm was Mr. X."

"You would have believed it if you could have seen him. He was so hateful." She reached up and stroked his cheek. "He wanted to destroy you."

"He must have been completely insane." He caught her fingers and pressed them to his lips. "I would have gladly thrown away my career and every legal ethic to save you, but I was so afraid it wouldn't be enough."

"Malcolm was a terrible person, and maybe it's wrong for me to feel this way, but I'm glad he's dead," she whispered, and Jack's arms tightened around her.

"Just try not to think about him," Jack advised.

They sat in silence for a few minutes before Beth asked, "How long will it take for the jury to decide?"

"It's hard to tell," Jack answered.

Beth turned her head so she could see his face. "I think Amber was telling the truth."

"I'm afraid you're right. Looking back, I can see that Ferris set me up from the beginning. I was flattered that he hired me. I thought he chose me for my reputation as a winner, and I knew the national attention would be good for my state senate hopes. But now I realize that he picked me because of Chloe. He knew when he accused Sean Ballard of molesting Jasmine, I'd be too blinded by fury to dig deeper."

"Let's just hope that the jury makes the right decision."

Jack nodded. "And speaking of Chloe, I'm going to call to see if she's made it home yet." Jack used his cell phone and in seconds he was talking to Winston Jones. Beth gathered from Jack's side of the conversation that Chloe was not there. Jack asked about the wounded policeman, then ended his phone call. "Winston says Arnold is in good condition. He lost some blood, but the bullet missed all his vital organs."

Mark joined them, carrying a legal pad and a pencil. "Agent Gray sent me to get your statement."

With a sigh, Beth retold her story. The men listened closely, but they didn't interrupt until she got to Malcolm's death. "So how did Lance get a knife to stab Malcolm?" Jack asked then.

"I'm not sure." Beth frowned, then shook her head and continued. "After Malcolm was . . . taken care of, Lance was in such a panic to get here . . ."

"Lance was anxious to bring in what he thought was a defense witness?" Jack asked skeptically.

"Well, he wasn't happy about that, but he didn't want the assistant DA to get credit for his closing argument. We couldn't find the hand-cuff keys, so Derrick had to shoot the chains. He protected Lance from powder burns using a technique he learned on an old episode of *The Brave and Relentless,*" she added for Jack's benefit.

He smiled. "I can't believe that silly show actually came in handy."

"Will there be a trial for Malcolm's death?" Beth dreaded the answer.

Mark shook his head. "There will be an investigation, but it was such a clear-cut case of self-defense that I can't imagine it going any further than that."

"Good," Beth said with relief. "I'd hate to think about testifying."

Roberta returned with bags full of deli sandwiches. "I called the house, and Beth's friend is there with Chloe. Winston said he'd hang around till you get home," the secretary reported. "I'm going up to the break room to get canned drinks. What does everybody want?" she asked the group in general.

"Something without caffeine for me," Mark requested.

"Me too," Beth said.

Jack shrugged. "Me too, I guess."

Roberta laughed, then walked out of the courtroom. She returned a few minutes later with her hands full of soft drinks. Agent Gray and Amber were following close behind her. Roberta distributed the drinks and passed around the sandwiches.

"I'll pay you for mine," Amber offered.

"Don't worry about it," Roberta waved this aside. "We'll charge it to Ferris."

Beth watched as Amber took a tentative bite of her sandwich. "If Ferris is convicted, maybe you could apply for custody of Jasmine."

A small smile drifted across the girl's lips, but she shook her head. "Jasmine's with a real nice foster family, and they want to adopt her. She'll be better off with them."

Jack spoke gently. "Well, you could at least ask for visitation rights."

"Seeing me would just remind her of the bad times. If Ferris goes to jail, I'll disappear again and hope he doesn't find me."

Beth looked up from her lunch. "Why would Mr. Burke want to find you?"

"To kill me," Amber said calmly. This comment attracted the shocked attention of the room's other occupants. "The night he killed Sean and Audrey, he told me if I testified against him he'd make sure I ended up as dead as my sister."

"Dear me," Roberta murmured.

Beth put her sandwich down, suddenly feeling ill. "Could Mr. Burke kill you from jail?"

Amber nodded. "Oh, yeah. He's got people everywhere."

The mood was dampened, and everyone finished the meal in silence. Afterward the men took turns pacing while the women watched them. Finally Roberta looked at the clock. "It's almost 6:30."

Mark sighed. "The judge is going to have to adjourn until Monday."

Jack agreed that it was getting too late to continue jury deliberations. "He might have them come in tomorrow," he suggested, but his tone wasn't hopeful.

Mark walked to the door. "I'm going to go see if there's any news." He was back a few minutes later. "The jury is returning," he announced. "They have a unanimous verdict."

CHAPTER 16

The doors were opened, and people poured back into the court-room. A sheriff's deputy brought Ferris in, and Jack went up to sit at the table with his client. Lance walked by a few minutes later. He was still wearing Jack's suit and looked exhausted but confident. Members of the press stood along the back wall, conferring excitedly with each other.

The crowd quieted when Judge Tate stepped up onto the bench, then everyone watched as the jury filed in. Amber leaned forward and grasped Beth's arm. "They didn't look at Ferris. On television that means they've found him guilty," she whispered.

Beth nodded as the judge told the jury foreman to give the verdict to the bailiff. Beth's eyes focused on the paper in the judge's hand. He read it, then looked up solemnly and returned the piece of paper to the bailiff. "Mr. Foreman, I'll ask you to read the verdict."

The paper exchanged hands, and the jury foreman cleared his throat. "We, the jury, find Ferris Burke . . ." the spectators held their breath, "guilty of murder in the first degree."

The courtroom dissolved into total confusion, and Judge Tate pounded his gavel vigorously until order was restored. "The sentencing hearing will be two weeks from Monday," he told Ferris. "And I want to give you some food for thought, Mr. Burke. As I am sure you know, some prisons are almost like resorts, while others are worse than living with the devil himself. I hold what's left of your future in my hands," the judge growled. "The degree of comfort you receive in a correc-tional facility will be in direct relationship to the continued safety of these jurors and their families. Do I make myself clear?"

Ferris gave the judge a brief nod. "Then this court is adjourned." The courtroom exploded with noise again, and Judge Tate left without even trying to restore order. Beth saw Lance smiling and accepting congratulations from the people gathered around him. The defense table was quiet as Jack made notes on a legal pad, and Roberta repacked his briefcase. A policeman came to get Ferris, and Jack looked up as his client walked by. The men regarded each other for a few seconds, then the country singer touched his forehead in salute. Jack made no response, and Ferris was led through a side door.

"Can I go now?" Amber asked Mark, pulling Beth's attention back to her companions.

"You said Ferris will try to kill you," Beth said in concern.

"That's why I figure I need to get out of sight quick."

Agent Gray shook his head. "I've talked to my boss in Atlanta and told him that you are part of the ongoing investigation of Felix Hummer. They've agreed to put you in protective custody. You'll be given a new identity until we're sure Ferris Burke can't find you."

Amber seemed skeptical. "That might be a long time."

"The FBI has the resources to protect you as long as necessary," the agent promised. "But we probably should leave before things in here get worse."

Beth surveyed the pandemonium around them, and as she glanced at the entrance to the courtroom she saw Hipolita walk in. The breath rushed from her lungs as she realized that the housekeeper's appearance could mean only one thing. Roberta saw Hipolita about the same time and put a hand on Jack's arm, directing his attention to the door. A hundred separate conversations continued, oblivious of this most recent tragedy.

Beth watched Jack's jaw tighten as Hipolita reached him. They spoke briefly, then Roberta and Hipolita went out the main door together while Jack walked to the back where the others were waiting.

"Roy?" Beth forced herself to say.

"He's gone," Jack said grimly.

She wanted to offer some comfort, but words seemed insufficient, so she moved into his arms instead.

Mark cleared his throat to get their attention. "You might want to slip out before the press finishes with Kilgore and starts looking for you," he suggested. Beth took Jack's hand as they moved quickly outside and stopped by Mark's car.

"I hate to leave Amber," Beth said as she watched the other woman climb into the sedan.

"We'll ride with them," Jack decided. "That is, if you don't mind going by our house," he directed to Mark.

"Winston's waiting there to ask us some questions anyway," Mark replied.

Agent Gray took Lance's spot in the front seat, and Beth slid into the back with Amber. When Jack settled beside her, she pressed close to him, and they rode in silence for a few minutes. Then he turned to her. "Roberta never was able to find a relative who expressed any interest in Roy. I thought maybe Bishop Sterling could do the funeral since sitting in the parking lot at the second ward was the closest Roy's come to attending church since he was a kid."

Beth nodded. "I'm sure he'd be glad to do it."

"I told Roberta to call him and set it up for Monday."

The gate was still open when they got home, and Mark parked between a silver van and a police vehicle. "Who do all these cars belong to?" Jack asked as he looked down the row at a luxury car and the big truck.

"The van is mine," Mark answered. "The police car is Winston's. The truck belonged to the dead guy."

"This must be Annabelle's," Beth remarked as they passed the BMW.

They walked in through the kitchen, and Beth averted her eyes from the corner where bullet holes marred the shining wood. They found their guests in the den. Emily was asleep in Kate's arms, and Chloe was sitting quietly on the couch.

"The Northcutts were here earlier," Kate explained in a hushed tone to keep from waking the baby. "Ellen helped me clean up the kitchen, and she wanted to stay until you got home, but it was time to put the children to bed."

"I'll call and thank her in the morning," Beth promised.

Mark paused beside Kate's chair long enough to give his wife's shoulder a squeeze, then crossed the room to stand by Winston. Amber and Agent Gray stayed near the door, and Jack sat on the couch next to Chloe.

"Hey, Daddy," the child greeted. "Miss Annabelle and Mr. Derrick took me to see a lot of bugs today."

"That was nice of them," Jack said as he pressed kisses along her forehead.

Beth decided to give Chloe a few minutes alone with her father and walked over to the love seat where Annabelle and Derrick were sitting close together. "Roy passed away this afternoon," she whispered.

Derrick nodded. "The hospital called."

"How's the policeman?" Beth asked Winston.

"Doctors say he's doing well."

"I guess you want to ask some questions." Beth tried to keep the dread from her voice.

"I will need to file a report, but I don't have to do it tonight. How about if I come over in the morning, and we can go over everything?" Winston offered with a smile.

"Really?" Beth hardly dared to hope.

Winston nodded. "We're all tired tonight. We'll have a better chance of figuring it all out when we're fresh."

"Would you be able to send a patrol car by our house occasionally during the night?" Mark asked the police chief. "Amber is going to stay with us, and I'd feel better if we had additional protection."

"Expecting trouble?" Winston asked, settling his hat on his head.

"I just want to be prepared," Mark responded with a glance at Agent Gray.

All the guests except Derrick and Annabelle moved toward the kitchen, and Beth could hear Jack thanking them for their help. When he returned, Annabelle sat forward on the love seat.

"Okay, start at the first and don't leave out any details."

"And I thought we were getting out of this tonight," Beth groaned.

"Consider it a practice run for your interview with Winston," Annabelle suggested.

With a sigh, Beth began explaining the day's events. When she reached Derrick's well-timed arrival, Annabelle cocked her head in confusion. "You said Mr. Kilgore stabbed this Malcolm person with a knife?" she asked and Beth nodded. "So where did he get a knife?"

Beth shrugged. "I have no idea."

"It must have been in the corner where Malcolm nailed him to the floor," Annabelle pointed out. "But your housekeeper is much too efficient to leave a knife just lying around."

"I'm sorry," Chloe spoke from the end of the couch, drawing everyone's attention.

Beth gave the child a reassuring smile. "Why are you sorry?"

Chloe climbed onto Jack's lap and burrowed her head into his neck. "What's the matter, Chloe?" he asked. "You don't have to be afraid anymore."

"I'm afraid you're going to be mad when I say I took Hipolita's knife out of the drawer in the kitchen," she whimpered. "The Scarecrow was really hurt bad and he needed to have a big operation so he wouldn't die. I looked in Dr. Barbie's bag, but she didn't have a knife. So I had to borrow one from Hipolita."

"Oh, Chloe!" Beth gasped. "I can't believe you were playing with a knife! You could have cut off a finger or . . ." Beth shuddered, all the horrible possibilities occurring to her at once.

Jack tilted Chloe's chin up. "You know better than to play with knives, but we'll discuss that later. Right now I'm going to take you upstairs and let you change for bed." He stood and lifted Chloe.

Annabelle moved closer as soon as the Gambles were gone. "Chloe tells us that you and her father are going to get married."

"Yes," Beth answered with a quick look at Derrick.

"Soon?" Annabelle pressed.

"Christmas at the earliest."

Annabelle considered this for a few seconds. "You know, it wouldn't be respectable for you to keep living here now that you're engaged, even with Hipolita and Chloe as chaperones."

Beth hadn't thought of this, but her heart sank. "I guess I could try to get my old apartment back." That prospect was depressing. "Or I could stay with my parents."

"You'd be too far away from Chloe," Annabelle dismissed this out of hand. "The only logical solution is for you to move in with me."

"That would be such an imposition," Beth started to decline.

"Nonsense. I'll enjoy the company, and Chloe needs to see that you intend to be a permanent part of her life."

In the quiet that followed this statement, they heard an announcer on the television say that they had a special report live from the Dougherty County Courthouse, where Ferris Burke had just been found guilty of first-degree murder. Derrick, Annabelle, and Beth all faced the television screen and watched as a young woman with a microphone addressed the camera. "I'm Veronica Smalls of Channel Five News, and I've got one of the jurors from Ferris Burke's trial with me." The camera angle widened to include another woman.

"Sandra Thomas," Beth said when she saw the juror. "Mother of three, PTA president, teaches a Sunday School class. Jack wanted her on the jury because he thought she'd sympathize with Ferris." Beth looked up at her friends. "Before we knew he was guilty."

"So, Mrs. Thomas," the reporter spoke again. "Would you tell us how the jury reached their verdict?"

"I can't give any specifics, but I don't think it would hurt to explain our general feelings. We all believed that Mr. Burke had killed his ex-wife's boyfriend, but most of us felt that he was somewhat justified because the man had threatened him and possibly abused his daughter." Mrs. Thomas paused here for a few seconds, and Ms. Smalls pushed her face into the camera.

"What changed your minds?" the reporter demanded.

"Well, in his closing argument, Mr. Gamble said that as parents none of us know what we would do if someone harmed our children. He mentioned his own daughter, and I could tell that he loved her very much. One of the other jurors brought this up when we were arguing about our verdict. He said 'If Jack Gamble thought someone had molested his daughter, what do you think he'd do?' I tried to imagine Mr. Gamble beating a man with a tennis racket, and I just couldn't."

The reporter interrupted again. "So what did Mr. Gamble's hypothetical reaction have to do with your final decision?"

"I believe that if someone hurt Mr. Gamble's daughter, he would do exactly what the district attorney said. He would call the police and have the man prosecuted through the court system. I believe that's what I would do too. It's what any responsible person would do. We can't take the law into our own hands. It's wrong, and we agreed on a guilty verdict."

The reporter summed up her segment, and Beth felt Annabelle and Derrick staring at her. "He always has a trick up his sleeve, but this is the first time I've ever seen him use one to try and lose," Derrick said quietly.

Annabelle turned to Derrick in surprise. "You think he said that about Chloe to make the jurors find Ferris Burke guilty?"

Derrick lifted an eyebrow expressively, but Beth shook her head. "Everyone is entitled to representation, and it was Jack's responsibility to do his best for Ferris."

"Lucky thing his best wasn't good enough today, then," Derrick said.

"Yeah," Jack spoke from the doorway. "I picked a good time to start losing."

Derrick blushed, but Annabelle laughed. "Well, let's get back to my place. We've got a whole backseat full of rancid casseroles to dispose of. I wonder if there is an appropriate thank-you phrase for this particular situation. 'Thank you so much for the casserole. We left it in the heat for twelve hours, and by the time we threw it away, it qualified as toxic waste.'" Annabelle pretended to consider. "I'll have to check with Eugenia. She's the etiquette expert."

Derrick stood and pulled Annabelle to her feet. Jack and Beth accompanied them through the kitchen, but Annabelle paused before they reached the door. "And speaking of Eugenia, can I use your phone?"

"Be my guest," Jack offered with a smile.

Annabelle picked up the receiver and dialed a number quickly. When Miss Eugenia answered, her voice echoed through the kitchen. "It's still on speaker phone from when Malcolm . . ." Beth whispered, but Annabelle put a finger to her lips.

"Eugenia, it's Annabelle."

"For heaven sakes! You think I can't recognize your voice? And who else would be rude enough to call so late?" Miss Eugenia demanded.

Annabelle ignored the reprimand. "You'll never guess where I am."

"Where?" Miss Eugenia's curiosity got the best of her.

"I am standing in Jack Gamble's kitchen."

"You don't mean it," Miss Eugenia's incredulous voice came through the speaker.

"I most certainly do. I'm standing right here looking at bullet holes Derrick made in the hardwood floor when he killed a madman."

"You *know* you don't mean it!"

"I wouldn't make up something like that! The dead person's name was Malcolm something-or-other, and he was a terrible, awful man. He was going to kill Beth and the district attorney and, well, it's too complicated for me to explain over the phone. But my Derrick is a hero, and I've seen the inside of Jack Gamble's house."

There was a brief silence before Miss Eugenia responded. "I do declare."

Annabelle laughed. "I'll come by in the morning and tell you the whole story." She disconnected the call, then waved to Beth and Jack. "See you kids tomorrow."

"Good night," Jack said, then glanced over at Beth. "I think I'll close the gate behind them." Beth tried to smile, but the horror of the day caught up with her and tears started streaming down her cheeks. He drew her into his arms. "Oh, Beth, don't cry."

Beth sniffled and tried to stop the flow of tears. "Roy would have been proud of you today," she said softly.

"Of me?" Jack asked. "I wanted to crawl under a rock after I made Amber Harper look like an idiot or worse." Jack shuddered. "I'll never try a criminal case again."

"You had an obligation to Ferris, which you fulfilled, and you could still try cases if you're a little more selective about the clients you choose to represent," Beth told him gently.

"I've represented guilty clients before, but today I was arguing to keep a murderer from going to jail. I don't think I could ever face another jury."

"So what will you do, assuming Lance gets Mr. Fuller's nomination for the senate seat?"

"Like Mark said, Oscar just makes a nomination, he doesn't pick the new senator. But if I don't get the appointment, I may look into hair-braiding as a career." He tightened his embrace.

"I'm sorry your winning record had to end," she whispered against his heart.

Jack cradled her head. "I don't care if I go down in Albany City history as the worst lawyer ever as long as I have you and Chloe, and you're both safe."

Beth looked up into his eyes. "I've been trying to make sense of all that has happened," she told him. "Now I really do believe that I am meant to be your wife and Chloe's mother, but why did David have to die? Couldn't we have just realized that we weren't right for each other? And what about Roy?"

"Sometimes there are no logical answers to the questions of life."

Beth shook her head. "I don't know if I can accept that." Then she said with a sigh, "Annabelle thinks people will talk if I continue to live here now that we're engaged. She offered to let me move in with her until the wedding."

"I don't care what people think," Jack objected mildly.

"I like this town, and I don't want the people here to have a bad opinion of me. And Christmas isn't that far away."

"It's seeming further and further," he muttered as the phone rang. "It's Oscar Fuller," he mouthed with his hand over the receiver. "Calling to apologize, I hope."

"Don't be too hard on him," Beth whispered. "Malcolm tricked us all."

Beth wanted to give Jack some privacy, so she went to check on Chloe. The child was curled up on her bed, sound asleep. Beth stretched out beside her, savoring the warmth. Then she closed her eyes just for a minute and woke up the next morning with Chloe's nose touching hers.

"You slept with me this time," she said with a delighted smile.

Beth glanced around to see that she was still wearing her clothes and shoes from the day before. "I was scared to sleep by myself after all the things that happened yesterday." Beth used a technique she learned in school, opening the door for Chloe to discuss her fears and concerns.

The child frowned. "Mr. Malcolm was a bad man. He hurt your face." Chloe reached out to touch the bruises on Beth's cheek.

"But he's dead now, and he can't hurt us anymore."

"Roy's dead too. They're going to have to put him in a grave." Chloe shuddered and Beth pulled her closer.

"Only Roy's body will be in the grave. His spirit will be up in heaven."

"What's his spirit?"

"His personality, his . . . oh, I don't know. You'll have to ask my dad when he comes."

Hipolita was particularly quiet during breakfast. Beth understood her grief and didn't force the housekeeper to make small talk. Finally, when they put their cereal bowls into the sink, Hipolita spoke. "You want me find another job? Since you and Mr. Jack get married?"

Beth reached out and touched the other woman's hand. "Hipolita, I can't even turn off the oven. I'd be very grateful if you'd stay."

Hipolita considered this for a few seconds, then nodded. "Okay."

Beth swallowed the lump in her throat. "You're a part of the family."

The corners of Hipolita's mouth turned up in her own special version of a smile, then she moved back to the sink as Jack walked in. He kissed Chloe on the top of the head, then kissed Beth more thoroughly. "Good morning, Hipolita," he said over Beth's head when he finished.

The housekeeper nodded in response, then gave him a cereal bowl and a spoon.

"Beth slept with me because she was scared," Chloe announced. "Since Mr. Malcolm is dead, we're not afraid anymore, but we're still sad about Roy."

"We'll always miss Roy," Jack acknowledged.

"But I'll bet he's real happy in heaven," Chloe proposed.

"And heaven will never be the same again," Jack said, putting a spoonful of cereal in his mouth. Then he stopped chewing and looked at Beth. "Why are you staring at me like that?"

"I love to watch you eat cereal," she said with a glance at the Cinnamon Toast Crunch box. "Froot Loops are the best." He raised an eyebrow, then smiled and let milk drip off his lips. Chloe screamed, Beth laughed, and Hipolita shook her head.

Winston arrived just as breakfast ended, and they went over the day before in agonizing detail. Then Jack went to meet Roberta and Bishop Sterling at a funeral home in Albany to make arrangements for Roy's graveside service. It was almost dark by the time Jack got home.

"So, is everything ready?" Beth asked.

Jack nodded. "Bishop Sterling is going to say a few words and a lady from the ward is going to sing a song. It will be short."

"Roy wouldn't have wanted a big fuss," Beth agreed.

He pulled her into his arms. "Are you staying here tonight?"

"I'll wait to move my things until after the funeral."

"I miss you already," he murmured against her forehead.

* * *

There was a chill in the air when Beth woke up on Monday. She took a deep breath, then climbed out of bed to face the day.

"Good morning," Jack greeted when she walked through the kitchen door. She was wearing the black dress she'd purchased for Annabelle's retirement party. Jack had on a dark suit, and Chloe was wearing her lacy French gown.

"Chloe doesn't have a black dress," Jack explained with a frown. "I tried to get her to wear navy blue, but she insisted on this one."

Beth smiled at the little girl. "I think she made the right choice. Roy wouldn't want to see her dressed in mourning colors."

"Is Roy going to see me today?" Chloe asked in surprise.

"My dad says that after someone dies, their spirit stays near their body until it's buried. So I think Roy will be at the funeral. He'll know we're there, and that we'll always love him," Beth struggled to keep her voice even.

"And that I'm wearing his favorite dress?" Chloe asked.

"That too," Beth nodded.

Roberta joined them for breakfast, and then they all rode together to the cemetery. "Roy's lawyer wants to come over to your house this afternoon and go over the will. I told him I'd check with you," Roberta said as they drove along. Beth was astounded that Roy had both a lawyer and a will, but Jack just nodded. "It's pretty straightforward and shouldn't take long," Roberta added.

"I can't imagine that Roy had much in the way of earthly possessions," Beth stated sadly.

"Actually, he had a fairly large estate," Roberta contradicted her.

"Roy? He didn't own a house or a car. I never saw him wear any expensive jewelry, and his clothes, well, they were as bad as mine. How could he have had any money?"

"Because he didn't have a house payment or a car payment, and he didn't buy jewelry or expensive clothes," Roberta said. "Jack paid him a nice salary, and he was good at picking stocks."

"Our Roy played the stock market?" Beth clarified.

"Yes, our Roy." Roberta's tone was gentle. Then she turned to her boss. "You remember those cousins I tracked down who said they barely knew Roy?"

"Yes," Jack answered.

"One of them called yesterday and said he wanted to know the size of Roy's estate and when he'd be getting his share. Can you believe that?"

Beth was horrified, but Jack just shrugged. "Let the lawyer handle him."

A large crowd of people had gathered by the time they arrived at the cemetery. Beth waved to her parents as Jack led the way up to the tent that covered the grave. Then the people who loved Roy most took seats in front of the gleaming silver casket. Bishop Sterling stepped forward and addressed the assemblage.

"On behalf of Mr. Gamble and his family, I'd like to thank all of you for coming here this morning to pay your respects to Roy Hankins. We'd like to begin with an opening prayer, which will be offered by Brother Mark Iverson."

Beth watched as Mark ducked under the canvas covering and stood near the end of the casket. After the prayer Bishop Sterling spoke again. "I have a regular funeral talk that I give on sad occasions such as this. But when I was reviewing it last night, it just didn't feel right. So I studied the scriptures and I prayed, and this is what I came up with." Bishop Sterling turned the pages in his quadruple combination and settled on a verse. "In 2 Nephi 10:24 and 25, we read: 'Wherefore, my beloved brethren, reconcile yourselves to the will of God and not to the will of . . . the flesh; and remember, after ye are reconciled unto God, that it is only in and through the grace of God that ye are saved. Wherefore, may God raise you from death by the power of the resurrection, and also from everlasting death by the power of the atonement, that ye may be received into the eternal kingdom of God, that ye may praise him through grace divine. Amen'."

Bishop Sterling closed his scriptures and faced the crowd. "My dear brothers and sisters, I submit to you that it is not ours to question why. Just as our Savior accepted the bitter cup in the Garden of Gethsemane and submitted to the will of His Father, we too must become reconciled to the will of God. And once we are truly reconciled, we can look forward to eternal life in the kingdom of Heaven. Brother Hankins is not gone from us, he has merely passed on to the next level of his progression toward salvation. We will see Roy again, and I pray that it will be a glorious reunion for us all, in the name of Jesus Christ, amen."

Bishop Sterling stepped back, and a woman Beth didn't recognize took his place. Then, in a sweet and clear soprano, she sang "Each Life That Touches Ours for Good." Beth couldn't hold back the tears, and Chloe looked up in concern. "It's okay, Beth," the child whispered earnestly.

"I know," Beth assured her.

After the service they stood to accept condolences from those in attendance. Beth invited her parents and Jack's to come home with them, but both declined. Beth walked them to their cars, then returned to the group of mourners and was surprised when Amber Harper stepped up beside her.

"I thought you'd be in places unknown by now," Beth teased.

"They let me stay for the funeral, but I'm flying . . . somewhere today." Amber tipped her head toward Agent Gray, who was standing near the Iversons.

"I probably won't ever see you again." Beth was saddened by the thought.

"I'll try to send you a postcard or something to show you that I'm okay."

"You don't even have to sign it. If I get a blank card in the mail, I'll know it's from you." Amber nodded and moved off with a little wave as Miss Eugenia charged up, her heels sinking into the soft damp ground.

"Real shame about Mr. Hankins," Miss Eugenia said, adjusting her black lace gloves.

"Yes, we'll miss him very much," Beth agreed.

"I . . ." Whatever Miss Eugenia was about to say was lost as someone gasped from behind them. They turned to see Derrick and Annabelle wrapped in a passionate embrace under a tree a few feet away. "Dear me! Kissing at a funeral," Miss Eugenia whispered in horror.

"Aren't you going to stop her?" Miss Polly Kirby demanded.

"If I holler across the cemetery, the few people who haven't already seen her in that disgraceful position will," Miss Eugenia pointed out. "So I'll pretend like I don't know her."

"For how long?" Miss Polly asked.

"The rest of her natural life," Miss Eugenia said grimly as she headed for her car.

After they left the cemetery, Jack drove to the courthouse. Once there, he, Beth, and Chloe transferred to the SUV while Roberta took Hipolita home in the Lexus. Jack went by his office to pick up some correspondence, then made a stop at the post office before returning to Haggerty. Chloe was asleep, and the house was crawling with people by the time they arrived.

"I hope you not mad," Hipolita said anxiously at the door. "But they bring so much food and say it is duty."

"I'm not mad," Jack assured the housekeeper. Hipolita looked relieved as she hurried down the hall to the safety of her room. "Do you know these people?" he asked Beth.

"Some of them," she replied as she saw Miss Eugenia taking a ham out of the oven.

Then Derrick walked through the dining room door. "I told you to leave that in until two o'clock," he said, putting the ham back into the oven. He was wearing one of Hipolita's aprons, and Beth had to put a hand to her mouth to keep from laughing.

"What I want to know is who put you in charge, Lover Boy?" Miss Eugenia demanded.

Derrick blushed but held his ground. "This is no time for a childish power struggle, Eugenia. The important thing is making sure that we have a nice meal ready for the mourners."

Miss Eugenia looked as if she might want to dispute this point, but before she could respond, Brother Stoops hobbled through the kitchen door leaning heavily on a cane. "Elmer!" she cried happily. "I'm so glad you came. Let me find you a comfortable place to sit."

"I don't want to take you away from your duties, Eugenia," the old man said with a look into the kitchen.

"I've got everything running smoothly. I guess I can leave the rest to him," she tipped her head at Derrick.

Jack shifted the child sleeping in his arms. "I'm going to put Chloe on her bed," Jack whispered to Beth.

"Hurry back," she pleaded, then moved over to stand beside Derrick. "It was so nice of everyone to do this." She waved at all the covered dishes.

"It's our pleasure," Derrick assured her. "Here, try some of this cranberry salad. It's in the new *Southern Living* and simply divine." He held out a spoonful.

"I've missed your cooking," Beth said as she chewed. "And our visits. We don't get a chance to talk much anymore."

"There's not much to say since you've quit reading library books and watching soaps."

"Maybe we can find some new common interests, and I'll get to see you more often once I move into your girlfriend's house."

Derrick blushed. "Annabelle and I are just good friends . . ."

"I was at the funeral, Derrick. I saw that kiss, and it was anything but friendly."

"You saw us too?" He sounded horrified at the thought.

"You were standing under a tree in broad daylight. Everyone saw you."

"Oh, no. I just didn't think. I . . ."

Beth smiled. "That's what love does—makes it so you can't think straight."

"Who can't think straight?" Annabelle asked as she walked in and took a sweet pickle off a relish tray. "I can't," Beth said with a smile at Derrick. "I haven't had a sensible thought since I met Jack Gamble."

"That's understandable," Annabelle nodded, then turned to Derrick. "Pauline Kirby is watching *The Brave and Relentless* in the den, and she says that they've taken the bandages off of Elena's eyes and she can see!"

"Jack will be so pleased to hear that," Beth murmured.

"And Marissa has agreed to go out on a date with Dr. Richards!" Annabelle continued.

"So soon after poor Cedric's death?" Derrick cried. "That's scandalous!"

Beth controlled a smile. "Cedric would want her to move on."

"Maybe." He didn't sound convinced.

"And the viewers were going to get sick and tired of watching Marissa plant flowers around his grave," Annabelle contributed.

"Blame it on the writers!" Beth agreed. "If it were up to Marissa, I'm sure she'd grieve for a respectable length of time."

"I guess you're right," Derrick replied doubtfully.

"Let's go see if anything else exciting happens," Annabelle suggested, grasping Derrick's hand and pulling him toward the den. Beth was just beginning to feel conspicuously alone when Kate Iverson walked in carrying a stack of paper plates.

"Everything is about ready," Kate reported with a sigh. "Derrick brought the ham, the Methodists brought drinks and bread, the Baptists brought salads and vegetables, and the second ward Relief Society provided dessert."

"Sounds like the ladies of Haggerty have already added a 'Mormon' category," Beth said, and Kate laughed. "Mark told me about the baby," Beth added quietly.

Kate looked around to be sure she couldn't be overheard, then smiled. "We're so excited. Some people will think we should have waited until Emily is older." Beth knew she meant Miss Eugenia. "And it's hard to explain, but the new baby is very important to our family."

"You have to decide what's best for you and try not to worry about what other people will think," Beth advised as Jack walked up.

"Does that mean you're not moving to Annabelle's?" he asked.

"No." Beth shook her head. "The bishop agreed with that decision. Which reminds me, I've still got a few more things to pack." She moved toward the hallway.

"I'll help," Jack said as he followed her.

"You'd better come back soon and eat some of this food!" Kate called after them.

Once they were away from the crowd, Jack pulled her into his arms.

"I thought we were going to pack," she protested.

"We'll pack later. Right now I just want to enjoy your company and the peace and quiet." Beth rested her head against his chest and listened to him breathe. "I thought the funeral was very nice," he said, and Beth agreed that it was. "Bishop Sterling gave a good talk."

"It was more than a good talk," she said softly. "It was the answer to my prayer."

Jack pulled back so that he could see her face. "Which prayer?"

"The one about David," Beth replied. "I realized when the bishop was reading from the scriptures that I was fighting the will of the Lord. I have to reconcile myself to the life He has given me and let go of the past."

"How long do you think this reconciliation is going to take?" Jack asked cautiously.

She smiled. "I should be ready by Christmas."

"How about Thanksgiving?" His face lowered toward her.

"There's always Veteran's Day," she whispered.

"Now you're talking," he murmured against her lips.

EPILOGUE

Nine Months Later

The first thing Beth saw when she woke up was her wedding dress hanging on the back of the closet door in Annabelle's guest room. It wasn't long and flowing like the first one, and the tightly woven linen fabric wouldn't let the morning sun shine through, but it did glow a little.

Beth took her shower and dressed carefully in the green dress she had purchased to impress Miss Hyde. She applied a light layer of makeup and was contemplating a hairstyle when she heard a soft knock on the door. Expecting Annabelle, she walked over and pulled the door open. Jack stood in the hallway outside her room.

"I thought I'd better come make sure you hadn't changed your mind," he said with a grin.

The sight of him took her breath away. "It's bad luck for a groom to see his bride before the wedding," she finally managed.

"You're the luckiest thing that's ever happened to me, and I don't plan to let you out of my sight again until you are my wife," Jack replied, then reached out and touched a damp lock of hair on her shoulder. "You need some help with your hair?"

She nodded mutely and he moved into the room. He went to work with her hairbrush and she closed her eyes. "Did you lose Chloe?"

"No, she's downstairs with Annabelle."

"Is she wearing Roy's favorite dress?"

"Of course."

Beth smiled. "I saw Oscar Fuller on the news last night. He's still taking full credit for your appointment to the state senate."

"Oscar's scrambling to hold onto his position as chairman of the Georgia Republican Party. If my appointment can help him, I don't mind."

"I'm not sure if I'm ready to be a politician's wife." Beth opened her eyes. "But I should have known that in spite of losing the Ferris Burke trial, you'd win the appointment. I mean, you always win."

Jack finished with her hair and turned her around to face him. "I'll admit that I'm a strong competitor, but lately the only thing I've cared about winning is your heart."

"That game has been over for a long time," Beth whispered, gazing into his blue eyes.

"Oh yeah?" he replied softly. "How long?"

Beth thought for a few seconds. "Since I found out that there really isn't a Volkswagen museum in Arkansas."

"Well, there should be," Jack said with a smile. "And don't feel too bad about surrendering your heart. Once I made up my mind, you didn't have a chance. Now I think it's time for me to kiss the bride."

"That comes later." Beth pulled back and looked over his shoulder at the sunrise. "Do you think Roy will be at the temple with us today?"

"I'd like to see the angel who could keep him away," Jack replied lightly.

Beth nodded. "That's what I think too. Even though we can't see him, I believe that Roy still looks out for us, just like always. In fact, sometimes I can almost feel his presence. Does that sound crazy?"

"Not to me," Jack answered. "And right now, if Roy's watching, I think it would make him real happy to see us kissing."

Beth laughed and didn't even try to object as his lips descended toward hers.

ABOUT THE AUTHOR

Betsy Brannon Green currently lives in a suburb of Birmingham, Alabama with her husband, Butch, and seven of their eight children. She is the secretary for Hueytown Elementary School's Kindergarten Campus and serves as Primary chorister for the Bessemer Ward.

Although born in Salt Lake, Betsy was raised in the South. Her life and her writing have both been strongly influenced by the small town of Headland, Alabama and the people who live there. In her characters you will see reflections of the gracious gentility unique to that part of the country.

Betsy's first book, *Hearts in Hiding*, was published in May of 2001 and *Never Look Back* followed in January of 2002. She loves to hear from readers and can be contacted at betsybrannongreen@yahoo.com or you may write her in care of:

Covenant Communications, Inc.
920 E. State Road, Suite F
American Fork, UT 84003-0416